Barry E. O'Meara

**Napoleon at St. Helena**

Volume 1

Barry E. O'Meara

**Napoleon at St. Helena**
*Volume 1*

ISBN/EAN: 9783337349684

Printed in Europe, USA, Canada, Australia, Japan

Cover: Foto ©Andreas Hilbeck / pixelio.de

More available books at **www.hansebooks.com**

# NAPOLEON
# AT ST. HELENA

BY

## BARRY EDWARD O'MEARA
### HIS LATE SURGEON

HOUSE IN WHICH NAPOLEON WAS BORN AT AJACCIO

IN TWO VOLUMES

VOL. I.

LONDON
RICHARD BENTLEY & SON, NEW BURLINGTON STREET
Publishers in Ordinary to Her Majesty the Queen

1888

# A Voice from St. Helena.

TO

# THE RIGHT HON. LADY HOLLAND

WHOSE HUMANE ATTENTIONS

TO

## NAPOLEON AT ST. HELENA,

DREW FROM HIM, IN HIS DYING MOMENTS,

THE GRATEFUL EXPRESSION OF HIS

'SATISFACTION AND ESTEEM,'

## THESE VOLUMES

ARE, WITH HER LADYSHIP'S PERMISSION,

MOST RESPECTFULLY INSCRIBED,

BY

HER LADYSHIP'S VERY OBEDIENT HUMBLE SERVANT,

## BARRY E. O'MEARA.

'Of these things
I was not unadvised, and my offence
Was voluntary ; in man's cause I drew
These evils on my head—but ills like these,
On this aërial rock to waste away,
This desart and unsocial precipice,
My mind presaged it not.'

# PREFATORY NOTE

THE cameo, an engraving from which is given as the frontispiece, was executed before the battle of Marengo, at a time when Napoleon had not become corpulent. *Madame Mère*,[1] when she presented it to me, informed me that it was then considered to be an excellent likeness : and indeed its resemblance to what he was when I saw him was striking, making allowance for his features having lost much of the sharpness shown in the cameo.

The engraving from the cameo[2] has been pronounced by M. Revelli, *Professore emerito* of the University of Turin, to be a most striking likeness of Napoleon at the period mentioned. It may be observed that no other painter was favoured with such opportunities of forming a correct judgment on the subject as M. Revelli; as, independently of having frequently seen Napoleon at an early age, he resided for several months with the Emperor at Elba, as his painter, and executed a beautiful portrait of him.

B. E. O'M.

[1] Napoleon's mother.
[2] This portrait has been fortunate in falling into the hands in succession of two such artists as Woolnoth and Stodart.

'O'MEARA'S work has increased my respect for Napoleon; since the days of Prometheus Viːctus I recollect no spectacle more moving and sublime than that of this great man in his dreary prison-house, captive, sick, despised, forsaken, yet arising above it all by the stern force of his own unconquerable spirit.'

CARLYLE.

# . AUTHOR'S PREFACE

*PLACED by circumstances arising from my profession, near the person of the most extraordinary man perhaps of any age, in the most critical period of his life, I determined to profit by the opportunities afforded me as far as I could consistently with honour. These volumes are the result. The reader will see in the outset of the work how I became attached as medical officer to the Household of the Emperor Napoleon in consequence of his own application, and with the full concurrence of the Lords of the Admiralty. I did not seek the situation; it was in some degree assigned to me; and most assuredly I should have shrunk from the acceptance of it, had I contemplated the possibility of being even remotely called upon to compromise the principles either of an officer or a gentleman. Before, however, I had been long scorched upon the rock of St. Helena, I learnt to appreciate the embarrassments of my situation. I saw that I must either become accessory to vexations for which there was no necessity, or incur suspicions of no very comfortable nature. Fortunately for my honour, my happiness, and indeed for everything except my interests, I did not hesitate. Humanity required of me consideration for my patient, the uniform I wore imperiously commanded that I should not soil it by indignities to a captive, and my country's character pledged me to hold sacred the misfortunes of the fallen. This I did. It is my pride to avow it : a pride inferior only to that which I feel in finding those men my enemies who consider it a crime.*

*The few alleviations which I had in my power to offer, Napoleon repaid by the condescension with which he honoured me ; and my necessary professional intercourse was soon increased into an intimacy, if I may speak of intimacy with so exalted a personage. Indeed, in the seclusion of Longwood, he almost entirely laid aside the Emperor ; with those about him he conversed familiarly on his past life, and sketched the characters, and detailed the anecdotes which are here presented faithfully to the reader. The unreserved manner in which he spoke of everything can only be conceived by those who heard him ; and though, where his own conduct was questioned, he had a natural human leaning towards himself, still truth appeared to be his principal, if not his only, object. In the delineation of character he was peculiarly felicitous. His mind seemed to concentrate its rays on the object he wished to elucidate, and its prominent features became instantly discernible. The intimate acquaintance which he necessarily possessed with all the great men who figured in Europe for the last thirty years gave to his opinions and observations more than ordinary interest; indeed, from no other source could such authentic information be acquired. Notwithstanding the interval which elapsed since many of the occurrences alluded to took place, and the distracting occupations which must have employed his mind, it was wonderful to see how freshly he remembered every transaction which became the subject of inquiry. If there was anything more extraordinary than this, it was the apathy with which he perused the libels which were written on him—he seemed inspired with a conviction of posthumous fame beyond the reach of contemporary depreciation.*

*I spoke as little and listened as attentively as I could, seldom interposing, except for the purpose of leading to those facts on which I wished for information. Though naturally having a retentive memory, I did not entirely trust to it; immediately on retiring from Napoleon's presence, I hurried to my chamber and committed to paper the topics of conversation, in, so far as I could, the exact words used. Where I had the least doubt as to my accuracy, I noted it in my journal, and contrived a recurrence to the topic when future opportunities offered. My long residence at Longwood rendered these opportunities frequent, and the facility of communication which Napoleon allowed, made the introduction of almost any subject easy. As my original journal increased in interest, it became of course to me an object of solicitude; and as nothing which could occur at St. Helena would have surprised me, I determined to place its contents beyond the power of that spoliation which afterwards was perpetrated on some of my other property. Having purchased in the island a machine for that purpose, I transmitted at intervals the portions copied to a friend on board one of His Majesty's ships in the roads, who forwarded them as opportunities occurred, to Mr. Holmes of Lyon's Inn, Napoleon's agent in London. The whole of this copy Mr. Holmes duly received previously to my return to England, as appears below by his own authentication,[1] and part of the silver paper manuscript as he received it, I have deposited with my publishers for the satisfaction of the sceptical. Perhaps, however, after all, the best proof of the authenticity of these volumes will be found in their own contents—independently of the internal evidence contained in the anecdotes themselves there was, on whatever came from Napoleon's mind, an inimitable*

---

[1]  3 LYON'S INN, *June* 22, 1822.

*I certify that I received all the papers alluded to by Mr. O'Meara in this Preface, a considerable time before his arrival in England.*

(*Signed*)    WILLIAM HOLMES.

*impress. On this subject, if I appear to many un-
necessarily minute, it is because I am aware that
every attempt will be made to deny the authenticity
of these conversations; there are too many implicated
—too many interested—too many who must wish to
cast an impenetrable veil over the transactions of
St. Helena, to suffer the truth to obtain an undis-
puted circulation. The following official letters will
show that it was at least the desire of His Majesty's
Ministers to bury Napoleon's mind with his body in
the grave of his imprisonment. If I have disobeyed
the injunction, it is because I thought that every
fragment of such a mind should be preserved to
history, because I despised the despotism which would
incarcerate even intellect: and because I thought
those only should become accessory to concealment
who were conscious of actions which could not bear
the light. The following creditable documents emanat-
ing from the Ministers of a free country were transmitted by authority to me at St. Helena soon after
the publication of Mr. Warden's book. Every one
will make his own comment on them.*

HIS MAJESTY'S SHIP 'CONQUEROR,'

ST. HELENA ROADS, *January* 2, 1818.

SIR—*I herewith enclose to you a copy of a letter I have just
received from Mr. Secretary Barrow (relative to a work published
by Mr. Warden, late surgeon of His Majesty's ship* Northumber-

c

land), *which I desire you will pay most particular attention to.—*
*I am, sir, your most obedient, humble servant,*

ROBT. PAMPLIN,
*Rear-Admiral, Commander-in-Chief.*

To Mr. Barry O'Meara, Surgeon, R.N.
Longwood, St. Helena.

(NO. XII.)        ADMIRALTY OFFICE, *September* 13, 1817.

SIR—*My Lords Commissioners of the Admiralty having had
under their consideration a work which has been published by Mr.
Warden, late surgeon of His Majesty's ship* Northumberland, *their
Lordships have commanded me to signify their directions to you to
acquaint all the officers employed under your orders that they are
to understand that if they should presume to publish any information which they may have obtained by being officially employed at
St. Helena, they will suffer their Lordships' heavy displeasure.—*
*I am, sir, your most obedient, humble servant,*

JOHN BARROW.

To Rear-Admiral Pamplin,
St. Helena.

*Despising the denunciation as I did, and from my
heart do, I have, however, thought it my duty not to
publish these conversations until after Napoleon's
death; nor have I done so even now without the
knowledge of his Executors.*

*B. E. O'M.*

# SIR HUDSON LOWE[1]

SIR HUDSON LOWE, *the subject of a most unenviable notoriety, was born in Galway on 28th July 1769. His father, a member of an old Lincolnshire family, obtained a medical appointment with the troops that served in Germany during the Seven Years' War, and was subsequently appointed Surgeon-Major and head of the Medical Department at Gibraltar. Hudson Lowe, before his twelfth year, and while still at school, was made Ensign in the East Devon Militia. In 1787 he obtained a commission as Ensign in the 50th Regiment, then stationed at Gibraltar, where Sir G. A. Eliott (afterwards Lord Heathfield) was Governor.*

*Sir George Eliott was succeeded by General O'Hara, of whom, in his fragment of autobiography, Lowe wrote:* ' *I was once proceeding with the escort to reach the barrier gate by daylight, moving with my head down to stem the tremendous gusts of wind and rain which opposed me, when I heard myself very sharply spoken to by a mounted officer, who desired me to hold up my head and look what I was about, for I was not ordered upon that duty as a matter of form. . . . This was the* only real rebuke *I ever experienced from a superior officer during the whole course of my military life.*'

[1] *This Memoir is not by Mr. O'Meara, and it appears for the first time in the 1888 edition.*

*After four years of very severe garrison duty, Lieutenant Lowe obtained leave of absence and travelled on the Continent, where he became a proficient in French and Italian. He was then sent to Corsica with his regiment, which was ordered to garrison Ajaccio. ' One of the best houses in the town,' he writes, 'was occupied by the mother and sisters of Bonaparte. Lieutenant de Butts of the Engineers had been sent forward to provide quarters, and to intimate to the family that as their sons were in the French service, or had quitted the island, they must surrender their house for the use of the English garrison. An officer of the 50th, named Ford, was quartered there, and spoke with much satisfaction of the kind manner in which the family treated him,—the young girls ran slipshod about the house, but hardly any notice was taken of them. . . . It is not from my own recollection I mention these circumstances, because, strange as it may appear, I was not aware of the residence of any part of the Bonaparte family in Ajaccio during nearly two years we were in garrison in that town. I used frequently to hear Napoleon spoken of, but not as connected with the exploit generally mentioned as having given the first celebrity to his name—his share in the expulsion of the British from Toulon.'*

*On the evacuation of Corsica, Lieutenant Lowe accompanied his regiment to Elba; in 1795 he was promoted to a company, and soon after appointed Deputy Judge Advocate to the troops. After about two years spent in Portugal he proceeded to Minorca, where he was entrusted with the command of a body of emigrants from Corsica organised into a corps called the ' Corsican Rangers,' which joined Sir Ralph Abercromby's expedition to Egypt as part of the reserve commanded by Major-General (afterwards Sir John) Moore. Major Lowe was present at the battle of Alexandria on 21st March 1801; during the*

*campaign a piquet, having mistaken Sir Sidney Smith for
a French officer, through his wearing a cocked hat, levelled
their pieces at him, when Major Lowe struck up their
muskets and saved his life.   His vigilance at the outposts
induced Moore to say to him : ' Lowe, when you're at the
outposts, I always feel sure of a good night's rest.'*

*The ' Corsican Rangers' were disbanded at the Peace of
Amiens, and after an interval of official work in Malta
and England Major Lowe was sent by the Government on
a secret mission to Portugal for the purpose of ascertaining
its military condition and resources.   He afterwards proceeded to the Mediterranean to raise another corps of ' Royal
Corsican Rangers,' of which he was appointed Lieutenant-
Colonel in December* 1803 ; *and in* 1806 *he was sent, at the
head of five companies of the ' Rangers' and a small detach-
ment of artillery, to garrison the island of Capri, where, after
the battle of Maida, the whole of his corps joined him.   The
system of employing ' Sicilian agents' brought him into contact
with a Corsican lawyer named Suzzarelli, who is said by Cipriani, Napoleon's* maître d'hôtel, *to have imposed on Colonel
Lowe and profited largely by his credulity.   The* Quarterly
Review (*No. LV. p.* 230) *summarising the matter says :
' Suppose the whole story were true, what does it amount to ?
That Suzzarelli was a double spy, who took money and
gave information on both sides.'   In October* 1807 *a
French expedition, commanded by General Lamarque, took
possession of Ana Capri, which was evacuated by Colonel
Lowe and his troops ' with all the honours of war,' after,
says Mr. Forsyth, a vigorous attack and brave defence.
Napier, in his* History of the Peninsular War, *cuttingly
observes that ' Sir Hudson Lowe first became known to
history by losing in a few days a post that, without any
pretensions to celebrity, might have been defended for as
many years.'   Referring to the same event, Napoleon said*

*that, at St. Helena, 'Sir Lowe' showed himself a better gaoler than general.*

*The 'Corsican Rangers' and their Colonel assisted at the fall of Ischia, and then took part in a successful expedition against the French in Cephalonia and Ithaca, the government of those islands being subsequently conferred on Colonel Lowe—without remuneration.*

*In 1813 he accompanied Sir Alexander Hope to Sweden, to inspect a corps called the Russian-German Legion, and negotiate with the Crown Prince, Bernadotte, with a view to placing him at its head and securing his co-operation with the Allied Powers. He then proceeded to Kalisch, to have an interview with the Emperor of Russia, crossing the Niemen on the raft on which Alexander and Napoleon had held their celebrated conference.*

*Colonel Lowe was an eyewitness of the battle of Bautzen, where he first saw Napoleon, then 'at the head of an immense and devoted army.' In January 1814 he joined Blucher at Vaucouleurs, and was present at thirteen actions, in eleven of which Napoleon himself led the opposing army. When Paris was entered by the Allies, Colonel Lowe took the news of Napoleon's abdication to England, and was knighted by the Prince Regent, receiving also the Prussian Order of Military Merit and the Russian Order of Saint George. His next appointment was that of Quartermaster-General to the British troops in the Low Countries, and after receiving high praise from Blucher and Count Gneisenau, and serving for a short time under the Duke of Wellington, he took command of the British troops at Genoa in June 1815. In July he sailed for Marseilles with Lord Exmouth, where he learnt that Napoleon was to be placed in his custody, and that he must at once return to England.*

*When he was appointed Governor of St. Helena by the*

Directors of the East India Company, he received his final and official 'Instructions' (substantially the same as those given to Sir George Cockburn) from Earl Bathurst, Secretary at War, who said, ' You will observe that the desire of His Majesty's Government is to allow every indulgence to General Bonaparte which may be compatible with the entire security of his person : that he should not by any means escape, or hold communication with any person whatever, excepting through your agency, must be your unremitted care ; and these points being made sure, every resource and amusement which may serve to reconcile Bonaparte to his confinement may be permitted.' The warmest defender of Sir Hudson Lowe must admit that · he did not interpret these instructions generously.

In January 1816, accompanied by his wife, two stepdaughters, and a rather numerous suite, Sir Hudson Lowe sailed from Portsmouth, landing at St. Helena in April.

No details of the following years need be given here, as they form the subject of Mr. O'Meara's pages. But it may be briefly owned that whatever Sir Hudson Lowe's military and diplomatic services may have been, the British Government could hardly have made a worse choice for the singularly difficult position in which they placed him. Granting that Napoleon and his comrades in captivity were prepared to detest him, and predetermined to place every obstacle in the way of an amicable performance of his invidious task, assuredly Sir Hudson Lowe lost no opportunity of further embittering his relations with them. He was not, of course, the ' assassin' they called him ; but almost every step he took was characterised by want of sympathy and want of tact. He has been leniently called ' an official machine' incapable of breaking down the barriers of red tape. But a machine would not have experienced

*those nervous panics in which some of his most undignified
and unnecessary 'precautions' seem to have originated.*

*Mr. Forsyth, Q.C., who considered himself authorised to
defend Sir Hudson Lowe against the severe censures of
Alison, Scott, and Lord Campbell, and from whose ex-
haustive and valuable* History of the Captivity of Napoleon
*these particulars of Sir Hudson's career have been chiefly
taken, says mildly: 'His manner was not prepossessing,
even in the judgment of favourable friends;' how little,
then, was it likely to conciliate those of whom Count Montholon said to Lieutenant-Colonel Jackson after their return
to Europe: 'An angel from Heaven could not have pleased
us as Governor of St. Helena!'*

*Napoleon died on the 5th of May 1821. On the 25th
of July Sir Hudson Lowe quitted St. Helena after receiving a complimentary address from the inhabitants. Lord
Bathurst and George the Fourth welcomed and congratulated him on his return to England, and he was made
Colonel of the 93d Regiment. The publication of O'Meara's*
Napoleon in Exile, *in July 1822, excited popular feeling
so strongly against Lowe that he resolved to endeavour to
obtain legal redress, retaining the Solicitor-General (afterwards Lord Lyndhurst) and Mr. Tindal. Sir Hudson
Lowe did not take any immediate action in the matter, and
when his application for a rule for a criminal information
was made in Hilary Term 1823, the book had gone through
a fifth edition, and Sir Hudson was informed that his
cause was 'lost in point of time.' He then consulted Mr.
Tindal as to the expediency of indicting O'Meara, or bringing an action for damages against him, but was dissuaded,
on the ground that he had cleared himself from every charge
upon his oath, and that if O'Meara challenged the truth of
his denials, he might test them by prosecuting Sir Hudson
Lowe for perjury. As to a civil action, Mr. Tindal said*

*O'Meara would certainly not justify, as a great portion of his work consisted of private communications from Bonaparte, which, of course, he could not prove.*

*Lord Bathurst advised Sir Hudson to draw up a full vindication of his government of St. Helena and publish it with documents. But instead of doing so, he 'wearied the Government with applications for redress,' says Mr. Forsyth, 'when he had in his own hands the amplest means of vindicating his character.' He received no pension ; but, after refusing the Governorship of Antigua, quitted England as Commander of the Forces at Ceylon in October 1825. On his way he saw Metternich at Vienna, who told him that Count Bertrand said at Paris that they had no complaint to make against the Governor of St. Helena personally, but that 'it was the island they were dissatisfied with.' In 1828 Sir Hudson Lowe returned to England (receiving a very cordial welcome at St. Helena, where he remained for three days* en route) *to consult Earl Bathurst as to the expediency of replying to the strictures on his conduct in Scott's* Life of Napoleon. *The Earl dissuaded him from any such attempt ; and after a fruitless endeavour to secure the interest of the Duke of Wellington to procure him either a pension or the Governorship of Ceylon,[1] Sir Hudson went back to his military duties. He finally returned to England in 1831, receiving no further public employment, and died there in 1844, seventy-five years old, and in such straitened circumstances that Sir Robert Peel recommended his unmarried daughter to the Queen for a small pension.* ·

---

[1] *The Duke, however, defended Sir Hudson Lowe's conduct against Lord Teynham in the House of Lords in* 1833.

The stiff surgeon who maintained his cause
Hath lost his place and gained the world's applause.

BYRON.

# BARRY EDWARD O'MEARA[1]

THE *author of the following work was born in Ireland in* 1778, *and was educated in Trinity College, Dublin. He studied surgery in the Royal College of Surgeons, Dublin, and also in London; at an early age he was appointed Assistant-Surgeon in the* 62d *Regiment, with which he served in Sicily, Egypt, and Calabria. As Assistant-Surgeon in the navy, Mr. O'Meara served on board the* Victorious, *commanded by Sir John Talbot, and was afterwards Surgeon on board the* Espiègle *sloop and the* Goliath *rasée, and was serving on the* Bellerophon *seventy-four, when Napoleon embarked in* 1815. *Mr. O'Meara's professional skill and knowledge of the Italian language attracted the attention of the Emperor, who proposed that he should accompany him to St. Helena as surgeon (see p.* 5). *Admiral Lord Keith sanctioning this proposal, it was accepted by Mr. O'Meara; and the following volumes, with six other works on Napoleon, are the results of his residence there. The importance which the French Government attached to the letters written from St. Helena by Mr. O'Meara is alluded to by Comte d'Hérisson, who says : ' Everything that came from . . . St. Helena, letters, papers, etc., was intercepted and delivered to· the* Black Cabinet. *If anything was allowed to escape, it*

[1] *This Memoir appears for the first time in the* 1888 *edition.*

*caused a veritable despair; and on* 10th April 1820 *Count Anglès expressed his regret at having the previous year missed the couriers of O'Meara, Balcombe, and the Bonaparte family. . . . To have missed O'Meara's correspondence was serious . . . everything from this physician, the Emperor's confidant, was especially coveted. . . . When O'Meara returned to Europe he was spied and tracked; a regular plot was laid, with a view to abstracting the precious documents of which he was the bearer.' After quoting the passage from O'Meara's book (vol. ii. pp.* 338, 339), *in which Napoleon urges O'Meara to go to his brother Joseph, obtain the confidential letters written to him (Napoleon) by the Emperors Alexander and Francis, and publish them, to shame the Imperial writers, Comte d'Hérisson adds: ' As soon as he returned to Europe, O'Meara hastened to execute Napoleon's orders and to inform his brother of them. But it was too late; the precious correspondence had been confided to unfaithful hands, and was already delivered to the different sovereigns who had so much interest to cause its disappearance'* (The Black Cabinet, *pp.* 156-158).[1]

*As some indication of the impression made by O'Meara on one of the most acutely critical and fastidious contemporary members of London society—a man by no means prepossessed in favour of O'Meara or his cause—we may quote a passage from the* Dudley Letters, *written in August* 1822: '*I forget whether you have read O'Meara's book. On Thursday last I dined in company with the author. He is a stout and not ill-looking man, as I should judge about four and thirty years old. He is cheerful, goodhumoured, and communicative, and in spite of an air of*

---

[1] ' *Amongst the Napoleon relics shown in the Saint Helena Section of the Colonial Exhibition in London in* 1887 *was a tiny autograph note sent by the Emperor to Prince Eugène, and concealed for safety by Barry O'Meara in the heel of his boot.*'

*confident vulgarity which is diffused over all his behaviour,
the impression he made upon me was rather favourable,
At least my belief in what he has told was strengthened
by having seen him, and still more so by some conversation
which I happened to have the very next day with Sir
G—— C——, whom I met at Gloucester Lodge. He
defends Sir Hudson Lowe only just as far as prudence and
decorum oblige an official man to do so. Indeed, he acknowledges that, with respect to what passed in St. Helena, he
was disposed to take O'Meara's part. He mentioned a
circumstance, however, since O'Meara's return to England,
which he thought disreputable—a letter addressed by him to
the Admiralty, containing a charge against Sir Hudson
Lowe which, if made at all, ought to have been made openly
and substantiated by proof. This, therefore, must be set
off against that appearance of credibility which is, as I
think, distinguishable in O'Meara's book and in his conversation.'* [1]*

 *For his services at St. Helena Mr. O'Meara received
the thanks of Lord Melville, and his conduct was approved
by Sir George Cockburn and Sir Pulteney Malcolm. On
his return to England he was well received by the Lords of
the Admiralty, and is said to have had the valuable post
of Surgeon to Greenwich Hospital offered to him. His
active and outspoken zeal on behalf of Napoleon is, however,
believed to have induced Ministerial interference, which
prevented this appointment being ratified. Disappointed
hopes possibly increased Mr. O'Meara's national antipathies,
for he ultimately became an extreme Liberal and a partisan
of O'Connell.* [2] *He died in 1836 at his house 'on' the
Edgware Road.*

---

[1] *Lord Dudley to the Bishop of Llandaff,* Dudley Letters, 1840, *pp.* 350, 351.
[2] *Perhaps a sense of injury at the hands of the English Government may
have accounted also for his occupation in September 1820, when we find in*

_At the sale of his effects on the_ 18th _and_ 19th _of July_
1836, _a few lines in Napoleon's handwriting sold for eleven
guineas, a lock of his hair for fifty shillings, one of his teeth,
extracted by O'Meara, for seven and a half guineas, and
the instrument with which it was extracted for three
guineas._

_His grand-daughter, Miss Kathleen O'Meara (who died
in_ 1888), _inherited the literary instincts of her ancestor, and was
known as the author of several bright and interesting works._

_O'Meara was bitterly attacked on his return to this
country for political reasons, and amongst others anonymously
in the_ Quarterly Review _by John Wilson Croker, who, however, offered to place the documents on which his attack was
founded, open to the inspection of the public. As he censures
O'Meara in his article for breach of trust, we suppose these
documents did not come into Croker's hands officially._

_A further onslaught was made upon O'Meara by a then
highly-esteemed critic, Christopher North, in_ Blackwood.

_A reply to these articles appeared in the pages of the_
Edinburgh Review, _in which it is stated that ' Mr.
O'Meara's work contained a body of the most interesting
and valuable information—information, the accuracy of
which stands unimpeached by any of the attacks lately
made against its author.'—XXXVIII._ 494.

_And Byron says—_

> ' _The stiff surgeon who maintained his cause_
> _Hath lost his place and gained the world's applause._'

_The accuracy of O'Meara's narrative is emphatically
endorsed by Count Las Cases ; those who are curious as to
' the history of Longwood may,' he says, ' seek for details in
the work of Mr. O'Meara. . . . The doctor, who was only_

_Thomas Moore's_ Diary: ' _O'Meara, the celebrated surgeon of Napoleon, is here,'
[in Paris] ' upon the Queen's business—forwarding witnesses, etc.,' vol. iii.
p._ 151.

*a witness, who was a stranger to us, and in some degree
one of the adverse party, can only have been actuated by the
impulse of a powerful feeling, and of generous indignation
which does honour to his heart. . . . All the facts which I
have seen stated in Mr. O'Meara's work which fell under
my knowledge when I was at St. Helena are strictly true;
and thence I naturally conclude, by analogy, that the remainder, which I have not seen, is also true. I do not
hesitate to say that I consider it such in my heart and
conscience.'* And its general interest and excellence received
the weighty approval of Carlyle :—*

*'O'Meara's work has increased my respect for Napoleon,'
he says; 'since the days of Prometheus Vinctus I recollect
no spectacle more moving and sublime than that of this
great man in his dreary prison-house, captive, sick, despised,
forsaken, yet rising above it all by the stern force of his
own unconquerable spirit. I declare I could almost love
the man! His native sense of honesty, the rude genuine
strength of his intellect, his lively fancy, his sardonic
humour, must have rendered him a most original and
interesting companion; he might have been among the
finest writers of his age if he had not chosen to be the first
Conqueror of any age.'*

# LIST OF ILLUSTRATIONS

# INTRODUCTION

THE reader will have learnt from the foregoing accounts of Sir Hudson Lowe and of O'Meara the outlines of the history of the two persons brought into notoriety by the publication of O'Meara's journal. That publication was felt as a blow, not only by Lowe, but also by the English Government. Lowe himself failed to meet the attack in the way that would have been most telling—that is, by going into Court and prosecuting O'Meara for libel. He professed indeed to be most eager to do so, but he delayed action till, when the case was brought on, the Judges refused to hear it after such a lapse of time. It is strange if it were news to his lawyers, as we are asked to believe it was to him, to know that an Englishman cannot let his conduct lie in the gutter for months, and then ask a Court of Law to clear him. The only reason given by Lowe for his delay was the time required for meeting charges in which truth was so artfully blended with falsehood; an admission that we have a good deal of truth in the journal.

It was obvious, however, that some attempt ought to be made to meet the charges brought by O'Meara, and the task was undertaken by Mr. Croker, the Secretary of the Admiralty, a post then more prominent than it is in our days; and Croker himself was a person carrying weight in the literary as well as in the political world.

*d*

His attack was delivered in the *Quarterly Review* of October 1822. It was written in a violent manner, apparently relying on countercharges against the Doctor to bear down his book, and it would hardly be looked on nowadays as a satisfactory attempt to meet charges which every Englishman would wish to see disproved. The personal attack on O'Meara, at page 220 of the article was, for example, grossly unfair, as no real charge against O'Meara's conduct, before he went to St Helena, was then or has since been made. The generation for whom Croker wrote would have thought nothing of an officer acting as second in a duel, or rather would probably have thought it creditable to him ; and Croker prudently did not name this, the real reason for O'Meara having to leave the army. Croker had all the official records of the army and of the navy open to him, and we should have something more than hints if he could have found anything really damaging to the Doctor. Besides all this, there runs through the article a complete misconception of Napoleon himself, which, for readers of the present day, will render the article valueless, as practically Croker trusts a good deal to sneers at O'Meara for being influenced by a man of the low type he imagined Napoleon to have been.

We can see how little Croker was fitted to judge of the real interest of O'Meara's work by a few of his comments thereon.

'His manners and conversation' (says Croker of Napoleon) 'were always vulgar and often brutal.' Often brutal, when angry, we quite allow ; but always vulgar ? Let the reader read the full passage in Croker, and then turn to Roederer. 'No one is a hero to his valet,' says the proverb. . . . But the proverb would be wrong for Bonaparte. 'The more you approach him the more you respect him. You find him always greater than yourself, when he speaks, when he thinks, when he acts.' Again Roederer describes him in the Council of State as always reverting to two points on every question—'Is it just? Is it useful?' and 'examining every question in itself under these two considerations, after having dissected it by the most exact and detailed analysis.' Again, how does Madame de Rémusat describe this vulgar conversation? We need fear no flattery from the woman who fawned on Napoleon, and ate his bread, in the days of his prosperity, and reviled him when dead. ' It was always, says Madame de Rémusat, 'a great pleasure for me to hear him converse, or rather speak,' and she goes on to refer to the originality of his ideas. If it be said these are opinions of members of his Court, let us turn to Metternich. 'What at first struck me most,' says that Minister, 'was the remarkable perspicuity and grand simplicity of his mind and its processes. Conversation with him always had a charm for me, difficult to define . . . always finding the fitting word for the thing, or inventing one where the usage of the language had not created it, his conversation was ever full of interest. He did not converse, he talked ; by the wealth of his ideas and the facility of his elocution, he was able to lead the conversation.' Is it any wonder that the surgeon, left much with him, should have fallen under his charm? and is there the slightest ground for the sneers of Croker at O'Meara for being influenced by such a man?

No, it is not to know Napoleon and all his dangerous charm, not to be aware that the man who would sometimes shower rough and coarse reproaches on any one who displeased him, could become as it were inspired by high and lofty thoughts, and could speak in a strain going to the hearts of the great, talented, and learned men, the

leaders of the nation, who had surrounded him. If Croker
had been sufficiently unprejudiced to see it, the pages of
O'Meara give proof that the conversation was often lofty
enough. O'Meara himself, apparently, was not possessed
of any special education, or of literary aptitude to originate
such topics, and he was not the man to invent the conversation he records. The coarse abuse of Lowe is only too
likely truly enough placed in Napoleon's mouth, but that
is not the part with which readers of the present day are
interested. It is the ideas on men and things, filtered of
course through the mind of O'Meara, which we value. We
must always remember O'Meara had everything to gain
by remaining on good terms with Lowe. He would have
led an easy and well-paid life, most likely rewarded by
both sides. In espousing altogether the side of Napoleon,
he was not influenced by a rough, low-bred upstart. As
so many other greater men had done, he fell under the
charm of one of the most fascinating minds the world has
ever produced.

How curiously unfit Croker was to judge O'Meara's
account of Napoleon's conversation can be seen by one
instance. Napoleon had said that he considered the
Archduke Charles the best Austrian general, and Prince
Schwarzenberg as not fit to command five thousand men.
This seems to Croker only amusing, and to be explained by
the fact that Napoleon had beaten the Archduke, and had
been defeated by the Prince. We would not venture to
define the exact number of men Schwarzenberg was fit to
command, but there is not a student of military history
in the world who would not acknowledge the correctness
of Napoleon's utterance. The Archduke was a general
of the first class, only prevented from being one of the
greatest by some strange failure of physical power, so at
least the Duke of Wellington explained his deficiency.

It is, by the bye, odd to remark that Croker apparently
forgot that the Archduke had defeated, or at least checked,
Napoleon at Essling.   What, however, is more pleasant is
to find Croker in 1826 recording a judgment of his
oracle, the Duke of Wellington, putting the Archduke on
an even higher level than' that Croker sneers at when he
finds it given as an opinion of Napoleon's.   Asking the
Duke whether the Archduke really was a great officer,
he was answered.   'A great officer? why, he knows
more about it (war) than Buonaparte or all of us put
together.   We are none of us worthy to fasten the latchets
of his shoes, if I am to judge from his book and his plans
of campaign.'   Could there be a more decisive proof of
the levity and ignorance displayed by Croker in the then
celebrated article?

What rank Schwarzenberg holds amongst generals, it
would be hard to say, assuredly not the third rank; his
highest praise probably being that he did not entirely
throw away the enormous forces placed in his hands in
1813 and 1814, but was gradually dragged, hustled, and
bullied into Paris by a sort of joint-committee of all
nations and of all armies.

We might take several instances of Croker's hasty
answers to statements in O'Meara, but two or three will
suffice.

He tries to get rid of any odium for the sale of
Napoleon's plate by asserting that there were large funds
in the Emperor's name in Europe, and to prove this he
gives an instance that Napoleon could pay a sailor
£300 without breaking up any plate.   But he himself says that this sum was paid by a draft, and the
Secretary of the Admiralty must have known that many an
officer abroad is often practically penniless while he may
have a good balance in England with his bankers.   We can

quite understand that Napoleon was unwilling to place his funds in Europe (exaggerated as the amount seems to have been) at the mercy of the Allies, but what we are concerned with is the question whether he really was in need of cash at St. Helena. Now Lowe at once came down on the proceeds of the sale of the plate, and insisted on retaining them, and on knowing how they were spent. We must, therefore, take Lowe as expressly acknowledging that the sum was required to defray proper expenditure. Lowe himself informed Lord Bathurst that, though the amount realised remained in deposit, the money had been advanced upon it—that is, the sum really had been used, and with Lowe's approval.

We must remember that though at first glance the sum allotted for the maintenance of Napoleon's establishment by the English Government seems large, it is not so when the high prices existing in the Island are considered. This will be seen by comparison with the other allowances granted there. None of the three Foreign Commissioners were of high rank or standing, nor were they required to make any show. Yet the Austrian got £1200, the Russian £2000, and the French £2400. Notwithstanding this, Lowe reported that the expense frightened them all, and would, he thought, soon drive them away. Lowe himself, only a local Major-General, got £12,000 a year; and Forsyth tells us that he could save little out of that. The expense for Longwood at first was from £13,000 to £16,000, the income of many an English squire, and that was for fifty-five persons. Thus, to men accustomed to luxury, the English grant was certainly not large. The Government were anxious to make Napoleon share in the expense, and whether they took his plate or his cash was not so important. The folly, however, of either driving or allowing him to fasten on the Government the odium of selling his plate was just a point which would have been saved by a Governor with any tact. But the real sting of Napoleon's act was his success in calling public attention to the intended economy of his jailers.

Again, Croker is indignant at one of Napoleon's ideas. The Emperor had said that if he 'were King of England, he would beautify London by building two great quays along the whole length of the Thames, by making two great streets, the one from Charing Cross to St. Paul's, the other from St. Paul's to the river.' This is sneered at by Croker. But on the subject of grand works, Napoleon, the great contractor, was a past master, and far in advance of English ideas of the time. We have done part of the work proposed by Napoleon, and perhaps a time may come when some generation of Englishmen will realise what a splendid effect would be gained by a street from St. Paul's to the river. The Corsican was only half a century ahead of the English; and we may dream of what would have been the result if we had gained the Empire and lost the Board of Works.

Again, Croker is very delighted at the course taken with regard to O'Meara's accusation against Lowe, that the Governor had tried to induce him to poison Napoleon. The Admiralty replied by summarily dismissing the Doctor from the service, on the ground that he was in the following dilemma: Either he had kept such a criminal project secret, or else the charge was false and calumnious. Now the dilemma is too obvious to be called a clever way of putting the matter, but it must be seen at once that if it seems telling against O'Meara it is no real answer to the charge. For instance, when Moreau at last reported the former traitorous projects of Pichegru, the Directory very properly dismissed him for having concealed his knowledge. But the charge against Pichegru was none the less true,

with this difference: Moreau, during his silence, could at
any time have reported directly to the Government with a
certainty that his report would have been heard by persons
to some degree impartial.  But O'Meara had no practical
possibility of reporting to the English Government except
through Lowe.  Any authorised communication, not sent
through Lowe, would have been to a certainty discredited
and returned to Lowe, to proceed against O'Meara at St.
Helena, O'Meara himself being the one witness against the
Governor.  The thing was impossible, and no one should
have known that better than the Secretary of the Admiralty.
The only really satisfactory way of answering O'Meara's
accusation was to try him by court-martial for it.  From
the case of Doctor Stokoe, who was tried at St. Helena,
there would probably have been no hesitation in doing this
in the Island, but O'Meara would have had to be tried in
England.  It is necessary to dwell on this point, for civilians
may not remember that the power given to the Crown
of summarily dismissing officers is one obviously open to
the grossest of abuses—abuses which have not occurred
in the army under the long, kindly, and just rule of
the present Commander-in-Chief, but which have existed
at certain periods.

It is not that we profess to believe that Lowe ever
really wished to poison Napoleon ; we do not believe he
even shared in Croker's longing for Napoleon's death ;
but we must insist on the fact that both the Government
and Lowe always shrank from bringing O'Meara before
any Court, martial or civil.

But to end with Croker, and to give his real thoughts,
we fortunately are now able to turn to his letters.  He
closes his indignant article on O'Meara by a sort of
virtuous tag, in which he professes to defend the nation,
which Napoleon never made responsible for his treatment.

We read his fine sentiments, and then turn to his correspondence (vol. i. p. 89), and find him writing to the Père
Elysée, for the benefit of the Royal Family of France :
' L'homme de Ste Hélène se porte assez bien—je dois
plutôt dire, trop bien.' This is strong, but we have something still stronger. On August 8, 1816, he informs Peel
that ' George Cockburn gives us no hope of Buonaparte's
dying.' This is the man who is shocked at O'Meara's
published diary not agreeing with the letters meant to be
seen by Lowe, and by the Ministers ; this is the man who
is horrified at the idea of charging an English officer with
a wish to shorten the life of Napoleon ; this is the literary
defender of Lowe and of Lord Bathurst.

At the moment Croker was thought by his admiring
friends to have crushed O'Meara, but as time went on the
weak points in Lowe's case became apparent, and it was
evident even to the advocates of Lowe that the charges of
O'Meara must be met in a different style. The task this
time was very wisely put in the hands of Mr. William
Forsyth, Q.C., who in 1853 published three volumes of
the *History of the Captivity of Napoleon at St. Helena, from
the letters and journals of the late Sir Hudson Lowe.* In
this work, written with an evident attempt at impartiality,
O'Meara's statements are dealt with in detail, and at some
length, so that to reply to it the whole of O'Meara would
have to be passed in review. It is impossible for us to
do this, but we may take specimens from Forsyth's work
to show that no attempt has yet succeeded in really
clearing Lowe from the charges made against him of
treating his prisoner with unnecessary severity, and of
placing Napoleon under restrictions utterly useless, but
made as irritating as possible.

It is, however, a great relief to turn from Croker to
Forsyth's defence of Lowe. Forsyth writes like a gentle-

man, and with an evident wish and intention to be fair.
He owns that some of Lowe's vagaries, the famous beans
for example, are too much for him ; he acknowledges that
Lowe's manner was not attractive, and he gives a variety
of documents most useful for the attack on Lowe. But
naturally he has to lean much on the superior credibility
of Lowe and of his staff (though we hear very little of
what we should like to know about, the opinion of the
officers of the garrison). In all probability if he had had
Baron Sturmer's correspondence before him, and had seen
how the general description of Lowe by O'Meara is repeated by the Austrian Commissioner, he would have
altered his opinion on many occurrences. Also, if one
may be allowed to say so, he, as a civilian, would naturally assume that some of Lowe's acts, his figuring about
with his staff, and hovering near Longwood when an
arrest was to be made, were part of military routine.
But all through Forsyth plods honestly on, giving us,
for example, the replies of Lord Bathurst to Lowe on
Napoleon's offer to drop his title, and other documents
telling against his own argument; and we should be
quite content to rest the case against Lowe on Forsyth's
three volumes checked by O'Meara and by Sturmer.

It is easy enough to realise the extraordinary task which
was undertaken by Lowe apparently without any idea of
what was before him. Napoleon's mind was one of the most
active possible. After a morning of laborious office work
he would for hours hold long interviews with Minister
after Minister ; his mind, when tired by one subject, re-
gaining complete freshness, not by rest, but by simply
turning to another subject with a fresh interlocutor. The
exhausted Ministers, when released by their master,
sought repose in their offices or houses, too often only to
find themselves followed by a shower of letters from the

Emperor, calling on them to satisfy his insatiable craving for information on details, weighty or trifling, it did not matter ; anything was welcome to his all-embracing mind. If he had by chance some minutes of compulsory leisure, say at the Opera, he occupied himself by planning every detail of the march of his army on some distant point. Further, no man probably was more a law to himself than Napoleon had been. No man had drunk more of what Clough calls the ' joy of eventful living.' Monarchs, however great, are almost always subject or subject themselves to an inexorable rule of custom, of routine, and of cere-monial, by which every minute and every action of their lives is governed. The life of a sailor on a man of war is a free and leisurely one compared to that passed by the Grand Monarque himself. But Napoleon was never restricted in his personal movements. With his new Empire, his new Court, and his new officials, he remained free in person, and unbound by the ceremonial to which he made others bow. When he rose, when he ate, when and where and how he went, were all matters ruled by the whim of the moment. Even the grandest processions of the Court were spoilt by his eagerness to get them finished, and we know the embarrassments of the courtiers placed between the graceful and slow pacing Josephine in front, and her restless lord pressing on in rear. When, too, he was in movement, he must see all and everything around him. If he were in a Dutch village, he must see even the kitchen of the mayor, and in the kitchen he must see what was in the *pot-à-feu*, though, to the delight of his attendants, he burnt his fingers in the process. Madame de Rémusat almost drops a tear as she describes how even the courtiers of the ancient nobility, who deigned to accept Court offices under the usurper, found that they too never had a moment of freedom or idleness, but lived under the uneasy influence of crowned restlessness. About twenty-four hours, passed under stress of weather in one of his own men of war, is the only quiet time we can say Napoleon had from 1799 till he stepped on board of the *Northumberland* in 1815. Thinking, planning, acting, and making all others in his mighty Empire think, move, and act in a way that no other Power has ever done or ever will do, Napoleon was the very spirit of movement and restlessness.

This man, of all men, Lowe was to keep in a lonely, desolate island, deprived of all the bustle and interest of life, without family, friends, or a proper supply of listeners: the very spirit of labour was to be condemned to lifelong idleness.

Something of what we have just said about Napoleon himself applies, of course, in a lesser degree, to his followers ; men accustomed to luxury, employment, and if not to the exercise of power, at least to be moving parts of the mighty machine which swayed France. Much that followed came, inevitably, and as a matter of course. Anger, irritability, jealousy, hatred, malice, all the evils which moralists from the beginning of morality have declared to be the works of idleness, flourished in St. Helena, as in many a small community and colony ; but in this instance much to the innocent surprise of the Governor, who seems to have gone out believing he would rule over a sort of happy family, his neighbour, 'General Buonaparte,' always ready to drop in to take potluck with him on the arrival of any distinguished visitor. One may be a fervent admirer of Napoleon without altogether losing the same feeling towards Lowe which the mother of Sir David Baird had for the compulsory companion of her son when, hearing that the captives of the Black Hole were chained two and two, she cried, 'The Lord help the man chained to my Davie!'

But Lowe himself, voluntarily undertaking the work, had no right to complain. A man might as well stand to stop an express train, and then feel aggrieved at the train hurting him : *that* it was sure to do.

To his and our misfortune, Lowe had some special personal disabilities for his task as jailer. In the first place, he had been in Corsica during the English occupation, when the Bonapartes, we beg his and Croker's pardon, the Buonapartes (how much there is in a vowel !), were in their days of poverty. He says he was not aware of their residence in the town of Ajaccio, though he displays an intimate knowledge of their way of life, telling us that the girls used to run about barefooted. (It is pleasant to think of the pretty Pauline bareshod, but even in her highest prosperity she was never careful about the extent of her clothing.) With a certain narrow-mindedness inherent in the man, this seems to have dwelt in his mind, and he was unable to realise that the brother of the barefooted girls could ever have been one of the great Princes of the world. Further, Napoleon, who knew how and where to apply the spur, seems to have struck at a sore place when he remarked that Lowe had not commanded an English regiment.

A regiment, far from being a machine obeying the least order of its commander, is an assemblage of individuals, often of strong idiosyncrasies, each and all nominally under perfect submission to any order, but each and all possessed of well-defined rights and privileges, given or confirmed by law and custom, and each individual, to the youngest drummer, well aware of the privileges he possesses. The English army, probably more than most armies, tends to preserve much valuable independence in its members from including amongst its officers such a large proportion of men of considerable fortune, serving only for honour, yielding to the touch of a man, but most troublesome to the fussy, meddlesome official. To rule such a body preserving the appearance and the reality of unlimited power, by never overstepping his proper limits, maintaining his own rights by respecting those of his subordinates, forms an experience and an education which must always tell on the character of any one who has undergone it. The results may be read at large in the history and in the customs of the English army. As a clever writer has pointed out, nothing is so remarkable as the constant and almost unconscious veiling of authority in the daily routine and in the phraseology of our army. 'Colonel A is requested to have his regiment formed on parade by ten to-morrow,' is the form in which an order is constantly given. The silk glove alone is shown, and never so much as when it covers the hand of steel. This training, this experience, this education, Lowe had never enjoyed; and in reading many of his admitted acts, his prowling in the neighbourhood when he had ordered an arrest, his suggesting the exclusion of an officer bearing a commission from the mess of a regiment, his extraordinary passion for secrecy, an English officer must say, 'This is not the way in the army.'

Nor can we believe that in such matters there has been any change since those days, our army being very conservative of its customs; and in these points of procedure, we may be sure, our fathers did not much differ from us, the present army, except of course in its knowledge of that useful branch of study, the higher mathematics, probably not being much of an improvement on the old one.

As for Lowe's whole system of restrictions, no one would have a right to complain if they had been necessary and effectual. Now they were not, and obviously never could have been effectual, and thus were assuredly unnecessary. Take, for example, the subject of correspondence. One thing which was more at Lowe's heart than any other was to prevent Napoleon and his staff communicating with the outer world except through him. Some fifty persons or more were employed about Longwood, there was constant going and coming between that place and the town, messengers and orderlies passed, and visitors had to be permitted to enter. Now you may possibly succeed in preventing a prisoner corresponding with his friends outside if you have him safe in a good cell, isolated as far as you can achieve it, and if you search his cell and his clothing from time to time. Even then the chances are you fail if much interest be taken in the prisoner by the outer world.

How could correspondence be stopped under the conditions which Lowe was forced to permit? At the time, even after the death of Napoleon, it would not have done for any of the Longwood party to acknowledge openly how much they had corresponded with Europe; and by this time the record is lost to us, but we can get an idea of how far Lowe's rules were successful.

In May 1818 Lowe does not find out, but is informed from England by Goulburn, on the authority of General Gourgaud, that 'there has always existed a free and inter- rupted communication between the inhabitants of Longwood and this country and the Continent, without the knowledge or intervention of the Governor;' and the letter goes to explain the full freedom of this correspondence. Thus, just as might be expected, while Lowe was making himself and every one in the Island miserable by his suspicions, inspecting a marble bust to see if letters were hidden in it, and made uneasy by the colour of beans, his system was an utter failure, and a whole correspondence was going on under his nose.   He now and then caught a letter, or some signs of the underground system, just enough to keep him on the fret.   Goulburn indeed need not have restricted the correspondence to this continent, it seems to have extended to America.   The reader will of course remark that the existence of this underground channel will explain what is sometimes wondered at—the apparent apathy of Napoleon's family about corresponding with their brother through Lowe.

A good specimen of Lowe's manner of acting is given by the arrest of Las Cases, the poor little Count who looks so small in Mr. Orchardson's picture of Napoleon on board the *Bellerophon*, and whose ears were so soundly boxed by hoydenish Miss Betsy Balcombe.   Lowe actually went to Longwood with the officers selected to make the seizure ; and it was only 'a short distance outside the barrier gate,' having given all the orders in case of resistance on the part of such a desperate criminal, that he left the ground.   How far off he went we are not told, but naturally not only O'Meara, but also Baron Sturmer, the Austrian Commissioner, treats him as present at the affair.   This does not read pleasantly to an Englishman of an English general ; there is a great deal too much of the fussy, suspicious jailer in it.   One thinks of Lowe, at a little distance, watching Longwood, just in the same ridiculously suspicious way as he did when one day the Commissioners, to his horror, got in there.

There had been some races near Longwood, and Baron Sturmer, his pretty wife, and the Russian Commissioner, seeing Napoleon watching on his balcony, went to the house with Lowe's permission.   Napoleon, as Lowe had prophesied, disappeared ; but all his staff came out, naturally enough, to have a chat.   Lowe, left outside, seems to have been driven wild by his restless suspicions.   ' Hardly

had the Governor lost sight of us,' says Sturmer, 'than he
was seized with his ordinary anxiety. He set off at the
fullest of gallops. As our servants had remained at the
gate of the enclosure with our horses, he could not resist
the craze to come and question them himself. ' How long
have your masters been inside ? ' he asked them in a
suspicious tone. ' Did they not tell you when they would
return ? ' Then he went to the height which commands
the enclosure to watch us. We walked to the railing of
the enclosure in which Bonaparte's house is placed. When
we got to this railing, a non-commissioned officer, thinking
we wished to enter, came to open the two wings of the
gate for us. This was the most critical moment for Sir
Hudson Lowe, but he was reassured when he saw us turn
round. He stuck his spurs in and went off like a dart as
soon as he thought we could see him. This ridiculous
scene was not lost to the inhabitants of Longwood.'

Are we to wonder that Napoleon despised the man
who acted in this manner ?

The arrest of Las Cases, indeed, to return to that matter,
throughout was a very clumsy and ill-advised affair. It was
well known that the Count had been employed by Napoleon
in composing the memoirs which lightened the weary hours
of the prisoner. Most men of any generosity would have
borne anything rather than have deprived his prisoner of
such an employment. Las Cases's own conduct also was of
a nature which should have led to his retention. Even now
it is not quite easy to say for certain whether, in leaving
the Island, he was going under orders from Napoleon to act
in Europe as an envoy, or whether, as seems most probable,
he was influenced by views of selfish interest. He had
amassed a good deal of valuable literary matter, and with
the craze of all men of the pen, he probably longed to get
it into print. The ease with which he communicated with

*e*

his messenger (an ease so great that Baron Sturmer hints that the affair looks like a trap laid by Lowe) showed how little the regulations really availed. It would have seemed much more natural and much safer to keep him in the Island. Certainly most governors, for the sake of their own characters, would have retained him till it was clear he left with Napoleon's approval, and that his place could be filled. There is in this, as in many of Lowe's acts, a readiness to deprive Napoleon of his French attendants, which is extraordinarily ungenerous. Lowe indeed was prepared to remove all the French from his prisoner if they had not given in to the insulting whim of objecting to the use by any one of the title 'Emperor.' Every one knows the story of a prisoner who tamed a mouse, and thus cheered himself in his lonely hour. The Governor of the prison had the mouse killed, and was no doubt really surprised at the consequent outburst of anger on the part of the prisoner. This is quite in Lowe's manner. He would have pointed out that pets were not allowed by the regulations; and he and his defenders would have been honestly horrified at any one who had sympathised with the prisoner.

The men who went with Napoleon to St. Helena were rather a chance collection; and it would have been more natural and more generous to have put pressure on them to remain, than to have tried to have helped them in leaving.

The retention of Napoleon's papers found amongst those of Las Cases is a good test case of Lowe's tact. He should have been prepared to find such papers, indeed he seems to have made the arrest in a manner as if he wished to seize all such documents in the Count's possession, otherwise the arrest could have been made more quietly and less offensively outside Longwood by sending for Las

Cases. Not only were the papers retained for some days, but also they were, most foolishly, returned piecemeal, thus naturally making Napoleon believe that they were being copied. Lowe surely must have known of the indignation of Frederick the Great when he thought Voltaire was carrying off his poetical trash ; and Napoleon was sure to be anxious and jealous about his own works—works of a great value, and the style of which is praised by two such different men as Sainte Beuve and the Duc de Broglie.

However O'Meara may have misrepresented Lowe, has he drawn a more ludicrous picture of the suspicious Governor than Lowe has done himself? Here we have it in the pages of his defender Forsyth. In May 1820 we learn of an occurrence which had given that worthy man ground for great uneasiness ; more, indeed, than finding that Napoleon had received a lock of his son's hair. Count Montholon had offered to send to the French Commissioner, the Marquis de Montchenu (we almost tremble to write the words, Croker alone could do justice to the incident), 'des haricots verts,' or 'des haricots blancs,' to which the Marquis answered that he might send to him a little of both ! Sir Hudson Lowe adds (we are really quoting verbatim from Forsyth, vol. iii. pp. 223, 224), 'Whether the "haricots blancs" and "haricots verts" bear any reference to the "drapeau blanc" of the Bourbons, and the "habit vert" of General Bonaparte himself, and the livery of his servants at Longwood, I am unable to say ; but the Marquis de Montchenu, it appears to me, would have acted with more propriety if he had declined receiving either, or limited himself to a demand for the white alone. He is not aware how much the question that was put by Count Montholon to Count Balmaine may be made to apply to his proceeding on this occasion.'

We have said Croker alone could do justice to this

incident. We were wrong. The late lamented Sergeant
Buzfuz was the man. 'Chops and tomato sauce.' Dickens
surely was a plagiarist from Lowe. The incident is too
much for the judicious Forsyth, who, with all his usual
fairness, acknowledges it 'does seem ludicrous.' It does ;
and all the more so when he goes on to tell us that Lowe
thought the matter of some importance and again alluded
to it in another letter to Lord Bathurst. What the
question put by Count Montholon to Count Balmaine was
neither Forsyth nor we know.

If ever a man wrote himself down an ass at large,
surely it was Lowe. Unfortunately, this suspicious
Governor, stalking up and down with his finger in his
mouth, perplexed with fears about similar dark doings,
was the man who was given power over the prisoner who
had trusted to our generosity. Like a true self-tormentor,
he was not contented with his actual difficulties, but
pondered over what might happen. What was to be
done if Napoleon killed a man? much exercised his
mind—a question apparently beyond the capabilities of
the English Government to settle.

A good illustration of the way in which Lowe and
the Government seemed to delight in using their power
to force on Napoleon and on his followers measures they
knew to be most offensive, is given by the objection
made to the use of the title Emperor. Napoleon, with
great good sense, was at first quite ready .to waive this
and to assume an incognito title, Colonel Muiron or
Duroc. The English Government had transformed him
into a general, and there would appear to be no reason
why they should not have accepted him as a colonel.
If there were, however, a real reason, they need not have
been ashamed to give that reason publicly. On the
contrary, we find Lord Bathurst writing privately to

Lowe that he probably would not give any instructions on this proposition of Napoleon. 'It appears harsh to refuse it, and there may arise much embarrassment in formally acquiescing in it. You will therefore not encourage any renewal of the conversation. As the proposition was not made officially, no official answer need be given,' —that is to say, the proposition was practically refused, and this Lord Bathurst owns appears 'harsh.' But, by not refusing formally, the harshness was concealed, and probably few persons now realise that all the irritation naturally raised by this question of the title was not caused by Napoleon insisting on having it given him, but by the English Government insisting on him and his staff acknowledging that he was only a general. Why a general? Heaven only knows. It would have been much more consistent to act as Dumouriez said Louis XVIII. wanted to do with him, and only give the rank he bore in the year 1789 or 1793—sacred years up to which only sovereigns of ancient dynasties made conquests.

But while the Minister in England was forced to attend to appearances, there was no such necessity at St. Helena, and we find Lowe writing on October 18, 1816, with an odious air of triumph, to Lord Bathurst, calling attention to the fact, that though Napoleon's attendants had at first refused to sign the declaration required without giving Napoleon his proper title, they had yielded when they found they would really be removed from the person of the Emperor. To be able to use the attachment of the French at St. Helena to Napoleon to force them to apparently acquiesce in his degradation from his Imperial style, surely was the vilest of triumphs.

It is only fair to Lowe to say, once for all, that though

the Ministry at home may not have fully understood the irritating and useless nature of many of the restrictions put on Napoleon, yet most, if not all, the discredit due to the system must be shared by them. They seem to have been quite ready to support the Governor in his acts.

A writer in the *Cornhill Magazine* of March 1887, in an account of the strange disappearance of Benjamin Bathurst in 1809, gives us a theory about Lord Bathurst, the immediate correspondent of Lowe, of which he must take the responsibility. 'In 1815,' he says, 'Lord Bathurst was Secretary for War and the Colonial Department. May we not suspect there was some mingling of personal exultation, along with political satisfaction, in being able to send to St. Helena the man who had not only been the scourge of Europe and the terror of kings, but who, as he supposed—quite erroneously, we believe—had inflicted on his own family an agony of suspense and doubt that was never to be wholly removed?'

One of the many irritating tricks of Lowe and of the Government was their habit of showing they thought their own rules to be so useless as to be waived at their pleasure. Lowe considered an invitation to dine with him carried with it permission to pass the bounds allotted to Napoleon. Lord Bathurst was willing to let the rules requiring all letters to be sent open to be suspended in case of a letter by which it was hoped Napoleon would send for money to pay part of the expenses of keeping him at St. Helena. In fact, Lord Bathurst would apparently have joined in the whimsical reflection of Forsyth that we should remember it was the money of the English tax-payer which was maintaining Napoleon at St. Helena. That Napoleon did not want the English tax-payer to maintain him at St. Helena is no doubt straying from the question. To condemn a man to perpetual imprisonment, and then to want to make him support himself, was surely one of the meanest of economies of an economical period.

One little incident will show what we mean by the unnecessary irritation kept up by Lowe, apparently in order to prove his power. In July 1818 Lowe appointed a Colonel Lyster as orderly officer at Longwood. Napoleon objected for different reasons, because Lyster had been in Corsica and was a personal enemy of his at Ajaccio, was not an officer in the regular forces, only held a militia commission, and so on : the main point was that Lyster was not an officer independent (during good behaviour) of Lowe—not an independent witness, in fact. Now all this may have been utterly unreasonable, but surely any fair-minded man would have consented to respect even an unreasonable personal objection to a person who was to be much with the French, and, practically, their immediate guardian, and surely the post ought to have been held by a regular officer. Lowe, however, refused to remove Colonel Lyster. It is significant that while Lowe had to use his authority to get the regular officers to stop O'Meara messing with them, Colonel Lyster at once began his residence at Longwood by refusing to mess with O'Meara, the Emperor's doctor. This act of his is the best commentary on Lyster's own statement that he was anxious to be on the most friendly terms with the exiles. Surely Napoleon was justified in wishing to get Lyster removed, and in considering his retention as simply one of the intentional insults of Lowe.

The end of the matter is good evidence of the character of Lowe and of Colonel Lyster. Lowe having received a letter from Count Bertrand, stating the personal objection to Lyster, proceeded with his usual tact. 'Unfortunately,' says Forsyth, 'Sir Hudson Lowe showed Bertrand's letter to Colonel Lyster. This was an act both uncalled for and indiscreet, for it could do no good, and the language there used was of a nature greatly to irritate the feelings of a susceptible soldier.' Lyster thereupon justified his selection for his difficult post, first, by sending a challenge to Count Bertrand, and then proposing to horsewhip the Count, and Lowe, thus beaten on his own ground, had to withdraw Colonel Lyster. This is just one incident taken at random out of Forsyth. Look at the matter from Napoleon's point of view and imagine him saying: 'Lowe appoints a man I strongly object to, as I believe him to be an enemy of mine, refuses to withdraw him, tries to make him still more bitter by showing him Bertrand's letter, and then he has to withdraw him when his agent lets his real disposition show itself.' Contests such as these were not likely to make life smooth for Lowe, but the incident is chiefly valuable as showing his utter want of tact, and his really curious dislike to allow any impartial person to be in a position to know what went on at Longwood.

It is to be noted also that Lowe's showing the letter would be the more resented by the French at Longwood, as he insisted on all correspondence passing through his hands unsealed. 'This,' they would say, 'is the man who is to read our private letters!' Lowe apparently had no idea of keeping secret any letters whose contents he obtained access to by this means. Forsyth, in a note at vol. iii. p. 185, of his work, regrets that he cannot quote a letter from Count Montholon to his wife, which, or a copy of which, he obviously had before him. 'Letters,' he says, 'written by a husband to a wife, or by a wife to a husband, in all the confidence of that intimate and affectionate relationship, and not intended to meet the public eye, ought to be held sacred.' Exactly, but if the letter *had* been kept sacred by Lowe, Forsyth would never have known its contents ; he is able to hint that they support his argument by some gross breach of trust of Lowe's in retaining or copying the letter.

Another private letter of Count Montholon is actually used by Forsyth, who assumes that there could be no objection on the part of the Count or of the Countess in the matter. Such an assumption is not a sufficient or satisfactory ground for using material obtained in this manner.

One of the most annoying things to an Englishman about the whole matter is, that we cannot help feeling it was not the undignified side of Napoleon's character which brought him most into conflict with Lowe. Napoleon was ready to acquiesce in most reasonable restrictions. He knew that some supervision might fairly be claimed over his rides, for example, and he was prepared not to *see* the officer who was to exercise that supervision. But he did not wish to be taken out like a dog with a string for a run. He was ready and anxious to talk with any visitor, but he did not wish to be let out for dinner, like a cadet, with a pass for the boundary, good for that night only. If he would have yielded in such matters, if he had been ready to have an orderly officer looking into his bedroom occasionally, as if he were a prisoner in the cells, Lowe might have been gracious. If Mordecai would but have bowed, Haman might have smiled on the ruined man. But Lowe, as Napoleon pointed out, never saw this side of the question. If the captives had food enough, all must be well. Their feelings, those common to most men, he did not regard. At first reading, the threat of Napoleon to use force to maintain his privacy seems a piece of bombast. Alas ! it was necessary, and it was effectual. Lowe himself told Sturmer he was ready to use force to get the

Commissioners introduced into Longwood (this was on
their first arrival, when he did not realise the part they
might play), but Bonaparte had threatened to fire on any
one forcing his door.    That, and that only, stopped
Lowe.

One final and disgraceful act of Lowe's must be re-
corded : When Napoleon was at last dead, we might then
have considered Lowe's task was over.    But no, he had his
eye fixed even on the coffin of his dead prisoner.    He would
not allow an inscription on the lid of the coffin unless the
word ' Bonaparte ' were added after ' Napoleon.'    Writing
to Montholon, he himself says (*Forsyth*, vol. iii. p. 296),
' To the addition of the word Bonaparte to that of Napoleon
you saw motives of objection which I did not seek to discuss, and thus no inscription whatever was placed.'    Mag-
nanimous Governor !    A present of white and green peas
passing between living men makes him anxious ; a father
receiving a lock of his son's hair or a bust of his child
disturbs him ; an inscription on a coffin cannot be allowed
unless it be framed to include what he well knew would be
taken as an insult on the dead Emperor !    Would not Dante
have assigned to him a place as perpetual sentinel at the
Invalides, to see generation after generation of soldiers of
all lands come to render their homage to the great warrior!

There are one or two little bits of indirect but significant
evidence against Lowe, showing that those in St. Helena
itself were not content with his proceedings.

When Lowe took what seems the extraordinary step
of getting O'Meara struck off the list of honorary members
of the 66th Regiment, O'Meara received an expression of
regret from some seven officers of the regiment present at
the mess.    Every attempt is made by Forsyth to whittle
down the significance of this.    By removing the officer
commanding the regiment, Colonel Lascelles, sending him

and another officer from the Island, and appointing a fresh commanding officer, it was possible to obtain a disclaimer of this letter from the officers of the regiment. The disclaimer given by Forsyth sounds oddly in the ears of an officer. When an English regiment guards a political prisoner, and a quarrel is known to be going on between their general and the prisoner, we may be sure the officers would not lightly show any sympathy with a surgeon disgraced by the Governor, unless his own character attached him to them, or unless they disliked the proceedings of their general, and whatever disclaimer was made under such severe pressure by Lowe with his great powers over the officers, the letter stands.

Had Lowe pushed his suit to trial, it would appear that O'Meara would have produced in his own support Major Poppleton (an officer praised by Lowe for the way he had performed his duty as orderly officer at Longwood, though he too had taken the accursed thing, one of those troublesome snuff-boxes), two captains of the 53d Regiment, and a captain and lieutenant of the 66th Regiment. We presume these officers must have shown readiness to support O'Meara ; and this is remarkable, as such a step must have been dangerously near ruin, when we remember the way O'Meara, Stokoe, and Colonel Lascelles had been dealt with, though of course it might not have been so easy to adopt the St. Helena methods in England.

There is, we believe, another bit of evidence to show that there must have been some feeling against Lowe amongst the residents and in the garrison. When the first attacks were made on Lowe, the Government, and even the King, took his part warmly. At that time they, of course, only had his own reports and those of his friends to go by. If nothing more had ever come to light, we should find Lowe in due time receiving the full reward of his conduct in an undoubtedly difficult and trying office; and the very fact of his being attacked would, in those days, have made his superiors the more anxious to show their continued confidence in him. But that confidence does not appear by Forsyth to have been continued. In 1823, when the Government were still warm in their belief in him, Lowe was offered a Governorship in the West Indies; this he did not accept. In 1825 he was made Commander-in-Chief in Ceylon, but he had set his heart on being Governor there. He never got that post, and when he came home and saw the Duke of Wellington he failed to get any promise or any real consideration from him. As Lowe himself puts it in 1843: 'The Government of the island of Ceylon had *thrice* fallen vacant, and the chief authority in the Ionian Islands (where my local services at their liberation, and in the discharge of *civil* and military duties subsequently, had contributed to form a strong claim for re-employment) *four* times during the period of which I have been speaking. Vacancies had also arisen on other stations; but on none of these occasions were either my local or general services, or any claim arising from past disappointments, taken into that consideration which I should have hoped might have been deemed to be their due. The several commands in India had also repeatedly fallen vacant during the above period, but although my name had been taken down as a candidate for employment in that quarter, no result followed.'

Now, though the administration had, as Forsyth says, changed, there were a good many changes of administration in that period, and not all in one direction, and the Duke of Wellington most certainly had full means of obtaining for Lowe some governorship or command which would have contented him. The Duke never did so, nor would he promise to do so.

There can only have been one or other of two causes for this : Either the books of O'Meara and of Las Cases were, if libels, then most successful libels, ruining Lowe, for (we say it with real regret) he died poor ; or else, in the course of time, as now an official, now an officer, now a regiment, came home from St. Helena, the dreaded evidence of impartial persons became known in England. Men whose mouths were sealed at St. Helena might speak in England. We acknowledge this is a mere inference ; any one who quarrels with it has to find some other reason for the undoubted neglect of Lowe.

We have willingly acknowledged that Lowe's position was a difficult and trying one, and whatever he did there probably would have been some complaints from Longwood, especially from Napoleon's attendants, always more unreasonable than the Emperor was. But Lowe had full power of defending himself. O'Meara, however, was in a very different position, and in considering the questions between him and Lowe it is but fair to remember the difficulties under which the surgeon was placed. He consented to join Napoleon as medical attendant with apparently no feelings of interest in him, and simply from love of change. Suspected at first by Napoleon, he had to gain his confidence if he were to be of use in his position. But exactly as he advanced in the favour of Napoleon, so was he sure to draw on himself the suspicion of such a man as Lowe, and also, probably, the ill-will of the little Longwood colony, broken up as it was by feuds and jealousies.

Another thing made his position one certain to give umbrage to Lowe, or, indeed, we must allow, probably to any Governor. By a meanness, which no one

would have suspected from the manner in which Croker
writes publicly of O'Meara, Croker was receiving the
surgeon's private letters from O'Meara's friend Mr. Finlaison, and was circulating copies of them amongst the
Cabinet Ministers. This correspondence was kept secret, not
only by O'Meara, but by the Ministers themselves. Thus
while Napoleon suspected O'Meara of being a spy on him,
and wished the surgeon to take up his side and act as his
medium of attacking the Governor, Lowe wanted O'Meara
to inform him, and him only, of everything which passed
at Longwood, and to act as confidential watchman there ;
and the Ministers were ready to receive O'Meara's accounts
of Napoleon, and to use him as an informant, not only of
the acts of Napoleon but also of those of Lowe.

That O'Meara should have sooner or later given offence
to some of those who were watching him was inevitable,
and, on the face of it, it is honourable to him that Lowe was
the person with whom he broke. It is to be noticed that the
break with Lowe practically began soon after the Governor
became aware of the correspondence sent secretly to the
Ministers. The fault of this correspondence must be laid
on the Ministers. It of course put O'Meara in a wrong
position. When he was told that his letters were read
with interest by the Ministers and by the Prince Regent,
when Croker was hoping that he 'would write in full
confidence, and in the utmost possible detail,' he was
given a position unfair to Lowe. But in his dealings with
Lowe, O'Meara cannot be said to have acted in any undignified manner. In one of the first disputes, Forsyth (vol. ii.
p. 162) acknowledges that there was 'nothing discreditable to O'Meara, who seems to have answered the questions put to him with candour and fairness.' Indeed
O'Meara assumed naturally a different tone with Lowe
from the officers actually dependent on the Governor,

checking him by offering his resignation, which Lowe was apparently unwilling to forward without other grounds than he could for long avow.

On this subject it is only necessary now to point out, if Finlaison were right, Lord Melville believed, 'it might even be advantageous to hear from an impartial and near observer the situation of Bonaparte and his suite' (*Forsyth*, vol. i. p. 308). Now not long before Lowe's discovery of the correspondence with the Ministers, he had solicited an increase of pay for O'Meara, 'having had experience of Dr. O'Meara's zeal and useful information' (*Forsyth*, vol. i. p. 281). Thus the first real ground of offence with Lowe was not anything connected with Napoleon, but with the discovery that O'Meara might act as a check on the Governor. Another ground of offence shows the strange ideas of honour possessed by Lowe. He was furious with O'Meara because the doctor had promised Napoleon not to repeat his conversations to Lowe, unless they referred to projects of escape—that is, O'Meara had promised to act as a gentleman and not as a spy. Forsyth seems to half own that O'Meara was right on this point, or at least calls it an error of judgment, but tries to blame him for repeating or recording anything which passed at Longwood. We think there can be no doubt that O'Meara kept the promise fully and honourably in the sense intended by Napoleon. He would have acted very dishonourably if he had done what Lowe wished —that is, listen to everything said at Longwood, to repeat it to Lowe.

Another cause for the bad relations which in time existed between O'Meara and the Governor was the fact that Lowe wished to replace the naval surgeon by his own doctor. This was told to O'Meara by Napoleon, and was reported to his Government by Baron Sturmer, the Austrian Commissioner. The wish was in keeping with Lowe's craze for having all communications with the French in his own hands or in those of men directly dependent on him ; and it would be intensified by the discovery of the use of O'Meara's correspondence by the Ministers in England. The doctors after Lowe's heart seem to have been Baxter, who drew up reports of Napoleon's state of health without seeing him, and Dr. Verling, who lived at Longwood for fourteen months, and who was praised by Lowe for his manner of performing his duties. That Dr. Verling had during that time never visited Napoleon does not seem to have detracted from Lowe's satisfaction in any way. In fact, not one of the English medical officers succeeded where O'Meara had eventually failed—that is, in getting Napoleon to trust him without incurring the suspicions of the Governor. Dr. Stokoe was sentenced to be dismissed the service, and Dr. Verling was, as we have just seen, utterly useless.

Had there really been anything bad in O'Meara's conduct, Lowe would have been able to state it at the time, and to have removed him on that ground. How Lowe did act towards him is worth referring to, as the conduct of the Governor is simply inexplicable, even by his own advocates, on any hypothesis creditable to him.

On April 10, 1818, O'Meara was ordered not to leave Longwood without permission of the Governor, except in certain specified cases, and was practically to be treated as one of the French prisoners. It was certain that O'Meara would not bear this, and his resignation which followed was a matter of course. Not only did he resign, but he also at once disobeyed the order, and, what is really curious, he did this with practical impunity. The irritable Governor having obtained his end seemed a little perplexed how to fill O'Meara's place.

But one curious and characteristic part of Lowe's conduct in this matter fairly puzzles Forsyth himself.

To Lord Bathurst Lowe represented that he gave the order confining O'Meara to Longwood because the doctor had taken a silver snuff-box from Napoleon to a clergy-man leaving the Island. It is the practice in the army to at once notify any offender of any offence charged against him. Now Lowe, while writing home to Lord Bathurst about this deep crime, kept silence to O'Meara about it. On April 10 Lowe gave the objectionable order, and it was only on May 3, so says Forsyth, that O'Meara was informed of the crime alleged against him. What was Lowe's object in this silence? Forsyth acknowledges that he cannot explain the reason, and also says that it is 'very remarkable' that in the tedious correspond-ence which ensued between O'Meara and Lowe 'no allusion whatever is made on either side to the affair of the snuff-box about which Sir Hudson Lowe wrote fully to Lord Bathurst on April 9.' O'Meara of course charged Lowe with simply wanting to get him to break the order about leaving Longwood, so as to have some good reason for sending him off. If this were not Lowe's object, why did he not mention the real crime? Surely never was an honest man more unfortunate in his conduct.

It is to be noted that Lowe distinctly misrepresents the case to Lord Bathurst, because, as Forsyth remarks, he wrote that 'neither Bonaparte nor O'Meara could controvert the fact of the present of the snuff-box, though they were both ready to defend it. But it does not ap-pear that O'Meara had at that time been taxed with the offence or that Bonaparte knew the cause of his disgrace.' This, however, is putting the case too leniently. O'Meara asked Lowe why no communication was made to him till twenty-three days afterwards. Lowe had, it would

*f*

seem, no answer to this, so we must take the concealment as admitted.

There are of course all sorts of counter-attacks on O'Meara with which we are not much concerned. Until he went to St. Helena there was nothing against his character ; and while there he seems to have been on very good terms with all the English except the special friends of Lowe ; certainly he got on with the officers of the garrison. He does not seem to have been on quite such good terms with the attendants of the Emperor as with their master,—a thing easy to be understood, but to be remembered when charges of inconsistency are brought against him for inserting sneers at them in his letters.

His selection by Napoleon as his surgeon, and, probably later, as a medium for an attack on the Government, is easily explained. Napoleon was, as Metternich remarks, 'gifted with a particular tact for recognising those men who could be useful to him. He discovered in them very quickly the side by which he could best attach them to his interest.' Limited as Napoleon was in the circle from whom he could choose, his selection was a good one for his purpose. O'Meara no doubt had a thousand imperfections. A calmer man would probably have made the attack on Lowe equally telling, and would have preserved his position in the service. But one thing Napoleon owes to O'Meara. If the doctor did not crush Lowe himself, he performed the still more useful office of making the Governor's friends give us a portrait of Lowe drawn by himself, which we now can find in the pages of Forsyth.

One of Forsyth's counter-charges against O'Meara is that the Journal does not agree with his other correspondence. But the details on which Forsyth seems to rely are all connected, not with Napoleon, but with the attendants of the Emperor. Now O'Meara never gives us the impression of being much in love with the French at Longwood ; we should rather gather from his journal that he either saw little of them or cared nothing for them. He began his duties with Napoleon in no very friendly spirit with the Emperor's staff. Further, O'Meara knew that his correspondence was seen by the Government, and whether writing to England or to Lowe, he may not have been averse to throwing in any sentiment pleasing to those he knew would read his letters, and who would have looked on him, as indeed they eventually did, as unfit for his position if he manifested any attachment. for the captive.

Other charges against O'Meara, such as, for instance, want of truthfulness, are of the nature certain to be made, and to have some apparent ground when a long and harassing correspondence and constant angry interviews take place. In the snuff-box affair, for instance, O'Meara's explanation was probably not in accordance with the facts ; but then, when was his explanation given ? Why, more than three weeks after the occurrence, Lowe having noted down his side, and fully corresponded about it with Lord Bathurst weeks before he thought of giving O'Meara any knowledge that a charge was being prepared against him. Few men do not get inaccurate under these circumstances. Take Lowe himself. He states that he had informed Baron Sturmer that 'an inhabitant might have been hanged for making such communications' as Sturmer's servants had been concerned in. On this Forsyth remarks, 'This may have been said *in terrorem ;* but the Governor must have known that the Act made it capital only to resist an attempt at *escape.*' Fancy if O'Meara had made a false statement *in terrorem !*

We assume O'Meara to have been wrong ; but Baron

Sturmer (p. 186) reported to his Government on this affair that the Governor was 'wrongly informed or is not telling the truth.' Obviously the Austrian Commissioner did not think highly of Lowe's veracity.

While any disagreements between O'Meara's letters and statements at different times are often explicable by this and other considerations, we must remember that he suffered under a great disadvantage in this matter, as his enemies had possession of his and of the private letters of others at Longwood. Where we can get at the private letters of the other side we also find some startling discrepancies.

We have given one instance from Croker's journal, and how much a man may vary in his ideas on the same subject at different times is shown by Lowe having afterwards stated that much difficulty was *not* caused by the question of the title of Emperor. Forsyth points out that this could only have been from forgetfulness, but similar alterations in the case of O'Meara are treated as intentional falsehoods.

In the case of a long controversy, resting on disputed facts, words, and intentions, we naturally wish to get the evidence of any impartial witnesses. Lowe was Governor and Commander-in-Chief at St. Helena. Any evidence he might produce in his favour from officers of the garrison or from the inhabitants would be liable to be attacked as being the words of men dependent on him or of his own creatures. Any man in Lowe's position, therefore, of ordinary honour and of ordinary foresight, would have wished to have always by his side some eye-witness of his every act, some confidant of all his intentions, who should be completely and above all suspicion independent of him and of the English Government. He had such men by his side. He did not use them. He did all in his power to prevent them seeing or knowing what was done. He and his Government did their best, successfully, to get rid of them from the Island.

The Allies did not acknowledge that the English Government held Napoleon as the captive of its own bow and spear ; they professed that England acted in the dignified position of jailer to the European Powers. Three of these—Austria, Russia, and France—sent Commissioners to the Island. What more natural than for Lowe to insist that these Commissioners were to know every measure he took, so as to be in a position to say, ' We have seen all that was done, and we testify that the French were well and considerately treated, and that the complaints made by them are unfounded ' ? Far from taking this view, the one anxiety of Lowe and of his Government seems to have been to prevent the Commissioners seeing or hearing anything except through the eyes and the ears of Lowe. So extremely anxious was Lowe to prevent free communication between the French and the Commissioners, that he actually gives as a reason for not granting the French the right of free correspondence with the inhabitants of the Island, that, if he did this, he could not exclude the Commissioners. Any ordinary man would have allowed free communication with the Commissioners, even if they objected to extending the right to the inhabitants. What would be thought of the Governor of a prison who was willing to let the prisoners communicate with his own tradesmen, but not with the visiting justices ? What is to be answered when the assailants of Lowe explain the difference in this treatment by pointing out that a tradesman or inhabitant, siding with the French, could be crushed by Lowe or by the Government : the Commissioners could not ?

Lowe had thus no impartial or independent witnesses

he could call, and his adversaries are much hampered on that point by the success of his and of the Government's measures to prevent such persons existing. It was the independence of the Commissioners that was their crime in the eyes of Lowe and of the Government. There was nothing specially wrong in their behaviour, at least all three seem to have been objected to. '*I cannot hang you*' was the delicate regret, repeated thousands of times by Lowe, says Baron Sturmer, when referring to their not being under the Act of Parliament by which Lowe ruled.

It is important that the reader should understand how determined Lord Bathurst was to prevent the Commissioners having free intercourse with Napoleon, practically, indeed, preventing any intercourse between them and Napoleon. Had the Commissioners been left to themselves, there can be no doubt they would have seen Napoleon by the simple plan of asking for an interview without insisting on their official position. Precautions against this were taken.

Lowe himself had, on July 29, 1816, described Napoleon as having ' no objection to see them (the Commissioners) privately,' meaning as private individuals, and the Commissioners were 'sick with their desire of seeing him.' As time went on, and as it became evident that there was a growing risk of one or more of the Commissioners dropping their office for the moment, or rather not insisting on it being formally acknowledged by Napoleon, fresh measures were taken by the English Government. Using the frivolous pretext that the unofficial presentation of the Commissioners would be acknowledging the dreaded principle that Napoleon was a Sovereign, Lord Bathurst wrote to Lowe in January 1818: 'His Royal Highness, therefore, has commanded me to instruct you not to allow any of the Commissioners to be presented to General

Buonaparte, except as a Commissioner of the Allied Powers, introduced by you in your official character as Governor of St. Helena.' That is, they were only to be permitted to see Napoleon under conditions it had first been ascertained would be refused by Napoleon. When such great anxiety is displayed to prevent intercourse with the captive, can we be surprised at the suggestion that the details of his treatment would not bear investigation?

Later, more stringent restrictions were adopted to prevent any possibility of the Commissioners succeeding in establishing free communication with Napoleon. When the French Commissioner claimed the right to this intercourse, Lord Bathurst, on November 30, 1820, though acknowledging the right of the Commissioner to ' see' Napoleon, ends by telling Lowe the claim to intercourse with the followers of Napoleon is to be resisted, ' so that, in all future cases in which an unrestricted intercourse with the followers of General Buonaparte, *or with General Buonaparte himself* ' (the italics are ours), ' may be claimed by any Commissioner, the claim may be resisted on the ground of general regulations, independent of any consideration or discussion of the particular reasons which render it objectionable.' The measure was really directed against the other two Commissioners ; but after this order, it would seem impracticable for the Commissioners to really ascertain the state of affairs at Longwood.

To do Lowe and the English Government full justice, we must readily acknowledge that, in their horror of any communication between Longwood and the independent witnesses, the Commissioners, they were supported not only by the English Ministry, but also by the Austrian Court. The man to whom the Emperor Francis had given his daughter was down, and the English heel well on him. Nothing could have been more unpleasant to the Court of Vienna than the reports their agent was making as to affairs at St. Helena. If the Commissioners were only out of the way, there would then be nothing heard from the Island except the report of Lowe himself describing that all his rules and regulations were excellent, and that all was for the best in the best of all possible prisons. Sturmer, much to his lamentation, was got rid of first in July 1818. The Russian, Balmaine, was then recalled in March 1820, though, as he was engaged to the stepdaughter of Lowe, and as he married that lady before he left, he may not have been looked on with great suspicion towards the end. Indeed, we find that he then believed Napoleon's health greatly improved, and that he heard the French had no reason to complain of anything at present. Still he went.

Nothing can be more significant of the intention of the Court of Vienna to play into the hands of the English Government, by depriving Napoleon of the presence and supervision of an independent witness, than the appointment of Montchenu, the French Commissioner, to represent them when they withdrew Sturmer. The Sovereign who had given his daughter to Napoleon, who knew that Napoleon was complaining of his treatment at St. Helena, who knew that his own Commissioner was reporting against the acts of Lowe, replied by withdrawing that Commissioner, his representative, and handing over the duties of that officer to a Frenchman, a former *émigré*, the representative of the Bourbons, the bitter enemies of Napoleon. This was simply saying, 'As our witness will report things that are not right at St. Helena, we withdraw him and shut our ears.' This, too, was done after Metternich knew that Napoleon wished, if dangerously ill, to make a communication to Baron Sturmer, to be repeated to the Austrian Emperor alone, about his wife and his son.

Is there any wonder that, as Sturmer reports, 'Bonaparte has bitterly complained of our august master, by whom he says he is abandoned, notwithstanding the ties of relationship which unite them'?   Can we be surprised when we find Napoleon turning to Alexander, declaring that all his hopes would thenceforward be placed on him, and adjuring him to always keep a Commissioner at St. Helena, whose mere presence only could alleviate his fate?   The English Government triumphed, and at last they had Napoleon alone in their power, without the inconvenient presence of any independent witness.

So determined was the Austrian Court to support Lowe, that it was even ready to give him the longed-for right of hanging their Commissioner, by placing him under the Act of Parliament, if only the other Powers would give Lowe the same rights over their representatives.

But the Marquis de Montchenu, probably remembering his disputes with Lowe, and feeling a crick in his neck, declared that *his* King would not allow a French Commissioner to be placed under the English laws ; and, indeed Louis XVIII., we may be sure, was too proud to suffer such a thing, and too clever not to know what would have been the effect in France of a Frenchman being strung up at St. Helena.

The view we take of the position of the Commissioners, as acting as a check on Lowe, and on his assailants, is the same as that submitted to Metternich by Baron Sturmer : 'Is it the truth he (Lowe) fears?' writes the Baron on February 11, 1818 ; 'in that case it is well it should be known.   Is it false reports?   The surest and the most loyal means of forestalling the effects, it seems to me, would be to keep us acquainted with what we ought to know.'   It is not pleasant reading for an Englishman, that sentence—'*Is it the truth he fears ?*'

Forsyth, as we have said, certainly tries to be impartial, but he does not see some of the weak points of Lowe's case. It is because he never seems to realise the position of the Commissioners, and the importance of their testimony, that we have dwelt on this part of the case against Lowe and against the English Government. Forsyth, we presume, never saw all Sturmer's correspondence, otherwise he, no doubt, would have brought forward that side of the question. As it is, he only agrees with Lowe's view of the matter, that the Commissioners, by communicating with the attendants of Napoleon—that is, fulfilling their most important duty, by learning the French side of the question, were obstructing Lowe. 'At the suggestion of the British Government,' Forsyth writes (vol. iii. p. 31), Baron Sturmer, 'the Austrian Commissioner, was removed from St. Helena at the end of June, in consequence of his persisting in unauthorised communications with the French at Longwood.' *Is it the truth he fears?*

It is for the advocates of Lowe or of the English Government to suggest any possible good or plausible reason for this intense desire to get rid of the independent witnesses. We know of none. If a man fears the light, we can only suppose he has good reason for doing so. One main object of all good prison systems is to prevent the prisoner being altogether at the mercy of the jailer, by instituting some supervision by impartial witnesses. A jailer who insists he cannot carry out his system if he be subjected to such supervision, *may* have good motives, but the world will suspect his motives ; and, if the prisoner complain, will side with the prisoner. And the world has sided with Napoleon against Lowe and against the English Government.

Fortunately, however, we have the evidence of one of these Commissioners, the Austrian, Baron Sturmer, whose reports and letters are published in a French edition, at Paris, as *Napoléon à Sainte Hélène. Rapports Officiels du Baron Sturmer, Librairie illustrée*, and in the German edition at Vienna, *Die Berichte des Kais Kön Commissärs Bartholomäus Freiherrn Von Stürmer aus St. Helena. Wien,* 1886, *Carl Gerold's Sohn, edited by Dr. Hanns Schlitter.* The main outline of his story agrees with that of O'Meara, though what O'Meara and Napoleon attributed to the desire of Lowe to annoy and injure, Sturmer would seem to put down to sheer fussy anxiety and to distrustfulness. In fact, we rise from Sturmer's book with a feeling of pitying contempt for the Governor, and concurring in Sturmer's opinion that 'it would have been difficult to find a clumsier, more extravagant, and disagreeable man.' Lowe's dislike to O'Meara, Sturmer attributes, as we have said, to a wish to replace him by another doctor ; and, in general, he takes much the same view of all occurrences as O'Meara.

We can indeed see good reason why Lowe should have been so anxious to get rid of the Commissioner in some of Sturmer's remarks to him. Asked for his opinion on O'Meara's conduct, Sturmer gives the advice of any frank, honest man. If he be guilty, O'Meara should be arrested. So far Lowe would agree. But Sturmer goes on, *And tried.* Precisely. If guilty, the English officers could have been trusted to do full justice on O'Meara. There was no trial, but O'Meara and the Commissioner were got out of the Island. 'Is it the truth he fears ?'

Now let us see what Sturmer says of O'Meara. He reports to Metternich : 'Your Highness will find in the papers attached hereto all the details of this matter (O'Meara's arrest). You will see that all the wrong appears to be on the part of the Governor. The letters of Dr. O'Meara bear the stamp of truth and of frankness.

When one knows his gentle and conciliatory character, his
sagacious and guarded conduct, his extreme prudence, and
if we consider that he is an Englishman, that he loves his
country, that confidence between him and the Governor
was established naturally, without art or effort on the part
of this latter, and that this confidence was founded on a
natural interest, it would seem that nothing were so easy
as to render it unchangeable.    But I know not what
fatality makes Sir Hudson Lowe always end by getting
on bad terms with every one.   Overwhelmed with the
weight of the responsibility with which he is charged, he
agitates and torments himself endlessly, and experiences
the necessity of tormenting others.'

 It is simply impossible to give here all the details with
which, stroke after stroke, Sturmer fills his sketch of the
anxious, fussy, moody Governor.   At every page we
understand more and more the anxiety of Lowe to get
rid of such a clearsighted witness.   He knew the
Austrian was condemning him, and the only thing was to
prevent his influencing the Austrian Government.

 Let us see Lowe through Sturmer's spectacles.   The
Austrian Commissioner has gone to see the Governor.
He first asks Lowe how he himself is.   This does not
much compromise the position of the Governor, so he
goes so far as to make a sign with his head, showing,
let us hope, he was well.   But then the Commissioner
goes on to ask a much more serious question.   He wants
to know how Bonaparte is.   To this question the Governor does not answer, but remains looking fixedly on the
ground, till Sturmer, having repeated his question without
eliciting any reply, proceeds to take his leave.   Lowe then
begs him to remain, pointing out that Sturmer must feel
that he has to weigh his response.   Sitting down at the
other end of the room, with his arms crossed, Lowe, for

twenty minutes, is plunged into a deep study. Then, after walking up and down a little, he at last is able to answer. 'I have nothing to say,' announced this worthy representative of our nation, 'since I am forestalled in information by the followers of Napoleon Bonaparte.' Then followed a long wrangle on the general wickedness of the Commissioners, especially of the Russian one, who saw the French of Longwood without Lowe being able to know all that was said. Sturmer had indeed only been at Longwood twice in seven months, though Lowe seems to have suspected him of more frequent visits. Sturmer himself ends by saying that the whole interview was so strange and improbable that he would not be surprised at being accused of inventing the matter himself.

Page after page might be filled with further confirmation of the general truthfulness of O'Meara's description of Lowe, taken from the despatches of Baron Sturmer, but perhaps one of the Baron's last reports will suffice.

'Your Highness,' Sturmer writes on June 1, 1818, to Metternich, 'will be more and more convinced that we (the Commissioners) shall never succeed in rendering our relations with the Governor as satisfactory as it is to be wished they should be. To please him, one must not think, see, or act, except in his way, and according to his fancies, approve all his absurdities, know nothing of what is done here, limit oneself to reporting that Bonaparte is alive, never put foot inside Longwood, be at daggers-drawn with every one who quarrels with him (and the number increases every day), act as his spy, and report faithfully to him everything said ; finally, put oneself on the rack every time he thinks fit, and undergo the most humiliating interrogations. All this is incompatible with our position, with the duties of our place, and even with honour. I doubt Sir Hudson Lowe maintaining himself

long in a post so much above his powers. Public opinion
is against him. He does nothing to make it favourable
to himself. The uprightness of his intentions justifies,
according to him, all his actions. On this principle he
spares no one, and makes himself odious. The English
fear and avoid him, the French laugh at him, the Commissioners complain of him, and every one agrees in
saying he is deranged.'

If any one believes that both Sturmer and O'Meara
have calumniated Lowe, and that Napoleon wished to
pass his time in solitude, fabricating charges against the
Governor, let him turn to the pages in which Mrs. Abell
gives her remembrances of the time when she, then the
hoydenish Betsy Balcombe, romped with the delighted
Emperor, threatened him with a sword, displayed her progress at billiards by the accuracy of her aim at his fingers,
delighted when she elicited some exclamation of pain ;
and, as we have said, when she boxed poor Las Cases's
ears while the Emperor held the unhappy Count.

We should certainly gather from her that Napoleon
had at first no settled purpose of making himself or others
miserable, but was only too glad to get society and amusement ; even going incognito to a fancy ball. With his
power of attaching persons to him, he was ready to take
an interest alike in the young high-spirited girl and in
the old Malay slave, both of whom became devoted to him.

But about Lowe we get a few hints, all agreeing with
the representations of O'Meara. Napoleon sends a horse
for the girl, the daughter of his purveyor, to ride, to
enable her to see some races ; and this gives great offence
to Lowe, who reprimanded Mr. Balcombe for letting one
of his family ride a horse belonging to Longwood.

Again, Napoleon is anxious to hear an air, the music
for which has been sent by the composer, his stepdaughter

Hortense, and which we may, we suppose, recognise as the 'Partant pour la Syrie.' The piano was out of tune, and what more natural than to send for the band-master of one of the ships to tune it? But our vigilant Governor was on the alert, and as the boat was leaving the ship's side, an order from him stopped the bandmaster. The introduction of a Bonapartist's air might, as Lord Bathurst would have said, have caused embarrassment. Beans, horses, busts, locks of hair, and pianos were all included in the strange mind of Lowe as objects of suspicion. How we long to hear of his feelings on the introduction by Madame Bertrand into Longwood of the baby, the first French subject who had entered Long-wood since Napoleon's arrival without Lord Bathurst's permission!

It may be said, of course, that Mrs. Abell's evidence is 'suspect,' because her father was one of the persons considered as having been won over by Napoleon. But if such a man, with permanent interests in the Island, threw himself into the side of what he knew must only be a transient party, against a man charged with the powers Lowe possessed, his attitude becomes the more significant. You cannot, in England at least, put aside all the evidence tending in a certain direction, because it is adverse evidence.

Excuse for Lowe and for the Government must not be sought by believing that the whole nation were so terror-stricken by Napoleon, and believed him to be such a villain, that no terms were to be kept with him, and were ready to approve everything, if only he were kept in his living grave. Napoleon knew better when he refused to ever reproach our nation with his treatment. Our fathers, the generation who faced a world in arms, and who by steady constancy beat down the greatest commander the world has yet seen, were not the rancorous cowards such a

theory would make them. The proofs lie ready on every
side. We take the first which comes to hand and turn
to no lover of military fame, the genial Elia. ' After all,'
writes Lamb to Southey in August 1815, ' Buonaparte is a
fine fellow, as my barber says, and I should not mind
standing bareheaded at his table to do him service in his
fall. They should have given him Hampton Court or
Kensington, with a tether extending forty miles round
London. Would not the people have ejected the
Brunswicks some day in his favour?' Lamb of course
must have his joke, but his words are significant. He
was not, as we have said, a lover of military glory. If he
had ever in later years seen the works of Napoleon, praised
though they be by Sainte Beuve, we fear he would have
slighted them as books which were no books. But we
know Lamb's real character, the true heroism, the finer for
the modesty and apparent unconsciousness with which he
took up his life's voluntary burden, and we put the words
of such a man against the sentiments of the Crokers and
Bathursts who, unfortunately, had the fate of Napoleon in
their power. Note, by the bye, the touch about the barber.
Napoleon was not the only man who believed he might
have been allowed to live in England. It was not so
many years afterwards when Soult passed through the
London streets amongst the cheers of the men who knew
how to appreciate a brave and skilful foe.

Against Lowe then we have this series of crushing facts.
He has no impartial witnesses to call in his favour, as he
himself succeeded in getting all such witnesses removed.
He has not the sentence of a court-martial in his favour,
for the Government preferred to crush O'Meara without
that ordeal; the doctor getting worse justice than he would
have done at Jedburgh, where the trial was at least
considered necessary at one stage of the proceedings. He

has not got the decision of a Civil Court in his favour, because he himself shrank from that ordeal after the most open attack on him. 'London juries,' as Lord Bathurst remarks with a sigh, when unable to prosecute the wicked *Morning Chronicle*, 'are very uncertain in their verdicts.' The independent witness sent by the Austrian Court testifies against him. The naval surgeon, selected at hazard by Napoleon to be with him, throws all his evidence against Lowe, taking up a position which he must know would lead to the loss of his commission, in order to openly attack the Governor. Dr. Stokoe has to be cashiered by court-martial. The Colonel of a regiment has to be removed before the officers can be got to cast any slur on his assailant O'Meara. Admiral Sir Pulteney Malcolm, having had some conversation with Napoleon, a 'coolness' arises between the Admiral and the Governor. If all this were only Lowe's misfortune, surely he was the most extraordinarily unlucky person the world has ever seen. Another fact to be carefully remembered is, that practically all Napoleon's anger was reserved for Lowe and the Government. The agents who carried out the numerous orders of the Governor must have been often irritating enough. With all his virtues, the British soldier, when on sentry, is one of the most marvellously inconsistent and puzzling of guardians. Napoleon and his staff had, it would seem, ample evidence of this, and part of his dislike to the numerous posts round him and round his permitted bounds no doubt came from dislike of being stopped by the men, puzzled as they were by Lowe and his verbal and written orders. But though his staff seem to have sometimes resented the acts of orderlies, etc., as personal to them, Napoleon is constant in his praise of the troops. What is more important even is, that the garrison seem to have liked and respected him.

*g*

These are only some of the facts which make us believe
that it would have been quite possible for any Governor
of fair sense and tact to have lived on friendly terms with
his captive. Napoleon would undoubtedly have every
now and then complained, and would have made the
best of any grievance which he could get reported to
Europe. That was only fair and to be expected. Few
captives pass their time in praising their jailer, and in
expatiating on the comforts of their prison. But the
bitter personal feeling which Lowe caused, surely could
have been avoided.

We believe that an impartial student of the whole
question will come to the following conclusions: Many of
the complaints of Napoleon were undoubtedly made with
a view to excite opinion against his detention, a perfectly
natural course and one to be expected. Others came
from or were increased by the irritating effects of disease
and the dreariness of his seclusion. But allowing all this,
most of the friction at St. Helena came from the injudicious
and suspicious nature of Lowe who was not a proper
person for the post. The regulations were not strict
enough to really prevent the French corresponding with
persons in the Island or in Europe. But while the rules
were useless they were also unnecessarily irritating, and
they were often enforced in an offensive manner.

There is, however, another and much more important
question for us to consider. The disputes at St. Helena
have no real permanent historical value, and most readers
will probably soon make up their decision on the questions
between the Emperor and his jailer, and be glad to pass on
to the record given by O'Meara of the opinions of Napoleon
on persons and on events of his time. That O'Meara
played well the part Napoleon selected him for as the
assailant of Lowe must be acknowledged. To the

English his book and not the *Mémorial* is the ground
of the condemnation of Lowe. It is of more interest to
us now to know whether he was equally good as a
recorder of Napoleon's ideas.

The fact that O'Meara really gives the opinions actually
expressed by Napoleon will be evident to any student of
the period. Thus, at vol. i. p. 171 of this edition of the
Doctor's Journal, we have a description of Carnot. Such
a man as O'Meara would either know little of Carnot, or
would simply be able to repeat the stock description of the
'Organiser of Victory.' Napoleon, on the contrary, gives
us an opinion with which most students will agree. Carnot
is constantly praised as if it were an unknown thing, before
his time, for France to have an army or to gain victories.
Much that he did, or tried to do, was simply to bring the
army back to something of its former order after the confusion
into which it had been thrown by the first Revolutionary
administrations, but he never succeeded in getting its
organisation on a really good basis. Napoleon had
served in the early Revolutionary armies, and knew what
they had suffered from the administration. Probably
those readers who accept the ordinary accounts of the
'Organiser of Victory' will be surprised to hear Jomini's
description of him: 'Carnot also directed the armies
from Paris; in 1793 he did well and saved France; in
1794 at first he did badly, and then by chance repaired
his faults; in 1796 he decidedly did badly.' At the
present moment, when the Carnot family, always an
honourable and patriotic one, has been again brought
into prominence, much of the former exaggerated praise
given to Lazare Carnot has been repeated, but whether
the reader may share Napoleon's estimate or not, he
may be sure it is Napoleon's and not the doctor's.

Many other examples might be given of similar descriptions of prominent characters where we, for our own part at least, recognise the opinion we should have expected to have been given by Napoleon, and which certainly would not have been given by O'Meara if left to himself. We have, of course, to allow for the medium through which Napoleon speaks, and we must make deductions for mistakes and confusions, O'Meara himself being so little up in the history of Napoleon as not to know the different characteristics of the battle of Eylau and of the battle of Essling, so that he is not sure to which Napoleon is referring, when it is of course of Eylau that Napoleon speaks. Also, without claiming the liberty we so gladly give to biblical critics, who inform us of the exact part of each canonical book we are to believe or discredit, we must always allow for the circumstances under which Napoleon's criticisms at St. Helena were made. Often an angry judgment was caused by some act of the person referred to who was still playing his part on the political stage. A spirit revisiting its former sphere, and seeing its former companions playing their parts under new conditions, might not be the most indulgent or most impartial of critics. Napoleon's voice in O'Meara is that of a man not dead, yet not in the world of the living, criticising the living and the dead, while the actions of the living still interest him and affect his fate.

The student of the Napoleonic period in going over the pages of O'Meara will have to say, ' Here speaks the prisoner acting his part for the moment.' Or again, ' Here speaks the Sovereign irritated by treachery or by ingratitude.' But then also he will have to say, ' Here speaks the great Captain and the great Statesman.' O'Meara must always hold a place in the books to be read to fully know the Napoleonic Age.

With O'Meara we leave Napoleon at a solemn period of his existence. The busy active life is done, the work of recording the history of his marvellous campaigns is soon to end. The shadow of death has reached his foot and is fast climbing upwards till it shall envelop him altogether. The man of St. Helena will no longer be too well for Croker. There will no longer be too much of time, the only thing he said there was too much of at St. Helena. Soon will come that day when a poor man can turn his face to the wall and die in peace, but when even a fallen Sovereign must have his last weaknesses watched by inquisitive eyes. None of his real friends will be by his side when he passes away in that great storm. Then comes the quiet funeral, with such ceremonial as the Island could furnish, and then the silence of the lonely grave, broken at last by the trumpet of Fame as the corpse of the Emperor takes its way through the reconquered capital. There, under the splendid dome, sits his great shade, more real than the flitting forms of Bourbon, Orleanist, and Republican Rulers, who have tried to fill the throne of the great CAPTAIN, the great LEGIS-LATOR, the great EMPEROR.

# The Emperor Napoleon

## STAFF AND ATTENDANTS

GRAND MARÉCHAL DU PALAIS—

GENERAL COMTE BERTRAND (*wife and three children,
another child born 17th January* 1817).

GENERAL COMTE MONTHOLON, *wife and one child
(Madame Montholon with her child left for France,
July* 1819).

GENERAL BARON GOURGAUD, *left for France at own
request,* 14th March 1818.

COMTE LAS CASES, *formerly one of the Chamberlains,
and his son* EMMANUEL, *both removed by* LOWE,
29th December 1816.

MARCHAND, *the Emperor's head valet, and the following
servants :*—SAINT DENIS *or* ALI, *chief chasseur;*
NOVARRE *or* NOVERRAZ, *chasseur;* SANTINI,
*usher, sent away by* LOWE, *October* 1816 ; ARCHAM-
BAUD (*senior*), *piqueur* (*outrider or groom*) ;
ARCHAMBAUD (*junior*), *piqueur, sent away by* LOWE,
*October* 1816 ; GENTILI, *footman;* CIPRIANI,
*maître d'hotel, died at St. Helena, February* 1818 ;
PEYRON *or* PIERRON, *butler;* LEPAGE, *cook, married
at St. Helena, June* 1816 ; *dismissed by* NAPOLEON,
*May* 1818 ; ROUSSEAU, *steward, sent away by*

LOWE, *October* 1816 ; JOSEPHINE, *and* BERNARD, *and his wife, servants to* COMTE BERTRAND. *A servant of* GENERAL GOURGAUD *was sent back by* LOWE, *November* 1815, *as clandestinely embarked on the* Northumberland.

CAPTAIN PIONTKOWSKI, *a Pole, a volunteer, arrived on* 30*th December* 1815 ; *sent away by* LOWE, *October* 1816.

DR. ANTOMMARCHI, *arrived* 18*th September* 1820, *sent by* CARDINAL FESCH, *with the* ABBÉ BUON-AVITA *or* BONAVISTA, *Almoner to* MADAME MÈRE, *and Chaplain of* PAULINE BONAPARTE [BONAVISTA *left* 17*th March* 1821], *and the* ABBÉ VIGNALE, *with* CHAUDELIN *or* CHANDELL, *the cook of* PAULINE BONAPARTE, *and* CAUSAL, *a valet of* MADAME MÈRE, *the successor of* CIPRIANI.

*FOREIGN COMMISSIONERS arrived* 17*th June* 1816.

AUSTRIA—BARON VON STURMER, *with wife, removed by his government,* 11*th July* 1818.

RUSSIA—COUNT BALMAINE, *removed by his government, March* 1820.

FRANCE—MARQUIS DE MONTCHENU, *remained until the death of the Emperor.*

## STAFF AT ST. HELENA.

GOVERNORS—

1. COLONEL WILKES, *for the East India Company until April* 1816.

2. SIR HUDSON LOWE, K.C.B., *lands 14th April* 1816, *appointed by the Crown.*

REAR-ADMIRALS—

1. SIR GEORGE COCKBURN, *until June* 1816 (*in charge of* NAPOLEON *and his attendants up to the arrival of* SIR HUDSON LOWE *in April* 1816).

2. SIR PULTENEY MALCOLM, K.C.B., *June* 1816 *to July* 1817.

3. ROBERT PLAMPIN, *July* 1817 *to July* 1820.

4. LAMBERT, *July* 1820 *to end.*

BRIGADIER-GENERALS—

1. SIR GEORGE BINGHAM, *leaves May* 1819.

2. COFFIN *arrives* 23d *August* 1820.

DEPUTY-ADJUTANT-GENERAL—

LIEUT.-COLONEL SIR THOMAS READE, C.B.

AIDE-DE-CAMP CAPTAIN *and* BT.-MAJOR GORRE-QUER, *Assistant Military Secretary in June* 1820.

ASSISTANT MILITARY SECRETARIES—

1. LIEUT.-COLONEL WYNWARD, *leaves June* 1820.

2. MAJOR GORREQUER, A.D.C.

INSPECTOR OF MILITIA—

LIEUT.-COLONEL LYSTER (*local rank*).

ORDERLY OFFICERS AT LONGWOOD—

1. CAPTAIN THOMAS POPPLETON, 53d *Regiment, December* 1815 *to July* 1817; *leaves with Regiment.*

2. *CAPTAIN BLAKENEY, 66th Regiment, to* 16th *July* 1818; *resigns.*

3. *LIEUT.-COLONEL LYSTER,* 16th *July* 1818 (*soon removed*), *assisted by LIEUTENANT BASIL JACKSON.*

4. *CAPTAIN BLAKENEY, reappointed, to September* 1818.

5. *CAPTAIN NICHOLLS, to* 9th *February* 1820.

6. *CAPTAIN LUTYENS,* 20th *Regiment, to April* 1821, *removed.*

7. *CAPTAIN CROKAT, to end.*

PURVEYORS—

1. *MR. BALCOMBE* (*went to England, March* 1818).

2. *MR. IBBETSON.*

DOCTORS IN CHARGE AT LONGWOOD—

1. *O'MEARA* (*Surgeon,* H.M.S. Bellerophon) *till* 25th *July* 1818; *removed; sent to England; summarily dismissed service.*

2. *VERLING* (*Assistant Surgeon, Royal Artillery*) *sent to Longwood when O'MEARA was removed, remains there* (*not seeing NAPOLEON,*) *until arrival of ANTOMMARCHI, then to England.*

3. *STOKOE* (H.M.S. Conqueror) *sees NAPOLEON* 17th *January* 1819; *soon forced to resign; sent to England; brought back to the island, tried, and sentenced to be dismissed.*

4. *ANTOMMARCHI* (*Italian*) *arrives* 20th *September* 1819; *in charge till the end.*

OTHER DOCTORS—

1. *DR. ARNOTT, Principal Medical Officer, saw NAPO-*

*LEON first professionally* 1*st April* 1821, *then attended him till the end.*

2. D*R.* B*AXTER,* *Deputy Inspector of Hospitals, left shortly before death of* N*APOLEON; succeeded by* D*R.* S*HORTT.*

3. D*R.* S*HORTT* (*successor of* D*R.* B*AXTER as Deputy Inspector of Hospitals*).

4. D*R.* M*ITCHELL.*

*Both* D*RS.* S*HORTT and* M*ITCHELL were at Longwood when the Emperor died, but did not see him.*

D*RS.* W*ARDEN and* M*AINGAUD do not come within the scope of these volumes.*

# THE COMPANIONS OF NAPOLEON

IT may be interesting to prefix to these volumes a very brief account of the antecedents of the men with whom Napoleon was brought into daily and intimate intercourse over several years, and had it been possible one could have wished to have supplemented it by some account of their personal characteristics.

It was fitting that the Emperor should have around him companions who had shared in nearly all his campaigns, and many must have been the reminiscences of the past recalled at table.

First in alphabetical order is

### Henri Gratien BERTRAND General and Count,

born at' Châteauroux (Indre) March 28, 1773, defended Louis XVI. as one of the National Guard on August 10, 1792, went to Egypt in 1798, took part subsequently in the battles of Austerlitz, Friedland, Wagram, the vicissitudes of the Russian Campaign, succeeded Duroc as Grand Marshal of the Palace, was present at Leipsic and during the arduous campaign of France in the following year. Attended the Emperor to Elba in 1814, and again to St. Helena in 1815. In apparent forgetfulness of his services in 1792 he was condemned to death by the Bourbons in 1816, but received permission in 1821, after closing the eyes of Napoleon, to return to France, and was ultimately reinstated in his rank. Bertrand died January 31, 1844. Napoleon dictated to him when at St. Helena the *Campagne d'Egypte et*

*Syrie*, which was published after Count Bertrand's death by his sons in 1847. One is able to infer one phase of Bertrand's character from a passage in the *Biog. Univer.*, 'Le Baron Gourgaud n'avait pas, il est vrai, *la modestie de Bertrand*, et faisait assez grand bruit de sa fidelité'—and his disinterestedness from his loyalty to two monarchs in their misfortunes.

### Gaspard GOURGAUD General and Baron,

just alluded to, follows next. His claims for services and his double rescue of the Emperor's life redeem him from the charge of gasconading. He was born at Versailles September 14, 1783, and entered the artillery school at Chalons at the age of fifteen. He was first attached to the camp at Boulogne, and was initiated into actual warfare under the dashing and gallant Lannes. He distinguished himself at the passage of the Bridge of Thabor, at Austerlitz, Friedland, the investment of Saragossa, Eckmühl, Essling, and Wagram. In the Russian Campaign he was directly under the superintendence of Napoleon, "il n'agissait que par ordre, et sous les yeux de l'Empereur," and though he was wounded at Smolensko, he did not return to France, but was present at the burning of Moscow, where he helped to save the Emperor's life imperilled by the explosion of a magazine, and to mitigate, however slightly, the horrors of the French retreat from Russia by plunging on horseback into the icy waves of the Beresina to seek a ford for the troops. General Gourgaud was present with the Eagles also at Lützen, Bautzen, and Wurzchen, and by his reconnoitring contributed valuable information to Napoleon leading to the victory at Dresden. In the campaign of 1814 he saved the Emperor's life when attacked by Cossacks, and received as his guerdon no less heirloom than the sword worn by Napoleon at Arcola, Lodi, and Rivoli. He was well received on account of his brilliant career by Louis XVIII. in 1814, but shared the fortunes of his former master at Fleurus and Waterloo in 1815, and accompanied him to St. Helena in the same year. He returned to France March 20, 1821, just before the Emperor's death, and subsequently co-operated with Montholon in the publication of *Memoirs of France under Napoleon*. In 1822 he married a daughter of Count Roederer, in 1825 fought a duel with Count Segur, and in 1827 he was engaged in an animated controversy with Sir Walter Scott. He died July 25, 1852.

### EMMANUEL AUGUSTIN DIEUDONNÉ MARTIN JOSEPH, LAS CASES, COUNT AND MARQUIS,[1]

was born at Château Las Cases in 1766, and was educated at Vendôme College. He entered the Royal Navy, was present at the siege of Gibraltar and the naval combat at Cadiz in 1782, and saw many parts of the world during his services afloat. After the outbreak of the great revolution he emigrated to England in 1790, and took part in the Royalist expeditions to Quiberon, etc. In 1802 he published under the *nom-de-guerre* of Le Sage his celebrated Atlas. He came back to France at the time of the Amnesty, and in 1808 was made one of the Chamberlains to Napoleon. In 1809 he served as a Volunteer at Flushing, when Antwerp was threatened by the English, and in the following year was placed in charge of Maritime affairs in the Kingdom of Holland. In 1811 the finances of Illyria and control of the Public Debt were entrusted to him. The Battle of Paris in 1814 found him enrolled among the National Guard, and in the same year he again returned to England. Present in France during the Cent Jours, he accompanied Napoleon to St. Helena. He was arrested there by Sir Hudson Lowe, November 27, 1816, and detained a prisoner for eight months at the Cape of Good Hope. He afterwards returned to Europe, and was placed for some time under surveillance at Frankfürt on Main. He died May 15, 1842. His son, Emmanuel Pons Dieudonné LAS CASES, born June 8, 1800, was at St. Helena with Napoleon and his father, and returned there in 1840 with the Prince de Joinville when the body of the Emperor was brought back to France. He took part in politics and matters affecting the Colonies and Marine, and is chiefly remembered by his attack upon Sir Hudson Lowe in London (see *Forsyth*, vol. iii. p. 316). He died July 8, 1854.

---

[1] "The Count de las Cases does not exceed five feet and an inch in height, and appears to be fifty years of age, of a meagre form, and with a wrinkled forehead. His dress was a French naval uniform . . . his diminutive appearance did not fail to invite observation from the inquisitive beholders."— *Warden Lettres*, p. 5.

CHARLES TRISTAN MONTHOLON, GENERAL, COUNT,
AND MARQUIS,

was born at Paris July 21, 1783, entered the Royal Army in a dragoon regiment, but, on the outbreak of the Revolution, was transferred to the Navy. Took part in the Expedition to Sardinia in 1797, after which he reverted to his former profession and was posted to an engineer corps. He served under General Championnet, took share in the campaigns of Italy and Holland, and afterwards made aide-de-camp to Generals Augereau and Macdonald. Montholon was present in the battles in Germany and in Poland in 1805, 1806, 1807, and was dangerously wounded at Jena. In 1808 he was sent to Spain, but in 1809 he was engaged at Eckmühl and Wagram, and in 1814 was on service in the Campaign of France. In 1811 he was employed by Napoleon as Minister Plenipotentiary to the Grand Duke of Würzburg for several years. He was aide-de-camp to the Emperor in the Waterloo Campaign, and accompanied him to St. Helena, and was appointed one of Napoleon's executors. He published in 1823 and succeeding years a *History of France under Napoleon*, and renewed later on his allegiance to Prince Louis Napoleon, whom he accompanied to Boulogne and Strasbourg, and whose captivity he shared at Ham.

In later years he is said to have dissipated the fortune left to him by the terms of Napoleon's will, and he died on August 22, 1853.

## THE AGE ON REACHING ST. HELENA

OF

| | | |
|---|---|---|
| Emperor Napoleon | was 46 | years. |
| COUNT BERTRAND | „ 42 | „ |
| BARON GOURGAUD | „ 32 | „ |
| COUNT LAS CASES | „ 49 | „ |
| COUNT MONTHOLON | „ 32 | „ |
| SIR HUDSON LOWE | „ 46 | „ |

# NOTE BY THE PUBLISHERS

(1888)

*WHEN the first edition of Dr. O'Meara's* Voice from St. Helena *was issued in 1822 by Messrs. Simpkin, Marshall, and Co., the interest excited by it was so great on the part of the public that the predecessors of the City Police were called into requisition, and posted round Stationers' Hall Court to keep off the crowd.*

*Mr. O'Meara's record still remains the most vivid if a most painful record of the latter days of Napoleon's eventful life, but during the many years which have elapsed since the earlier editions of the work were issued, several important works have appeared—such as* De Rémusat *and* Metternich *—dealing with the events of the First Empire, and notably two bearing especially upon the St. Helena period, viz. the narrative of Baron Sturmer and the* Life of Governor Lowe *by Forsyth. Advantage has been taken of these publications to supplement any important passages or events by the impressions of other observers at the moment—since made accessible.*

*Many parallel passages of Las Cases's narrative have also been quoted or referred to in footnotes, and*

h

*one or two discrepancies between the various editions
of O'Meara's work—English and French—have been
indicated,[1] and the proof-sheets have had the advantage
of careful perusal by more than one person whilst
passing through the press.*

*In the present edition some purely repetitory pass-
ages have been omitted, and also the story of the
early days of Napoleon's butler, Cipriani, in Italy,
which was both uninteresting and irrelevant to the
main narrative of O'Meara.*

*Amongst the new matter in this edition may be
observed some account of the principal personages on
the island, which should afford a better knowledge of
their past services and qualifications.  There is also
an introduction touching upon the revelations of
Sturmer, and the conduct of Croker and Lowe; a
chapter briefly continuing the work from* 1818 *to*
1821 *for purpose of casual reference.  The bulk of
the notes throughout the book are new.  There is a
fresh portrait of Napoleon at St. Helena, taken only
three months before his death, and a copy of a picture
by Horace Vernet,—the new Indices, the Bonapartist
Kalendar, interesting only from the association of so
many redoubtable persons and events with the glorious
career of one man,—and the reference List of Titles,
which, it is hoped, may prove serviceable to Napoleonic
readers generally.*

---

[1] *See for example vol. i. p.* 259; *vol. ii. pp.* 164, 350.  *In
previous editions also the dates have not been clearly shown.*

# DR. O'MEARA'S DIARY

NAPOLEON AT PLYMOUTH

# CHAPTER I

## 1815

In consequence of the resolution adopted by the British Government to send the former Sovereign of France to a distant settlement,[1] the Emperor Napoleon, accompanied by such of his suite as were permitted by our Government, was removed on the 7th of August 1815 from the *Bellerophon* to the *Northumberland*, 74, Captain Ross.

The latter vessel bore the flag of Rear-Admiral Sir George Cockburn, G.C.B., who was entrusted with the charge of conveying Napoleon to St. Helena, and of regulating all measures necessary to the security of his personal detention after his arrival at the place of his confinement. Out of the suite that had followed his fortunes on board the

---

[1] Communicated to him by Major-General Sir Henry Bunbury, Under-Secretary of State, on board the *Bellerophon*, 74, Captain Maitland, at Plymouth, a few days before.—B. E. O'M.

*Bellerophon* and *Myrmidon*, His Majesty's Government permitted four of his officers, his surgeon, and twelve of his household to share his exile. The undermentioned persons were consequently selected, and accompanied him on board the *Northumberland:* Counts Bertrand, Montholon, and Las Cases, Baron Gourgaud, Countess Bertrand and her three children, Countess Montholon and child; Marchand, *premier valet de chambre;* Cipriani, *maître d'hôtel;* Peyran, St. Denis, Noverraz, Le Page, two Archambauds, Santini, Rousseau, Gentilini; Josephine, Bernard, and his wife, domestics to Count Bertrand. A fine youth of about fourteen, son to Count Las Cases, was also permitted to accompany his father.

Previous to their removal from the *Bellerophon,* the swords and other arms of the prisoners were demanded,[1] and their luggage was subsequently examined, in order that possession might be taken of their property, whether in bills, money, or jewels. After paying those of his suite who were not permitted to accompany him, only four thousand Napoleons in

---

[1] When Napoleon was about to leave the *Bellerophon* for the *Northumberland,* 'I inquired,' says Las Cases, 'whether it was probable that those appointed to search would go so far as to deprive the Emperor of his sword. He' (Lord Keith) 'said that it would be respected, but that Napoleon was the only person exempted, as all his followers would be disarmed. I showed him that I was already so, my sword having been taken from me before I left the *Bellerophon.* A secretary who was writing near us observed to Lord Keith, in English, that the order stated that Napoleon himself was to be disarmed; upon which the Admiral drily replied, also in English, as well as I could comprehend : " Mind your own business, sir, and leave us to ours." '—*Memoirs of the Emperor Napoleon,* by the Comte de Las Cases, 1824, edition vol. i. pp. 35, 36, 68.

gold were found, which were taken possession of by persons authorised by His Majesty's Government.

When the determination of the British ministers to send Napoleon to St. Helena was communicated to his suite, M. Maingaud, the surgeon who had accompanied him from Rochefort, refused to follow him to the tropics. M. Maingaud was a young man unknown to Napoleon, and had been at the moment chosen to attend him until M. Fourreau de Beauregard, who had been his surgeon in Elba, could join him ; and I was informed that even had he been willing to proceed to St. Helena, his services would not have been accepted.

On the day that Napoleon first came on board the *Bellerophon*, after he had gone round the ship, he addressed me on the poop, and asked if I were the *chirurgien major ?* I replied in the affirmative, in the Italian language. He then asked in the same language, of what country I was a native ? I replied, of Ireland. 'Where did you study your profession ?' —'In Dublin and London.'—'Which of the two is the best school of physic ?' I replied that I thought Dublin the best school of anatomy, and London of surgery. 'Oh,' said he, smiling, 'you say Dublin is the best school of anatomy because you are an Irishman.' I answered that I begged pardon, that I had said so because it was true ; as in Dublin the subjects for dissection were to be procured at a fourth of the price paid for them in London, and the professors were equally good. He smiled at this reply, and asked what actions I had been in, and in what parts of the globe I had served? I mentioned several, and amongst others, Egypt. At the word Egypt he commenced a series of questions, which I answered to the best of my ability. I mentioned to him that the corps of officers to which I then belonged messed in a house that had formerly served as a stable for his horses. He laughed at this, and ever afterwards noticed me when walking on deck, and occasionally called me to interpret or explain.[1] On the passage from Rochefort to Torbay, Colonel Planat, one of his orderly officers, was taken very ill, and attended by me, as M. Maingaud was incapable, through sea-sickness, of offering any assistance. During the period of his illness, Napoleon frequently asked about him, and conversed with me on the nature of his malady and

---

[1] 'Napoleon was in fact,' says Las Cases, 'an Emperor on board the *Bellerophon*. The captain, officers, and crew soon adopted the etiquette of his suite, showing him exactly the same attention and respect. The captain addressed him either as " Sire " or " Your Majesty " ; when he appeared on deck every one took off his hat and remained uncovered while he was present. There was no entering his cabin except by passing the attendants ; no persons but those who were invited appeared at his table. . . .

'On our leaving the *Bellerophon* to visit the *Superb*, the Emperor stopped short in front of the guard drawn up on the quarter-deck to salute him. He made them perform several movements, giving the word of command himself; having desired them to charge bayonets, and perceiving this motion was not performed altogether in the French manner, he advanced into the midst of the soldiers, put the weapons aside with his hands, and seized a musket from one of the rear rank, with which he went through the exercise himself, according to our method. A sudden movement and change of countenance amongst the officers and others who were present sufficiently expressed their astonishment at seeing the Emperor thus carelessly place himself amidst English bayonets.'

the mode of cure.    After our arrival at Plymouth, General Gourgaud also was very unwell, and did me the honour to have recourse to me for advice.

All those circumstances had the effect of bringing me more in contact with Napoleon than any other officer in the ship, with the exception of Captain Maitland ; and the day before the *Bellerophon* left Torbay, the Duke of Rovigo (Savary), with whom I was frequently in the habit of conversing, asked me if I were willing to accompany Napoleon to St. Helena as surgeon, adding, that if I were, I should receive a communication to that effect from Count Bertrand, the Grand Maréchal.[1]    I replied that I had no objection, provided the British Government and my captain were willing to permit me, and also under certain conditions.    I communicated this immediately to Captain Maitland, who was good enough to favour me with his advice and opinion, which were, that I ought to accept the offer, provided the sanction of Admiral Lord Keith and of the English Government could be obtained, adding, that he would mention the matter to his lordship.    On our arrival at Torbay, Count Bertrand made the proposal to Captain Maitland and to myself, which was immediately communicated to Lord Keith.    His lordship sent for me on board the *Tonnant*, and after some preliminary conversation, in which I explained the nature of the stipulations I

---

[1] It is best to explain once for all here that Bertrand was 'Grand Maréchal du Palais,' having succeeded Duroc, Duc de Frioul, in that office, a purely court employment, and having nothing to do with the rank of Marshal often erroneously given to him and to Duroc, though in this book Bertrand is sometimes called 'Marshal' for brevity's sake.

was desirous of making, did me the honour to recommend me in strong terms to accept the situation,
adding, that he could not order me to do so, as it was
foreign to the naval service, and a business altogether
extraordinary ; but that he expressed his conviction
that Government would feel obliged to me, as they
were very anxious that Napoleon should be accompanied by a surgeon of his own choice.   His lordship
added, that it was an employment perfectly consistent
with my honour, and with the duty I owed to my
country and my sovereign.

Feeling highly gratified that the step which I had
in contemplation had met with the approbation of
characters so distinguished in the service as Admiral
Lord Keith and Captain Maitland, I accepted the
situation, and proceeded on board the *Northumberland*, stipulating, however, by letter to his lordship,
that I should be always considered as a British
officer, and upon the list of naval surgeons on full
pay, paid by the British Government, and that I
should be at liberty to quit so peculiar a service,
should I find it not to be consonant with my wishes.

During the voyage, which lasted about ten
weeks, Napoleon did not suffer much from sea-
sickness after the first week.   He rarely made his
appearance on deck until after dinner.   He breakfasted in his own cabin *à la fourchette* at ten or
eleven o'clock, and spent a considerable portion of
the day in writing and reading.   Before he sat
down to dinner he generally played a game at chess,
and remained at that meal, in compliment to the

Admiral, about an hour ; at which time coffee was
brought to him, and he left the company to take a walk
upon deck, accompanied by Counts Bertrand or Las
Cases, while the Admiral and the rest continued
at table for an hour or two longer.   While walking
the quarterdeck, he frequently spoke to such of the
officers as could understand and converse with him ;
and often asked Mr. Warden (the surgeon of the
*Northumberland*) questions touching the prevailing
complaints and mode of treatment of the sick.[1]   He

[1] Mr. Warden in his *Letters from St. Helena* (edition 1816,
pp. 10, 11) thus describes Napoleon's appearance when he went
on board the *Northumberland:* 'His dress was that of a general
of French infantry.   The coat was green, faced with white ; the vest
was white, with white silk stockings and a handsome shoe with gold
oval buckles.   He was decorated with a red ribbon and a star, with
three medals suspended from a button-hole. . . . His face was pale,
and his beard unshaven.   His forehead is thinly covered with dark
hair, as well as the top of his head, which is large, and has a singular
flatness.   What hair he has behind is bushy, and I could not discern
the slightest mixture of white in it.   His eyes, which are gray, are in
continual motion ; his teeth are regular and good ; his neck is short,
but his shoulders of the finest proportion.   The rest of his figure,
though a little blended with the Dutch fulness, is very handsome.'
(See also P. W. Clayden's *Early Life of Samuel Rogers*, p. 431,
for another portrait of Napoleon.)   Compare with the foregoing
Madame de Rémusat's description of Napoleon's appearance and
dress at an earlier period : 'Napoleon Bonaparte is of low stature
and ill-made ; the upper part of his body is too long in proportion to
his legs.   He has thin chestnut hair, his eyes are grayish-blue, and
his skin, which was yellow whilst he was slight, has become of late
years a dead-white without any colour.   His forehead, the setting of
his eye, the line of his nose,—all are beautiful, and remind one of an
antique medallion ; his mouth, which is thin-lipped, becomes pleasant
when he laughs ; the teeth are regular ; his chin is short, and his
jaw heavy and square ; he has well-formed hands and feet ; I
mention them particularly, because he thought a good deal of them.
He has an habitual slight stoop ; his eyes are dull, giving to his face

occasionally played a game at whist, but generally retired to his cabin at nine or ten o'clock. Such was the uniform course of his life during the voyage.

The *Northumberland* hove to off Funchal, and the *Havannah* frigate was sent in to procure refreshments. During the time we were off the anchorage a violent *scirocco levante* prevailed, which did great mischief to the grapes. We were informed that some of the ignorant and superstitious inhabitants attributed it to the presence of Napoleon. Fourteen or fifteen hundred volumes of books were ordered from England for Napoleon's use by Count Bertrand.[1]

a melancholy and meditative expression when in repose. When he is angry, his looks are fierce and menacing . . . when he laughs, his countenance improves. He was always simple in his dress, and generally wore the uniform of his own guard . . . the precipitation with which he did everything did not admit of his clothes being put on carefully ; and on full-dress occasions his attendants were obliged to consult together as to when they might snatch a moment to dress him. He could not endure the wearing of ornaments. He would tear off or break anything that gave him the least annoyance, and the poor valet, who had occasioned him a passing inconvenience, would receive violent proofs of his anger. . . . His hair was cut short, smoothed down, and generally ill-arranged. With his crimson and gold coat he would wear a black cravat, a lace frill to his shirt, but no sleeve-ruffles. Sometimes he wore a white vest embroidered in silver, but more frequently his uniform waistcoat, his uniform sword, breeches, silk stockings, and boots. This extraordinary costume and his small stature gave him the oddest possible appearance, which, however, no one ventured to ridicule. When he became Emperor, he wore a richly-laced coat, with a short cloak and a plumed hat ; and that costume became him very well. He also wore a magnificent collar of the Order of the Legion of Honour, in diamonds, on state occasions ; but on ordinary occasions he wore only the silver cross.'— *Memoirs of Madame de Rémusat*, vol. i. pp. 1-3, 72,

[1] It may be interesting here to refer to the list of books taken out by General Bonaparte to Egypt in 1798, to be found in the first

We arrived at St. Helena on the 15th of October. Nothing can be more desolate than the appearance of the exterior of the island.[1] When we had anchored, it was expected that Napoleon would

volume of Bourrienne's *Memoirs* (English edition of 1885); also to a project of the Emperor Napoleon for reprinting, uniformly, in cabinet size, the best standard and current works of all countries in about three thousand volumes, described in the *Academy*, 4th April 1885.

[1] 'Its appearance from the sea is gloomy and forbidding. Masses of volcanic rock, with sharp and jagged peaks, tower up round the coast, and form an iron girdle which seems to bar all access to the interior. And the few points where a landing can be effected were then bristling with cannon, so as to render the aspect still more formidable. The whole island bears evidence of having been formed by the tremendous agency of fire, but so gigantic are the strata of which it is composed, and so disproportioned to its size, that some have thought it the relic and wreck of a vast submerged continent. Its seared and barren sides, without foliage or verdure, present an appearance of dreary desolation.'—Forsyth's *Lowe*, vol. i. pp. 26, 27.

The island of St. Helena is situated in latitude 15° 55′ S., and longitude 5° 46′ W., in the south-east trade wind. It is about ten miles and a half in length, six and three-quarters in breadth, and twenty-eight in circumference. The highest part of it is Diana's Peak. From the nearest land (Ascension) it is distant about six hundred miles, and twelve hundred from the nearest continent, the Cape of Good Hope. Jamestown, the only one in the island, is situated in the bottom of a deep wedgelike ravine, flanked on each side by barren and tremendous overhanging precipices. The one on the left from the sea is called Rupert's Hill, and that on the right, Ladder Hill. There is a steep and narrow road, called the side path, cut along the former, and a good zigzag road leads along the latter to the country-seat of the Governor. Opposite to the town is James's Bay, the principal anchorage, where the largest ships lie perfectly secure, as the wind never varies more than two or three points, and is always off the land and favourable for sailing. The town consists of a small street along the beach, called the Marina, and the main street, commencing from this and extending in a right line to a distance of about three hundred yards, where it branches off into two lesser ones. There are about one hundred and sixty have been invited to stop at Plantation House, the country-seat of the Governor, until a house could have been got ready for him, as heretofore passengers of distinction had invariably been asked to pass the time they remained on the island there.

On the evening of the 17th, about seven o'clock, Napoleon landed at Jamestown, accompanied by the Admiral, Count and Countess Bertrand, Las Cases, Count and Countess Montholon, etc., and proceeded to a house belonging to a gentleman named Porteous, which had been taken for that purpose by the Admiral, and was one of the best in the town. It was not, however, free from inconvenience, as Napoleon could not make his appearance at the windows, or even descend from his bedchamber, without being exposed to the rude and ardent gaze of those who wished to gratify their curiosity with a sight of the imperial captive. There was no house in the town at all calculated for privacy, except the Governor's, to which there belonged a court, and in front there was a walk upon the ramparts facing the sea, and overlooking the Marina, which proximity to the ocean probably was the cause of its not having been selected for him.

The inhabitants of the island were in very anxious expectation during the greatest part of the day to obtain a sight of the exiled Ruler when he

houses, chiefly built of stone, cemented with mud, lime being scarce on the island. There is a church, a botanical garden, a hospital, a tavern, and barracks. On the left from the beach stands the castle, the town residence of the Governor.

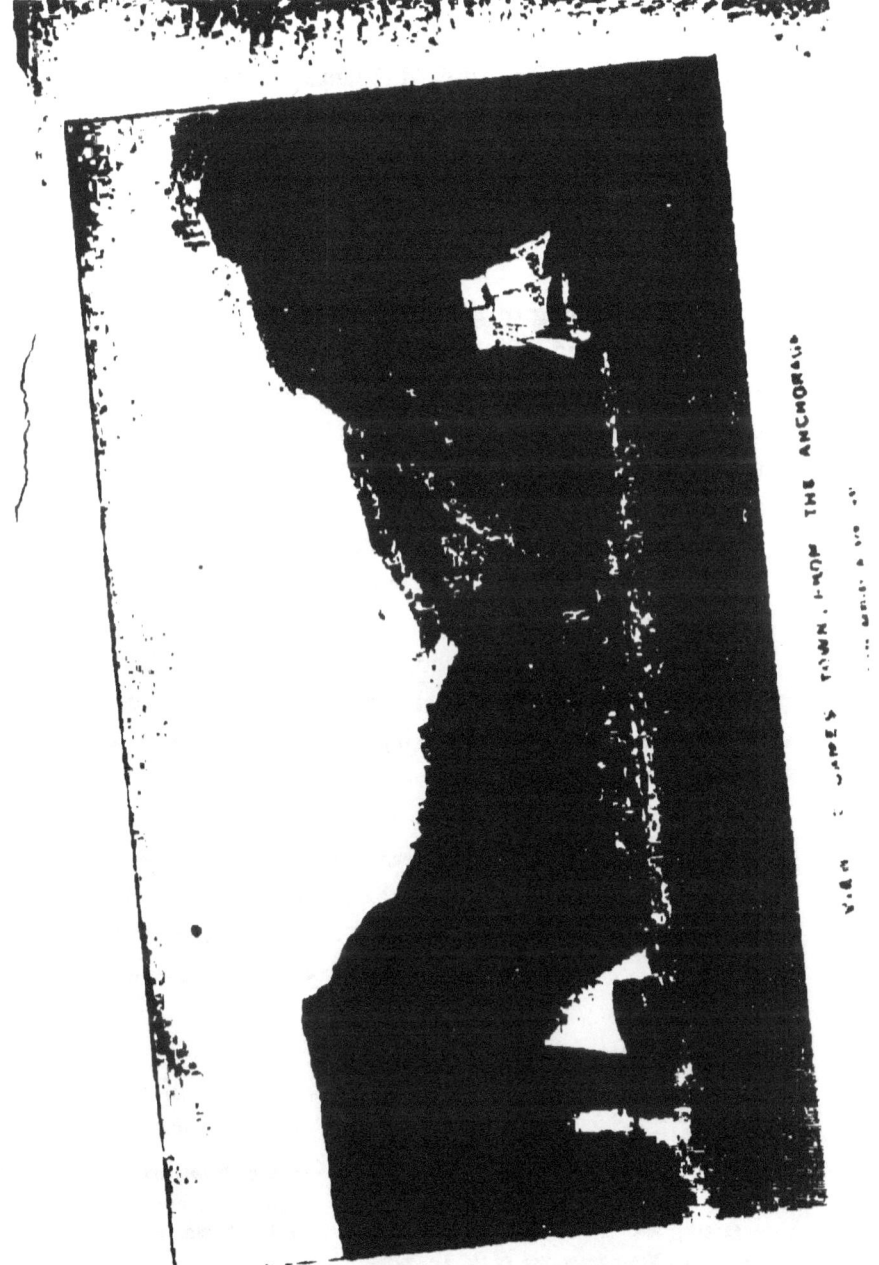

VIEW : JAMES TOWN FROM THE ANCHORAGE

have been invited to stop at Plantation House, the country seat of the Governor, until a house could have been got ready for him, as heretofore passengers of distinction had invariably been asked to pass the time they remained on the island there.

On the evening of the 17th, about seven o'clock, Napoleon landed at Jamestown, accompanied by the Admiral, Count and Countess Bertrand, Las Cases, Count and Countess Montholon, etc., and proceeded to a house belonging to a gentleman named Porteous, which had been taken for that purpose by the Admiral, and was one of the best in the town. It was not, however, free from inconvenience, as Napoleon could not make his appearance at the windows or even descend from his bedchamber, without being exposed to the rude and ardent gaze of those who wished to gratify their curiosity with a sight of the imperial captive. There was no house in the town at all calculated for privacy, except the [...] to which there belonged a court [...] in [...] upon the rampart [...] the [...] the Marina [...] proximity to [...] the [...] having [...]

The inhabitants [...] island were in very anxious [...] the greatest part of the day to see [...] Ruler when he [...], [...] time being scarce on the island. There is a church [...] of garden, a hospital, a tavern, [...]. On the [...] beach stands the castle, the town residence of the Governor.

VIEW OF JAMES TOWN, FROM THE ANCHORAGE

LONDON RICHARD BENTLEY & SON 1887

should make his *entrée* to the place of his confinement. Numbers of persons of every description
crowded the Marina, the street, and the houses by
which he was to pass, in the eager hope of catching
a glimpse of him. The expectations of most of
them were, however, disappointed, as he did not land
till after sunset, at which time the majority of the
islanders, tired of waiting, and supposing that his
landing was deferred until the following morning,
had retired to their homes. It was also at this time
nearly impossible to recognise his person in the
dusk.

Counts Bertrand and Montholon, with their
ladies, Count Las Cases and son, General Gourgaud, and myself, were also accommodated in Mr.
Porteous's house.

At a very early hour on the morning of the 18th,
Napoleon, accompanied by the Admiral and Las
Cases, proceeded up to Longwood, a country-seat
of the Lieutenant-Governor's, which he was informed was the place deemed most proper for his
future residence. He was mounted on a spirited
little black horse, which was lent for the occasion
by the Governor, Colonel Wilks. On his way up
he observed a neat little spot called the Briars,
situated about two hundred yards from the road,
belonging to a gentleman named Balcombe, who,
he was informed, was to be his purveyor, and
appeared pleased with its romantic situation.

Longwood is situated on a plain, formed on the
summit of a mountain about eighteen hundred feet

above the level of the sea, and, including Deadwood,
comprises fourteen or fifteen hundred acres of land,
a great part of which is planted with an indigenous
tree called gumwood.    Its appearance is sombre
and unpromising.[1]    Napoleon, however, said that
he should be more contented to fix his residence
there than to remain in the town as a mark for the
prying curiosity of importunate spectators.    Un-

[1] When it was understood that Longwood had been fixed upon
for the abode of Napoleon, it at first excited some surprise in the
minds of the islanders, as the situation was so bleak and exposed
that it had never been inhabited by any family for more than a few
months in the year; but this surprise soon subsided, as it was
supposed that a suitable winter residence would be provided for him
when the new Governor arrived.    Longwood is on the summit
of a mountain on the *windward* side of the island, containing a
number of gumwood trees (*Conyza gummifera*), which, being nearly
all of the same size and inclination, in consequence of the trade-wind
continually blowing from the south-east, present a monotonous and
melancholy appearance.    There is no water, except what is brought
from the distance of nearly three miles—no continuous shade.
Exposed to a south-east wind constantly charged with humidity,
its elevated situation causes it to be enveloped in fog, or drenched
with rain for the greatest part of the year.    For a month or six weeks
during the year there is fine weather, for two or three a powerful
vertical sun prevails, and for seven or eight the weather is wet
and most disagreeable.    Extreme changes of temperature often
occur several times in the course of the day, and are one cause of
the unhealthiness of St. Helena.    One frequently left Longwood in fog
and rain, and found fine weather on Plantation Estate; indeed, the
change generally began after having passed the mountains above
Hut's Gate.    This may be accounted for by the clouds having been
attracted by the high mountains, called the backbone of the island.
Fine weather in the town and very bad in the mountains at the
same time was an everyday occurrence.    It is singular that thunder
and lightning are unknown in St. Helena.    This arises probably
from the electric fluid being attracted by Diana's Peak and the
other conical hills and conducted into the sea.

fortunately the house only consisted of five rooms on a ground-floor, which had been built one after the other, according to the wants of the family, and were totally inadequate for the accommodation of himself and his suite. Several additions were consequently necessary, which it was evident could not be accomplished for some weeks, even under the superintendence of so active an officer as Sir George Cockburn. Upon his return from Longwood, Napoleon proceeded to the Briars, and intimated to Sir George that he should prefer remaining there, until the necessary additions were made to Longwood, to returning to town, provided the proprietor's consent could be obtained. This request was immediately granted.

The Briars is the name of an estate picturesquely situated about a mile and a half from Jamestown, comprising a few acres of highly-cultivated land, excellent fruit and kitchen-gardens, plentifully supplied with water, adorned with many delightful shady walks, and long celebrated for the genuine old English hospitality of the proprietor, Mr. Balcombe. About twenty yards from the dwelling-house stood a little pavilion, consisting of one good room on the ground-floor and two garrets, which Napoleon, not willing to cause any inconvenience to the family of his host, selected for his abode. In the lower room his camp-bed was put up, and in this room he ate, slept, read, and also dictated the records of a portion of his eventful life. Las Cases and his son were accommodated in one of the garrets above, and

Napoleon's *premier valet de chambre* and others of
his household slept in the other and upon the floor
in the little hall opposite the entrance of the lower
room.   At first his dinner was sent ready cooked
from the town, but afterwards Mr. Balcombe found
means to get a kitchen fitted up for his use.   The
accommodation was so insufficient that Napoleon
frequently good-naturedly walked out after he had
finished his dinner, in order to allow his domestics
an opportunity of eating theirs in the room which
he had just quitted.

Mr. Balcombe's family consisted of his wife, two
daughters,[1] one about twelve and the other fifteen
years of age, and two boys of five or six.   The
young ladies spoke French fluently, and Napoleon
frequently dropt in to play a rubber of whist or hold
a little *conversazione*.   On one occasion he indulged
them by participating in a game of blindman's-buff,
very much to the amusement of the young ladies.
Nothing was left undone by this worthy family that
could contribute to lessen the inconveniences of his
situation.[2]   A Captain of Artillery resided at the

[1] One of whom, afterwards Mrs. Abell, has since published her
*Recollections of the Emperor* when at St. Helena, to. which we shall
have occasion immediately to refer.

[2] 'The Emperor's habits, during the time he stayed with us,
were very simple and regular.   His usual hour for getting up was
eight, and he seldom took anything but a cup of coffee until one,
when he breakfasted.   He dined at nine, and retired about eleven to
his own rooms.   His manner was so unaffectedly kind and amiable
that in a few days I felt perfectly at ease in his society, and looked
upon him more as a companion of my own age than as the
mighty warrior at whose name "the world grew pale."   His spirits
were very good, and he was at times almost boyish in his

Briars as orderly officer ; and at first a serjeant and some soldiers were also stationed there as an additional security ; but upon a remonstrance being made to Sir George Cockburn, the latter, convinced of their inutility, ordered them to be removed. Counts Bertrand and Montholon, with their respective ladies and children, General Gourgaud, and myself, lived together at Mr. Porteous's, where a suitable table in the French style was provided by Mr. Balcombe. When any of them were desirous of paying a visit to the Briars or of going out of the town elsewhere, no further restriction was imposed upon them than causing them to be accompanied by myself or by some other British officer, or followed by a soldier. In this manner they were permitted to visit any part of the island they pleased except the forts and batteries. They were visited by Colonel and Mrs. Wilks, Lieutenant-Colonel and Mrs. Skelton, the Members of Council,

mirth, not unmixed sometimes with a tinge of malice. . . . One evening he strolled out, accompanied by General Gourgaud, my sister, and myself, into a meadow in which some cows were grazing. One of these, the moment she saw our party, put her head down and advanced *à pas de charge* against the Emperor. He made a skilful and rapid retreat, and leaping nimbly over a wall placed this rampart between himself and the enemy. But General Gourgaud valiantly stood his ground, and, drawing his sword, threw himself between his sovereign and the cow, exclaiming, "This is the second time I have saved the Emperor's life !" Napoleon laughed heartily when he heard the General's boast, and said, "He ought to have thrown himself into square to repel cavalry !" I told him the cow appeared tranquillised the moment he disappeared, and he replied, "She wished to save the English Government the expense and trouble of keeping him."'—*Recollections of the Emperor Napoleon,* by Mrs. Abell, third edition (1873), pp. 41-44.

and by most of the respectable inhabitants, and the
officers, both military and naval, belonging to the
garrison and squadron, and by their wives and
families.  Little evening parties were occasionally
given by the French to their visitors, and matters
were managed in such a manner that there was not
much *appearance* of constraint.  Sometimes the
Countesses Bertrand and Montholon, accompanied
by one or two casual island visitors, passed an hour
or two in viewing and occasionally purchasing some
of the productions of the East and of Europe
exhibited in the shops of the tradesmen, which,
though far from offering the variety or the magnificence of those of the Rue Vivienne, tended nevertheless to distract them a little from the tedious
monotony of a St. Helena residence.  Sir George
Cockburn gave several well-attended balls, to all
of which they were invited ; and, with the exception
of Napoleon, they frequently went.

It would, perhaps, have been better and more
consistent with propriety had Napoleon been accommodated at Plantation House until the repairs
and additions to Longwood were finished, instead
of being so indifferently provided for in point of
lodging at the Briars.  I must, however, do the
Admiral the justice to say, that upon this point I
have reason to believe he was not at liberty to carry
his own wishes into effect.[1]  In the meantime no

[1] Sir George Cockburn, in his despatch of 22d October 1815,
seems to take all the responsibility for the choice of Longwood.  See
Forsyth's *Lowe*, vol. i. p. 32.

exertions were spared by Sir George Cockburn[1] to enlarge and improve the old building, so as to render it capable of containing so great an increase of inmates. For this purpose all the workmen, not only of the squadron, but in the island, were put in requisition; and Longwood for nearly two months presented as busy a scene as has ever been witnessed during the war in any of His Majesty's dockyards, whilst a fleet was fitting out under the personal directions of some of our first naval commanders. The Admiral, indefatigable in his exertions, was frequently seen to arrive at Longwood shortly after sunrise, stimulating by his presence the St. Helena workmen, who, in general lazy and indolent, beheld with astonishment the despatch and activity of a man-of-war succeed to the characteristic idleness which, until then, they had been accustomed both to witness and to practise.

Every day bodies of two or three hundred seamen were employed in carrying up from Jamestown timber and other materials for building, together with furniture, which, though the best was purchased at an enormous expense wherever it could be procured, was paltry and old-fashioned. So deficient was the island in the means of transport,

---

[1] Sir George writes: 'Having visited the different houses and estates throughout the island, and the Governor, as well as the Members of the Council and every other person I have consulted here, most fully concurring with me in considering Longwood not only the best but the only place on the island calculated to answer for the future residence of General Bonaparte, I have not hesitated in fixing upon it for the purpose.'

that almost everything, even the very stones for
building, were carried up the steep side-paths on the
heads and shoulders of the seamen, occasionally
assisted by fatigue - parties of the 53d Regiment.
By means of incessant labour Longwood House was
enlarged so as to admit, on the 9th of December,
Napoleon and part of his household, Count and
Countess Montholon and children, Count and young
Las Cases.

[The accompanying plan is an exact transcript of
the one of the enlarged building at Longwood, as it
was drawn by young Las Cases, first for his mother,
and subsequently enclosed to Maria Louisa, in a letter
which was intercepted; it is also the same mentioned
in a letter of the Count to Prince Lucien, relating the
events at St. Helena : on account of these circumstances it is presented here without alteration :—

A. *The Emperor's Bedroom.*

 *a. Small camp-bedstead of iron on which the Em-
  peror slept.*

 *b. Sofa on which the Emperor sat a great part of
  the day, turned towards the fireplace.*

 *c. Small table on which the Emperor's breakfast
  was served. He often made my Father come
  to it, particularly when he took his English
  lessons.*

 *d. Chest of drawers between the windows.*

 *e. Fireplace, over which were suspended two portraits
  of the Empress, five of the King of Rome (one
  of which was embroidered by Maria Louisa),
  also a small marble bust of the King of Rome.*

 *f. Large ewer brought from the Elysée.*

Scale of English Feet.

Scale of French Feet.

Tent in which the Emperor often breakfasted and dictated during the day, in fine weather.

Library

Parlour.

Antichamber and Waiting room for Visitors.

D

E

B        C

A

Servants' hall.

Court yard frequently muddy

Servants' room.

Lea Case's Servants' room.

G        F

Kitchen.

Apartments

Orderly Officer.

of General Gourgaud

Count Lea Case's 1st Apart.

Dr. O'Meara.

General Gourgaud.

Officers.

Count Montholon.

220 English Feet.

PLAN OF LONGWOOD.

The Grand Marshall's apartment was 400 yards from Longwood.

RICHARD BENTLEY & SON.

LONDON 1867.

B. *STUDY.*

   *g. Bookshelves.*

   *h. Second small bed like the other; when the
      Emperor could not sleep he often removed from
      one bed to the other.*

   *i. Table on which the Emperor wrote—(1) the
      Emperor's place; (2) that of my Father; (3)
      myself, to whom he dictated the campaigns of
      Italy; each of us had our particular depart-
      ment and different hours.*

C. *CLOSET*
   *in which the valet de chambre attended.*

   *j. Bath in which the Emperor bathed whenever
      there was not a scarcity of water.*

D. *DINING-ROOM.*
   *(1) The Emperor's place; (2) my Father's; (3) self;
   (4) Montholon; (5) Gourgaud; (6) Mad^e. Montholon.
   Count and Countess Bertrand, living in another house
   at some distance from Longwood, only came to dine on
   Sundays. After dinner, which never lasted more than
   from 15 to 18 minutes, the Emperor dismissed all the
   attendants, exercising his English by telling them to
   'go out, go to supper.' He would then turn to us
   and ask whether we wished to visit the theatre, upon
   which I was sent to the library for a book; this the
   Emperor read aloud. One of our great authors was
   always chosen, generally Corneille, Racine, or Molière;
   when the reading was over, he withdrew to his bedroom. If he read till 11 o'clock, or midnight, he
   considered himself fortunate, and called this a victory
   over time.*

E. *Small table on which the Emperor generally played a
   game of chess before dinner.*

F. *MY FATHER'S BEDROOM.*
   *(1) His bed; (2) mine. The room was so small that
   there was scarcely space enough for two chairs.*

G. *Our Study.*

> *(1) My Father's desk ; (2) table on which I wrote to you, my Mother; (3) table for Ali, the Emperor's valet, who frequently came to transcribe for my Father ; (4) sofa on which my Father lay a great part of the day. These rooms are so low that you may touch the ceilings with your hands ; they are covered with tarred paper. If the sun was shining we were almost suffocated ; when it rained we were almost drowned. How often have we walked about here till a late hour talking of you, my dear Mother!]*

Napoleon himself had a small narrow bedroom on the ground-floor, a writing-room of the same dimensions, and a sort of small antechamber, in which a bath was put up. The writing-room opened into a dark and low apartment, which was converted into a dining-room. The opposite wing consisted of a bedroom larger than that of Napoleon's, which, with an antechamber and closet, formed the accommodation for Count and Countess Montholon and son. From the dining-room a door led to a drawing-room, about eighteen feet by fifteen. In prolongation of this, one longer, much higher, and more airy was built of wood by Sir George Cockburn, with three windows on each side, and a verandah leading to the garden. This, although it became intolerably hot towards the evening, whenever the sun shone forth in tropical splendour, by the rays penetrating the wood of which it was composed, was the only good room in the building.

Las Cases had a room next the kitchen,[1] which

[1] Some time afterwards an apartment was built for the Count

had formerly been occupied by some of Colonel
Skelton's servants, through the ceiling of which
an opening was cut so as to admit a very narrow
stair, leading to a sort of cockloft above, where
his son reposed.  The garrets over the old building were floored and converted into apartments
for Marchand, Cipriani, St. Denis, Josephine, etc.
From the sloping structure of the roof, it was
impossible to stand upright in those garrets
unless in the centre, and the sun, penetrating
through the slating, rendered them occasionally
insupportably hot.   Additional rooms were constructing for them and for General Gourgaud, the
orderly officer, and myself, who, in the meantime,
were accommodated with tents.   Lieutenant Blood
and Mr. Cooper, carpenter of the *Northumberland*,
with several artificers from the ship, also resided
upon the premises; the two former under an old
studding sail, which had been converted into a tent.

A very liberal table (considering St. Helena)
was found by order of Sir George Cockburn for the
orderly officers and myself.[1]

Las Cases and his son at the back of the house, which was subsequently divided into a bed and sitting room, with one for their
servant.   They were so small that there was not room for a chair
between the bedsteads of the father and son; and so low that the
ceiling could be touched by a person standing on the floor.

[1] We found on our arrival that provisions were very scarce;
indeed the necessaries of life were to be procured with great difficulty,
and at an exorbitant rate.   Such was the scarcity of cattle, that
killing a bullock was an affair of state, and a regulation existed
prohibiting the inhabitants from slaughtering even their own cattle,
without first having obtained official permission from the Governor
and Council.   Hence 'accidents' were frequent to the bullocks, who

Count and Countess Bertrand and family [1] were lodged in a little house at Hut's Gate, about a mile from Longwood, which, though uncomfortable, was nevertheless hired at their own request, and was the only one which could be procured at a moderate rate in the neighbourhood, as it was found impossible to accommodate them at Longwood until a new house, the foundation of which was immediately laid down by Sir George Cockburn, could be finished.

During the time that Napoleon resided at the

were sometimes abruptly helped over the edge of a rocky ravine and sustained injuries necessitating immediate slaughter. The sheep are very small, weighing from twenty to thirty pounds each. Mutton, when to be had, sold from about one shilling and sixpence per pound to two shillings. Fowls were very dear, from six to ten shillings each. Ducks, ten shillings; geese, fifteen; and a turkey, from one pound five to two pounds sterling. Veal very difficult to be had, and about two shillings per pound. Pork, one shilling and threepence. Cabbages, from tenpence to half a crown each. Carrots, a shilling per dozen. Potatoes, six to eight shillings per bushel. Eggs per dozen, five to six shillings. Peas sometimes to be had, but exorbitantly dear. The principal supply of fish was mackerel, which was caught in abundance. There were albicore, bonetta, bulls' eyes, cavalli, and many other kinds, and at times, but very rarely, turtle. There were also a kind of cray-fish and some species of crabs. A few wild peacocks, some partridges, and pheasants constitute the only game on the island. These last are royal game, and are solely reserved for the Governor, there being a penalty liable to be levied upon any person killing one who does not immediately send it to him.

[1] 'The little Bertrands are interesting children. The youngest is three or four years old; the eldest was born at Trieste during the time his father was Governor of the Illyrian Provinces; the other is a lively little girl who gives evidences of a violent disposition. Military instincts are already dominant in these little urchins' characters. They pass their time from morning until night in drilling or galloping as if on horseback.'—*Hérisson*, p. 169.

Briars I kept no regular journal, and consequently
can give only a brief outline of what took place.
His time was occupied principally in dictating to
Las Cases and his son, or to Counts Bertrand,
Montholon, and Gourgaud, some of whom were in
daily attendance upon him. He occasionally received
visitors (who came to pay their respects to him)
on the lawn before the house; and, in a few
instances, some who had received that permission
were presented to him when at Mr. Balcombe's in
the evening. During the whole time he was there
he never left the grounds but once, when he strolled
down to the little residence of Major Hodson of the
St. Helena regiment, where he conversed for half
an hour with the Major and Mrs. Hodson, taking
great notice of their children, who were extremely
handsome. He frequently, however, walked for
hours in the shady paths and shrubberies of the
Briars, where care was taken to prevent his being
intruded upon. During one of these walks he
stopped and pointed out to me the frightful precipices which environed us and said : ' Behold your
country's generosity ; *this* is their liberality to the
unfortunate man who, blindly relying on what he
so falsely imagined to be their national character,
in an evil hour unsuspectingly confided himself
to them ! '

At another time he discovered, through the
interpretation of Las Cases, that an old Malay, who
was hired by Mr. Balcombe as gardener, had been
enticed from his native place on board an English

ship several years before, brought to St. Helena, smuggled on shore, illegally sold for a slave, let out to whoever would hire him, and his earnings chiefly appropriated to his master. This he communicated to the Admiral, who immediately set on foot an inquiry; the probable result would have been the emancipation of poor Toby had the Admiral remained in command.[1]

Arrangements were made with the purveyor to supply certain quantities of provisions, wines, etc. The scale of allowances was liberal, and such as was deemed sufficient for the service of the house by Cipriani, the *maître d'hotêl*. It is true that sometimes the provisions were deficient in quantity or bad in quality, but this was often caused either by the absolute want of resources on the island, or by accident, and was generally remedied, wherever such remedy could be applied, by Sir George Cockburn.

A space of about twelve miles in circumference was allotted to Napoleon, within which he might ride or walk, without being accompanied by a British officer. Within this space was placed the camp of the 53d, at Deadwood, about a mile from Longwood House, and another at Hut's Gate,

[1] When Napoleon discovered, some time after the departure of Sir George Cockburn, that the poor man had not been emancipated, he directed Mr. Balcombe to purchase him from his master, set him at liberty, and charge the amount to Count Bertrand's private account. Sir Hudson Lowe, however, thought proper to prohibit this, and the man was still in a state of slavery when I left St. Helena.—B. E. O'M.

opposite Count Bertrand's, close to whose door there
was an officer's guard.   An arrangement was made
with Bertrand, by means of which persons furnished
with a pass from him had permission to enter the
grounds of Longwood.   This was not productive of
inconvenience, as no person could, in the first
instance, go to Bertrand's without permission from
the Admiral, the Governor, or Sir George Bingham,
and consequently no improper persons were permitted to have access to him.   The French also
were allowed to send sealed letters to the inhabitants
and others *residing* upon the island—a regulation
not likely to prove injurious, as it was evident that
if they wished to transmit letters to Europe, this
could only be attempted after previous arrangements
had been made ; and it was highly improbable that
they would send, through the medium of an English
servant or dragoon, letters, the contents of which
would compromise either themselves or their friends,
when the more simple and natural mode of delivering
them *personally* to the individuals for whom they
were intended, and with whom they were at liberty
to visit and converse at pleasure, was entirely in
their power.[1]

A subaltern's guard was posted at the entrance
of Longwood, about six hundred paces from the
house, and a cordon of sentinels and picquets were
placed round the limits.   At nine o'clock the sentinels

[1] A strong proof of this is, that during the nine months Sir
George Cockburn had this system put in force, not a single letter
was ever sent to Europe, unless through the regular Government
channels.

were drawn in and stationed in communication with each other; surrounding the house in such positions that no person could come in or go out without being seen and scrutinised by them. At the entrance of the house double sentinels were placed, and patrols were continually passing backward and forward. After nine Napoleon was not at liberty to leave the house unless in company with a field-officer; and no person whatever was allowed to pass without the countersign. This state of affairs continued until daylight in the morning. Every landing-place in the island, and, indeed, every place which .presented the semblance of one, was furnished with a picquet, and sentinels were even placed upon every *goat-path* leading to the sea, though, in truth, the obstacles presented by nature in almost all the paths in that direction would of themselves have proved insurmountable to so unwieldy a person as Napoleon.

From the various signal-posts on the island ships are frequently discovered at twenty-four leagues' distance, and always long before they can approach the shore. Two ships of war continually cruised, one to windward and the other to leeward, to whom signals were made as soon as a vessel was discovered from the posts on shore. Every ship, except a British man of war, was accompanied down to the road by one of the cruisers, who remained with her until she was either permitted to anchor or was sent away. No foreign vessels were allowed to anchor unless under circumstances of great distress, in which case no person from them was permitted to land, and an officer and party from one of the ships of war was sent on board to take charge of them as long as they remained, as well as in order to prevent any unauthorised communication. Every fishing-boat belonging to the island was numbered and anchored every evening at sunset, under the superintendence of a lieutenant in the navy. No boats, excepting guard-boats from the ships of war, which pulled about the island all night, were allowed to be down after sunset. The orderly officer was also instructed to ascertain the actual presence of Napoleon twice in the twenty-four hours, which was done with as much delicacy as possible. In fact, every human precaution to prevent escape, short of actually incarcerating or enchaining him, was adopted by Sir George Cockburn.

The officers of the 53d and several of the most respectable inhabitants, the officers of the St. Helena corps and their wives, were introduced to Napoleon, at whose table some were weekly invited to dine, and amongst them Mr. Doveton, Miss Doveton, Colonel and Mrs. Skelton, Captain and Mrs. Younghusband, Mr. Balcombe and family, etc. Officers and other respectable passengers from India and China came in numbers to Longwood to request a presentation to the fallen chief; in which expectation they were rarely disappointed, unless indisposition on his part or the shortness of their stay on the island prevented it. Many ladies and gentlemen who came up at an inconvenient time have remained in my room long after the foretop-sail of the ship which was to waft them to England was loosed, in the hope of Napoleon's presenting himself at the windows of his apartments.

# CHAPTER II

## 1816

SOME short time after his arrival at Longwood, I communicated to the Emperor the news of Murat's death.[1] He heard it with calmness, and immediately inquired if he had perished on the field of battle? At first I hesitated to tell him that his brother-in-law had been executed by military law. On his repeating the question, I informed him of the manner in which Murat had been put to death, to which he listened without any change of countenance. I also communicated the intelligence of the death of Ney.[2] 'He was a brave man, nobody more so; but he was a madman,' said he. 'He betrayed me at Fontaine-bleau: the proclamation against the Bourbons which he said in his defence I caused to be given to him was written by himself, and I never knew anything about that document until it was read to the troops. It is true that I sent him orders to obey me. What

[1] Murat was shot at Pizzo, 13th October 1815, the news reaching St Helena early in 1816.

[2] The Marshal Prince of the Moskwa, 'the bravest of the brave,' was executed 7th December 1815, in the grey of the morning, by his own countrymen.

could he do ?   His troops abandoned him.   Not
only the troops, but the people wished to join me.'
I had lent him Miss Williams's *Present State of
France* to read.   Two or three days afterwards he
said to me, while dressing, 'That is a vile production
of that countrywoman of yours.   It is a heap of
falsehoods.   This,' opening his shirt and showing
his flannel waistcoat, 'is the only coat of mail I ever
wore.   My hat lined with steel too!   There is the
hat I wore,' pointing to the one he always carried.[1]
Napoleon's hours of rising were uncertain, much
depending upon the quantum of rest he had enjoyed
during the night.   He was in general a bad sleeper,
and frequently got up at three or four o'clock, in

---

[1] Doctor O'Meara was introduced to him ; it was the usual hour of
his being admitted.  ' Dottore,' said the Emperor to him in Italian,
whilst he was shaving himself, 'I have just read one of your fine
London productions against me.'  The Doctor's countenance indicated
a wish to know what it was.  I showed him the book at a distance ;
it was himself who had lent it to me : he was disconcerted.  ' It is a
very just remark,' continued the Emperor, 'that it is the truth only
which gives offence.  I have not been angry for a moment, but I
have frequently laughed at it.'  The Doctor endeavoured to reply,
and puzzled himself with high-flown sentences ; it was, he said, an
infamous, disgusting libel ; everybody knew it to be such, nobody
paid any attention to it ; nevertheless, persons might be found who
would believe it from its not having been replied to.  ' But how can
that be helped?' said the Emperor.  'If it should enter any one's
head to put in print that I had grown hairy, and walked on four paws,
there are people who would believe it, and would say that God had
punished me as He did Nebuchadnezzar.  And what could I do?
There is no remedy in such cases.'  The Doctor went away, hardly
able to believe the gaiety, the indifference, the good nature, of which
he had just been witness : with regard to ourselves, we are now
accustomed to it.—*Las Cases*, vol. i., part ii., p. 121, English
edition.

which case he read or wrote until six or seven, at which time, when the weather was fine, he sometimes went out to ride, attended by some of his generals, or lay down again to repose for a couple of hours.[1] When he retired to bed, he could not sleep unless the most perfect darkness was obtained, by the closing of every cranny through which a ray of light might pass, although I have sometimes seen him fall asleep on the sofa, and remain so for a few minutes in broad daylight. When ill, Marchand occasionally read to him until he fell asleep.[2]

[1] 'He very often woke during the night, called for one of his secretaries, and worked until sleep returned. Day and night in the kitchen of the Tuileries, or even in a campaign, three fowls were always kept in different stages of roasting. One was always to be ready for immediate eating on the Emperor's demand.'—D'Hérisson's *Black Cabinet*, p. 189.

[2] 'I have known the Emperor to be engaged in business in the Council of State for eight or nine hours successively, and afterwards rise with his ideas as clear as when he sat down. I have seen him at St. Helena peruse books for ten or twelve hours in succession, on the most abtruse subjects, without appearing in the least fatigued. He has suffered, unmoved, the greatest shocks that ever man experienced. On his return from Moscow or Leipzig, after he had communicated the disastrous event in the Council of State, he said: "It has been reported in Paris that this misfortune turned my hair grey; but you see it is not so (pointing to his head); and I hope I shall be able to support many other reverses." But these prodigious exertions are made only, as it were, in despite of his physical powers, which never appear less susceptible than when his mind is in full activity. The Emperor eats very irregularly, but generally very little. He often says that a man may hurt himself by eating too much, but never by eating too little. He will remain four-and-twenty hours without eating, only to get an appetite for the ensuing day. But if he eats little, he drinks still less. A single glass of Madeira or Champagne is sufficient to restore his strength and to produce cheerfulness of spirits. He sleeps very little and very irregularly, generally rising at

At times he rose at seven and wrote or dictated until breakfast time, or, if the morning was very fine, he went out to ride. When he breakfasted in his own room, it was generally served on a little round

daybreak to read or write, and afterwards lying down to sleep again.

'The Emperor has no faith in medicine, and never takes any. He had adopted a peculiar mode of treatment for himself. Whenever he found himself unwell, his plan was to run into an extreme, the opposite of what happened to be his habit at the time. This he calls restoring the equilibrium of nature. If, for instance, he had been inactive for a length of time, he would suddenly ride about sixty miles, or hunt for a whole day. If, on the contrary, he had been harassed by great fatigues, he would resign himself to a state of absolute rest for twenty-four hours. These unexpected shocks infallibly brought about an internal crisis, and instantly produced the desired effect ; the remedy, he observed, never failed.

'The Emperor's lymphatic system is deranged, and his blood circulates with difficulty. Nature, he said, had endowed him with two important advantages : the one was the power of sleeping whenever he needed repose, at any hour, and in any place ; another was that he was incapable of committing any injurious excess either in eating or drinking. "If," said he, "I go the least beyond my mark, my stomach instantly revolts." He is subject to nausea from very slight causes ; a mere tickling cough is sufficient to produce that effect on him.'—*Las Cases*, vol. i., part i., p. 368, English edition.

'Here the Grand Marshal added that he could safely say he had seen Napoleon sleep, not only on the eve of an engagement, but even during the battle. "I was obliged to do so," said Napoleon, "when I fought battles that lasted three days ; Nature was also to have her due : I took advantage of the smallest intervals and slept where and when I could." He slept on the field of battle at Wagram, and at Bautzen, even during the action, and completely within the range of the enemy's balls. On this subject he said that, independently of the necessity of obeying Nature, these slumbers afforded a general, commanding a very great army, the important advantage of enabling him to await, calmly, the reports and combinations of all his divisions, instead of perhaps being hurried away by the only event which he himself could witness.'—*Ibid.* vol. i., part ii., p. 337.

table at between nine and ten ; when along with the
rest of his suite at eleven : in either case *à la
fourchette*. After breakfast he generally dictated to
some of his suite for a few hours, and at two or three
o'clock received such visitors as, by previous
appointment, had been directed to present themselves. Between four and five, when the weather
permitted, he rode out on horseback, or in the
carriage for an hour or two, accompanied by all his
suite, then returned, and dictated or read until eight,
or occasionally played a game at chess, at which
time dinner was announced, which rarely exceeded
twenty minutes or half an hour in duration. He ate
heartily and fast, and did not appear to be partial
to high-seasoned or rich food. One of his most
favourite dishes was a roasted leg of mutton, of
which I have seen him sometimes pare the outside
brown part off; he was also partial to mutton chops.[1]
He rarely drank as much as a pint of claret at his
dinner, which was generally much diluted with water.
After dinner, when the servants had withdrawn,
and when there were no visitors, he sometimes
played at chess or at whist, but more frequently sent
for a volume of Corneille, or of some other standard
author, and read aloud for an hour, or conversed

---

[1] The habit of eating fast and carelessly is supposed to have
paralysed Napoleon's powers upon two critical occasions of his life,—
the battles of Borodino and of Leipzig, upon both of which occasions
he is known to have suffered from indigestion. The German novelist
Hoffman states also that the Emperor's energies were impaired during
the battle of Dresden from the effects of a shoulder of mutton stuffed
with onions.

with the ladies and the rest of his suite. He usually
retired to his bedroom at ten or eleven, and to rest
immediately afterwards. When he breakfasted or
dined in his own apartment (*dans l'intérieur*) he
sometimes sent for one of his suite to converse with
him during the repast. He never ate more than
two meals a day, nor, since I knew him, had he ever
taken more than a very small cup of coffee after each
repast, and at no other time. I have also been
informed by those who have been in his service
for fifteen years that he had never exceeded that
quantity.[1]

On the 14th of April the *Phaeton* frigate, Captain
Stanfell, arrived from England, having on board
Lieutenant-General Sir Hudson Lowe, Lady Lowe ;
Sir Thomas Reade (Deputy-Adjutant-General);
Major Gorrequer, aide-de-camp to Sir Hudson
Lowe; Lieutenant-Colonel Lyster, Inspector of
Militia; Major Emmett of the Engineers; Mr.
Baxter, Deputy Inspector of Hospitals ; Lieutenants

---

[1] 'Bonaparte drank little wine, always either claret or Burgundy,
and the latter by preference. After breakfast as well as after dinner
he took a cup of strong coffee. I never saw him take any between
his meals, and I cannot imagine what can have given rise to the
assertion of his being particularly fond of coffee. When he worked
late at night he never ordered coffee, but chocolate, of which he made
me take a cup with him. . . . All that has been said about
Bonaparte's immoderate use of snuff has no more foundation in truth
than his pretended partiality for coffee. It is true that at an early
period of his life he began to take snuff, but very sparingly, and
always out of a box ; and if he bore any resemblance to Frederick the
Great, it was not in filling his waistcoat pockets with snuff, for he
carried his notions of personal neatness to a fastidious degree.'—
Bourrienne's *Memoirs of Napoleon*, edition 1885, vol. i. p. 281.

Wortham and Jackson of the Engineers and Staff Corps, and other officers.

The following day Sir Hudson Lowe landed and was installed as Governor with the customary forms. A message was then sent to Longwood that the new Governor would visit Napoleon at nine o'clock on the following morning. Accordingly, a little before that time, Sir Hudson Lowe arrived, in the midst of a pelting storm of rain and wind, accompanied by Sir George Cockburn, and followed by his numerous staff. As the hour fixed upon was rather unseasonable, and one at which Napoleon had never received any person, intimation was given to the Governor on his arrival that Napoleon was indisposed and could not receive any visitors that morning. This appeared to disconcert Sir Hudson Lowe, who, after pacing up and down before the windows of the drawing-room for a few minutes, demanded at what time on the following day he could be introduced : two o'clock was fixed upon for the interview, at which time he arrived, accompanied as before by the Admiral, and followed by his staff. They were at first ushered into the dining-room, behind which was the salon, where they were to be received. A proposal was made by Sir George Cockburn to Sir Hudson Lowe that the latter should be introduced by him, as being, in his opinion, the most official and proper manner of resigning to him the charge of the prisoner ; for which purpose Sir George suggested that they should enter the room together. This was acceded to by Sir Hudson. At the door of the drawing-room stood Noverraz, one of the French valets, whose business it was to announce the persons introduced. After waiting a few minutes, the door was opened and the Governor called for. As soon as the word Governor was pronounced, Sir Hudson Lowe started up and stepped forward so hastily that he entered the room before Sir George Cockburn was well apprised of it. The door was then closed, and when the Admiral presented himself, the valet, not having heard his name called, told him that he could not enter.[1] Sir Hudson Lowe remained about a quarter of an hour with Napoleon, during which time the conversation was chiefly carried on in Italian, and subsequently the officers of his staff were introduced. The Admiral did not again apply for admittance.

On the 18th of April I brought up some newspapers to Napoleon, who, after asking me some questions concerning the meeting of Parliament, inquired who had lent the newspapers? I replied that the Admiral had lent them to me. Napoleon said, ' I believe that he was rather ill-treated the day

---

[1] ' Sir Hudson Lowe, writing to Sir Henry Bunbury, the Under-Secretary of State, says that the Admiral attributed his exclusion to the rudeness of Bertrand and "a servant," and this is confirmed by Count Las Cases, who, in his *Journal*, describes the Emperor as "*ravi*" at the circumstance: "Ah, my good Noverraz," said he, "you have done a clever thing for once in your life. He heard me say that I would not see the Admiral again, and thought he was bound to shut the door in his face. This is delightful ! " Count Montholon, however, says, and with greater probability, as the Emperor was partial to Sir George Cockburn, " The oversight of the valet grieved him." He charged O'Meara to say so to Sir George, and even sent one of us to express to him his regret.'—See Forsyth's *Life of Lowe*, vol. i. p. 142.

he came up with the new Governor : what does he
say about it ?' I replied, 'The Admiral considered it
an insult offered to him, and certainly felt greatly
offended at it. Some explanation, has however, been
given by General Montholon upon the subject.'
Napoleon said, ' I shall never see him with pleasure,
but he did not announce himself as being desirous
of seeing me.' I replied, ' He wished to introduce
officially to you the new Governor, and thought that,
as he was to act in that capacity, it was not necessary
to be previously announced.' Napoleon answered,
' He should have sent me word by Bertrand that he
wanted to see me ; but,' continued he, ' he wished to
embroil me with the new Governor, and for that
purpose persuaded him to come up here at nine
o'clock in the morning, though he must have known
that I never received any person at that hour. It
is a pity that a man who really has talents—for I
believe him to be a very good officer in his own
service—should have behaved in the manner he has
done to me. Insulting those who are in your power,
and consequently cannot make any opposition, is
a sign of an ignoble mind.' I said that I was
convinced it was quite a mistake, and that the
Admiral never had the smallest intention of insulting
or embroiling him with the Governor. He resumed,
' I, in my misfortunes, sought an asylum, and instead
of that I have found contempt, ill-treatment, and
insult. Shortly after I came on board his ship, as I
did not wish to sit at table for two or three hours
drinking wine, I got up and walked out upon deck.

While I was going out he said in a contemptuous manner, "I believe the *General* has never read Lord Chesterfield;" meaning that I was deficient in politeness, and did not know how to conduct myself at table.' I endeavoured to explain to him that the English, and above all naval officers, were not in the habit of going through many forms, and that it was wholly unintentional on the part of the Admiral. '.If,' said he, 'Sir George wanted to see Lord St. Vincent, or Lord Keith, would he not have sent beforehand and asked at what hour it might be convenient to see him ; and should not I be treated with at least as much respect as either of them ? Putting out of the question that I have been a crowned head, I think,' said he, laughing, 'that the actions which I have performed are at least as well known as anything they have done.' I endeavoured again to excuse the Admiral, upon which he recalled to my mind what he had just related about Lord Chesterfield, and asked me 'What could *that* mean ?' [1]

General Montholon came in at this moment with

---

[1] 'The English Ministry warmly censured the respect which had been shown to the Emperor on board the *Bellerophon*, and issued fresh orders in consequence, so that a totally different style of manner and expression was affected on the *Northumberland*. The crew seemed to betray a ridiculous anxiety to be covered before the Emperor ; it had been strictly enjoined to give him no other title than that of " General," and only to treat him as such. . . . I need scarcely observe that the English are accustomed to remain a long time at table after the dessert drinking and conversing. The Emperor, already tired by the tedious dinner, could never have endured this custom, and he rose, therefore, from the first day, immediately after coffee had been handed round, and went out on deck, followed by the Grand Marshal and myself. This disconcerted

a translation of a paper sent by Sir Hudson Lowe, which the domestics, who were willing to remain, were required to sign ; it was accompanied by the following letter :—[1]

DOWNING STREET, 10 *Janvier* 1816.

Je dois à present vous faire connaître, que la plaisir de S. A. R. le Prince Regent, est, qu'à votre arrivée à Ste. Hélène, vous communiqueriez à toutes les personnes de la suite de Napoléon Bonaparte, y compris les serviteurs doméstiques, qu'ils sont libres de quitter l'isle immediatement pour rétourner en Europe; ajoutant, qu'il ne sera permis à aucun de rester à Ste. Hélène, excepté ceux qui déclareront par un écrit que sera déposé dans vos mains, que c'est leur désir de rester dans l'isle et de participer aux restrictions qu'il est nécessaire d'imposer sur Napoléon Bonaparte personnellement.

Ceux qui parmi eux se détermineront à retourner en Europe, devront être envoyé par le premier occasion favorable au Cap de Bonne Espérance, le gouverneur de cette colonie sera chargé de pourvoir aux personnes des moyens de transport en Europe.

(Signé)    BATHURST.

This declaration was not approved of by Napoleon, who, moreover, pronounced it to be too

the Admiral, who took occasion to express his surprise to his officers. But Madame Bertrand, whose maternal language is English, warmly replied : " Do not forget, Admiral, that your guest is a man who has governed a large portion of the world, and that kings once contended for the honour of being admitted to his table."—" Very true," replied the Admiral ; and this officer, who possesses good sense, a becoming pliability of manners, and sometimes much elegance, did his utmost from that moment to accommodate the Emperor in his habits. He shortened the time of sitting at table, ordering coffee for Napoleon and those who accompanied him even before the rest of the company had finished their dinner. The moment Napoleon had taken his coffee he left the cabin ; upon which everybody rose until he had quitted the room, and then continued to take their wine for another hour.'— *Journal of the Private Life of the Emperor Napoleon at St. Helena*, by the Comte de Las Cases, edition 1824, vol. i. pp. 72, 91.

[1] The reader will not consider me accountable for the accuracy of the French sent from Plantation House to Longwood.—B. E. O'M.

literally translated to be easily comprehended by
a Frenchman. He accordingly desired Count
Montholon to retire into the next room, where the
following was substituted :—

Nous soussignés, voulant continuer à rester au service de S.
M. l'Empereur Napoléon, consentons, quelqu'affreux que soit le
séjour de Ste. Hélène, à y rester, nous soumettant aux restrictions, quoiqu' injustes et arbitraires, qu'on a imposées à S. M. et
aux personnes de son service.

'There,' said he, 'let those who please sign that ;
but do not attempt to influence them either one way
or the other.'

The request to the domestics to sign the paper
sent by Sir H. Lowe had produced a wish for
further explanation amongst them ; and some who
applied to Sir Thomas Reade for that purpose
received answers of a nature to inculcate a belief
that those who signed it would be compelled
to remain in the island during the lifetime of Bonaparte. This, however, did not prevent any of
them from signing the paper which was presented
to them.

*April* 19.—The weather has been extremely bad
for some days, which has contributed, with other circumstances, to make Napoleon a little dissatisfied. 'In
this *isola maladetta*,' said he, 'there is neither sun nor
moon to be seen for the greatest part of the year.
Constant rain and fog. It is worse than Capri. Have
you ever been at Capri ?' continued he. I replied in
the affirmative. 'There,' said he, 'you can have
everything you want from the continent in a few hours.'

He afterwards made a few remarks upon some absurd falsehoods which had been published in the ministerial papers respecting him ; and asked if it were 'possible that the English could be so foolishly credulous as to believe all the stuff we published about him.'

*April* 21.—Captain Hamilton of the *Havannah* frigate had an audience with Napoleon in the garden. Napoleon told him that when he (Napoleon) had arrived on the island, he had been asked what he desired to have? He therefore begged of him to say that he desired his liberty, or *le bourreau ;* that the English ministers had unworthily violated the most sacred rights of hospitality towards him by declaring him a prisoner, which savages would not have done in the situation in which he stood.

Colonel and Miss Wilks were to proceed to England in the *Havannah.* Before their departure they came up to Longwood and had a long interview with Napoleon. He was highly pleased with Miss Wilks (a highly accomplished and elegant young lady), and gallantly told her that 'she exceeded the description which had been given of her to him.'

*April* 24.—The weather still gloomy. Napoleon at first was out of spirits, but gradually became enlivened. Conversed much about the Admiral, whom he professed to esteem as a man of talent in his profession. 'He is not,' said he, 'a man of a bad heart; on the contrary, I believe him to be capable of a generous action; but he is rough, overbearing, vain, choleric, and capricious; never consulting anybody; jealous of his authority; caring little for the manner in which he exercises it, and sometimes violent without dignity.'

He then made some observations about the bullocks which had been brought from the Cape of Good Hope by the Government, and amongst which a great mortality had taken place. 'The Admiral,' said he, 'ought to have contracted for them, instead of making them Government property. It is well known that whatever belongs to a Government is never taken any care of, and is plundered by everybody. If he had contracted with some person, I will venture to say very few would have died, instead of a third, as has been the case.' He then asked me many questions about the relative price of articles in England and St. Helena, and concluded by inquiring if I took any fees for attending sick people on the island. I replied in the negative, which seemed to surprise him. 'Corvisart,' said he, 'notwithstanding his being my first physician, possessed of great wealth, and in the habit of receiving many rich presents from me, took a Napoleon for each visit he paid to the sick. In your country particularly every man has his trade; the member of Parliament takes money for his vote, the ministers for their places, the lawyers for their opinion.'

*April* 26.—Napoleon asked several questions relative to the ships which had been seen to approach the island; was anxious to know if Lady Bingham, who had been expected for some time, had arrived; observed how anxious Sir George Bingham must be about her; asked me if the ship was furnished

with a chronometer by Government; to which I
replied in the negative.    He observed that the
vessel might very probably miss the island through
the want of one.    'How shameful it is,' said he,
'for your Government to put three or four hundred
men on board a ship destined for this place without
a chronometer, thereby running the risk of ship and
cargo, of the value perhaps of half a million, together
with the lives of so many *poveri diavoli*, for the sake
of saving three or four hundred francs for a watch.
I,' continued he, 'ordered that every ship employed
in the French service should be supplied with one.
It is a neglect on the part of your Government not
to be accounted for.'    He then asked me if it were
true that a court of inquiry was then sitting upon
some officer for having made too free with the bottle.
'Is it a crime,' added he, 'for the English to get
drunk, and will a court-martial be the consequence?
for if that were the case, you would have nothing
but courts-martial every day. —— was a little
merry on board every day after dinner.'    I observed
that there was a wide difference between being
merry and getting drunk.[1]    He laughed and repeated

[1] 'The Emperor had formed an exaggerated idea of the quantity
of wine drunk by English gentlemen, and used always to ask me,
after we had had a party, how many bottles of wine my father drank?
and then laughing, and counting on his fingers, generally made the
number five.    One day, to annoy me, he said that my countrywomen
drank gin and brandy, and then added in English, "You laike veree
mosh dreenk, meess, sometimes brandee, geen."    Though I could
not help laughing at his way of saying this, I felt most indignant at
the accusation, and assured him that the ladies of England had the
utmost horror of drinking spirits. . . . At last he confessed, laughing,

what he had said relative to courts-martial. 'Is it true,' he then said, 'that they are sending out a house and furniture for me, as there are so many false reports in your newspapers that I have my doubts, especially as I have heard nothing about it officially?' I told him that Sir Hudson Lowe had assured me of the fact, and that Sir Thomas Reade professed to have seen both the house and the furniture.

Many changes relative to the treatment of the French took place after the arrival of Sir Hudson Lowe. Mr. Brooke, the colonial secretary, Major Gorrequer, Sir Hudson's aide-de-camp, and other official persons, went round to the different shop-keepers in the town, ordering them, in the name of the Governor, not to give credit to any of the French, or to sell them any article, unless for ready money, under pain of not only losing the amount of the sum so credited, but suffering such other punishment as the Governor might think proper to award. They were further directed to hold no communication whatsoever with them without special permission from the Governor, under pain of being expelled from the island.

Many of the officers of the 53d who were in the habit of calling to see Madame Bertrand at Hut's Gate, received hints that their visits were not pleasing to the lately-arrived authorities ; and the

that he had made the accusation only to tease me. When I was going away he repeated : " You like dreenk meess Betsee,—dreenk, dreenk!"'—*Recollections of Napoleon*, by Mrs. Abell, third edition, pp. 101, 102.

officer of the Hut's Gate guard was ordered to report the names of all persons entering Bertrand's house. Sentinels were placed in different directions to prevent the approach of visitors, several of whom, including some ladies, were turned back. A sensation of unwillingness to approach the exiles, very different from the feeling which existed a few days ago, appeared to be general amongst the inhabitants, and even amongst the military and naval officers. The Governor was very minute in his inquiries to those persons who had formerly conversed with Napoleon or any of his suite. Several of the officers of the 53d went to Hut's Gate to take leave of Countess Bertrand, as (to use their own words) they declared that it was impossible for men of honour to comply with the new regulations. It was required that all persons who visited at Hut's Gate or at Longwood should make a report to the Governor or to Sir Thomas Reade of the conversations they had held with the French. Several additional sentinels were placed around Longwood House and grounds.

*May* 3.—The weather has been extremely wet and foggy, with high winds for several days, during which time Napoleon did not stir out of doors. Messengers and letters continually arrived from Plantation House. The Governor was apparently very anxious to see Napoleon, and seemingly distrustful, although the residents of Longwood were assured of his actual presence by the sound of his voice. He had some communications with Count

Bertrand relative to the necessity which he said there was that some of his officers should see Napoleon daily. He also came to Longwood frequently himself, and finally, after some difficulty, succeeded in obtaining an interview with Napoleon in his bed-chamber, which lasted about a quarter of an hour.

Some days before he sent for me, he asked a variety of questions concerning the captive, walked round the house several times and before the windows, measuring and laying down the plan of a new ditch, which he said he would have dug, in order to prevent the cattle from trespassing. On his arrival at the angle formed by the union of two of the old ditches he observed a tree, the branches of which considerably overhung it. This appeared to excite considerable alarm in His Excellency's breast, as he desired me to send instantly for Mr. Porteous, the Superintendent of the Company's gardens. Some minutes having elapsed after I had despatched a messenger for that gentleman, the Governor, who had his eyes continually fixed upon the tree, desired me, in a hasty manner, to go and fetch Mr. Porteous instantly myself. On my return with him, I found Sir Hudson Lowe walking up and down, contemplating the object which appeared to be such a source of alarm. In a hurried manner he ordered Mr. Porteous to send some men instantly to have the tree grubbed up, and before leaving the ground directed me in an undertone to 'see that it was done.'[1]

[1] 'About three o'clock the Emperor, with whom I breakfasted this morning, sent for me. He wished to take the air, and he en-

On the 4th Sir Hudson Lowe went to see Count Bertrand, with whom he had an hour's conversation, which did not appear to be of a nature very pleasing to him, as, on retiring, he mounted his horse, muttering something, and evidently out of humour. Shortly afterwards I learned the purport of his

deavoured to walk as far as the wood; but the air was too keen for him. He then called at the Grand Marshal's, and he sat for a considerable time in an arm-chair, apparently quite exhausted. We remarked the colour of his countenance, his thinness, and his evident debility; and we were much distressed at the change observable in him.

'As we passed through the wood the Emperor saw the fortifications with which we are about to be surrounded; and he could not forbear smiling at these useless and absurd preparations. He remarked that the ground in our neighbourhood had been entirely disfigured by the removal of the kind of turf with which it was covered, and which had been carried away for the purpose of raising banks. In fact, for the last two months, the Governor has been incessantly digging ditches, constructing parapets, planting palisadoes, etc. He has quite blockaded us in Longwood, and the stable at present presents every appearance of a redoubt. We are at a loss to guess where will be the advantage equivalent to the expense and labour bestowed on these works, which by turns excite the ill-humour and ridicule of the soldiers and Chinese who are employed upon them, and who now distinguish Longwood and the stable by the names of *Hudson Fort* and *Lowe Fort.* We are assured that Sir Hudson Lowe often starts out of his sleep to devise new measures of security. " Surely," said the Emperor, " this seems something like madness. Why cannot the man sleep tranquilly and let us alone? Has he not sense enough to perceive that the security of our local situation here is sufficient to remove all his panic terrors?"—" Sire," said an individual present, " he cannot forget Capri, which, with two thousand men, thirty pieces of cannon, and batteries mounted to the clouds, was taken by twelve hundred Frenchmen, commanded by the brave Lamarque, who could only reach Sir Hudson Lowe by the help of a triple escalade."—" Well," said the Emperor, " this only proves that our Governor is a better jailor than a general." '—*Las Cases*, vol. iv., part vii., p. 204, English edition.

visit. He commenced by saying that the French made a great many complaints without any reason ; that, considering their situations, they were very well treated, and ought to be thankful, instead of making any complaints. It appeared to him, however, that instead of being so, they abused the liberal treatment which was practised towards them. That he was determined to assure himself of General Bonaparte's actual presence daily, by the observation of an officer appointed by him, and that this officer should visit him at fixed hours for such purpose. During the whole of it he spoke in a very authoritative and indeed contemptuous manner, frequently referring to the great powers with which he was invested.

*May* 5.[1]—Napoleon sent Marchand for me at about nine o'clock. I was introduced by the back-door into his bedroom, a description of which I shall endeavour to give as minutely and as correctly as possible.[2] It was about fourteen feet by twelve, and ten or eleven feet in height. The walls were lined with brown nankeen, bordered and edged with common green bordering paper, and destitute of surbase. Two small windows, without pulleys, looked towards the camp of the 53d Regiment, one of which was thrown up and fastened by a piece of notched wood. Window-curtains of white long-

---

[1] Las Cases put this as happening on 6th May, not 5th May. As the 5th was Sunday there ought to be no mistake in O'Meara's account. The subject was, however, referred to again by the Emperor on the following day, see p. 55.

[2] See also Plan of Longwood on p. 19.

cloth, a small fireplace, a shabby grate, and fire-irons to match, with a paltry mantelpiece of wood, painted white, upon which stood a small marble bust of his son.   Above the mantelpiece hung the portrait of Marie Louise, and four or five of young Napoleon, one of which was embroidered by the hands of the mother.   A little more to the right hung also a miniature picture of the Empress Josephine, and to the left was suspended the alarum chamber-watch of Frederick the Great,[1] brought by Napoleon from Potsdam ; while on the right the Consular watch, engraved with the cypher B, hung by a chain of the plaited hair of Marie Louise from a pin stuck in the nankeen lining.

The floor was covered with a second-hand carpet, which had once decorated the dining-room of a lieu-tenant of the St. Helena artillery.   In the right-hand corner was placed the little plain iron camp-

[1] 'This morning, when I was in the Emperor's apartment, being unemployed, I took a fancy to examine Frederick the Great's large watch, which hangs beside the chimney-piece.   This led the Em-peror to say, "I have been the possessor of glorious and valuable relics.   I had the sword of Frederick the Great ; and the Spaniards presented to me at the Tuileries the sword of Francis I.   This was a high compliment, and it must have cost them some sacrifice.   The Turks and Persians have also sent me arms, which were said to have belonged to Gengis-Khan, Tamerlane, Shah Nadir, and I know not whom ; but I attached importance not to the fact but to the intention."

'I expressed my astonishment that he had not endeavoured to keep Frederick's sword.   "Why, I had my own," said he smiling, and gently pinching my ear.   He was right : I certainly made a very stupid observation.'—*Las Cases*, vol. iv., part vii., p. 181, English edition.

bedstead, with green silk curtains, upon which its master had reposed on the fields of Marengo and Austerlitz. Between the windows there was a paltry second-hand chest of drawers, and an old bookcase with green blinds stood on the left of the door leading to the next apartment. Four or five cane-bottomed chairs, painted green, were standing here and there about the room. Before the back-door there was a screen covered with nankeen, and between that and the fireplace an old-fashioned sofa covered with white long-cloth, upon which Napoleon reclined, clothed in his white morning gown, white loose trousers and stockings all in one, —a chequered red Madrás handkerchief upon his head, and his shirt-collar open without a cravat. His air was melancholy and troubled. Before him stood a little round table with some books, at the foot of which lay, in confusion upon the carpet, a heap of those which he had already perused, and at the foot of the sofa, facing him, was suspended a portrait of the Empress Marie Louise, with her son in her arms. In front of the fireplace stood Las Cases with his arms folded over his breast, and some papers in one of his hands. Of all the former magnificence of the once mighty Emperor of France nothing was present except a superb wash-hand-stand, containing a silver basin and water-jug of the same metal, in the left-hand corner.

Napoleon, after a few questions of no importance, asked me in both French and Italian, in the presence of Count Las Cases, the following questions : 'You

are aware that it was in consequence of my application that you were appointed to attend upon me.
Now I want to know from you precisely and truly,
as a man of honour, in what situation you conceive
yourself to be, whether my surgeon, as M. Maingaud was, or the surgeon of a prison-ship ? Whether
you have orders to report every trifling occurrence
or illness, or what I say to you, to the Governor?
Answer me candidly: What situation do you conceive yourself to be in ?'

I replied, 'As your surgeon and to attend upon
you and your suite. I have received no other
orders than to make an immediate report in case of
your being taken seriously ill, in order to have
promptly the advice and assistance of other physi-
cians.'—'First obtaining my consent to call in
others,' demanded he : 'is it not so?' I answered
that I would certainly obtain his previous consent.

He then said, 'If you were appointed as surgeon
to a prison, and to report my conversations to the
Governor, whom I take to be *un capo di spioni*, I
would never see you again. Do not,' continued he
(on my replying that I was placed about him as a
surgeon and by no means as a spy), 'suppose that
I take you for a spy ; on the contrary, I have never
had the least occasion to find fault with you, and I
have a friendship for you and an esteem for your
character, a greater proof of which I could not give
you than asking you candidly your own opinion of
your situation; as you, being an Englishman, and

paid by the English Government, might perhaps be obliged to do what I have asked.'

I replied as before, and that in my professional capacity I did not consider myself to belong to any particular country. 'If I am taken seriously ill,' said he, 'then acquaint me with your opinion, and ask my consent to call in others. This Governor, during the few days that I was melancholy and had a mental depression in consequence of the treatment I receive, which prevented me from going out, in order that I might. not *ennuyer* others with my afflictions, wanted to send his physician to me under the pretext of inquiring after my health. I desired Bertrand to tell him that I had not sufficient confidence in his physician to take anything from his hands; that if I were really ill I would send for you, in whom I have confidence; but that a physician was of no use in such cases, and that I only wanted to be left alone. I understand that he proposed an officer should enter my chamber to see me if I did not stir out. Any person,' continued he, with much emotion, 'who endeavours to force his way into my apartment shall be a corpse the moment he enters it. If he ever eats bread or meat again, I am not Napoleon. This I am determined on; I know that I shall be killed afterwards, as what can one do against a *camp*? I have faced death too many times to fear it. Besides, I am convinced that this Governor has been sent out by Lord —— I told him a few days ago, that if he wanted to put an end to me, he would have a very good opportunity by

sending somebody to force his way into my chamber.
That I would immediately make a corpse of the
first that entered, and then I should be of course
despatched, and he might write home to his
Government that "*Bonaparte*" was killed in a
brawl. I also told him to leave me alone, and not
to torment me with his hateful presence. I have
seen Prussians, Tartars, Cossacks, Kalmucks, etc.,
but never before in my life have I beheld so
ill-favoured and so forbidding a countenance. *Il
porte le diable empreint sur son visage.'*

I endeavoured to convince him that the English
Ministry would never be capable of what he supposed, and that such was not the character of the
nation. 'I had reason to complain of the Admiral,'
said he; 'but though he treated me roughly, he
never behaved in such a manner as this *Prussian*.
A few days ago he, in a manner, insisted upon
seeing me when I was undressed in my chamber,
and a prey to melancholy. The Admiral never
asked to see me a second time, when it was intimated to him that I was unwell or undressed; as
he well knew that, although I did not go out, I was
still to be found.'

After this he mentioned his apprehensions of
being afflicted with an attack of gout. · I recommended him to take much more exercise. 'What
can I do,' replied he, 'in this execrable island, where
you cannot ride a mile without being wet through;
an island that even the English themselves complain of, though used to humidity?' He concluded

by making some severe remarks upon the Governor's conduct in having sent his aide-de-camp and secretary round the shops, forbidding the shopkeepers to give the French credit, under pain of severe punishment.[1]

*May* 6.—Had some conversation with Napoleon upon the same subject as yesterday, which commenced by my submitting to him, that according to the strict letter of the conversation of yesterday, it would be impossible for me to reply to any question addressed to me relative to him or to his affairs, whether made by the Governor or any one else, which he must be aware was, in my situation, impossible. Moreover, that I had been, from the time of my arrival, and was then, frequently employed as a medium of communication to the authorities of the island, which I hoped I had executed to his satisfaction. He replied that all he wanted of me was to act as a *galantuomo*, and 'as you would do were you surgeon to Lord St. Vincent. I do not mean to bind you to silence, or to prevent you from repeating any *bavardage* you may hear me say ; but I want to prevent you from allowing yourself to be cajoled and made a spy of, unintentionally on your part, by this Governor. After that to your God, your duty is to be paid to your own country and sovereign, and your next, to your patients.'

'During the short interview that this Governor had with me in my bed-chamber,' continued he,

---

[1] Compare Forsyth, *Lowe* vol. i. p. 80.

'one of the first things which he proposed was to
send you away, and to take his own surgeon in your
place.   This he repeated twice ; and so earnest was
he to gain his object, that although I gave him a
most decided refusal, when he was going out he
turned about and again proposed it.   I never saw
such a horrid countenance.   He sat on a chair
opposite to my sofa, and on the little table between
us there was a cup of coffee.   His physiognomy
made such an unfavourable impression upon me,
that I thought his evil eye had poisoned it, and I
ordered Marchand to throw it out of the window ;
I could not have swallowed it for the world.'

*May* 14.—Saw Napoleon in his dressing-room ;
he complained of being affected with catarrhal
symptoms, which I attributed to his having walked
out in the wet with very thin shoes, and recommended him to wear galoshes, which he ordered
Marchand to provide.   'I have promised,' added
he, 'to see a number of people to-day ; and though
I am indisposed, I shall do so.'   Just at this moment
some of the visitors came close to the window of his
dressing-room, which was open, tried to put aside
the curtain and peep in.   Napoleon shut the window,
asked some questions about Lady Moira, and observed, 'The Governor sent an invitation to
Bertrand for General Bonaparte to come to Plantation House to meet Lady Moira.   I told Bertrand
to return no answer to it.   If he really wanted me
to see her, he would have put Plantation House in
the limits ; but to send such an invitation, knowing

that I must go in charge of a guard if I wished to avail myself of it, was an insult. Had he sent word that Lady Moira was ill or fatigued, I would have gone to see her; although I think that, under all the circumstances, she might have come to see me, or Madame Bertrand, or Montholon, as she was free and unshackled. The first Sovereigns in the world have not been ashamed to pay me a visit.'[1]

'It appears,' added he, 'that this Governor was with Blucher, and is the writer of some official letters to your Government, descriptive of part of the operations of 1814. I pointed them out to him the last time I saw him, and asked him, *Est-ce vous, Monsieur?* He replied, "Yes." I told him that they were *pleines de faussetés et de sottises.* He shrugged his shoulders, appeared confused, and replied, "*J'ai cru voir cela.*" If,' continued he, 'those letters were the only accounts he sent, he betrayed his country.'

Count Bertrand came in, and announced that several persons had arrived to see him, besides those who had received appointments for the day. Amongst other names that of Arbuthnot was mentioned. Napoleon asked me who he was. I answered, that I believed him to be brother to the person who had been ambassador at Constantinople. 'Ah, yes, yes,' said Napoleon with a sly smile, 'when Sebastiani was there. You may say that I shall receive them.'

[1] For the extraordinary form of this invitation, see Forsyth, *Lowe*, vol. i. p. 168.

'Have you conversed much with the Governor's physician?' said Napoleon. I replied in the affirmative, adding, that he was the chief of the medical staff, but not attached to the Governor as his body physician. 'What sort of a man is he?—does he look like an honest man, or a man of talent?' I replied that his appearance was very much in his favour, and that he was considered to be a man of talent and of science.

*May* 16.—Sir Hudson Lowe had an interview of about half an hour with Napoleon, which did not appear to be satisfactory. Saw Napoleon walking in the garden in a very thoughtful manner a few minutes subsequent to the Governor's departure, and gave to him the *Dictionnaire des Girouettes* and a few newspapers. After he had asked me from whom I had procured them, he said, 'Here has been this *viso di boja a tormentarmi*. Tell him that I never want to see him, and that I wish he may not come again to annoy me with his hateful presence. Let him never again come near me, unless it is with orders to despatch me; he will then find my breast ready for the blow; but until then, let me be free of his odious countenance; I cannot accustom myself to it.'

*May* 17.—Napoleon in very good spirits. Demanded what the news was. I informed him that the ladies he had received a few days before were highly delighted with his manners, especially, as from what they had read and heard, they had been prepossessed with opinions of a very different nature. 'Ah,' said he, laughing, 'I suppose that they imagined I was some ferocious horned animal.'

Some conversation occurred touching what Sir Robert Wilson had written respecting him about Jaffa, Captain Wright, etc. I observed that as those assertions had never been fully contradicted, they were believed by numbers of English. 'Bah,' replied Napoleon, 'those calumnies will die of themselves, especially now that there are so many English in France who will soon find out that they are all falsehoods. Were Wilson himself not convinced of the untruth of the statements which he had once believed, do you think that he would have assisted Lavalette to escape out of prison?'[1]

*May* 19.—Napoleon in very good humour. Told him that the late Governor of Java,[2] Mr. Raffles, and his staff, had arrived on their way to England, and were very desirous of the honour of paying their respects to him. 'What kind of a man is the Governor?' I replied, Mr. Urmston informed me that he is *un bravissimo uomo*, and possessed of great learning and talents. 'Well, then,' said he, 'I shall see them when I am dressed.'

'This Governor,' said he, '*è un imbécile.* He

---

[1] Count Lavalette was Postmaster-General under Napoleon, and was sentenced by the Bourbons to be shot. His wife being allowed to see him in prison, persuaded him to change dresses with her and pass out, hiding his face in his handkerchief, to where a sedan chair was waiting. Then entering a cabriolet he again changed his dress, and obtained shelter from an employé in the Foreign Office in the Hotel of the Ministry! Whilst there Sir Robert Wilson and other officers arranged his escape from Paris in the uniform of an English officer.

[2] Java was held by the English from 1811 to 1814.

asked Bertrand the other day if he (Bertrand) ever had asked any of the passengers bound to England whether they intended to go to France, as, if he had done so, he must not continue such a practice. Bertrand replied that he certainly had, and, moreover, had begged of some to tell his relations that they were in good health. "But," says this imbecile, "you must not do so."—"Why," says Bertrand, "has not your Government permitted me to write as many letters as I like, and can any Government deny me the liberty of speaking?" Bertrand,' continued he, 'ought to have replied that galley-slaves and prisoners under sentence of death were permitted to inquire after their relations.'

He then observed how unnecessary and vexatious it was to require that an officer should accompany him, should he be desirous of visiting the interior of the island. 'It is all right,' continued he, 'to keep me away from the town and the sea-side. I would never desire to approach either the one or the other. All that is necessary for my security is to guard well the sea-borders of this rock. Let him place his picquets round the island close by the sea and in communication with each other, which he might easily do with the number of men he has, and it would be impossible for me to escape. Cannot he, moreover, put a few horsemen in motion when he knows I am going out? Cannot he place them on the hills, or where he likes, without letting me know anything about it? *I will never appear to see them.* Cannot he do this without obliging me to tell Poppleton that I want to ride out—not that I have any objection to Poppleton—I love a good soldier of any nation ; but I will not do anything which may lead people to imagine that I am a prisoner,—I have been forced here contrary to the law of nations, and I will never recognise their right to detain me. My asking an officer to accompany me would be a tacit acknowledgment of it. I have no intention to attempt an escape, although I have not given my word of honour not to try. Neither will I ever give it, as that would be acknowledging myself a prisoner, which I will never do. Cannot they impose additional restrictions when ships arrive ; and above all, not allow any ship to sail until my actual presence is ascertained, without inflicting such useless, and, because useless, vexatious restrictions ? It is necessary for my health that I should ride seven or eight leagues daily, but I will not do so with an officer or a guard over me. It has always been my maxim, that a man shows more real courage by supporting and resisting the calamities and misfortunes which befall him than by making away with himself. *That* is the action of a losing gamester, or a ruined spendthrift, and is a want of courage, instead of a proof of it. Your Government will be mistaken if they imagine that, by seeking every means to annoy me, such as sending me here, depriving me of all communication with my nearest and dearest relatives, so that I am ignorant if one of my blood exists, isolating me from the world, and imposing useless and vexatious

restrictions which are daily getting worse, they will
weary out my patience and induce me to commit
suicide. Even if I ever had entertained a thought
of the kind, the idea of the gratification it would
afford to them would prevent me from completing it.'

'That *palace*,' said he, laughing, 'which they say
they have sent out for me, is so much money thrown
into the sea. I would rather that they had sent me
four hundred volumes of books than all their furniture and houses. In the first place, it will require
some years to build it, and before that time I shall
be no more. All must be done by the labour of
those poor soldiers and sailors. I do not wish it—I
do not wish to incur the hatred of those poor fellows,
who are already made sufficiently miserable by having been sent to this detestable place, and harassed
in the manner they are. They will load me with
execrations, supposing me to be the author of all
their hardships, and perhaps may wish to put an
end to me.' I observed that no English soldier
would become an assassin. He interrupted me by
saying : 'I have no reason to complain of the English
soldiers or sailors ; on the contrary, they treat me
with every respect, and even appear to feel for me.'

He then spoke of some English officers.
'Moore,' said he, 'was a brave soldier, an excellent
officer, and a man of talent. He made a few
mistakes, which were probably inseparable from the
difficulties with which he was surrounded, and
caused perhaps by his information having misled
him.' This eulogium he repeated more than once ;

and observed that he had commanded the reserve in
Egypt, where he had behaved very well, and displayed talent.   I remarked that Moore was always
in front of the battle, and was generally unfortunate
enough to be wounded.   'Ah!' said he, 'it is necessary sometimes.   He died gloriously—he died like a
soldier.   Menou was a man of courage, but no
soldier.   You ought not to have taken Egypt.   If
Kléber had lived, you would never have conquered it.
An army without artillery or cavalry!   The Turks
counted for nothing.   Kléber was an irreparable loss
to France and to me.   He was a man of the bright-
est talents and the greatest bravery.   I have composed the history of my own campaigns in Egypt
and of yours while I was at the Briars.   But I want
the *Moniteurs* for the dates.'

The conversation then turned upon French naval
officers.   'Villeneuve,' said he, 'when taken prisoner
and brought to England, was so much grieved at
his defeat, that he studied anatomy on purpose to
destroy himself.   For this purpose he bought some
anatomical plates of the heart and compared them
with his own body, in order to ascertain the exact
situation of that organ.   On his arrival in France
I ordered that he should remain at Rennes, and not
proceed to Paris.   Villeneuve, afraid of being tried
by a court-martial for disobeying orders, and consequently losing the fleet—for I had ordered him not
to sail or to engage the English,—determined to
destroy himself, and accordingly took his plates of
the heart and compared them with his breast.

Exactly in the centre of the plate he made a mark with a large pin, then fixed the pin as near as he could judge in the same spot in his own breast, shoved it in to the head, penetrated his heart, and expired. When the room was opened, he was found dead ; the pin in his breast and a mark in the plate corresponding with the wound in his breast. He need not have done it,' continued he, 'as he was a brave man, though possessed of no talent.'

' Barré,' said he, ' whom you took in the Rivoli, was a very brave and good officer. When I went to Egypt I gave directions, after I had disembarked and had taken Alexandria in a few hours, to sound for a passage for the fleet. A Venetian sixty-four (and a fifty-gun ship, I think he said) got in, which I suppose you have seen there, but it was reported that the large ships of the line could not. I ordered Barré to sound. He reported to me that there was a sufficiency of water in one part of the channel. Brueys, on the contrary, said there was not enough of water for the eighty-gun ships. Barré insisted that there was. In the meantime I had advanced into the country after the Mamelukes. All communication with the army from the town by messengers was cut off by the Bedouins, who took or killed them all. My orders did not arrive, or I would have obliged Brueys to enter; for I had the command of the fleet as well as of the army. In the meantime, Nelson came and destroyed Brueys and our fleet. By what I have learned from you, I see that Barré was right, as you saw the *Tigre* and *Canopus* enter.'

After this he made some observations upon the island. 'Such,' said he, 'is the deplorable state of this rock, that the absence of actual want or starvation is considered as a great blessing. Piontkowski[1] went down to Robinson's the other day, where they said to him, "Oh, how lucky you are to have *fresh meat* every day for dinner. If we could enjoy *that*, how happy should we be!"'

*May* 28.—Napoleon asked me if I had not had a very large party to dinner yesterday. I replied, 'A few.'—'How many of you were drunk?' I said, 'None.'—'Bah! what, none? Why, they could not have done any honour to your entertainment. Was not Captain Ross a little gay?' I replied, 'Captain Ross is always gay.' He laughed at this and said, 'Ross is a very fine fellow, and the ship's company are very happy in having such a captain. I saw,' said he, 'that poor clergyman, Jones.[2] They have used that poor man most cruelly in depriving him of his employment. For the sake of his family, if not for himself, they ought not to have superseded him. He is a good man, is he not?' I replied that he was a man of good heart, but that he was accused of being too fond of meddling with what did not concern him.

---

[1] Captain Piontkowski or Piontowski, a Pole, who had served under Napoleon, and had been left at Plymouth, had arrived as a volunteer on 30th December 1815. See *Warden*, p. 204.

[2] Mr. Jones had been a tutor to Mr. Balcombe's children during Napoleon's residence at the Briars.

I told him that news had arrived that the Queen of Portugal was dead, and also that a French frigate had arrived at Rio Janeiro to demand one of the King's daughters in marriage for the Duc de Berri. ' The Queen,' said he, ' has been mad for a long time, and the daughters are all ugly.'

*May* 29.—A ship arrived from England. Went to town ; saw the Governor, and on my return went to Napoleon, who was playing at nine-pins with his generals in his garden. I told him (by desire of the Governor) that a Bill concerning him had been brought into Parliament, to enable Ministers to detain him in St. Helena, and to provide the necessary sums of money for his maintenance. He asked if it had met with opposition ? I replied, ' Scarcely any.' —' Brougham or Burdett,' said he, ' did they make any ? ' I replied, ' I have not seen the papers, but I believe that Mr. Brougham said something.' Gave him some French newspapers, which the Admiral had given me before he had read them himself. ' Who gave you those papers ? '—' The Admiral.' —' What, for me ? ' (with some surprise). ' He told me to give them to Bertrand, but in reality they were intended for you.' After some conversation he desired me to endeavour to procure the *Morning Chronicle*, the *Globe*, or any of the opposition or neutral papers.

*June* 7.—Breakfasted with Napoleon in the garden. Had a long medical argument with him, in which he maintained that *his* practice in case of malady, viz. to eat nothing, drink plenty of barley-water and no wine, and ride for seven or eight leagues to promote perspiration, was much better than mine.[1]

Some conversation took place about the mode of solemnising marriages, in which I said that in England when a Protestant and Catholic were married, it was necessary that the ceremony should be performed first by a Protestant clergyman, and afterwards by a Roman Catholic priest. 'That is wrong,' said he ; 'marriage ought to be a civil contract ; and on the parties going before a magistrate in the presence of witnesses and entering into an engagement, they should be considered as man and wife. This is what I caused to be done in France. If they wished it, they might go to the church afterwards and get a priest to repeat the ceremony : but this ought not to be considered indispensable. It was always my maxim that those religious ceremonies should never be above the laws. I also ordained that marriages contracted by French subjects in

---

[1] 'The Emperor's chief physician, Corvisart, or his surgeon in ordinary, Ivan, were sometimes present at his toilet. The Emperor liked challenging Corvisart about medical matters, and he always did so by sallies and bitter remarks against doctors. Corvisart, while acknowledging the uncertainty of medicine, defended its utility with arguments strong enough often to stop the sarcasms of his antagonist on his very lips.'—*Meneval*, tome i. pp. 143, 144. See also *Bourrienne*, vol. i. p. 279. 'When at the Tuileries,' says Madame de Rémusat, 'while dressing he was usually silent, unless a discussion arose between him and Corvisart on some medical subject. He liked to go straight to the point in everything ; and if any one was mentioned as being ill, his first question was always, "Will he die ?" A hesitating answer displeased him, and he would then declaim on the inefficiency of medical science.'—*Memoirs*, vol. ii. p. 103.

foreign countries, when performed according to the laws of those countries, should be valid on the return of the parties to France.'

*June* 15.—Napoleon at breakfast in his bath ; a little sliding-table was put over the bath, upon which the dishes were placed. I told him that Warden had found a book belonging to him, which was supposed to have been lost on board of the *Northumberland.* 'Ah! Warden, *ce brave homme*, how is he ? Why does he not come and see me—I shall be glad to see him ? How is the *médecin en chef ?*' I said that he would feel highly honoured by being presented to him, if he would consent to see him as a private person and not as a physician. 'As you say that he is *un galantuomo*, I shall see him ; you may introduce him to me in the garden any day you like. Have you seen Miladi Lowe ? I have been told that she is a graceful and a fine woman.' I replied that I had heard so, and also that she was very lively. 'It is a pity,' said he, 'that she cannot bestow a portion of her wit and grace upon her husband—as, for a public character, I never saw a man so deficient in both.' He asked me a number of questions about London, of which I had lent him a history, which had been made a present to me by Captain Ross. He appeared to be well acquainted with the contents of the book, though he had not had it in his possession many days ; described the plates, and tried to repeat several of the cries,—said that if he had been King of England he would have made a grand

street on each side of the Thames, and another
from St. Paul's to the river.[1]

The conversation afterwards turned upon the
manner of living in France and England. 'Which
eats the most,' said he, 'the Frenchman or the
Englishman ?' I said, 'I think the Frenchman.'—
'I don't believe it,' said Napoleon. I replied that
the French, though they nominally make but two
meals a day, really have four. 'Only two,' said he. I
replied, 'They take something at nine in the morning,
at eleven, at four, and at seven or eight in the evening.'—'I,' said he, 'never eat more than twice daily.
You English always eat four or five times a day.
Your cookery is more healthy than ours. Your soup
is, however, very bad : nothing but bread, pepper,
and water. You drink an enormous quantity of
wine.' I said, 'Not so much as is supposed by the
French.'—'Why,' replied he, 'Piontkowski, who
dines sometimes in camp with the officers of the
53d, says that they drink by the hour ; that after
the cloth is removed, they pay so much an hour and
drink as much as they like, which sometimes lasts
until four o'clock in the morning.' I said, 'This is
so far from the truth, that some of the officers do not
drink wine more than twice a week, and that on days
in which strangers are permitted to be invited.
There is a third of a bottle put on for each member
who drinks wine, and when that is exhausted, another

[1] One portion of Napoleon's design has been carried out half
a century subsequently by the embankment on the north side of the
Thames. A proper approach to St. Paul's is yet to be made.

third is put on, and so on. Members only pay in proportion to what they drink.' He appeared surprised at this explanation, and observed how easily a stranger, having only an imperfect knowledge of the language, was led to give a wrong interpretation to the customs and actions of other nations.

*June* 17.—Told Napoleon that the *Newcastle* frigate was in sight, with the new Admiral. He desired me to fetch my glass and point her out to him. Found the Emperor on my return on his way to the stables. Pointed out the vessel beating up to windward. Shortly afterwards Warden came up, and Napoleon invited me to breakfast with him, and to bring Warden and Lieutenant Blood with me. At breakfast some conversation took place about the Abbé de Pradt,[1] etc.; and some of the absurd falsehoods detailed in the *Quarterly Review* respecting General Bonaparte's conduct when at the Briars were repeated to him. '*Cela amusera le public*,' replied Napoleon. Warden observed that all Europe was very anxious to know his opinion of Lord Wellington as a general. To this he made no reply, and the question was not repeated.

Three commissioners arrived in the *Newcastle :* Count Balmaine for Russia ; Baron Sturmer for Austria, accompanied by the Baroness, his wife ;

---

[1] A clever but conceited man. At a dinner on one occasion at which the Duke of Wellington was present, the Abbé de Pradt reremarked—' Un seul homme a sauvé l'Europe.' He paused, and all eyes were turned to the Duke. But he added, to the no small astonishment of all present—' C'est *Moi !* '—See Moore's *Diary*, vol. ii. p. 247.

the Marquis de Montchenu for France ; with Captain
Gor, his aide-de-camp. An Austrian botanist also
accompanied Baron Sturmer.[1]

*June* 18.—Told Napoleon that I had been to
town, and that the Commissioners for Russia, France,
and Austria had arrived. ' Have you seen any of
them ? '—' Yes, I saw the French Commissioner.'—
' What sort of a man is he ?'—' He is an old *emigré*
named the Marquis de Montchenu, extremely fond
of talking ; but his looks are not against him.
While I was standing in a group of officers on the
terrace opposite the Admiral's house, he came out,
and addressing himself to me, said in French, " If
you or any of you speak French, for the love of
God make it known to me, for I do not speak a

---

[1] ' The Austrian Commissioner shows himself a true *élève* of Prince
Metternich. No chameleon could change his hue more frequently
than he has done on observing any desire or opinion he has ventured
upon not meeting my assent. He was at first all for free intercourse
with Bonaparte, to learn everything he could from him and his
followers, to make up a budget for Prince Metternich. He now
reprobates anything like communication, and is absolutely indifferent
as to anything he can learn from him. In other respects he appears
a gentlemanly, pleasant, and well-informed man. The French
Marquis, who has been thirty years an emigrant, says : *" Ce sont les
gens d'esprit qui ont causé la Révolution !"* *He* evidently has had
no hand in it. The Russian appears to laugh at the other two, and
really seems to have much more in him than either of them. He is
descended from a Scotch family. The expense of this place frightens
them all, and, I think, will soon drive them all away, except perhaps
the Austrian, who may be retained here *in petto* until it may be
determined what shall be the fate and fortunes of the King of Rome,
of whose beauty, intelligence, and the dignity of whose infantine .
manner, the Baroness, his wife, seems quite full.' Sir Hudson Lowe
to Sir Henry Bunbury.—Forsyth's *Lowe*, vol. i. pp. 191, 192

word of English. I have arrived here to finish my days amongst those rocks (pointing to Ladder Hill), and I cannot speak a word of the language." ' Napoleon laughed very heartily at this, and repeated *bavard, imbécile,* several times. 'What folly it is,' said he, 'to send those Commissioners out here. Without charge or responsibility, they will have nothing to do but to walk about the streets and creep up the rocks. The Prussian Government has displayed more judgment and saved its money.' I told him that Drouot had been acquitted, which pleased him much.[1] Of Drouot's talents and virtues he spoke in the highest terms, and observed, that by the laws of France he could not be punished for his conduct.

*June* 20.—Rear-Admiral Sir Pulteney Malcolm, Captain Meynel (the flag-captain), and some other naval officers, were presented to Napoleon.

*June* 21.—Saw Napoleon walking in the garden, and went down to meet him with a book that I had procured for him. After he had made some inquiries about the health of Mrs. Pirie, a respectable old lady whom I visited, he said that he had seen the new Admiral. 'Ah, there is a man with a countenance really pleasing, open, intelligent, frank, and sincere. There is the face of an Englishman. His countenance bespeaks his heart, and I am sure he is a good man : I never yet beheld a man of whom I

[1] General Drouot, not to be confused with Drouet, Comte d'Erlon, had accompanied Napoleon to and from Elba, and fought at Waterloo. Tried by the Bourbons, to whom he had never sworn allegiance, he was acquitted.

so immediately formed a good opinion as of that fine soldier-like old man. He carries his head erect, and speaks out openly and boldly what he thinks, without being afraid to look you in the face. His physiognomy would make every person desirous of a further acquaintance, and render the most suspicious confident in him.'

Some conversation now passed relative to the protest which had been made by Lord Holland against the Bill for his detention.[1] Napoleon expressed that opinion of Lord Holland to which his talents and virtues so fully entitle him. He was highly pleased to find that the Duke of Sussex had joined his lordship in the protest, and observed, that when passions were calmed, the conduct of those two peers would be handed down to posterity with as much honour as that of the proposers of the measure would be loaded with ignominy. He asked

---

[1] PROTEST

*To the second Reading of Bonaparte's Detention Bill.*

BECAUSE, without reference to the character or previous conduct of the person who is the object of the present bill, I disapprove of the measure which it sanctions and continues.

To consign to distant exile and imprisonment a foreign and captive chief, who, after the abdication of his authority, relying on British generosity, had surrendered himself to us in preference to his other enemies, is unworthy of the magnanimity of a great country; and the treaties by which, after his captivity, we have bound ourselves to detain him in custody, at the will of sovereigns to whom he had never surrendered himself, appear to me repugnant to the principles of equity, and utterly uncalled for by expedience or necessity.

           (*Signed*)        VASSALL HOLLAND.

And, on the third reading, His Royal Highness the Duke of Sussex entered his protest for the same reasons.

several questions concerning the reduction of the
English army, and observed that it was absurd in
the English Government to endeavour to establish
the nation as a great military power, without having
a population sufficiently numerous to afford the
requisite number of soldiers to enable them to vie
with the great or even the second-rate continental
powers, while they neglected and seemed to under-
value the navy, which was the real force and bulwark
of England. 'They will yet,' said he, 'discover
their error.'

*June* 23.—Several cases of books which had
been ordered by Bertrand at Madeira, and were
brought out in the *Newcastle* by Sir Pulteney
Malcolm, were sent up to him the day before.
Found the Emperor in his bed-chamber surrounded
with heaps of books; his countenance was smiling,
and he was in perfect good humour. He had been
occupied in reading nearly all the night. 'Ah,' said
he, pointing to some books that he had thrown on
the floor, according to his custom, after having read
them, 'what a pleasure I have enjoyed! What a
difference! I can read forty pages of French in the
time that it would require me to comprehend two of
English.' I found afterwards that his anxiety to
see them was so great, that he had laboured hard
himself, with a hammer and chisel, in opening the
cases which contained them.

*June* 24.—Saw Napoleon in the garden. Told
him that Sir Thomas Reade had sent up seven cases
of books to me for him, and that the Governor had

sent me two guns on the percussion principle for his use, and had desired me to explain the manner in which they were constructed. ' It is useless,' replied he, ' to send me guns, when I am confined to a place where there is no game.' I told him that Mr. Baxter had come up to have the honour of being introduced to him. He desired me to call him. On being presented he said, smiling, ' Well, *signor medico*, how many patients have you killed in your time?' Afterwards he conversed with him for nearly an hour on various subjects.

Sir Hudson Lowe told me that ' he was so far from wishing to prevent any letters or complaints being sent to Europe, that he had offered to Bonaparte to forward any letters or statements he wished to England, and not only would he do so, but he would have them printed in the newspapers, in French and English.'

*June* 28.—A proclamation issued by Sir Hudson Lowe, declaring that any person holding any correspondence or communication with Napoleon Bonaparte, his followers or attendants, receiving from or delivering to him or them letters or communications, without express authorisation from the Governor, under his hand, was guilty of an infraction of the Acts of Parliament for his safe custody, and would be prosecuted with all the rigour of the law. Also, that any person or persons who received any letters or communications from him, his followers, or attendants, and did not immediately deliver or make known the same to the Governor, or who should furnish the said Napoleon Bonaparte, his followers, or attendants, with money, or any other means whatever, whereby his escape might be furthered, would be considered to be aiding and assisting in the same, and would be proceeded against accordingly.

*July* 1.—A letter sent by Sir Hudson Lowe to Count Bertrand, prohibiting all communications, either written or verbal, with the inhabitants, except such as shall have been previously made known to him (the Governor) through the orderly officer.

Since the arrival of the books, the Emperor has been daily occupied for several hours in reading and collecting dates and other materials for the history of his life, which is written up to his landing in France in 1799 from Egypt. The state of the weather also, the almost constant rain or fog, with the strong wind continually blowing over the bleak and exposed situation of Longwood, have contributed much to keep him within doors, and disgust him with his present residence. He expressed a wish to be removed to the leeward side of the island, which is warmer and protected from the eternal sharp south-east wind.

*July* 4.—Sir Pulteney and Lady Malcolm had an interview of nearly two hours with Napoleon, who was much pleased with both. During the conversation he entered deeply into a description of the battle of Waterloo, naval tactics, etc. The officers of the *Newcastle* were also presented to him. The meat, which has generally been of a bad quality, is to-day so detestable that Captain Poppleton felt

himself obliged to send it back, and write a complaint
to the Governor.

*July* 8.—The servants from Longwood bringing
the provisions to Bertrand's, stopped by the sentinels, and not allowed to enter the court. The
viands were, at last, handed over the wall, in presence of a sentinel, who said he could not permit
any conversation to take place. A similar scene
occurred when my servant brought some medicines
for Bertrand's servant (Bernard), who was dangerously ill. Round one of the bottles there was a
label in my handwriting, containing directions how
to take the medicine. This was written in French,
and the sentinel, not being able to understand it,
thought it his duty not to suffer it to enter, and it
was accordingly torn off. A sentinel was relieved
the day before, and sent to camp to be tried by a
court-martial for having allowed a black to go into
Bertrand's court to get a drink of water, which
probably has given rise to this increased rigour on
the part of the soldiers.

*July* 9.—A letter of expostulation sent this
morning to Sir Hudson Lowe. Some conversation
at Longwood relative to a machine for making ice,
said by some of the officers of the *Newcastle* to have
been sent by Lady Holland for Napoleon's use, but
which has not yet made its appearance.

*July* 10.—A great deficiency has existed for
several days in the quantity of wine, fowls, and other
necessary articles. Wrote to Sir Thomas Reade
about it. Captain Poppleton also went to town

himself to lay the matter before Sir Hudson Lowe.

*July* 11.—While at Hut's Gate, a serjeant came in with a message from Sir Hudson Lowe, desiring me to follow him. His Excellency inquired of me in what part of the island General Bonaparte would wish to have his new house built? I replied, ' He would like the Briars.' Sir Hudson said that would never do, that it was too near the town, and in fact out of the question. He then asked me if I thought he would prefer any part of the island to Longwood? I said, ' Most certainly he would prefer a habitation on the other side of the island.' His Excellency then desired me to find out from himself what part of the island he would prefer. He also said that Napoleon had refused to see the Commissioners,[1] and desired me to ascertain whether he was still of that opinion. Sir Hudson observed that he would report Las Cases to the British Government, for having contemptuously refused to receive or accept some articles sent for the supply of the generals and others with Bonaparte ; while at the same time he wrote a letter to Lady Clavering, desiring that some articles of a similar nature to those so offered might be purchased and sent out to him. He then again assured me of his readiness not only to transmit their complaints to His Majesty's Government, but also to cause them to be published ; and told me that he much wished me to let him know General Bonaparte's wants and wishes, in

[1] See *Sturmer*, p. 34.

order that he might communicate them to his Government, which would thus know how to anticipate and provide for any demands. After this he went to Longwood, where he had a long conversation with General Montholon, chiefly about altering, enlarging, and improving Longwood House.

*July* 12.—Napoleon rather out of spirits. I informed him that the Governor had been at Longwood yesterday, in order to see if he could afford greater comfort and accommodation to him, either by building some additional rooms to the house already existing at Longwood, or erecting a new house in some other part of the island; and that the Governor had charged me to inquire from him which he would prefer. He replied, ' I hate this Longwood. Let him put me on the Plantation House side of the island, if he really wishes to do anything for me. But what is the use of his coming up here proposing things and doing nothing. There is Bertrand's house not the least advanced since his arrival. The Admiral at least sent his carpenter here, who made the work go on.' I replied that the Governor had desired me to say that he did not like to undertake anything without first knowing that it would meet with his approval; but that if he (Napoleon) would fix on or propose a plan for the house, he would order every workman on the island, with a proportionate number of engineer officers, etc., to proceed to Longwood, and set about it. That the Governor feared that making additions to the present building would annoy him by the noise of the workmen. He replied, ' Certainly it would. I do not wish him to do anything to this house, or on this dismal place. Let him build a house on the other side of the island, where there is shade, verdure, and water, and where I may be sheltered from this *vento agro*. If it is determined to build a new house for my use, I would wish to have it erected on the estate of Colonel Smith, which Bertrand has been to look at, or at Rosemary Hall. But his proposals are all a delusion. Nothing advances since he came. Look there' (pointing to the window). ' I was obliged to order a pair of sheets to be put up as curtains, as the others were so dirty I could not approach them, and none could be obtained to replace them. Remark his conduct to *quella povera dama*, Madame Bertrand. He has deprived her of the little liberty she had, and has prevented people from coming to visit and *bavarder* for an hour with her, which was some little solace to a lady who had always been accustomed to see company.' I observed that the Governor had said it was in consequence of Madame Bertrand's having sent a note to the Marquis de Montchenu, without having first caused it to pass through the Governor's hands. 'Trash!' replied he. 'By the regulations in existence when he arrived, it was permissible to send notes to residents, and no communication of an alteration having taken place was made to them. Besides, could not she and her husband have gone to town to see Montchenu? Weak men are always timorous and suspicious.'

*July* 13.—Went to town, and communicated Napoleon's reply to Sir Hudson Lowe, who did not seem to like it, and said that he could not so easily be watched. I observed that I thought easier, as he would then be in the midst of his (Sir Hudson's) staff; and, moreover, as the spots in question were nearly surrounded with high and unequal rocks, it would be extremely easy to place picquets in such a manner as to preclude the possibility of escape, and at the same time be unseen by the captive. His Excellency at first assented to this; but a moment afterwards observed that he should not know where to place the Austrian Commissioner, who had taken Rosemary Hall. I ventured to suggest to him that however desirable an object the accommodation of the Baron Sturmer might be, still it was one of quite minor importance to that of the principal *détenu*.

*July* 16.—Napoleon, who had gone down to the stables at an early hour and himself ordered the horses to be put to, overtook me in the park, and made me get into the carriage. Complained of his teeth. Breakfasted with him. During the meal the subject of the Commissioners was introduced. He asked if Madame Sturmer had ever seen him at Paris. I replied that she had, and was very desirous to see him again. 'And who prevents her?' said he. I replied that she and her husband, as well as the rest of the Commissioners, believed that he would not receive them. 'Who told them so?' said he; 'I am willing to receive them whenever they please to ask through Bertrand. I shall receive them in a private capacity. I never refuse to see any person, when asked in a proper way, and I should always be especially glad to see a lady.'

'It appears,' said he, 'that your Ministers have sent out a great many articles of dress for us, and other things, which it was supposed might be wanted. Now if this Governor was possessed of the feelings of a gentleman, he would have sent a list of them to Bertrand, stating that the English Government had sent a supply of certain articles which it was thought we might want, and that if we stood in need of them, we might order such as we pleased. But, instead of acting in a manner pointed out by the rules of politeness, he selects what things he himself pleases, and sends them up in a contemptuous manner, without consulting us, as if he were sending alms to a set of beggars, or clothing to convicts. I am astonished that he allows you or Poppleton to remain near me. He would willingly watch me himself always, were it in his power. Have you any galley-slaves in England?' I replied, No; but that we had some convicts who were condemned to work at Portsmouth and elsewhere. 'Then,' said he, 'he ought to have been made keeper of them. It would be exactly the office suited to him.'

Sir Hudson Lowe came to Longwood, and had a brief interview with the Emperor.

*July* 17.—Napoleon called me into the garden. Informed me that he had told the Governor that he had unnecessarily increased their restrictions; that he had insulted them by his manner of sending up the articles sent for their use; that he had insulted Las Cases, by telling him that he had read his letters, and by informing him that if he wanted a pair of shoes or stockings, he must first send to him. 'I told him,' added he, 'that if Bertrand or Las Cases wanted to plot with the Commissioners (which he appeared to be afraid of), he had nothing more to do than to go to the town and make an appointment with any of them to come up inside the alarm-house and meet him.'

He then spoke about the new house, and said that if he expected to remain long in St. Helena, he should wish to have it erected at the Plantation House side; 'but,' continued he, 'I am of opinion that as soon as the affairs of France are settled, and things quiet, the English Government will allow me to return to Europe and finish my days in England. I do not believe that they are foolish enough to be at the expense of eight millions of francs annually, to keep me here, when I am no longer to be feared; I therefore am not very anxious about the house.'

*July* 18.—Sir Hudson came to Longwood and arranged some matters with General Montholon relative to the house. Everything connected with the alterations in the building put under the direction of Lieutenant-Colonel Wynyard, assisted by Lieutenant Jackson of the staff corps. A billiard-table brought up to Longwood.

*July* 19. — The drawing-room of Longwood House was discovered to be on fire at about five o'clock in the morning. It was extinguished in about half an hour by great exertions on the part of

Captain Poppleton and the guard, aided by the household. The flames had reached within a few inches of the upper flooring, which was formed of a double boarding. Had this caught fire it would have been nearly impossible to have saved the building, as there is no water at Longwood.

*July* 20.—Some curtains for the Emperor's bed sent up to me by Sir Thomas Reade.

*July* 22.—Dined in camp, on occasion of the anniversary of the battle of Salamanca. Present, His Excellency and staff, heads of departments, etc.

*July* 24.—The Admiral sent up a lieutenant and party of seamen to pitch a tent, formed of a lower studding-sail, as no shade was afforded by the trees at Longwood. Colonel Maunsell, of the 53d, asked me to exert myself in order to procure, through Count Bertrand, for Dr. Ward (who had been eighteen years in India) an interview with Napoleon. Count Bertrand accordingly made the application to the Emperor, who replied that ' Dr. Ward must apply in person to Count Bertrand.'

*July* 25.—Told Napoleon that the *Griffin* had arrived from England the night before, and had brought the news of the condemnation of General Bertrand to death, though absent.[1] He appeared for a moment lost in astonishment and much concerned, but, recollecting himself, observed that by

[1] Bertrand had accompanied Napoleon to Elba in 1814, and had never sworn allegiance to the Bourbons, nor had he taken any office under them. In 1815 he had accompanied his lawful sovereign to France. This condemnation could not be maintained, even by the Bourbons, and it was annulled when Bertrand returned to France in 1821.

the laws of France a man accused of a capital
offence might be tried and condemned to death *par
contumace*, but that they could not act upon such a
sentence ; that the individual must be tried again
and be actually present ; that if Bertrand were now
in France, he would be acquitted, as Drouot had
been.   He expressed, however, much regret at it,
on account of the effect which it might probably
produce upon Madame Bertrand.

*July* 26. — Saw Napoleon at his toilette.[1]

[1] 'The Emperor, it was well known, was in the habit of taking
snuff almost every minute : this was a sort of mania which seized him
chiefly during intervals of abstraction.   His snuff-box was speedily
emptied ; but he still continued to thrust his fingers into it, or to
raise it to his nose, particularly when he was speaking.   Those
chamberlains who proved themselves most expert and assiduous in
the discharge of their duties would frequently endeavour, unobserved
by the Emperor, to take away the empty box and substitute a full
one in its stead ; for there existed a great competition of attention
and courtesy among the chamberlains who were habitually employed
in services about the Emperor's person : an honour which was very
much envied.   These individuals were, however, seldom changed,
either because they intrigued to retain their places, or because it was
naturally most agreeable to the Emperor to continue them in posts
with the duties of which they were acquainted.   It was the business
of the Grand Marshal (Duroc) to make all these arrangements.
The following is an instance of the attentions evinced by the Emperor's
chamberlains.   One of them having observed that the Emperor on
going to the theatre frequently forgot his opera-glass, of which he
made very great use, got one made exactly like it, so that the first time
he saw the Emperor without his glass he presented his own to him, and
the difference was not observed.   On his return from the theatre the
Emperor was not a little surprised to find that he had got two
glasses exactly alike.   Next day he inquired how the new opera-
glass had made its appearance, and the chamberlain replied that it
was one he kept in reserve in case it might be wanted.'—*Las Cases*,
vol. ii., part. iv., p. 232, English edition.

While dressing he is attended by Marchand, St.
Denis, and Noverraz. One of the latter holds a
looking-glass before him, and the other the necessary
implements for shaving, while Marchand is in waiting to hand his clothes, *eau de Cologne*, etc. When
he has gone over one side of his face with the razor,
he asks St. Denis or Noverraz, 'Is it done?' and
after receiving an answer commences on the other.
After he has finished, the glass is held before him to
the light, and he examines whether he has removed
every portion of his beard. If he perceives or feels
that any remains, he sometimes lays hold of one of
them by the ear, or gives him a gentle slap on the
cheek, in a good-humoured manner, crying, 'Ah,
*coquin*, why did you tell me it was done?' (This,
probably, has given rise to the report of his having
been in the habit of beating and otherwise ill-treating
his domestics.) He then washes with water, in which
some *eau de Cologne* has been mingled, a little of
which he also sprinkles over his person, very carefully
cleans his teeth, frequently has himself rubbed with
a flesh-brush, changes his linen and flannel waistcoat, and dresses in white kerseymere (or brown
nankeen) breeches, white waistcoat, silk stockings,
shoes and gold buckles, and a green single-breasted
coat with white buttons, black stock, with none of
the white shirt-collar appearing above it, and a three-
cornered small cocked hat, with a little tricoloured
cockade. When dressed he always wears the
cordon and grand cross of the Legion of Honour.
When he has put on his coat, a little *bonbonnière*,

his snuff-box, and handkerchief scented with *eau de Cologne*, are handed to him by Marchand, and he leaves the chamber.[1]

Napoleon complained of a slight pain in his right side. I advised him to get it well rubbed with *eau de Cologne* and flannel, and also suggested a dose of physic. At this last he laughed, and gave me a friendly slap on the cheek. He asked the causes of the liver complaint now very prevalent in the island. I enumerated several, and amongst others inebriety and hot climates. ' If,' said he, ' drunkenness be a cause, I ought never to have it.'

*July* 27.—Colonel Keating, late Governor of the Isle of Bourbon, had an interview with Napoleon, which lasted for nearly an hour.

*July* 28. — Informed by Cipriani that in the beginning of 1815 he had been sent from Elba to Leghorn, to purchase one hundred thousand francs' worth of furniture for Napoleon's palace. During his stay he became very intimate with a person named ——, who had a —— at Vienna, from whom a private intimation was sent to him, that it was the determination of the Congress of Vienna to send the Emperor to St. Helena, and who even had sent him a paper containing the substance of the agreement, a copy of which he gave to Cipriani, who departed instantly for Elba to communicate the information he had received to the Emperor. This,

---

[1] ' Napoleon never made use of any perfume except *eau de Cologne*, but of that he would get through sixty bottles in a month.' —*Memoirs of Madame de Rémusat*, vol. ii. p. 103.

with the confirmation which he afterwards received
from M—— A—— and M—— at Vienna, contributed to determine Napoleon to attempt the recovery of his throne. [1]

Accompanied Napoleon in his evening drive.
Informed him that Sir Thomas Reade had begged
me to acquaint him that the Russian Commissioner
had taken no part in the official note addressed to
the Governor, and containing a request to see him
(Napoleon). He observed that if they wished to
see him, they had taken very bad measures, as all
the powers of Europe should not induce him to receive them as official persons. They might break
open the door or level the walls of the house down
and find him. He then observed that a book [2]
relative to his last reign in France had been lately
sent out by the author (an Englishman) to Sir
Hudson Lowe, with a request that it should be
delivered to him. On the back was inscribed, in
letters of gold, *To the Emperor Napoleon*, or *To
the Great Napoleon*. 'Now,' continued he, 'this
*galeriano* would not allow the book to be sent to me,
because it had the "Emperor Napoleon" written
upon it ; because he thought that it would give me
some pleasure to see that all men were not like him,
and that I was esteemed by some of his nation.'

Since the arrival of Sir Hudson Lowe there has
been a great alteration in the number of newspapers

[1] For the manner in which the Bourbons failed to carry out their
pledges to the Emperor of Elba, see footnote in *Bourrienne's
Napoleon*, 1885 edition, vol. iii. p. 237.

[2] *The last Reign of the Emperor Napoleon*, by Mr. Hobhouse.

sent to Longwood. Instead of receiving, as heretofore, a regular series of some papers, as well as
many detached ones, only a few irregular numbers
of the *Times* have arrived, and occasionally a *Courier*.
This has caused great anxiety at Longwood to those
who have relations in France, and given much
displeasure to Napoleon, to whom Sir George
Cockburn frequently sent up papers, even before
perusing them himself.

*August* 2.—Made a complaint to the purveyors
that no vegetables except potatoes had been sent
up for three days, and requested that if they were
not permitted to furnish any more, my letter might
be transmitted to Major Gorrequer.

*August* 3.—Received an answer from Mr.
Fowler, clerk to the purveyors, informing me that
they had been ordered to send no more vegetables,
which they had been informed by Major Gorrequer
were in future to be furnished from the Honourable
Company's garden.[1]

*August* 5.—Sir Hudson Lowe came to Longwood, and calling me aside in a mysterious manner,
asked if I thought that ' General Bonaparte' would
take it well if he invited him to come to a ball at
Plantation House on the Prince Regent's birthday?
I replied that under all circumstances I thought it
most probable that he would look upon it as an

---

[1] St. Helena was a depot of the Hon. East India Company
for provisioning their ships when on the voyage to and from Europe,
and has since been transferred from the Indian Government to the
Crown. The neighbouring *Island of Ascension* is entered in the books
of the Admiralty as a ship of war.

insult, especially if addressed to '*General Bonaparte.*' His Excellency remarked that he would avoid that by asking him in person. I said that I would recommend him to consult Count Bertrand on the subject, which he said he would do. He then referred to a previous conversation, and informed me that he was of opinion my salary ought to be augmented to £500 per annum, and that he would certainly write to Lord Bathurst and recommend it. After this he spoke about Mr. Hobhouse's book ; observed that he could not send it to Longwood, as it had not been forwarded through the channel of the Secretary of State ; moreover, that Lord Castlereagh was extremely ill-spoken of, and that he had no idea of allowing General Bonaparte to read a book in which a British Minister was treated in such a manner, or even to know that a work containing such reflections could be published in England. I ventured to observe to His Excellency that Napoleon was very desirous to see the book, and that he could not confer a much greater favour than to send it up. Sir Hudson replied that Mr. Hobhouse, in the letter which accompanied it, had permitted him to place it in his own library, if he did not think himself authorised to send it to its original destination.

*August* 6.—A lieutenant, two midshipmen, and a party of seamen employed in repairing the tent, which had suffered materially in the late bad weather. Napoleon went up and conversed for a short time with the midshipmen, one of whom, by a strange coincidence, happened to be the son of Mr. Drake, notorious for his conduct at Munich.[1]

*August* 10.—Sir Hudson Lowe came up while Napoleon was at breakfast in the tent, in order to see him, but did not succeed.

*August* 12.—Grand field-day at camp in honour of the Prince Regent. Explained to Napoleon that in all our colonies his Royal Highness's birthday was celebrated. '*Naturalmente*,' said he. Asked if I was to dine with the Governor? I replied, No; but that I was asked to the ball in the evening.

*August* 14.—Napoleon went out to ride this morning for the first time for eight weeks. Informed me that he had so severe a headache that he had determined to try the effect of a little exercise.[2] ' But,' continued he, ' the limits are so circumscribed that I cannot ride for more than a hour; and in order to do me any good, I should ride very hard for three or four. That *sbirro Siciliano*,' continued he, ' has been here. I would have remained in the tent an hour longer if I had not been informed of his arrival. *Mi ripugna l'anima il vederlo.* He is perpetually unquiet, and appears always in a passion with somebody, or uneasy, as if something tormented

[1] Mr. Drake, an energetic British Minister at Munich, was particularly active in gathering information, and also in organising the opposition of the smaller German States to Napoleon.

[2] On one occasion when out riding the Emperor appears to have taken additional exercise. ' We arrived at a field where some labourers were engaged in ploughing. The Emperor alighted from his horse, seized the plough, and, to the great astonishment of the man who was holding it, he himself traced a furrow of considerable length.'—*Las Cases*, vol. i., part ii., p. 87, English edition.

his conscience, and he was anxious to run away
from himself.   A man, to be well-fitted for the post
of Governor of St. Helena,' he observed, 'ought to
be a person of great politeness, and at the same
time of great firmness,—one who could gloss over
a refusal and lessen the miseries of the *détenus*,
instead of eternally putting them in mind that they
were considered prisoners.'

*August* 15.—Anniversary of Napoleon's birthday.   Breakfasted in the tent with the ladies and
all his suite, including Piontkowski and the children.
There was, however, no change of uniform or
additional decorations.   In the evening the second
class of domestics, including the English, had a grand
supper and a dance afterwards.   To the astonishment of the French not an Englishman got drunk.

*August* 16.—Sir Hudson Lowe came up and
had a long conversation with General Montholon
and myself, principally about the necessity of
reducing the expenses of the establishment, which,
he observed, was not conducted with a due regard
to economy.   Amongst other examples of what he
considered wasteful expenditure, he stated to General
Montholon that he had observed, on looking over
the accounts of Plantation House and Longwood,
that there was a much greater quantity of basket-
salt consumed at the latter than at the former; he
desired, therefore, that in future common salt should
be used as much as possible in the kitchen and at
the table of the servants.

One of Leslie's pneumatic machines for making

ice sent up to Longwood this day. As soon as it
was put up, I informed Napoleon, and told him that
the Admiral was at Longwood. He asked several
questions about the process, and it was evident that
he was perfectly acquainted with the principles upon
which air-pumps are formed. He expressed great
admiration of the science of chemistry, spoke of the
great improvements which had of late years been
made in it, and observed that he had always promoted and encouraged it to the best of his power.
I then left him and proceeded to the room where
the machine was, in order to commence the experi-
ment in the presence of the Admiral. In a few
minutes Napoleon, accompanied by Count Montholon, came in and accosted the Admiral in a very
pleasant manner, seemingly gratified to see him.
A cupful of water was then frozen in his presence
in about fifteen minutes, and he waited for upwards
of half an hour to see if the same quantity of
lemonade would freeze, which did not succeed.
Milk was then tried, but it would not answer.
Napoleon took into his hand the piece of ice produced from the water, and observed to me what a
gratification that would have been in Egypt. The
first ice ever seen in St. Helena was made by this
machine, and was viewed with no small degree of
surprise by the natives—some of whom could with
difficulty be persuaded that the solid lump in their
hands was really composed of water, and were
not fully convinced until they had witnessed its
liquefaction.

*August* 17.—Went to Hut's Gate to visit
Bertrand's servant Bernard, who was very ill. The
serjeant of the guard ordered the sentry to be confined for letting me in. Went out to inquire, and
was informed by the serjeant that he had orders to
prevent every one from going in except the general
staff. Sir Hudson Lowe had, it appeared, given
some directions yesterday himself on going out of
Bertrand's, to whom he showed a letter from Lord
Bathurst, stating that the expenses of the establishment must be reduced to £8000 per annum for
everything. The men who brought the provisions
were not allowed to enter, but were obliged to hand
them over the wall. The servants from Longwood
were also refused admittance. Mr. Brookes, the
Colonial Secretary, was also denied entrance. A
letter sent by Sir Hudson Lowe to Count Montholon, making a demand of £12,000 a year for the
maintenance of Napoleon and suite.

*August* 18. — The Governor and Admiral,
accompanied by Sir Thomas Reade and Major
Gorrequer, arrived at Longwood, while Napoleon
was walking in the garden with Counts Bertrand,
Montholon, Las Cases, and his son. His Excellency
sent to ask an interview, which was granted. It
took place in the garden. The three principal
personages, Napoleon, Sir Hudson, and Sir Pulteney,
were a little in front of the others. Captain Poppleton and myself stood at some distance from them,
but sufficiently near to observe their gestures. We
remarked that the conversation was principally on

the part of Napoleon, who appeared at times considerably animated, frequently stopping and again
hurried in his walk, and accompanying his words
with a good deal of action. Sir Hudson's manner
also appeared hurried and greatly agitated. The
Admiral was the only one who seemed to discourse
with calmness. In about half an hour we saw Sir
Hudson Lowe abruptly turn about and withdraw
without saluting Napoleon.[1] The Admiral took off
his hat, made his bow, and departed. Sir Hudson
Lowe came up to where Poppleton and myself were
standing, paced up and down in an agitated manner,
while his horses were coming, and said to me,
'General Bonaparte has been very abusive to me.
I parted with him rather abruptly, and told him,
*Vous êtes malhonnête, monsieur.*' He then mounted
his horse and galloped away. The Admiral appeared
troubled and pensive. It was evident that the interview had been very unpleasant.

*August* 19.—Saw Napoleon in his dressing-
room. He was in very good humour,—asked how
Gourgaud was, and on being informed that I had
given him some medicine, he laughed and said,
' He would have done better to have *dieted* himself
for some days : let him drink plenty of water and
eat nothing. Medicines,' he said, 'were only fit for
old people.'

He then said, ' That Governor came here yes-

---

[1] Lowe acknowledged having turned away without a salutation
after having expressed his '*pity*' for the rudeness of Napoleon's
manners.—*Forsyth*, vol. i. p. 251.

terday to annoy me. He saw me walking in the
garden, and in consequence I could not refuse to
see him. He wanted to enter into some details
with me about reducing the expenses of the establishment. He had the audacity to tell me that
things were as he found them, and that he came
up to justify himself; that he had come up two
or three times before to do so, but that I was in a
bath. I replied, " No, sir, I was not in a bath, but
I ordered one on purpose not to see you. In
endeavouring to justify yourself you make matters
worse." He said that I did not know him; that if
I knew him, I should change my opinion. " Know
you, sir," I answered, " How could I know you?
People make themselves known by their actions;
by commanding in battles. You have never commanded in battle. You have never commanded
any but vagabond Corsican deserters, Piedmontese
and Neapolitan brigands. I know the name of
every English general who has distinguished himself, but I never heard of you except as a *scrivano*
to Blucher, or as a commandant of brigands. You
have never commanded, or been accustomed to men
of honour." He said that he had not sought for
the employment. I told him that such employments
were not asked for; that they were given by Governments to people who had dishonoured themselves.
He said that he only did his duty, and that I ought
not to blame him, as he only acted according to his
orders. I replied, " So does the hangman. He
acts according to his orders. But when he puts a

rope round my neck to finish me, is that a reason
that I should like that hangman, because he acts
according to his orders ?    Besides, I do not believe
that any Government could be so mean as to give
such orders as you cause to be executed." I told
him that if he pleased, he need not send up anything to eat.  That I would go over and dine at the
table of the brave officers of the 53d ; that I was
sure there was not one of them who would not
be happy to give a plate at the table to an old
soldier.   That there was not a soldier in the regiment who had not more heart than he had.   That
in the iniquitous Bill of Parliament they had
decreed that I was to be treated as a prisoner,
but that he treated me worse than a condemned
criminal,  or  a  galley-slave,  as  they  were  permitted to receive newspapers and printed books,
which he deprived me of.   I said, "You have
power over my body, but none over my soul.
That soul is as proud, fierce, and determined at
the  present  moment  as  when  it  commanded
Europe."   I told him that he was a *sbirro
Siciliano* and not an Englishman, and desired him
not to let me see him again until he came with
orders to despatch me, when he would find all the
doors thrown open to admit him.

'It is not my custom,' continued he, 'to abuse
any person, but that man's effrontery made my blood
boil, and I could not help expressing my sentiments.
When he had the impudence to tell me before the
Admiral that he had changed nothing ; that all was

the same as when he had arrived, I replied, " Call the captain of *ordonnance* here, and ask *him*.   I will leave it to his decision."   This struck him dumb; he was mute.

'He told me that he had found his situation so difficult that he had resigned.   I replied that a worse man than himself could not be sent out, though the employment was not one which a *galantuomo* would wish to accept.   If you have an opportunity,' added Napoleon, ' or if any one asks you, you are at liberty to repeat what I have told you.'

Gave the Emperor Sarrazin's *Account of the Campaign in Spain.*   'Sarrazin,' said he, 'was a traitor, and a man without honour, truth, or probity. When I returned from Elba to Paris, he wrote to offer his services to me, and proposed, if I would forgive and employ him, to betray to me all the secrets and plans of the English.   It was my intention to have had him tried as a traitor, as he deserved, instead of accepting his offer, but I was so much occupied that it escaped my memory.'[1]

*August* 21.—A ship arrived from England. Went to town, where I saw Captain Stanfell, to whom I mentioned in the course of conversation that a very unpleasant conversation had taken place

---

[1] Jean Sarrazin deserted to the English on the 14th June 1810, when a brigadier-general serving at Boulogne under Vandamme, at the moment Vandamme reported most favourably of his past conduct (Du Casse's *Vandamme*, vol. ii. p. 340).   Sarrazin afterwards wrote several books—*History of the War in Spain and Portugal*, etc.   In 1819 he was sentenced in France to ten years' hard labour for bigamy, but he did not undergo all the sentence.   He had already been sentenced to death, in 1810, by a court-martial in his absence.

between the Governor and Napoleon, and that Sir
Hudson Lowe had told the latter that he had given
in his resignation. On my return, called at Hut's
Gate, along with Captain Maunsell of the 53d,
and Captain Poppleton. Madame Bertrand asked
if there were any letters. Captain Maunsell said
that he had seen some for them at the post-office.
On my arrival at Longwood, Napoleon asked me
the same question, to which I replied that Captain
Maunsell had informed Madame Bertrand there
were some at the post-office. It was not my
intention to have mentioned them until I had
ascertained whether they would be sent to Longwood, as I did not wish to embroil him further with
the Governor ; but as I was assured that he would
hear it from Hut's Gate, I could not conceal my
knowledge of the fact.

*August* 22.—Sir Hudson Lowe sent for me
to Plantation House. Found him walking in the
path to the left of the house. He said that he
had some communication to make to Government,
wished to know the state of General Bonaparte's
health, and whether I had anything to say. 'I
understand,' continued he, 'that Bonaparte told
you I had said that I had given in my resignation
as Governor of this island : is it true ?' I replied,
'He told me that you had said so to him.' Sir
Hudson added, 'I never said any such thing, nor
ever had an idea of it. He has either invented it,
or perhaps mistaken my expressions. I merely
said that if the Government did not approve of my

conduct I would resign. I wish you therefore to explain to him that I never either said so, or had any intention of doing it.' He then asked me if I had heard the subject of their conversation. I replied, 'Some part of it.' He wished to know what it was. I replied, 'That I supposed he remembered it, and that I did not wish to repeat what must be disagreeable to him.' He observed that I had mentioned it elsewhere, and that he had a right to hear it from my own lips. Although I had permission to communicate it, I was not pleased to be obliged to repeat to a man's face opinions such as those which had been expressed of him; but under the circumstances I did not think proper to refuse; I therefore repeated some parts. Sir Hudson said that though he had not commanded an army against Napoleon, yet he had probably done him more mischief by the advice and information which he had given, prior to and during the Conferences at Chatillon, some of which had not been published, as the Conferences were going on at the time, than if he had commanded against him. That what *he* had pointed out had been acted upon afterwards, and was the cause of his downfall from the throne. 'I should like,' added he, 'to let him know this, in order to give him some cause for his hatred. I shall probably publish an account of the matter.'

Sir Hudson Lowe then walked about for a short time biting his nails, and asked me if

Madame Bertrand had repeated to strangers any of
the conversation which had passed between General
Bonaparte and himself? I replied that I was not
aware that Madame Bertrand was yet acquainted
with it. 'She had better not,' said he, 'lest it may
render her and her husband's situation much more
unpleasant than at present.' He then repeated
some of Napoleon's expressions in a very angry
manner, and said, 'Did General Bonaparte tell you,
sir, that I told him his language was impolite and
indecent, and that I would not listen any longer to
it?' I said, 'No.'—'Then it showed,' observed the
Governor, 'great littleness on the part of General
Bonaparte not to tell you the whole. He had
better reflect on his situation, for it is in my power
to render him much more uncomfortable than he is.
If he continues his abuse, I shall make him feel his
situation. He is a prisoner of war, and I have a
right to treat him according to his conduct. I'll
build him up.'

He walked about for a few minutes repeating
again some of the observations, which he characterised as ungentlemanlike, etc., until he had worked
himself into a passion, and said, 'Tell General
Bonaparte that he had better take care what he
does, as, if he continues his present conduct, I
shall be obliged to take measures to increase the
restrictions already in force.' After observing
that he had been the cause of the loss of the lives
of millions of men, and might be again if he
got loose, he concluded by saying, 'I consider

Ali Pacha to be *a much more respectable scoundrel than Bonaparte.*[1]

*August* 23.—Told Napoleon in the course of conversation that the Governor had said that he had mistaken his expressions, as he had never said, or intended to say, that he had given in his resignation ; that he had certainly said that if the Government did not approve of his conduct, he would resign, etc. 'That is very extraordinary,' said Napoleon, 'as he told me himself that he had resigned—at least I understood him so. *Tanto peggio.*' I then observed that in consequence of what had occurred at the last interview, it was probable that he would not seek another. '*Tanto meglio*,' said the Emperor, 'as then I shall be freed from the embarrassment *del suo brutto viso.*'

*August* 26.—Napoleon asked me 'if I had seen the letter written by Count Montholon to Sir Hudson Lowe, containing a list of their grievances.' I replied that I had. 'Do you think,' said he, 'that this Governor will send it to England?' I assured him that there was not a doubt of it. That, moreover, the Governor told me that he had offered to him not only to send their letters home, but even to get them published in the newspapers. 'It is a falsehood,' replied the Emperor. 'He said that he would send letters to Europe, and have them published, with this proviso, however, that *he approved of their contents*. Besides, even if he

---

[1] Mr. Baxter came up and joined us about the moment that this expression was used.—B. E. O'M.

wished to do so, his Government would not permit
it.   Suppose, for example, that I sent him an
address to the French nation ?   I do not think,' continued he, 'that they will allow a letter which covers
them with so much disgrace to be published.   The
people of England want to know why I call myself
Emperor after having abdicated,—I have explained
it in that letter.[1]   It was my intention to have lived
in England *incognito;* but as they have sent me
here, and want to make it appear that I was never
Chief Magistrate or Emperor of France, I still retain
the title : —— told me that he heard Lords
Liverpool and Castlereagh say that one of the
principal reasons why they sent me here was a
dread of my caballing with the Opposition.   It is
likely enough that they were afraid of my telling the
truth of them, and of my explaining some things
which they would not like, as they knew that if I
remained in England they must permit people of
rank to see me.'

He afterwards complained of the unnecessary
severity exercised in depriving him of a series of
newspapers, and restricting him to some uncon-
nected numbers of 'the Bourbon paper,' the *Times.*

Within a few days some more picquets have
been established, and several additional sentinels
placed, some in sight of Napoleon, if he chose to
walk after sunset.   Ditches, of eight or ten feet
deep, nearly completed round the garden.

*August* 27.—Napoleon asked me if the French

[1] See also *Las Cases*, English edition, vol. iii. p. 247.

Commissioner and Madame Sturmer had not had a quarrel? I replied that Montchenu had said that Madame Sturmer did not know how to come into a drawing-room. He laughed at this, and said, 'I will venture to say that the old booby says so because she is not sprung from some of those *imbéciles*, the old *noblesse*. These old *emigrés* hate and are jealous of all who are not hereditary asses like themselves.' I asked him if the King of Prussia was a man of talent. 'Who,' said he, 'the King of Prussia?' He burst into a fit of laughter. '*He* a man of talent! The greatest blockhead on earth. *Un ignorantaccio che non ha nè talento, nè informazione.* A Don Quixote in appearance. I know him well. He cannot hold a conversation for five minutes. Not so his wife. She was a very clever, fine woman, but very unfortunate. *Era bella, graziosa, e piena d'intelligenza.*' He then conversed for a considerable time about the Bourbons. 'They want,' said he, 'to introduce the old system of nobility into the army. Instead of allowing the sons of peasants and labourers to be eligible to be made generals, as they were in my time, they want to confine it entirely to the old nobility, to *emigrés* like that old blockhead, Montchenu. When you have seen Montchenu, you have seen all the old nobility of France before the Revolution. Such were all the race, and such they have returned, ignorant, vain, and arrogant as they left. *Ils n'ont rien appris, ils n'ont rien oublié.* They were the cause of the Revolution and of so much bloodshed ; and now, after twenty-five years of exile and disgrace, they return loaded with the same vices and crimes for which they were expatriated, to produce another revolution. I know the French. Believe me, that after six or ten years[1] the whole race of *emigrés* will be massacred and thrown into the Seine. They are a curse to the nation. It is of such as these that the Bourbons want to make generals. I made most of mine, *de la boue.* Wherever I found talent and courage, I rewarded it. My principle was, *la carrière ouverte aux talens*, without asking whether there were any quarterings of nobility to show. It is true that I sometimes promoted a few of the old nobility, from a principle of policy and justice, but I never reposed especial confidence in them. The mass of the people,' continued he, 'now see the revival of the feudal times,—they see that soon it will be impossible for their progeny to rise in the army. Every true Frenchman reflects with chagrin that a family for so many years odious to France *has been forced upon them by foreign bayonets.*

'What I am going to recount will give you some idea of the imbecility of the family. When the Comte d'Artois came to Lyons, although he threw himself on his knees before the troops, in order to induce them to advance against me, he never put on the cordon of the Legion of Honour, although he

[1] This was in 1816. Napoleon underestimated the time. It was in 1830 that France shook herself free for ever from the legitimate monarchy, since which, under whatever Government, she has really been ruled on the principles of 1789.

knew that the sight of it would be most likely to excite the minds of the soldiers in his favour, as it was the order so many of them bore on their breasts, and required nothing but bravery to obtain it. But no, he decked himself out with the order of the Holy Ghost, to be eligible for which you must prove one hundred and fifty years of nobility,— an order formed purposely to exclude merit, and one which excited indignation in the breasts of the old soldiers. "We will not," said they, "fight for orders like that, nor for *emigrés* like those;" he had ten or eleven of these *imbéciles* as aides-de-camp. Instead of showing to the troops some of those generals who had so often led them to glory, he brought with him a set of *misérables*, who served no other purpose than to recall to the minds of the veterans their former sufferings under the *noblesse* and the priests.

'To give you an instance of the general feeling in France towards the Bourbons, I will relate to you an anecdote. On my return from Italy,[1] while my carriage was ascending the steep hill of Tarare, I got out and walked up, without any attendants, as was often my custom. My wife and my suite were at a little distance behind me. I saw an old woman, lame, and hobbling about with the help of a crutch, endeavouring to ascend the mountain. I had a greatcoat on and was not recognised. I went up to her and said, "Well, *ma bonne*, where are you going with a haste which so little belongs to your

---

[1] After the Coronation.

years ?   What is the matter ?"—"*Ma foi,*" replied
the old dame, "they tell me the Emperor is here,
and I want to see him before I die."   Bah, bah!
said I, what do you want to see him for ?   What
have you gained by him ?   He is a tyrant as well
as the others.   You have only changed one tyrant
for another—Louis for Napoleon.   "*Mais, monsieur,*
that may be ; but, after all, he is the King of the
*people,* and the Bourbons were the Kings of the
*nobles.   We* have chosen *him,* and if we are to
have a tyrant, let him be one chosen by ourselves."
There,' said he, 'you have the sentiments of the
French nation expressed by an old woman.'

I asked his opinion about Soult, and mentioned
that I had heard some persons place him in the
rank next to himself as a general.   He replied, ' He
is an excellent Minister for War, or Chief of the
Staff : one who knows much better the arrangement
of an army than how to command in chief.'

Some officers of the 53d told Madame Bertrand
that Sir Thomas Reade had said that Bonaparte
did not like the sight of them, or of any other red-
coat, as it put him in mind of Waterloo.   Madame
Bertrand assured them that it was directly contrary
to everything that he had ever expressed in her
hearing.   The same was mentioned to me yesterday
by Lieutenants Fitzgerald and Mackay.

*August* 30.—Napoleon rose at 3 A.M.   Continued writing until six ; when he retired to rest
again.   At five o'clock Count Bertrand came to
Captain Poppleton and told him that the Emperor

desired to see him. Poppleton, being in his morning walking-dress, wished to retire and change, but was desired to come *sans cérémonie.* He was accordingly ushered into the billiard-room in his dishabille. Napoleon was standing with his hat under his arm. 'Well, *M. le capitaine,*' said he, ' I believe you are the senior captain of the 53d?'—'I am.'—'I have an esteem for the officers and men of the 53d. They are brave men, and do their duty. I have been informed that it is said in camp that I do not wish to see the officers. Will you be so good as to tell them, that whoever asserted this told a falsehood. I never said or thought so; I shall be always happy to see them. I have been told also that they have been prohibited by the Governor from visiting me.' Captain Poppleton replied that he believed the information which he had received was groundless, and that the officers of the 53d were acquainted with the good opinion which he had previously expressed of them, which was highly flattering to their feelings. That they had the greatest respect for him. Napoleon smiled and replied, '*Je ne suis pas vieille femme.* I love a brave soldier who has undergone *le baptême du feu,* whatever nation he may belong to.'[1]

[1] 'After dinner the Emperor good-humouredly related the remark made by an old soldier of the 53d, who, having seen him yesterday for the first time, went back to his comrades and said: "What lies they told me about Napoleon's age; he is not old at all; the rogue has at least sixty campaigns in his body yet." We thought this expression savoured very much of the Frenchman, and we laid claim to it as having proceeded from one of our grenadiers. We then related to him a number of *bons-mots* made by our soldiers during

*September* 1. — Sir Hudson Lowe came to Longwood. Two or three days ago the '*letter*' had been shown and read by Count Las Cases to Captain Grey of the Artillery, and some other officers. Sir Hudson was very desirous to know whether any of them had taken a copy of it. I informed him that any person at Longwood who liked might get one. His Excellency appeared greatly alarmed at this, and observed that it was an infraction of the Act of Parliament in any person, not belonging to Longwood, to receive it. He then asked if I had communicated to General Bonaparte what he had directed me to say on the 22d instant. I replied that I had; that Napoleon had said, ' That he might act as he pleased ; that the only thing left undone now was to put sentinels at the doors and windows to prevent him from going

his absence and on his return, with which he was much entertained. But what particularly excited his risibility was the answer made by a grenadier at Lyons. A Grand Review was held there, just after the Emperor had landed on his return from Elba. The commanding officer remarked to his soldiers, that they were well clothed and well fed, that their pay might be seen upon their persons. "Yes, certainly," replied the grenadier to whom he addressed himself. "Well!" continued the officer, with a confident air, "it was not so under Bonaparte. Your pay was in arrears; he was in your debt?"— "And what did that signify," said the grenadier smartly, "if we chose to give him *credit ?*"'—*Las Cases*, vol. ii., part iii., p. 69, English edition.

Forsyth (vol. i. p. 278) tries to make capital against O'Meara or against Poppleton for a difference in the account of the conversation as given here, and as reported by Poppleton. This seems over-strained. The closing remark of Napoleon is just what he would have said, and as for the conversation, when did two people agree as to what each had said ?

out ; that as long as he had a book he cared but little about it.' The Governor remarked that he had sent his letter of complaints to the British Government, and that it rested with the ministers how to act. That he had put them in full possession of everything, which he desired me to tell him.[1]

*September* 5. — Major Gorrequer came up to Longwood to discuss with General Montholon the proposed reduction of the expenditure, and begged me to be present. The purport of his communication was, that when the British Government had fixed £8000 as the maximum of the whole of the expenses attendant upon General Bonaparte's establishment, they had contemplated that a great reduction would take place in the number of persons composing it, by some of the general officers and others returning to Europe. But as that had not taken place, the Governor had, on his own responsibility, directed that an additional sum of £4000 should be added, making in the whole £12,000 for all and every expense ; that General Montholon must therefore be informed that on no account could the expenditure be allowed to exceed £1000 per month. Should General Bonaparte be averse to the reductions necessary to bring the disbursements within that sum, the surplus must be paid by himself, by bills drawn upon some banker in Europe, or by such of his friends as were willing to pay them. Count Montholon replied that the Emperor was ready to pay all the expenses of the establishment, if they

[1] This I had an opportunity of doing on the 4th.—B. E. O'M.

would allow him the means of doing so ; and that
if they permitted a mercantile or banking-house in
St. Helena, London, or Paris, chosen by the British
Government itself, to serve as intermediaries, through
whom they could send sealed letters and receive
answers, he would engage to pay all the expenses.
That on the one side his honour should be pledged
that the letters should relate solely to pecuniary
matters ; and on the other that the correspondence
should be held sacred. Major Gorrequer replied
that this could not be complied with ; that no sealed
letters would be suffered to leave Longwood.

Major Gorrequer shortly afterwards told Count
Montholon that the intended reductions would take
place on the 15th of the present month, and
begged him to arrange matters with Mr. Balcombe,
the purveyor, about the disposition of the £1000
monthly, unless he chose to give drafts for the
surplus. Count Montholon replied that he would
not meddle with it ; that the Governor might
act as he pleased ; that at the present moment there
was not any superfluity of provisions supplied ; that
as soon as the reductions took place, he, for his part,
would give up charge, and would not interfere
further in the matter. That the conduct of the
English Ministry was infamous, in declaring to
Europe that the Emperor should not be suffered to
want anything, and refusing the offers of the Allied
Powers to defray a part of the expenses, and now
reducing him and his suite nearly to rations. Major
Gorrequer denied that the Allied Powers had ever

made such an offer.   Montholon replied that he had
read it in some of the papers.   Major Gorrequer
then observed that a great reduction could be made
in the wine, viz. that it could be reduced to ten
bottles of claret daily and one of Madeira; that at
Plantation House the consumption was regulated
on the average of one bottle to each person.   Montholon replied that the French drank much less
than the English; and that he had already done at
the Emperor's table what he never had done in his
own private house in France, viz. corked up the
remnants of the bottles of wine, in order to produce
them on the table the next day; that, moreover, at
night there was not a morsel of meat remaining in
the pantry.   Gorrequer observed that £12,000 a
year was a very handsome allowance.   'Equal to
about as much as £4000 would be in England,'
replied Montholon.   The business was then deferred
until Saturday.   Before leaving Longwood, Major
Gorrequer himself allowed to me that the establishment could not be carried on for £12,000 annually;
but that he thought a reduction of about £2000
yearly might be made.   I observed that it might,
provided a store of everything necessary was established at Longwood, together with a stockyard,
under the direction of a proper person.

*September* 7.—Major Gorrequer came up and
had a long conversation with Count Montholon in
my presence.   The latter told him that orders had
been given to discharge seven servants, which, with
the consequent saving of provisions and a reduction

of wine, would diminish the expenses of the establishment to about £15,194 annually ; but that sum was the *minimum of minimums*, and that no further reductions could possibly take place. Major Gorrequer observed that it was nearly what he had calculated himself. However, he still persisted in declaring that on the 15th not more than £1000 per month would be allowed. Count Montholon then, after renewing the offer made on the last conversation, said, that as the Emperor was not permitted by the British Government to have access to his property, he had no other means left than to dispose of it to some one else ; and that accordingly a portion of his plate would be sent to the town for sale, in order to obtain the sum required monthly, in addition to that allowed by Sir Hudson Lowe, to provide them with the necessaries of life. Major Gorrequer said that he would acquaint the Governor with these observations.[1]

[1] 'Few facts connected with the captivity of Napoleon have excited more sympathy than the sale by him of his plate. As the case has been generally represented, it did seem a pitiable thing that he should have been reduced to the necessity of parting with his silver plate in order to keep himself and his followers from starvation at St. Helena. And if any necessity for the sale existed, it must have inflicted indelible reproach on the British Government. . . . But was there such a necessity ?. . . That the plate was sent from Longwood for sale is indisputable ; but the alleged cause was a fiction, and the whole affair was a manœuvre of Napoleon to create false sympathy for himself and draw public odium upon Sir Hudson Lowe. . . . O'Meara himself shall reveal the truth. . . . In a private letter to his friend, Mr. Finlaison, after mentioning that the French at Longwood daily spent more than the Government allowance, to meet which outlay Napoleon had caused some of his plate to be broken up, he adds : " In this he has also a wish to

Sir Hudson Lowe, accompanied by General Meade (who had arrived a day or two before), came up and rode round Longwood. He appeared to point out to the General the limits, and other matters connected with the prisoners.

At night Napoleon sent for me. He was sitting in his bedroom, with only a wood fire burning, the flames of which, alternately blazing and sinking, gave at moments a most singular and melancholy expression to his countenance, as he sat opposite to it with his hands crossed upon his knees, probably reflecting upon his forlorn condition. After a moment's pause, '*Dottore,*' said he, '*potete dar qualcosa a far dormire un uomo che non può?* This is beyond your art. I have been trying in vain to procure a little rest. I cannot,' continued he, 'well comprehend the conduct of your Ministers. They go to the expense of £60,000 or £70,000 in sending out furniture, wood, and building materials for my use, and at the same time send orders to put me nearly on rations, and oblige me to discharge my servants, and make reductions incompatible with the decency and comfort of the house. Then we have aides-de-camp making stipulations about a bottle of wine and two or three pounds of meat, with as much gravity and consequence as if they were treating about the distribution of kingdoms. I see contradictions that I cannot reconcile : on the one hand, excite an odium against the Governor, by saying that he has been obliged to sell his plate in order to provide against starvation, as he himself told me was his object."'—Forsyth's *Lowe*, vol. i. pp. 288, 289.

enormous and useless expenditure; on the other, unparalleled meanness and littleness. Why do not they allow me to provide myself with everything, instead of disgracing the character of the nation? They will not furnish my followers with what they have been accustomed to, nor will they allow me to provide for them, by sending sealed letters through a mercantile house even of their own selection. For no man in France would answer a letter of mine, when he knew that it would be read by the English Ministers, and that he would consequently be denounced to the Bourbons, and his property and person exposed to certain destruction. Moreover, your own ministers have not given a specimen of good faith in seizing upon the trifling sum of money that I had in the *Bellerophon;* which gives reason to suppose that they would do the same again if they knew where any of my property was placed. It must be,' continued he, 'to gull the English nation. John Bull, seeing all this furniture sent out, and so much parade and show in the preparations made in England, concludes that I am well treated here. If they knew the truth, and the dishonour which it reflects upon them, they would not suffer it.'

He then asked who was 'that strange general officer?' I replied, General Meade, who, with Mrs. Meade, had arrived a few days back. That I had been under his command in Egypt, where he had been severely wounded. 'What, with Abercrombie?'—'No,' I replied, 'during the unfortunate

attack upon Rosetta.'[1]—'What sort of a man is he?'
I replied that he bore a very excellent character.
'That Governor,' said he, 'was seen stopping him
frequently, and pointing in different directions. I
suppose that he has been filling his head with *bugie*
about me, and has told him that I hate the sight of
every Englishman, as some of his *canaille* have said
to the officers of the 53d. I shall order a letter to
be written to tell him that I will see him.'

*September* 8.—A letter written by Count Montholon to General Meade, containing an invitation
to come to Longwood. This was given to Captain
Poppleton, who was also requested to inform Mrs.
Meade that Napoleon could scarcely request a lady
to visit him ; but that, if she came, he should be
happy to see her also. Captain Poppleton delivered
this letter open to Sir Hudson Lowe. His
Excellency handed the note to General Meade.
On the road down to Jamestown General Meade
reined back his horse, and informed Captain Poppleton that he should have been very happy to have
availed himself of the invitation, but that he
understood restrictions existed, and that he must
apply to the Governor for permission, and in the
next place the vessel was under weigh, and he could
not well detain her.

[1] An English force was defeated here by a superior body of
Turkish horse, April 22, 1807. The prisoners were treated with
extraordinary barbarity. 'Among other things too horrible to relate,
says Mr. Madox, in his *Excursions in the Holy Land*, vol. ii. p. 47,
'every English captive was obliged to carry in his hands the head of
one of his slain companions as a present to the Pasha.'

*September* 9.—Napoleon complained of headache, colic, etc. I wished him to take a doze of
physic, which he declined, saying that he would
cure himself by diet, and restricting himself to
chicken-broth. He said that General Meade had
written to Count Montholon, expressing his inability
to accept the invitation; 'but I am convinced,'
continued he, 'that in reality he was prevented
by the Governor. Tell him the first time you see
him that I said he prevented General Meade from
coming to see me.'

General Gourgaud and Count Montholon complained of the wine, which they suspected contained
lead, as it gave them the colic, and desired me to
get some tests in order to analyse it.

Young Las Cases and Piontkowski went to town
this day, and had a conversation with the Russian
and French Commissioners. On their return
Piontkowski said, that on their arrival Sir Thomas
Reade had sent orders to the lieutenant who
accompanied them, not to allow them to separate;
and that he must follow them everywhere, and
listen to their conversation. While they were
speaking to 'the Rosebud' (a very pretty young
lady, so denominated from the freshness and fineness
of her complexion), one of Sir Thomas Reade's
orderlies brought out their horses by his command,
with directions to inform them that their servant
was drunk, and that if they did not leave the town
directly, he (Sir Thomas) would confine him, as he
was a soldier, and punish him for being drunk.

That young Las Cases, who was cooler, had desired
him to demand an order in writing to that effect ;
but that in his passion he could not help saying that
he would horsewhip any person who attempted to
lead the horses away.

*September* 10.—Napoleon, after some conversation touching the state of his health, said that
'while young Las Cases was speaking to the Russian
Commissioner yesterday, the Governor was walking
up and down before the house where they were,
watching them. I could not have believed it
possible before that a Lieutenant-General and a
Governor could have demeaned himself by acting as
a *gendarme.* Tell him so the next time you see him.'

Napoleon then made some observations upon the
bad quality of the wine furnished to Longwood, and
remarked that when he was a *sous lieutenant* of
artillery he had a better table, and drank better wine
than at present.

I saw Sir Hudson Lowe afterwards, who asked
me if General Bonaparte had made any observations
relative to General Meade's not having accepted
the offer made to him ? I replied that. he had said
he was convinced that he (Sir Hudson) had prevented him from accepting it, and had desired me to
tell him that such was his opinion. No sooner had
I said this than His Excellency's countenance
changed, and he exclaimed in a violent tone of voice,
' He is a d——d lying rascal. I wished General
Meade to accept it, and told him to do so.' He
then walked about for a few minutes in an agitated

manner, repeating, ' That none but a black-hearted villain would have entertained such an idea ;' then mounted his horse and rode away.   He had not proceeded more than about a hundred paces when he wheeled round, rode back to where I was standing, and said in a very angry manner, ' Tell General Bonaparte that the assertion that I prevented General Meade from going to see him, *è una bugia infame, e che è un bugiardone chi l'ha detto.*   Tell him my exact words.'[1]

Sir Thomas Reade informed me that Piontkowski's account of the transaction in town was false ; that the only orders he had given to Lieutenant Sweeny were not to lose sight of them.   That seeing their servant was so drunk that he could not sit on horseback, he had sent his own orderly to assist in bringing the horses out, merely as an act of civility.

*September* 12.—Napoleon still unwell.   Recommended him strongly to take a dose of Epsom salts. In a good-humoured manner he gave me a slap in the face and said, if he was not better to-morrow he would take his own medicine, crystals of tartar.[2]

---

[1] ' *An infamous lie, and the person who said it is a great liar.*' It is unnecessary for me to say that I did not deliver this message in the manner I was directed to convey it.—B. E. O'M.

[2] 'The Emperor played a game at piquet with Madame de Montholon.   The Grand Marshal having entered, he left off playing, and asked him how he thought he looked.   Bertrand replied, "Only rather yellow ;" which was indeed the case.   The Emperor rose good-humouredly, and pursued Bertrand into the salon, in order to catch him by the ear, exclaiming, " Rather yellow, indeed !   Do you intend to insult me, Grand Marshal ?   Do you mean to say that I

During the conversation I informed him that the Governor had assured me that he had not only not prevented General Meade from seeing him, but that he had recommended him to accept the invitation. ' I do not believe him,' said Napoleon ; 'or if he did, it was done in such a manner as to let the other know that he would rather that he did not avail himself of it.'

I related afterwards to him the explanation given to me by Sir Thomas Reade of Piontkowski's affair. 'What I complain of,' said he, 'is the disingenuous manner in which they act, in order to prevent any of the French from going to the town. Why do they not say at once manfully, "You cannot go to town," and then nobody will ask, instead of converting officers into spies and *gendarmes*, by making them follow the French everywhere, and listen to their conversation. But their design is to throw so many impediments in the way, and render it so disagreeable to us as to amount to a prohibition, without giving any direct orders, to enable this Governor to say that we have the liberty of the town, but that we do not choose to avail ourselves of it.'

I saw Sir Hudson Lowe in town, to whom I explained what I had said to Napoleon about Piontkowski, his reply, also the complaint made by Generals Gourgaud and Montholon of the wine,

am bilious, morose, atrabilious, passionate, unjust, tyrannical ? Let me catch hold of your ear, and I will take my revenge." '—*Las Cases*, vol. iii., part vi., p. 149, English edition.

and their request that I might procure some tests to analyse it. A few bottles of claret have been borrowed from Captain Poppleton for the Emperor's own use.

*September* 13.—Napoleon much better. Had a conversation with Mr. Balcombe relative to the concerns of the establishment.

A large quantity of plate weighed for the purpose of being broken up for sale. Information given of this by Captain Poppleton to Sir Hudson Lowe. Complaints made by Count Montholon and Cipriani of the state of the copper saucepans at Longwood. Found them, on examination, to be in want of immediate tinning.[1] Communicated the above to Major Gorrequer, with a request that a tradesman might be sent forthwith to repair them. A letter came from Mr. Balcombe to Count Montholon, containing the scale of provisions, etc., which had been fixed for their daily use, according to the reduction ordered by the Governor. Montholon refused to sign any more receipts.

In the evening Cipriani went to Captain Maunsell and requested him to obtain for him a dozen or two of the same claret which for two or three days they had borrowed from Captain Poppleton for the Emperor, and which had been got from the 53d's mess, as that sent up from Jamestown had given him the colic, adding that they would either pay for

---

[1] This should be remarked as a full explanation of the symptoms which made some of the Longwood party complain they were poisoned by the wine.—See *Forsyth*, vol. i. p. 294.

it, or return an equal quantity. This request was interpreted by me to Captain Maunsell, who said that he would endeavour to procure it.

Received an answer from Major Gorrequer, acquainting me that he had ordered a new *batterie de cuisine* to be sent to Longwood.

Sir Hudson Lowe and staff in camp; he was very angry at the request which had been made to Captain Maunsell to procure the wine. It appeared that Captain Maunsell had mentioned it to his brother, and to the wine committee of the regiment, who proposed to send a case of claret to Napoleon. This was told to Sir George Bingham, and reported by him to the Governor, who sent for me, and said that I had no business to act as interpreter on such an occasion. Major Gorrequer observed that the wine had been sent out for the use of General Bonaparte, and that he ought to be obliged to drink it, or get nothing else.

*September* 15.—Wrote to Major Gorrequer in answer to some points of his last letter, and stated that General Gourgaud had affirmed that there was lead in the wine, and had begged me to procure some tests for the purpose of ascertaining the fact; adding, that I had acquainted Sir Hudson Lowe with this request the last time I had seen him in town. I hinted also that it was very natural for Napoleon to believe General Gourgaud's assertion (who was considered to be a good chemist), until it was proved not to be correct. This letter I requested him to lay before the Governor.

*September* 17.—This day Major Gorrequer, in the course of conversation with me relative to the provisioning of Longwood, said that Sir Hudson Lowe had observed, that any soldiers who would attend at Longwood as servants to General Bonaparte *were unworthy of rations.* Sir Thomas Reade begged me to try and get him some of Napoleon's plate *whole*, which, he observed, would *sell* better in that state than if it were broken up.

*September* 18.—Sir Hudson Lowe at Longwood. Sir Thomas Reade told me that Bertrand had injured himself very much in his conversation with the Governor, as the latter had found it to be his duty to write a strong letter on the subject to Lord Bathurst.

*September* 19.—A large portion of Napoleon's plate broken up, the imperial arms and the eagles cut out and put by. Count Montholon applied to Captain Poppleton for an officer to accompany him to Jamestown, for the purpose of disposing of the plate, with which the latter acquainted the Governor forthwith by an orderly. Received back an order to acquaint Count Montholon 'that the money produced by the sale of the silver should not be paid to him, but be deposited in the hands of Mr. Balcombe, the purveyor, for the use of General Bonaparte.'

*September* 21.—Sir Pulteney Malcolm came up to Longwood in order to take leave of Napoleon, prior to his departure for the Cape of Good Hope, which was expected to take place in a few days.

Had a long interview, and was received very graciously by Napoleon; the conversation was chiefly relative to the Scheldt, Antwerp, battles in Germany, the Poles, etc.

Wrote last night to Sir Thomas Reade, by request of Madame Bertrand, to know whether permission would be granted for a phaeton, which had been purchased with Napoleon's own money, and afterwards given by him to Madame Bertrand, to be sent to the Cape for sale by Sir Pulteney Malcolm's ship. Concluded by requesting him to let me know, before he applied to the Governor, if there was any impropriety in the request, as in that case it should not be made.

*September* 23.—Received an answer from Sir Thomas Reade, announcing that the Governor had given his consent to the sale of the phaeton, with a proviso that the money derived from it should not be paid to themselves, but deposited in Mr. Balcombe's hands.[1] Three of Bertrand's servants very seriously ill.

Heard a curious anecdote of General Vandamme. When made prisoner by the Russians, he was brought before the Emperor Alexander, who reproached him in bitter terms with being a robber, a plunderer, and a murderer; adding, that no favour could be granted to such an execrable character. This was followed by an order that he should be

---

[1] Sir Thomas Reade's letter to Dr. O'Meara—a very courteous one—is given *in extenso* in Forsyth's *Lowe*, vol. i. p. 296, and contains no 'proviso.'

sent to Siberia, whilst the other prisoners were sent to a much less northern destination. Vandamme replied, with great *sang froid*, ' It may be, sire, that I am a robber and a plunderer ; but at least I have not to reproach myself with having soiled my hands with the blood of a father !!'[1]

Met Sir Hudson Lowe on his way to Longwood, who observed that General Bonaparte had done himself a great deal of mischief by the letters which he caused Count Montholon to write, and that he wished him to know it. That by conducting himself properly for some years, the Ministers might believe him to be sincere, and allow him to return to England. He added that he (Sir Hudson) had written such letters to England about Count Las Cases as would effectually prevent his ever being permitted to return to France. On his arrival at Longwood, the fowls which had been sent up for the day's consumption were shown to His Excellency by Captain Poppleton. He was obliged to admit that they were very poor.[2]

---

[1] The better story is that Vandamme, after his capture at Kulm, indignant at Alexander's reproaches for plundering, exclaimed that Alexander could not have treated him worse if he had murdered his (Alexander's) father, Alexander being always suspected of having been privy to the plot against Paul. But Vandamme himself, on his return from Russia, always professed himself thoroughly satisfied with his treatment by Alexander, who received him kindly, and also complimented him on his defence.—Du Casse's *Vandamme*, vol. ii. p. 550.

[2] O'Meara, writing to Sir Thomas Reade, after mentioning the scarcity and inferior quality of the meat, wine, etc. sent to Longwood, adds : ' They '—the Emperor's French attendants—' are sufficiently malignant to impute all these things to the Governor, instead of setting them down as being owing to the neglect or carelessness of

*September* 27.—The Commissioners came up to Longwood gate and wanted to enter, but were refused admission by the officer of the guard, as their passes did not specify Longwood, but merely 'wherever a British officer might pass.'

*September* 28.—Napoleon occupied in reading Denon's large work on Egypt, from which he was making some extracts with his own hand.

*October* 1.—Repeated to Napoleon what Sir Hudson Lowe had desired me on the 23d. He replied, 'I expect nothing from the present Ministry but ill-treatment. The more they want to lessen me, the more I will exalt myself. It was my intention to have assumed the name of Colonel Muiron, who was killed by my side at Arcola, covering me with his body, and to have lived as a private person in England, in some part of the country, without ever desiring to mix in the grand world. I would never have gone to London, nor have dined out. Probably I should have seen very few persons. Perhaps I might have formed a friendship with some *savans*. I should have ridden out every day, and then returned to my books.'

I observed that as long as he kept the title of Majesty, the English Ministers would have a pretext for keeping him in St. Helena. He replied, 'They force me to it. I wanted to assume an *incognito* on my arrival here, which was proposed to some of Balcombe's people. Every little circumstance is carried directly to Bonaparte, with every aggravation that malignity and falsehood can suggest to evil-disposed and cankered minds.'— Forsyth's *Lowe*, vol. i. pp. 237, 238.

the Admiral, but they will not permit it. They insist on calling me General Bonaparte. I have no reason to be ashamed of that title, but I will not take it from them. If the Republic had not a legal existence, it had no more right to constitute me General than First Magistrate.[1] If the Admiral had remained,' continued he, 'perhaps matters might have been arranged. He had some heart, and, to do him justice, was incapable of a mean action. Do you think,' added he, 'that he will do us an injury on his arrival in England?' I replied, 'I do not think that he will render you any service, particularly in consequence of the manner in which he was treated when he last came up to see you, but he will strictly adhere to the truth.'

I also observed that during the empire he had caused Sir George Cockburn's brother to be arrested, when envoy at Hamburg, and conveyed to France, where he was detained for some years.[2] He appeared surprised at this, and endeavoured to recollect it. After a pause he asked me if I was sure that the person so arrested was Sir George Cockburn's brother.[3]

---

[1] See *Thiers*, vol. iv. p. 577, Bentley edition of 1854. Also see *Forsyth*, vol. i. p. 319, where Lowe says that Napoleon should have himself dropped his title.

[2] A mistake of O'Meara's. The person really arrested was Sir George Rumboldt, who, however, was released after a few days' confinement.—*Alison*, chap. xxxvii. para. 49. Perhaps Sir George Cockburn's brother may really have been arrested when so many English were in 1803.

[3] It has just been communicated to me that I am in error in having stated above that it was *Sir G. Cockburn's brother* that was seized in Hamburg by order of Napoleon; the person, according to

I replied that I was perfectly so, as the Admiral had told me the circumstance himself. 'It is likely enough,' replied he, 'but I do not recollect the name. I suppose, however, that it must have been at the time when your Government had seized upon all the French ships, sailors, and passengers they could lay their hands upon in harbour, or at sea, before the Declaration of War. I, in my turn, seized upon all the English that I could find on land, in order to show them that if they were all-powerful at sea, and could do what they liked there, I was equally so on land, and had as good a right to seize people on my element as they had upon theirs. *Now*,' said he, 'I can comprehend the reason why your Ministers selected him. I am surprised, however, that he never told me anything about it.'

Sir Hudson Lowe, accompanied by Sir Thomas Reade, Major Gorrequer, Wynyard, and Prichard, and followed by three dragoons and a servant, rode into Longwood, alighted in front of the billiard-room, and demanded to 'see General Bonaparte.' A reply was given by General Montholon that he was indisposed. This did not satisfy His Excellency, who sent again, in rather an authoritative manner, to say that he had something to communicate, which he wanted to deliver in person to General Bonaparte, and to no other person would he give it. An answer

the information of the gentlemen who write to me, was *Sir George Rumboldt*. Although I can scarcely believe that I was mistaken, yet I think it my duty to put the public in possession of this friendly correction.—B. E. O'M. *21st August* 1822.

was sent that notice would be given to him when he could be received—that Napoleon was then suffering from toothache ; and at 4 P.M. Napoleon sent for me, and desired me to look at one of the *dentes sapientiæ*, which was carious and loose. He then asked me if I knew what the Governor wanted, or why he wished to see him ? I replied that he had perhaps some communication from Lord Bathurst, which he did not like to deliver to any other person. ' It will be better for us not to meet,' said Napoleon. ' It is probably some *bêtise* of Lord Bathurst, which he will make worse by his ungracious manner of communicating it. I am sure it is nothing that is good, or he would not be so anxious to deliver it himself.

' The last time I saw him he laid his hand upon his sabre two or three times in a violent manner,[1] therefore go to him or to Sir Thomas Reade to-morrow, and tell him that if he has anything to communicate, he had better send it to Bertrand, or Bertrand will go to his house ; assure him that he may rely upon Bertrand's making a faithful report. Or let him send Colonel Reade to me to explain what he has to say ; I will receive and hear him, because he will be only the bearer of orders and not the giver of them ; therefore if he comes upon a bad mission, I shall not be angry, as he will only obey the orders of a

[1] Lowe indignantly denied this. See *Forsyth*, vol. i. p. 318, and O'Meara on 5th October. Nothing more likely than he did accidentally place his hand on the hilt of his sword (see 10th October), and Napoleon, accustomed to officers speaking to him at strict ' attention,' would remark the action. See also p. 141.

superior.' I endeavoured to induce him to meet
the Governor, in order, if possible, to make up the
differences between them ; but he replied, 'To meet
him would be the worst mode of attempting it, as he
was confident it was some *bêtise* of Lord Bathurst's
which he would make worse, and convert into an
insult by his brutal mode of delivering it.'—'You
know,' added he, ' I never got into a passion with the
Admiral, because even when he had something bad
to communicate, he did it with some feeling ; *but
this man treats us as if we were so many deserters.*'

Sir Thomas Reade being incapable of explaining
to him in either French or Italian the purport of
any communication exceeding a few words, I asked
him, 'In case Sir Thomas Reade should not find
himself capable of explaining perfectly every particular, and should commit what he had to say to
paper, if he would read it, or allow it to be read to
him ?' He replied, 'Certainly, let him do this, or
send it to Bertrand. As to me, perhaps I shall not
see him for six months. Let him break open the
doors or level the house, I am not subject to the
English laws, because they do not protect me. I
wish they would give orders to have me despatched.
I do not like to commit suicide ; it is a thing that I
have always disapproved of. I have made a vow
to drain the cup to the last draught ; but I should
be most rejoiced if they would send directions to
put me to death.'[1]

[1] Nevertheless, Napoleon is said to have attempted his own life
shortly after his abdication : 'When Napoleon departed for his

*October* 2.—Saw Napoleon in the morning.
A toothache, he said, had prevented him from
sleeping a great part of the night: his cheek was
swelled. After having examined the tooth, I recommended the extraction of it. Hé desired me
to inform the Governor that in consequence of
indisposition, pain, and want of sleep, he found
himself unfit to listen calmly to communications, or
to enter into discussions ; therefore that he wished the

second campaign in Russia, Corvisart gave him some prussic acid,
enclosed in a little bag hermetically sealed, which he constantly wore
round his neck. . . . Napoleon was confident of the efficacy of this
poison, and regarded it as the means of being master of himself.
He swallowed it on the night above mentioned, after having put his
affairs in order and written some letters. The poison was extremely
violent in its nature, but liable to lose its power by being kept for
any length of time. This happened in the present instance. It
caused the Emperor dreadful pain, but did not prove fatal. When
the Duc de Bassano saw him in a condition closely resembling death,
he knelt down at his bedside and burst into tears. "Ah, sire," he
exclaimed, " what have you done ?" The Emperor, stretching to him
his cold and humid hand, said, " You see, God has decreed that I shall
not die. He too condemns me to suffer !"'—*Memoirs of Napoleon,*
by the Duchesse d'Abrantés, 1883 edition, vol. iii. pp. 407, 408.

And when on board the *Bellerophon* Napoleon said to Comte de
Las Cases, ' My friend, I have sometimes an idea of quitting you,
and this would not be very difficult ; it is only necessary to create a
little mental excitement, and I shall soon have escaped. All will be
over, and you can then quietly rejoin your families. This is the
more easy since my internal principles do not oppose any bar to it.
I am one of those who conceive that the pains of the other world
were only imagined as a counterpoise to those inadequate allure-
ments which are offered to us there. God can never have willed
such a contradiction to His infinite goodness, especially for an act of
this kind ; and what is it after all, but wishing to return to Him a
little sooner ?'—*Journal of the Private Life of the Emperor Napoleon
at St. Helena,* by the Comte de Las Cases, 1824 edition, vol. i.
p. 56.

Governor would communicate to Count Bertrand whatever he had to say. That Count Bertrand would faithfully report it to him. If he would not communicate it to Count Bertrand, or to any other resident at Longwood, Napoleon would have no objection to receive it from Colonel Reade.

'Sir Hudson Lowe came up here yesterday, surrounded by his staff, as if he were going in state to assist at an execution, instead of asking privately to see me.[1] Three times has he gone away in a passion, therefore it will be better that no more interviews should take place between us, as no good can arise from them ; and as he represents his nation here, I do not like to insult or make severe remarks to him, similar to those I was obliged to utter before.'

Went to Sir Hudson Lowe, to whom I made known the message with which I had been charged, but moderating some of the expressions. His

---

[1] Forsyth (vol. i. p. 317) founds a charge against O'Meara for not inserting here what he wrote at the time to Mr. Finlaison. ('This, I suppose, was invented and told him by Montholon,' etc.) But surely this was no invention ; the statement was quite true. See O'Meara himself on 1st October, a little farther back. ('Sir Hudson Lowe, accompanied by Sir Thomas Reade, Major Gorrequer, Wynyard, and Prichard, and followed by three dragoons and a servant.') See also Forsyth himself, vol. i. p. 313 ('accompanied by the officers of his staff'). An English general usually would take with him one aide-de-camp, and perhaps a mounted orderly to hold his horse if he intended to dismount. It will be seen that Napoleon was right, and that Lowe did intend the interview to be a special one. O'Meara, if he appears inconsistent, is only correcting his own first erroneous statement. Later on, 25th November, Lowe again appears in similar state, for mere ostentation's sake.

Excellency desired me to give it to him in writing, and then told me that the Secretary of State had sent directions to him to inquire very minutely concerning a letter which had appeared in one of the Portsmouth papers concerning Bonaparte, and which had given great offence to His Majesty's Ministers; particularly as it had been reported to them by Captain Hamilton, of the *Havannah* frigate, that I was either the author, or had brought it on board. His Excellency then asked me who I had written to, adding, 'There is no harm in the letter. It is very correct in general, but the Ministers do not like that anything should be published about him. Everything must come through them;' also that Captain Hamilton had reported that it was an anonymous letter, and expressly intended for publication. I replied to Sir Hudson Lowe that I had never written an anonymous letter in my life, and that several letters had been published in the newspapers of which I had been supposed the author, until another individual had acknowledged them to have been written by him. Sir Hudson Lowe desired me to write a letter of explanation to him on the subject; after which he dictated to Sir Thomas Reade what he wished me to express in answer to General Bonaparte, of which I took the following copy; which the Governor read before I left the house.

'The principal object of the Governor's visit to Longwood to see General Bonaparte was from a sense of attention towards him, in order to acquaint

him, first, with instructions received concerning his
officers, which could only be decided by him, before
informing them.   The Governor would wish the
communication to General Bonaparte should be
made by himself, in the presence of Sir Thomas
Reade, or some of his own staff, and one of the
French generals.   He never intended to say
anything which would affront or insult General
Bonaparte; on the contrary, he wished to conciliate,
and to modify the strict letter of his instructions,
with every attention and respect to him, and cannot
conceive the cause of so much resentment manifested
by General Bonaparte towards him.   If he would
not consent to an interview with the Governor, in
the presence of other persons, the Governor would
send Sir Thomas Reade (if he consented to it) to
communicate the general purport of what he had to
say, leaving some points for future discussion.   If
Count Bertrand was sent to the Governor, some
expression of concern would be required from
him for the language made use of by him to the
Governor, on the last interview which the Governor
undertook, by desire of General Bonaparte himself;
and the Governor conceives the same expression of
concern necessary from Count Bertrand, on the part
of General Bonaparte himself, for his intemperate
language in the last interview with the Governor;
and *then*, the latter will express his concern for any
words made use of by him in reply, which may have
been deemed unpleasant, as there was no intention
on his part of saying anything offensive, his words

being merely repelling an attack made upon him, and this he would not do to a person in any other situation than that of General Bonaparte. But if the latter is determined to dispute with the Governor for endeavouring to execute his orders, he sees little hope of a proper understanding between them.'

On my return to Longwood I minutely explained the above to Napoleon, both alone and in the presence of Count Bertrand. Napoleon smiled contemptuously at the idea of *his* apologising to Sir Hudson Lowe.

*October* 3.—Saw Napoleon in the morning. After I had inquired into the state of his health, he entered upon the business of yesterday. 'As this Governor,' says he, 'declares that he will not communicate the whole to Reade, but intends to reserve some future points for discussion, I shall not see him, for I only agree to see Reade in order to avoid the sight of the other; and by reserving the points he speaks of, he might come up again tomorrow or next day, and demand another interview. If he wants to make any communication, let him send his Adjutant-General to Bertrand, or Montholon, or Las Cases, or Gourgaud, or to you; or send for one of them and explain it himself; or let him communicate the *whole* to Reade, or to Sir George Bingham, or somebody else; and then I will see the person so chosen. If he still insists on seeing me, I will write myself in answer, "The Emperor Napoleon will not see you, because the three last times you were with him you insulted him, and he

does not wish more communication with you." I
well know that if we have another interview there
will be disputes and abuse; a suspicious gesture
might produce I know not what. He, for his own
sake, ought not to desire one after the language
which I applied to him the last time. I would
sooner have an interview with the corporal of the
guard than with that *galeriano*. How different it
was with the Admiral! We used to converse together sociably on different subjects, like friends.'

According to his desire, I wrote an account of
what he had said to Sir Hudson Lowe; avoiding,
however, repeating the strongest of his expressions.

*October* 4.—Sir Thomas Reade came up to
my room at Longwood, with a written paper from
the Governor, containing the new instructions which
the latter had received from England. I went to
Napoleon and announced him. He asked me 'if
he was in full possession of everything?' I replied
that he had told me so. He desired me to introduce
him. When I went back, Sir Thomas Reade told
me that his mission was not a very pleasant one, and
that he hoped 'Bonaparte would not be offended
with him,' and asked me how he should explain it
to him. I told him how to express himself to
this effect in Italian. We then went into the garden where Napoleon was: I introduced him, and
left them together. In a few minutes Napoleon
called Count Las Cases and told him to translate
aloud, in French, the contents of the paper as Reade
repeated it.

When Reade came to my room, on his return, he said that Napoleon had been very civil to him, and that so far from being offended, he had asked him the news and laughed, and only observed (as the knight repeated in his Italian), '*Più mi si perseguiterà, meglio andrà e mostrerà al mondo che rabbia di persecuzioni. Fra poco tempo mi si leveranno tutti gli altri, e qualche mattina m'ammazzeranno.*' Sir Thomas then allowed me to read the paper, the contents of which were as follows : 'That the French, who wished to remain with General Bonaparte, must sign the simple form, which would be given to them, of their willingness to submit to whatever restrictions might be imposed upon General Bonaparte, without making any remarks of their own upon it. Those who refused would be sent to the Cape of Good Hope. The establishment to be reduced in number four persons ; those who remained were to consider themselves to be amenable to the laws, in the same manner as if they were British subjects, especially to those which had been framed for the safe custody of General Bonaparte, and declaring the aiding and assisting him to escape felony. Any of them abusing, reflecting upon, or behaving ill to the Governor, or the Government they were under, would be forthwith sent to the Cape, where no facilities would be afforded for their conveyance to Europe.' It explained also that it was not to be understood that the obligation was to be perpetual on those who signed. There was also a demand for £1400 paid for books, which had been sent out. The whole was couched in peremptory language. Sir Thomas then told me that Count Bertrand was to go the following day to Plantation House, and that I might hint to him that, if he behaved himself well, perhaps none but domestics would be sent away, but that all depended upon his '*good behaviour.*'

*October* 5.—Count Bertrand went to Plantation House, where he learned that Piontkowski and three of the domestics were to be sent away.

*October* 9.—Sir Hudson Lowe came up to Longwood, accompanied by Colonel Wynyard. They went into Captain Poppleton's room, where they appeared to be very busily occupied for two hours. During this time the Governor frequently came out, and walked up and down before the door, with one of his arms elevated, and the end of a finger in the corner of his mouth, as was his general custom when in thought. When they had finished, a sealed packet was given to Captain Poppleton, to be delivered to Count Bertrand; after which His Excellency came to me, and after some conversation, asked if I thought that any copies of·Montholon's letter to him had been distributed? I replied that it was very probable, as there was no secret made of its contents; and that the French, as he well knew, publicly avowed their intention to circulate copies of it. He asked me if I thought that the Commissioners had got a copy. I replied, 'Very likely.' He appeared uneasy at this at first; but afterwards said that he had shown the letter to them himself. He then asked me if I had got a copy. I replied, I had. This alarmed His Excellency much; who demanded to see it, and said that it would be *felony* to send it to England.

After some discussion upon the subject, during which I observed that, considering my situation, and my being employed as I was between Longwood and Plantation House, I could not be ignorant of the principal part of what was passing, His Excellency said, True; and that it was my duty to tell him everything that occurred between General Bonaparte and myself. I replied that if there was any plot for his escape, or correspondence tending to it, or anything suspicious, I should conceive it my duty to give him notice of it; also if anything of political importance was uttered by Napoleon, or anecdote, clearing up any part of his history, or which might prove serviceable to him, I would make him acquainted with it; but that I could not think of telling him everything, especially anything abusive or injurious, that passed between us, or whatever might tend to generate bad blood, or increase the difference already unhappily exist-ing between them, unless ordered so to do. Sir Hudson at first agreed that it would not be proper to tell him any abuse of himself; but immediately afterwards said that it was essential for me to repeat it; that *one of the means which General Bonaparte had of escaping was vilifying him; that abusing and lowering the character of the Ministry was an underhand and base way of endeavouring to escape from the island ;* and, therefore, that it was incumbent on me to communicate everything of the kind instantly. That as to himself, he did not care about abuse, and would never be actuated by vindictive feelings ; but that he wished to know everything : that nothing ought to be made known or communicated in England, except through him ; and that he himself only communicated with Lord Bathurst.

Not perfectly agreeing with His Excellency's sophistry (especially when I reflected upon the conversation which I had had with him under the trees at Plantation House two days after his last interview with Napoleon), I replied that it did not appear that all the members of His Majesty's Government were of a similar opinion, as I had received letters from official persons, with a request to communicate circumstances relative to Bonaparte, and returning thanks for my former letters, which had been shown to some of the Cabinet Ministers. The Governor was excessively uneasy at this, and observed that those persons had nothing to do with Bonaparte ; that the Secretary of State, with whom he corresponded, was the only one who ought to know anything about the matter ; that *he* did not even communicate what passed to the Duke of York. That none of the Ministers, excepting Lord Bathurst, ought to know what passed ; and that all communication, even to his lordship, ought to go *through him only.* His Excellency then observed that my correspondence ought to be subject to the same restrictions as those on the attendants of General Bonaparte. I replied that if he was not satisfied with the manner in which matters stood, I was ready to resign the situation I held, and go on board ship as soon as he liked, as I was determined not to give up my rights as a British officer. Sir Hudson said that there was no necessity for this; that it would be very easy to arrange matters; and concluded by observing that it was a business which required consideration, and that he would revert to the subject on another day.

*October* 10.—Had some conversation with Napoleon in his dressing-room, during which I endeavoured to convince him that Sir Hudson Lowe might in reality have intended to offer civilities at times when his conduct was supposed to be insulting; that his gestures sometimes indicated intentions far from his thoughts; and particularly explained to him that Sir Hudson Lowe's having laid his hand upon his sword, proceeded entirely from an involuntary habit which he had of seizing his sabre, and raising it between his side and his arm (which I endeavoured to show him by imitation).

This evening Count Bertrand came to my room in order that I should assist him in translating some part of the new restrictions, which were, he said, of a nature so outrageous to the Emperor that he was induced to flatter himself with the idea that he had not understood them. They were those parts where Napoleon was prohibited from going off the

high-road ; from going on the path leading to Miss
Mason's ; from entering any house, and from
conversing with any person whom he might meet
in his rides or walks. Prepared as I was by the
Governor's manner, and by what I had observed
this day, to expect something very severe, I confess
that at the first sight of these restrictions I
remained thunderstruck, and even after reading
them three or four times could scarcely persuade
myself that I had properly understood them.
While I was employed in assisting Count Bertrand
in the translation, Colonel Wynyard came into my
room. When the Count had gone, I told the
Colonel what he wanted, and asked him if I was
right in the construction which I had given, which
I explained to him. Colonel Wynyard replied that
I was perfectly correct.

*October* 11.—Sir Hudson Lowe sent for me to
town. Breakfasted in company with him at Sir
Thomas Reade's ; after which he told me that he
had something particular to say, but that the place
was not a proper one, and another time would do.
Showed to him and to Sir Thomas the translation
which I had made of those points in the restriction of which Count Bertrand had been doubtful.
Sir Hudson observed that I had translated one
part rather too strongly, viz. ' will be required to
be strictly adhered to,' but that I had given a
perfectly correct explanation of the sense. That
the French were not to go down into the valley,
or separate from the high-road, as space was given

them for exercise only to preserve their health. That they were not to speak to any person, or enter any house ; and that no further explanation was needed, as every restriction upon General Bonaparte equally applied to his followers. He concluded by observing that I had better take an opportunity of telling Bonaparte that I had heard the Governor say that the orders originated with the British Government, and that *he* was merely the person who carried them into execution, and not the framer.

*October* 12. — Napoleon, after asking many questions concerning a trial which took place yesterday, at which I had appeared as a witness, spoke about the new restrictions, and observed that Bertrand could not be brought to think that he had rightly comprehended them, and asked me my opinion, which I explained to him as briefly and delicately as I could. When I had finished, ' *Che rabbia di persecuzioni !* ' exclaimed Napoleon. I observed that I had heard the Governor say yesterday that the orders had originated with the British Government, and that he was merely the person who carried them into execution, and not the framer. Napoleon looked at me in a most incredulous manner, smiled, and gave me in a good-natured manner a slap in the face.

A quantity of plate sent to town to-day, and sold in the presence of Sir Thomas Reade to Mr. Balcombe, who was ordered by Reade to pay a certain sum an ounce for it, and the money which

it produced, viz. about £240, was to lie in
Balcombe's hands, and to be drawn for in small
sums, as their necessities required.

Two letters arrived from Sir Hudson Lowe for
Bertrand. I did not see their contents, but was
informed that one related to the new restrictions,
and contained assertions that but little alteration
had taken place in them, and that very little change
in the limits had been ordered. The other a
reprimand to Count Las Cases for having presumed to give Mr. Balcombe (the purveyor) an
order on the Count's banker in London, without
having first asked the Governor's permission, and
also containing a demand for the price of the books
sent out by Government for General Bonaparte's
use. Notwithstanding this, it appeared that Las
Cases had acquainted the Governor with his
intentions, and obtained his consent, which
His Excellency had forgotten, and detained
Las Cases's order when presented to him by Mr.
Balcombe.

*October* 13. — Napoleon in his bath. He
railed against the island, and observed that he
could not walk out when the sun was to be seen
for half an hour without getting a headache, in
consequence of the want of shade, and repeated his
complaints against the Governor. ' In the tribunals
of the inquisition,' he said, 'a man is heard in his
own defence ; but I have been condemned unheard,
and without trial, in violation of all laws, divine and
human ; detained as a prisoner of war in a time of

peace; separated from my wife and child, violently
transported here, where arbitrary and hitherto unknown restrictions are imposed upon me, extending even to the privation of speech. I am
sure,' continued he, 'that none of the Ministers
except Lord Bathurst would give their consent
to this last act of tyranny.[1] His great desire for
secrecy shows that he is afraid of his conduct being
made known, even to the Ministers themselves.
Instead of all this mystery and espionage, they
would do better to treat me in such a manner as
not to be afraid of any disclosures being made.
They profess in England to furnish all my wants,
and in fact they send out many things: this man
then comes out, reduces everything, obliges me
to sell my plate in order to purchase those necessaries of life which he either denies altogether, or
supplies in quantities so small as to be insufficient;
imposes daily new and arbitrary restrictions; insults
me and my followers; concludes with attempting
to deny me the faculty of speech, and then has
the impudence to write that he has changed
nothing! He says that if strangers come to visit
me they cannot speak to any of my suite, and
wishes that they should be presented by him. If
my *son* came to the island, and it were required
that he should be presented by him, I would not
see him. You know,' continued he, 'that it was

---

[1] Napoleon's suspicions as to Lord Bathurst's conduct may not
have been altogether unwarranted if the Emperor had any cognisance
of the fate of Mr. Benjamin Bathurst. For an interesting paper on
this subject see the *Cornhill Magazine* for March 1887.

more a trouble than a pleasure for me to receive
many of the strangers who arrived, some of whom
merely came to gaze at me, as they would at a
*curious beast;* but still it was consoling to have the
right to see them, if I pleased.'

*October* 14.—The paper sent by the Governor
to Longwood, containing an acknowledgment from
the French of their willingness to submit to such
restrictions as had been or might be imposed upon
Napoleon Bonaparte, was signed by all, and sent
to Sir Hudson Lowe.   The only alteration made
by them was the substitution of '*l'Empereur
Napoléon,*' for '*Napoleon Buonaparte.*'

*October* 15.—The papers sent back by the
Governor to Count Bertrand, with a demand that
*Napoleon Buonaparte* should be inserted in the
place of *l'Empereur Napoléon.*

Saw Napoleon, who told me that he had advised
them not to sign it, if altered, but rather to quit
the island, and go to the Cape.

Sir Hudson Lowe came up to Longwood.   I
informed him that I believed the French would not
sign the declaration worded in the manner he
wished.   'I suppose,' replied His Excellency, 'that
they are very glad of it, as it will give them a
pretext to leave General Bonaparte, which I shall
order them to do.'   He then sent for Count
Bertrand, Count Las Cases, and the remainder of
the officers (except Piontkowski), with whom he
had a long conversation.   At eleven o'clock at
night a letter was sent by Sir Hudson Lowe to

Count Bertrand, in which he informed him that in consequence of the refusal of the French officers to sign the declaration with the words *Napoleon Buonaparte*, they and the domestics must all depart for the Cape of Good Hope *instantly*, in a ship which was ready for their reception; with the exception of a cook, *maître d'hôtel*, and one or two of the valets; that in consideration of the delicate state of the Countess Bertrand's health, her husband would be permitted to remain until she was able to bear the voyage.

The prospect of separation from the Emperor caused great grief and consternation among the inmates of Longwood, who, without the knowledge of Napoleon, waited upon Captain Poppleton after midnight and signed the obnoxious paper (with the exception of Santini, who refused to sign any in which his master was not styled *l'Empereur*), which was transmitted to the Governor.

*October* 16.—Napoleon sent Noverraz for me at half-past six in the morning. On my arrival he looked very earnestly at me, and said, laughing, 'You look as if you had been drunk last night.' I replied, No; but that I had dined at the camp, and sat up very late. '*Quante bottiglie, tre?*' he added, holding up three of his fingers. He then told me that Count Bertrand had had a conversation with the Governor yesterday, which partly related to him. That he had sent for me in order that I might explain to the Governor his real sentiments on the subject; and 'here,' continued he, taking up a piece of paper, in which were contained words, in his own handwriting, of a meaning similar to the paper which he subsequently gave to me, ' is what I have written, and which I intend to send to him.'  He then read it out aloud, asking me every now and then if I comprehended him, and said, ' You will take a copy of this to the Governor, and inform him that such are my intentions.  If he asks you why it is not signed by me, you will say that it was unnecessary, because I have read it out and explained it to you from my own handwriting.'  After observing that the name of Napoleon was *troppo ben conosciuto*, and might bring back recollections which it were better should be dropped, he desired me to propose his being called Colonel Muiron, who had been killed at his side at Arcola, or Baron Duroc ; that as colonel was a title denoting military rank, it might perhaps give umbrage, and therefore probably it would be better to adopt that of Baron Duroc, which was the lowest feudal title.  ' If the Governor,' continued he, ' consents, let him signify to Bertrand that he acquiesces in one of them, and such shall be adopted.  It will prevent many difficulties and smooth the way.'  He then rang the bell, called St. Denis, took the paper which he had copied from him, made me read it aloud, underlined some passages with his own hand, gave it to me, and gently pushing me out of the room in a smiling manner, told me to go to the Governor, and tell him that such were his intentions.

The paper was as follows :—

'*In conversations which have taken place with General Lowe and several other gentlemen, statements have been made relative to my position, which are at variance with my own views.*

'*I placed my abdication in favour of my Son in the hands of the Representatives of the Nation. I went with confidence to England, with the intention of living there, or in America, in the most profound retirement, and taking the name of a colonel, killed at my side,* resolved to remain a stranger to every political occurrence, of whatever nature it might be.

'*As soon as I had embarked on the* Northumberland, *I was informed that I was a prisoner of war; that I was to be transported beyond the Line; and that I was to be styled General Bonaparte. In self-vindication and contradistinction to the name of General Bonaparte, which it was wished to impose upon me, I was obliged to maintain on all occasions my title of Emperor.*

'*Seven or eight months ago, Count Montholon proposed to remedy the daily inconveniences thus caused by my adoption of an ordinary name. The Admiral thought it to be his duty to write on the subject to London; there the matter at present rests.*

'*A name is at present given to me, which has the advantage of not wholly obliterating the past, but which is not according to the forms of society.* I am at any time prepared to retire into private life, *and I reiterate, that when it shall be judged proper to discontinue this cruel place of Exile,* I am willing to remain a stranger to politics, whatever events may occur in the world. *This is my intention, and any-thing which may have been said to the contrary is incorrect.'*

I proceeded immediately to Plantation House, where I delivered the paper to the Governor, and made known to him the conversation which I had had. His Excellency appeared much surprised, and said that it was a very important communication, and one which required consideration. After I had made a deposition, the Governor wrote on a sheet of paper the following words : ' The Governor will lose no time in forwarding to the British Government the paper presented to him this day by Dr. O'Meara. He thinks, however, that it would be more satisfactory if it was signed by the person in whose name it was presented. The Governor does not, however, intend to cast by this the slightest doubts upon the authenticity or validity of the paper, either as to the words or spirit, but merely that it would be better to send it in a form to which no objection could be offered. The Governor will consider attentively whether the tenor of his instructions will permit him to adopt either of the names proposed. He would naturally, however, be desirous to defer the use of them in any public communication, until he obtains the sanction of his Government for that purpose. The Governor will be ready at any time to confer with General Bertrand on the subject.' This communica-tion he desired me to show to Napoleon, and added, ' Indeed it is no great matter if you leave it with him.' He then asked me if I thought Napoleon would sign it. I replied perhaps he might, particularly if he (Sir Hudson) would authorise him to use either of the names in question. This, however, he said, he could not yet decide upon. After this, His Excellency told me that I must have no communication whatever with any official persons in England about General Bonaparte ; therefore he insisted that I would not mention a word to them of the proposal which I had just made ; that he had written to Lord Bathurst about me, and that there was no doubt I should do well ; that my situation was one of great confidence, and that none of the Ministers, except the one he communicated with, ought to know anything about what passed at St. Helena. After which he desired me to go back and endeavour to get Napoleon to sign the paper.

On my return to Longwood, I explained to Napoleon the Governor's reply and wishes. He observed, he had not intended that the paper should be left with the Governor, but merely read and shown to him, and then returned, as had taken place once before. That he wished to communicate his sentiments to him, in order to know if he were inclined to meet him half-way. That after communication with Bertrand, a proper letter would be written, and that would be the time to sign. He concluded by directing me to get back the paper.

I went accordingly to Plantation House and acquainted Sir Hudson Lowe that I was directed to bring back the paper, which he returned to me, after some expression of surprise on the part of the Governor, and a hint that such a demand had been caused by shuffling or want of sincerity on the part of Bonaparte, or bad advice from some of his generals. He then asked my opinion whether 'Count Montholon imagined himself secure to remain in the island because he had signed the declaration?' He desired me to say that applying to the British Government was not asking permission for General Bonaparte to change his name, but merely a demand whether they would recognise such a change.

I returned the paper to Napoleon and explained the Governor's sentiments. He observed that if Sir Hudson Lowe would make known to Bertrand, or even to me, that he authorised the change of name, and would address him accordingly, he (Napoleon) would write a letter, declaring that he would adopt one of the names which had been proposed, which he would sign and send to the Governor. 'One half of the vexations that I have experienced here,' said he, 'have arisen from my title.' I observed that many were surprised at his having retained the title after abdication. He replied, 'I abdicated the throne of France, but not the title of Emperor. I do not call myself Napoleon, Emperor of France, but the Emperor Napoleon. Sovereigns generally retain their titles. Thus Charles of Spain retains the title of King and Majesty, after having abdicated in favour of his son. If I were in England, I would not call myself

Emperor. But they want to make it appear that the French nation had not a right to make me its Sovereign. If they had not a right to make me Emperor, they were equally incapable of making me General. A man, when he is at the head of a few, during the disturbances of a country, is called a chief of rebels ; but when he succeeds, performs great actions, and exalts his country and himself, from being styled chief of rebels, he is called general, sovereign, etc. It is only success which makes him such. Had he been unfortunate, he would be still chief of rebels, and perhaps perish on a scaffold. Your nation,' continued he, 'called Washington a leader of rebels for a long time, and refused to acknowledge either him or the constitution of his country ; but his successes obliged them to change and acknowledge both. It is success which makes the great man.'

He then spoke in terms of great praise of Counts Bertrand, Montholon, Las Cases, and the rest of his suite, for the heroic devotion which they had manifested, and the proofs of attachment to his person which they had given, by remaining with him contrary to his desire.

I asked him later on, the conversation passing to the topic, which he thought had been the best Minister of Police, Savary[1] or Fouché,[2] adding, that both of them had a bad reputation in England. 'Savary,' said he, 'is not a bad man ; on the contrary, Savary is a man of a good heart, and a

[1] Duke of Rovigo.          [2] Duke of Otranto.

brave soldier.   You have seen him weep.[1]   He loves me with the affection of a son.

'Fouché is a miscreant of all colours, a priest, a terrorist, and one who took an active part in many bloody scenes in the Revolution.[2]   He is a man who can worm all your secrets out of you with an air of the most perfect unconcern.   He is very rich,' added he, 'but his riches were badly acquired.   There was a tax upon gambling-houses in Paris, but as it was an infamous way of gaining money, I did not like to profit by it, and therefore ordered that the amount of the tax should be appropriated to an hospital for the poor.   It amounted to some millions, but Fouché, who had the collecting of the impost, put many of them into his own pockets, and it was impossible for me to discover the real yearly total.'

I observed to him that it had excited considerable surprise that, during the height of his glory, he had never given a dukedom in France to any person, although he had created many dukes and princes elsewhere.[3]   He replied, 'Because it would have

---

[1] Scene at Plymouth on taking leave of the Emperor.   See *Las Cases*, vol. i., part i., p. 70, 1824, English edition.   .

[2] 'Confiscations, proscriptions, massacres, attended his ' [Fouché's] 'path in the departments of the Aube and Nièvre . . . eighty-three of the clergy he sent to Nantes to figure in the famous *noyades;* and the churches were everywhere plundered and laid waste.   Not only was the guillotine kept constantly at work, but hundreds of victims were despatched at once by grape-shot.'—*Court and Camp of Buonaparte*, p. 64.

[3] A list of the Sovereign and other titles conferred by the Emperor Napoleon (above that of Count or Baron) will be found in the Appendix to the 1885 English edition of Bourrienne's *Memoirs of Napoleon*.

produced great discontent amongst the people. If, for example, I had made one of my marshals Duke of Burgundy, instead of giving him a title derived from one of my victories, it would have excited great alarm in Burgundy, as they would have conceived that some feudal rights and territory were attached to the title, which the duke would claim ; and the nation hated the old nobility so much, that the creation of any rank resembling them would have given universal discontent, which I, powerful as I was, dared not venture upon. I instituted the new nobility to *écraser* the old, and to satisfy the people, as the greatest part of those I created had sprung from themselves, and every private soldier had a right to aspire to the title of Duke. I believe that I acted wrongly in doing even this, as it lessened that system of equality which pleased the people so much ; but if I had created dukes with French titles, it would have been considered as a revival of the old feudal privileges, with which the nation had been cursed so long.'

He complained of his general health, and added that he felt convinced that, under all the circumstances, he could not last long. I advised exercise and the diet I had formerly recommended. He observed that he had put in practice the diet and the other remedies, but as to taking exercise (which was the most essential), the restrictions presented an insurmountable obstacle. He asked many anatomical questions, particularly about the heart, and observed, 'I think that my heart does not beat; I have

never felt it pulsate.' He then desired me to feel
his heart. I tried for some time, but could not
perceive any pulsation, which I attributed to obesity.
I had before observed that his circulation was
very feeble, rarely exceeding fifty-eight or sixty in
a minute, and most frequently fifty-four.

*October* 18.—Captain Piontkowski, Rousseau, Santini, and Archambaud cadet, were the persons named
by Sir Hudson Lowe to be removed from Longwood. Count Montholon desired me to inform the
Governor that the Emperor did not wish to separate
the brothers Archambaud, which, moreover, would
totally disorganise the carriage, and must consequently deprive him of the little means he had of
taking exercise, as the Governor was aware that in
such a place as St. Helena, where the roads were so
dangerous, it was very necessary to have careful
drivers. He added, that if the choice of those who
were to go were left to Napoleon, he would fix upon
Rousseau, Santini, and Bernard, who was a useless
subject, and much given to intoxication, or Gentilini,
as he thought that it would be great cruelty to separate two brothers.

Communicated this to Sir Hudson Lowe, who
replied that the choice was not left to General
Bonaparte ; that the servants were to be taken from
Longwood, and not from Count Bertrand ; and,
moreover, that the orders were to send away *Frenchmen*, and not natives of other countries. That
Bernard was a Flamand, and Gentilini an Italian,
and therefore did not come within the strict applica-

tion of his orders ; that if Santini had not refused to sign the paper, he would not have accepted him as one, as he was a Corsican, and *not* a Frenchman. He had no objection, however, that all the *Frenchmen* in General Bonaparte's service should draw lots. These circumstances he desired I might impress upon General Bonaparte's mind. He added that, as by his instructions the choice was left to him, he would give written directions to Captain Poppleton to send away Piontkowski, and both of the Archambauds, if Rousseau remained, or one of them, if Rousseau were to go.

He then directed me to ask if he were to expect any further communication respecting the change of name, as the vessel containing his despatches on the subject would sail for England in the evening.[1]

On my return to Longwood, communicated this to Napoleon, who replied, ' Is it in the Governor's power to authorise the change ? In the note he sent the contrary appears.' I answered that I knew nothing more than what I had already communicated. ' Then,' said he, ' before any further steps are taken,

---

[1] The only reply which His Majesty's Ministers condescended to make to this proposal was contained in a virulent article in the *Quarterly Review*, No. XXXII., which Sir Hudson Lowe took care should be sent to Longwood as soon as a copy had reached the island. I think that I am justified in attributing the article alluded to to some ministerial person, as the transaction was known only to officers in their employment, and to the establishment at Longwood, and it is evident that the persons composing the latter could not have been the authors of it.—B. E. O'M.

It will be remembered that Croker, the Secretary of the Admiralty, the man who expressed his regret at the continued health of Napoleon, was a regular contributor to the *Quarterly*.

let him reply positively whether he is authorised or not, *Si o no.*' Informed him of His Excellency's opinion and decision relative to the domestics who were to leave St. Helena. 'Santini not a Frenchman?' said he, 'Doctor, you cannot be imbecile enough not to see that this is a pretext to convey an insult to me. All Corsicans are Frenchmen. By taking away my drivers, he wants to prevent me from taking a little carriage exercise.'

*October* 19.—Piontkowski, Santini, Rousseau, and Archambaud the younger, sent by order of Sir Hudson Lowe to town in order to embark. Santini had a pension of £50, Archambaud and Rousseau £25 each, annually, settled upon them; Piontkowski had also a pension and a letter of recommendation. On embarkation, their persons and baggage were searched by Captain Maunsell and the prevost serjeant. They sailed in the evening for the Cape. Piontkowski was stripped to the skin by Captain Maunsell.

Communicated to Sir Hudson Lowe Napoleon's last remarks concerning the change of name, who replied, 'I believe that it is in my power to approve of it.' I then recommended him to see Count Bertrand upon the subject, and his Excellency proceeded to Hut's Gate accordingly.

*October* 20.—Count and Countess Bertrand and family moved from Hut's Gate to Longwood.

*October* 21.—Dined at Plantation House in company with the Russian and Austrian Commissioners, the botanist, and Captain Gor. They

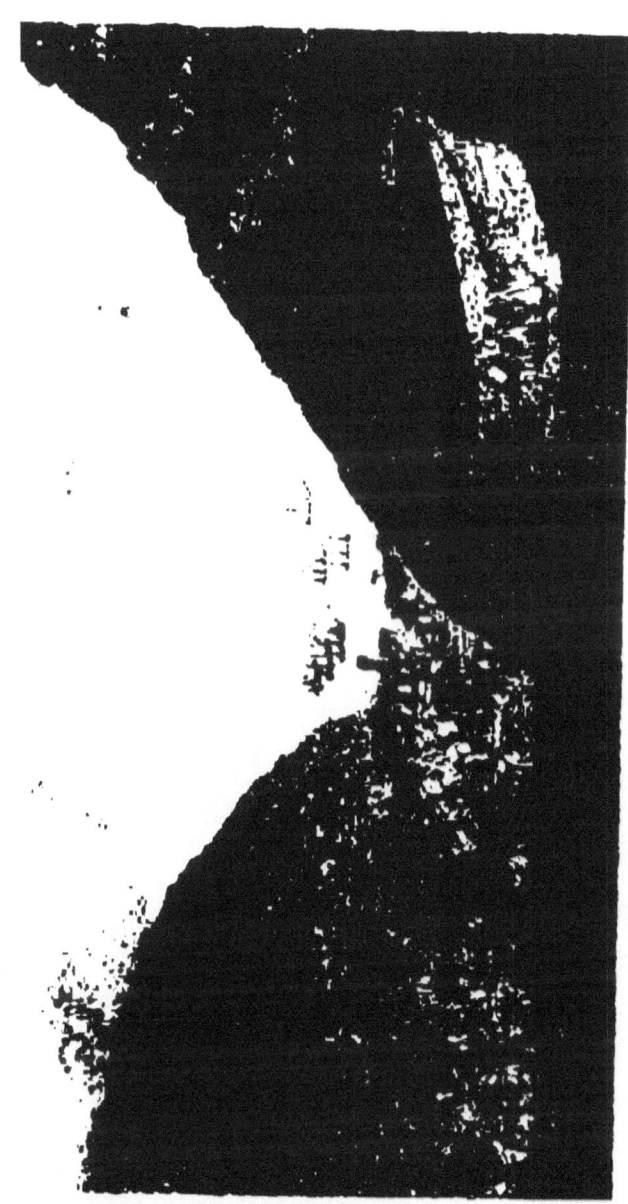

VIEW OF St HELENA ROADS, FROM THE HEIGHTS BEHIND JAMES TOWN.

ned him of His Ex
relative to the dome
ena. 'Santini not a
tor, you cannot be
this is a pretext to c
rsicans are Frenchr
rs, he wants to pr
riage exercise.'
tkowski. Santini. I
rounger, sent by ord
in order to embark.
. Archambaud and
ted upon them . Pic
r . letter of recomm

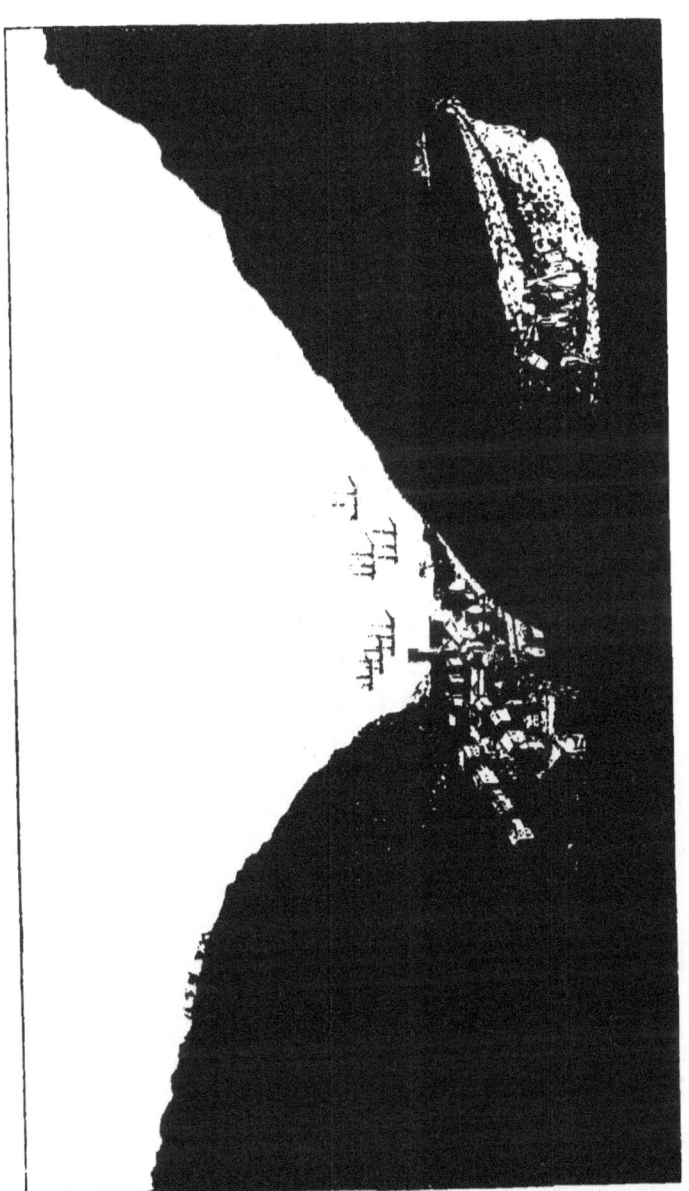

VIEW OF ST HELENA ROADS, FROM THE HEIGHTS BEHIND JAMES TOWN.

LONDON. RICHARD BENTLEY & SON. 1887.

generally expressed great dissatisfaction at not
having yet seen Napoleon.   Count Balmaine in
particular observed that they (the Commissioners)
appeared to be objects of suspicion ; that had he
been aware of the manner in which they should have
been treated, he would not have come out.   That
the Emperor Alexander had great interest in preventing the escape of Napoleon, but that he wished
him to be well treated,[1] and with that respect due to
him : for which reason he (Count Balmaine) had
only asked to see him as a private person and not
officially as Commissioner.   That they should be
objects of ridicule in Europe as soon as it was known
they had been so many months in St. Helena without ever once seeing the individual to ascertain
whose presence was the sole object of their mission.
That the Governor always replied to their questions
that Bonaparte had refused to receive any person
whatsoever.   The botanist held language of a similar tendency, and remarked that Longwood was '*le
dernier séjour du monde*,' and in his opinion the
worst part of the island.

*October* 22. — Sir Hudson Lowe sent for me,
and observed that the Commissioners seemed to
have paid me much attention ; that he should think
nothing of their speaking as long as they had done

---

[1] Balmaine himself wrote to Lowe, 21st July 1816 : '*La volonté
de l'empereur* (Alexander) *mon maître, étant que je ne blesse en aucune
circonstance les égards personnels qui lui sont dus.*'—*Sturmer*, p. 155.
Had similar orders been given to any ordinary English officer entrusted with the custody of Napoleon, these volumes would never have
been written.

to me, to any other person, but that it had an appearance as if they wished something to be conveyed to General Bonaparte, and advised me to be very cautious in my conversations with them. He also informed me that Count Bertrand had confirmed to him every communication that I had made relative to the change of name.[1]

*October* 26.—Napoleon out in the carriage for the first time for a considerable period. Observed to me afterwards that he had followed my prescription. His face much better.

'English soldiers,' said the Emperor in course of our conversation, 'are not equal in address, activity, or intelligence to the French. When they get from under the fear of the lash, they obey nobody. In a retreat, they cannot be managed; and if they meet with wine, they are so many devils, and adieu to subordination. I saw the retreat of Moore, and I never witnessed anything like it. It was impossible to collect or to make them do anything. Nearly all were drunk. Your officers depend for promotion upon interest or money. Your soldiers are brave, nobody can deny it; but it was bad policy to encourage the military mania instead of sticking to your marine, which is the real force of your country, and one which, while you preserve it, will always render

---

[1] '*Friday, October* 25, 1816.—I attended the Emperor at his toilette. The weather was tolerably fine, and he went out, and walked as far as the wood. He was very feeble; for it was now ten days since he had stirred out. He felt a weakness in his knees; and remarked that he should soon be obliged to lean on me for support.'—*Las Cases*, vol. iv., part vii., p. 1, English edition.

you powerful. In order to have good soldiers a nation must *always be at war.'*

'If you had lost the battle of Waterloo,' continued he, 'what a state would England have been in! The flower of your youth would have been destroyed; for not a man, not even Lord Wellington, would have escaped.' I observed here that Lord Wellington had determined never to leave the field alive. Napoleon replied, ' He could not retreat. He would have been destroyed with his army if, instead of the Prussians, Grouchy had come up.'[1] I asked him if he had not believed for some time that the Prussians who had shown themselves were a part of Grouchy's corps. He replied, 'Certainly; and I can now scarcely comprehend why it was a Prussian division and not that of Grouchy.' I then took the liberty of asking whether, if neither Grouchy nor the Prussians had arrived, it would not have been a drawn battle. Napoleon answered, 'The English army would have been destroyed. They were defeated at mid-day. But accident, or more likely destiny, decided that Lord Wellington should gain it. I could scarcely believe that he would have given me battle ; because if he had retreated to Antwerp, as he ought to have done, I must have been over-whelmed by the armies of three or four hundred thousand men that were coming against me. By giving me battle there was a chance for me.

' It was the greatest folly to divide the English and Prussian armies. They ought to have been united ;

---

[1] See footnote on p. 334 ; also vol. ii. p. 25.

and I cannot conceive the reason of their separation. It was folly in Wellington to give me battle in a place where, if defeated, all must have been lost, for he could not retreat. There was a wood in his rear, and but one road to gain it. He would have been destroyed. Moreover, he allowed himself to be surprised by me. This was a great fault. He ought to have been encamped from the beginning of June, as he must have known that I intended to attack him. He might have lost everything. But he has been fortunate; his destiny has prevailed; and everything he did will meet with applause. My intentions were to attack and to destroy the English. This I knew would produce an immediate change of Ministry. The indignation against them for having caused the loss of forty thousand of the flower of the English army would have excited such a popular commotion that they would have been turned out. The people would have said, " What is it to us who is on the throne of France, Louis or Napoleon; are we to sacrifice all our blood in endeavours to place on the throne a detested family? No, we have suffered enough. It is no affair of ours,—let them settle it amongst themselves." They would have made peace. The Saxons, Bavarians, Belgians, Wurtembergers, would have joined me. The coalition was nothing without England. The Russians would have made peace, and I should have been quietly seated on the throne. Peace would have been permanent, as what could France do after the treaty of Paris? What was to be feared from her ?'

' Pitt and his politics,' continued he, ' nearly ruined
England by keeping up a continental war with
France.' I remarked that it was asserted by many
able politicians in England that, if we had not carried
on that war, we should have been ruined and ultimately have become a province of France. ' It is
not true,' said Napoleon ; ' England being at war
with France, gave the latter a pretence and an
opportunity of extending her conquest under me, to
the length she did, until I became Emperor of nearly
all the world, which could not have happened if
there had been no war.' The conversation then
turned upon the occupation of Malta. ' Two days,'
said he, ' before Lord Whitworth left Paris, an offer
was made to the Minister and to others about me of
thirty millions of francs, and to acknowledge me as
King of France, provided I would give up Malta to
you.' He added, however, that the war would have
broken out had Malta been out of the question.

Some conversation then took place relative to
English seamen. Napoleon observed that the
English seamen were as much superior to the
French as the latter were to the Spaniards. I
ventured to say that I thought the French would
never make good seamen, on account of their im-
patience and volatility of temper. That especially
they would never submit without complaining, as
we had done at Toulon, to blockade ports for years
together, suffering from the combined effects of bad
weather, and of privations of every kind. ' I do not
agree with you there, *Signor dottore*,' said he, ' but I

do not think that they will ever make as good seamen as yours. The sea is yours,—your seamen are
as much superior to ours as the Dutch were once to
yours. I think, however, that the Americans are
better seamen than yours, because they are less
numerous.' I observed that the Americans had a
considerable number of English seamen in their
service who passed for Americans, which was remarkable, as, independently of other circumstances,
the American discipline on board of men-of-war was
much more severe than ours. And that if the
Americans had a large navy, they would find it
impossible to have so many able seamen in each
ship as they had at present. When I observed that
the American discipline was more severe than ours,
he smiled and said, ' *Sarebbe difficile a credere.*'

Five P.M.—Napoleon sent for me. Found him
sitting in a chair opposite to the fire. He had gone
out to walk, and was seized with rigors, headache,
severe cough. Examined his tonsils, which were
swelled. Cheek inflamed. Had severest rigors
while I was present. ' *Je tremble,*' said he to Count
Las Cases, who was present, ' *comme si j'eusse peur.*'
Pulse much quickened. He asked a great many
questions about fever.

Saw him again at nine in bed. He had strictly
complied with my directions ; I was desirous that
he should take a diaphoretic, but he preferred trusting
to warm diluents. He imputed his complaint to the
*ventaccio* eternally blowing over the bleak and
exposed site of Longwood. ' I ought,' said he, ' to

be at the Briars, or at the other side of the
island, instead of being on this horrid spot. While
I was there last year at this season I was very
well.' He asked what I thought was the easiest
mode of dying, and observed that death by cold
was the easiest of all others, because '*si muore
dormendo.*' [1]

Sent a letter to Sir Hudson Lowe, acquainting
him with Napoleon's indisposition.

*October* 27.—A free perspiration took place in
the night, and Napoleon was considerably better.
Had some conversation with him relative to the
Empress Josephine, of whom he spoke in the most
affectionate terms. His first acquaintance with
Madame Beauharnais commenced after the disarm-
ing of the sections in Paris, subsequently to the 13th
of Vendemiaire 1795. 'A boy of twelve or thirteen
years old presented himself to me,' continued he,
'and entreated that his father's sword (who had
been a General of the Republic) should be returned.[2]
I was so touched by this affectionate request that
I ordered it to be given to him. This boy was
Eugene Beauharnais. On seeing the sword he
burst into tears. I felt so much affected by his
conduct that I noticed and praised him much. A
few days afterwards his mother came to return me
a visit of thanks. I was much struck with her
appearance, and still more with her *esprit.* This

---

[1] Probably from what he had seen in Russia, when men fell dead
while marching, or were found dead round the fires by which they
had slept.

[2] The possibility of this is denied.

first impression was daily strengthened, and marriage was not long in following.'[1]

Saw Sir Hudson Lowe. Informed him of Napoleon's state of health, that he had attributed his complaints to the bleak and exposed situation of Longwood, and that he had expressed a desire to be removed either to the Briars, or to the other side of the island. His Excellency replied, ' The fact is, that General Bonaparte wants to get Plantation House ; but the East India Company will not consent to have so fine an estate given to a set of Frenchmen, to destroy the trees and ruin the gardens.'

*October* 30.— Napoleon consented to make use of a gargle of infusion of roses and sulphuric acid. He inveighed against the barbarous climate of Longwood, and again mentioned the Briars.[2]

Again informed Sir Hudson Lowe of the state of Napoleon's health, and of his desire to be removed to the Briars. His Excellency replied that if General Bonaparte wanted to make himself comfortable, and to get reconciled to the island, he ought to draw

---

[1] ' Napoleon often looked at my mother for a long time very earnestly and then apologised, saying that she reminded him so much of Josephine. Her memory appeared to be idolised by him, and he was never weary of dwelling on her sweetness of disposition and the grace of her movements. He said she was the most truly feminine woman he had ever known,—the most amiable, elegant, charming, and affable woman in the world. . . . And, moreover, she was so humane, and was the *best* of women. . . . " Josephine was grace personified ; everything she did was marked with it. She never acted inelegantly during the whole time we lived together ! " '—Mrs. Abell's *Recollections of the Emperor Napoleon*, 1873 edition, pp. 97, 98.

[2] The Briars is nearly two miles distant from the seashore.

upon some of those large sums of money which he possessed, and lay them out in purchasing a house and grounds. I said that Napoleon had told me he did not know where his money was placed. Sir Hudson replied, ' I suppose he told you that, in order that you might repeat it to me.'

*November* 1.—Napoleon better. Some tumefaction of the legs and enlargement of the glands of the thigh. Recommended him to take some sulphate of magnesia, or Glauber's salts. Another portion of plate broken up, in order to be sent to town for sale.

*November* 2. — Nearly the same. Again recommended him in the strongest terms to take exercise as soon as the state of his cheeks and of the weather would admit of it.

During the conversation I took the liberty of asking the Emperor his reasons for having encouraged the Jews so much. He replied, ' I wanted to make them leave off usury and become like other men. There were a great many Jews in the countries I reigned over ; by removing their disabilities, and by putting them upon an equality with Catholics, Protestants, and others, I hoped to make them become good citizens, and conduct themselves like the rest of the community.[1] I believe that I should have succeeded in the end. My reasoning

---

[1] The Jewish disabilities in England were not totally removed till 1858, 'the Corsican' having anticipated us in that as in many other matters. The great meeting of the Sanhedrim was held in Paris in September 1806, and February and March 1807.

with them was that, as their rabbins explained to them, they ought not to practise usury against their own tribes, but were allowed to practise it with Christians and others ; therefore, as I had restored them to all their privileges, and made them equal to my other subjects, they must consider me, like Solomon or Herod, to be the head of their nation, and my subjects as brethren of a tribe similar to theirs. That, consequently, they were not permitted to deal usuriously with them or me, but to treat us as if we were of the tribe of Judah. That, enjoying similar privileges to my other subjects, they were, in like manner, to pay taxes and submit to the laws of conscription, and to other laws. By this I gained many soldiers. Besides, I should have drawn great wealth to France, as the Jews are very numerous, and would have flocked to a country where they enjoyed such superior privileges.

'Moreover, I wanted to establish an universal liberty of conscience. My system was to have no predominant religion, but to allow perfect liberty of conscience and of thought, to make all men equal, whether Protestants, Catholics, Mahometans, Deists, or others ; so that their religion should have no influence in getting them employments under Government. In fact, that it should neither be the means of serving nor of injuring them ; and that no objection should be made to a man's getting a situation on the score of religion, provided he were fit for it in other respects. I made everything independent of religion. All the tribunals were so. Marriages were independent of the priests; even the burying-grounds were not left at their disposal, as they could not refuse interment to the body of any person, of whatsoever religion.[1] My intention was to render everything belonging to the State and the Constitution purely civil, without reference to any religion. I wished to deprive the priests of all influence and power in civil affairs, and to oblige them to confine themselves to their own spiritual matters and meddle with nothing else.' I asked if uncles and nieces had not a right to marry in France. He replied, 'Yes, but they must obtain a special permission.' I asked if the permission were to be granted by the Pope. 'By the Pope?' said he; 'No,' catching me by the ear and smiling, 'I tell you that neither the Pope nor any of his priests had power to grant anything.—By the Sovereign.'

[1] The stinging reproof in the columns of the *Moniteur* from the pen of Napoleon (Junot's *Memoirs*, English edition of 1883, vol. ii. p. 274) to the Curé of St. Roche will not be readily forgotten: 'The Curé of St. Roche, in a temporary aberration of reason, has refused to pray for Mademoiselle Chameroi, and to admit her remains within the church. One of his colleagues, a sensible man, versed in the true morality of the Gospel, received the body into the church of the Filles St. Thomas, where the service was performed with all the usual solemnities. The Archbishop has ordered the Curé of St. Roche three months' suspension, to remind him that Jesus Christ commands us to pray for even our enemies, and in order that— recalled to a sense of his duty by meditation—he may learn that all the superstitious practices preserved by some rituals, but which— begotten in times of ignorance, or created by the overheated imagination of zealots—degrade religion by their triviality, were proscribed by the Concordat and by the law of the 18th Germinal.'

I asked some questions relative to the Freemasons, and his opinions concerning them. 'A set
of imbeciles who meet, · *à faire bonne chère*, and
perform some ridiculous fooleries. However,' said
he, 'they do some good actions. They assisted in
the Revolution, and latterly to diminish the power
of the Pope and the influence of the clergy. When
the sentiments of a people are against the Government, every society has a tendency to do mischief
to it.' I then asked if the Freemasons on the Continent had any connection with the Illuminati. He
replied, ' No, that is a society altogether different,
and in Germany is of a very dangerous nature.' I
asked if he had not encouraged the Freemasons?
He said, ' Rather so, for they fought against the
Pope.' I then asked if he ever would have permitted the re-establishment of the Jesuits in
France? ' Never,' said he ; ' it is the most dangerous of societies, and has done more mischief than
all the others. Their doctrine is, that their General
is the Sovereign of sovereigns, and master of the
world ; that all orders from him, however contrary
to the laws, or however wicked, must· be obeyed.
Every act, however atrocious, committed by them pur-
suant to orders from their General at Rome, becomes
in their eyes meritorious. No, no ; I would never
have allowed a society to exist in my dominions
under the orders of a foreign General at Rome.
In fact, I would not allow any *frati*. There were
priests sufficient for those who wanted them without having monasteries filled with *canaglie*, who did

nothing but gormandise, pray, and commit crimes.'
I observed that it was to be feared the priests and
the Jesuits would soon have great influence in
France.   Napoleon replied, 'Very likely.   The
Bourbons are fanatics, and would willingly bring
back both the Jesuits and the Inquisition.   In reigns
before mine the Protestants were as badly treated
as the Jews; they could not purchase land—I put
them upon a level with the Catholics.   They will
now be trampled upon by the Bourbons, to whom
they and everything else liberal will always be
objects of suspicion.[1]   The Emperor Alexander
may allow them to enter his empire, because it is
his policy to draw into his barbarous country men
of information, whatsoever their sect may be, and,
moreover, they are not to be much feared in Russia,
because the religion is different.'

The following was his description of Carnot.[2]   A
man laborious and sincere, but liable to be deceived.
He directed the operations of war without having
merited the eulogiums which were pronounced upon
him, as he had neither the theory nor the experience of war.   When Minister of War he had many
quarrels with the Minister of Finance and the
Treasury; in all of which he was wrong.   He left
the Ministry, convinced that he could not maintain
his station for want of money.   He afterwards
voted against the establishment of the Empire, but

[1] The attacks on the Protestants in 1815, after the second
Restoration, in the south of France, will be remembered.   See
*Guizot*, vol. viii. p. 247.

[2] The grandfather of the present President of the French Republic.

as his conduct was always upright, he never gave
any umbrage to the Government. During the
prosperity of the Empire he never asked for anything; but after the misfortunes in Russia he demanded employment, and got the command of
Antwerp, where he acquitted himself very well.
After my return from Elba, he was Minister of the
Interior; and I had every reason to be satisfied
with his conduct. He was faithful, a man of truth
and probity, and laborious in his exertions. At my
abdication he was named one of the Provisional
Government, but he was *joué* by the intriguers by
whom he was surrounded. He was thought eccen-
tric by his companions when he was young. He
hated the nobles, and on that account had several
quarrels with Robespierre, who latterly protected
many of them. He was Member of the Committee
of Public Safety along with Robespierre, Couthon,
St. Just, and the other butchers, and was the only
one who was not denounced. He afterwards
demanded to be included in the denunciation,
and to be tried for his conduct as well as the others,
which was refused; but his having asked to share
the fate of the rest gained him great credit.

'Barras,' Napoleon said, 'was a violent man, and
possessed of little knowledge or resolution; fickle,
and far from meriting the reputation which he enjoyed, although from the violence of his manner
and loudness of tone in the beginning of his
speeches, one would have thought otherwise.'

*November* 5.—Sir Hudson Lowe at Longwood.

Informed him that although Napoleon was much better, it was my opinion that, if he persisted in the system of confining himself to his room, and in not taking exercise, he would soon be attacked by some serious complaint, and that in all probability his existence in St. Helena would not be protracted for more than a year or two. Sir Hudson asked with some degree of asperity, 'Why did he not take exercise?' I briefly recapitulated to him some of his own restrictions :[1] amongst others, that of placing sentinels, with orders to let nobody out, at the gates of the garden in which he had formerly walked, at six o'clock in the afternoon, which, being the cool of the evening, was the most desirable time to walk. Sir Hudson said they were not placed at six o'clock, but only at sunset. I observed to His Excellency that the sun set immediately after six, and that in the tropics the twilight was of a very short duration.

[1] We had cleared our valley as usual, and were reascending it at the back part opposite Longwood, when a soldier from one of the heights, where there had hitherto been no post, called out several times, and made various signs to us. As we were in the very centre of our circuit we paid no attention to him. He then came running down towards us, out of breath, charging his piece as he ran. General Gourgaud remained behind to see what he wanted, while we continued our route. I could see the General, after dodging the fellow many times, collar and secure him ; he made him follow him as far as the neighbouring post by the Grand Marshal's, which the General endeavoured to make him enter, but he escaped from him. He found that he was a drunken corporal who had not rightly understood his watchword. He had frequently levelled his piece at us. This circumstance, which might have been very easily repeated, made us tremble for the Emperor's life : the latter looked upon it only as an affront and a fresh obstacle to the continuance of his exercises on horseback.—*Las Cases*, vol. i., part ii., p. 113, English edition.

The Governor then sent for Captain Poppleton, and made some inquiries concerning the posting of the sentinels and their orders. Captain Poppleton informed him that the orders which were issued to the sentinels being verbal were continually liable to be misunderstood.

After some further conversation Sir Hudson Lowe observed, he thought it very extraordinary that General Bonaparte would not ride out with a British officer. I remarked that he would in all probability, if matters were well managed. For example, if, when he mounted his horse, an officer was sent after him at a short distance to watch his motions, I could answer to His Excellency that Napoleon, although he should well know what the officer's business was, would never appear to be aware of it, and that he would be just as secure as if an officer rode by his side. I went so far as to say that Napoleon had himself intimated to me that he would not *see* any person following him, provided it were not officially made known that he was a guard over him. Sir Hudson replied that he would consider it, and desired me to write him a statement of my opinion of the health of General Bonaparte ; cautioning me that in writing it I must bear in mind that the life of one man was not to be put into competition with the mischief which he might cause were he to get loose ;[1] and that I must

---

[1] This being an awkward statement, Forsyth (vol. i. p. 365) gets rid of it by simply disbelieving it ; but surely it is only in accordance with Lowe's whole conduct, and he himself certainly would have agreed with the statement that anything was allowable to prevent Napoleon's escape.

recollect, General Bonaparte had been already a curse to the world, and had caused the loss of many thousands of lives. That my situation was very peculiar and one of great political importance.

A quantity of plate which had been broken up, taken to town by Cipriani, and deposited with Balcombe, Cole, and Co. in the presence of Sir Thomas Reade, to whom the key of the chest containing it was delivered.

*November 7.*—Napoleon much better, and nearly free from complaint.

*November 8.*—Napoleon asked me many ana-tomical and physiological questions, and observed that he had studied anatomy himself for a few days, but had been sickened by the sight of some bodies that were opened, and abandoned any further pro-gress in that science. Later, upon an opportunity arising, I made a few remarks upon the Poles who had served in his army, who, I observed, were greatly attached to his person. 'Ah!' replied the Emperor, 'they *were* much attached to me. The present Viceroy of Poland was with me in my campaigns in Egypt.[1] I made him a General. Most of my old Polish guard are now through policy employed by Alexander. They are a brave nation, and make good soldiers. In the cold which prevails in the northern countries the Pole is better than the Frenchman.' I asked him if in less rigorous climates the Poles were as good soldiers as the French. 'Oh no, no. In other places the French-

[1] General Prince Joseph Zayonchek.

man is much superior. The commandant of Dantzic
informed me that during the severity of the winter,
when the thermometer indicated eighteen degrees
of frost, it was impossible to make the French
soldiers keep their posts as sentinels, while the
Poles suffered nothing. Poniatowsky,' continued
he, 'was a noble character, full of honour and
bravery. It was my intention to have made him
King of Poland had I succeeded in Russia.'

I asked to what he principally attributed his
failure in that expedition. 'To the cold, the premature cold, and the burning of Moscow,' replied
Napoleon. 'I was a few days too late—I had made
a calculation of the weather for fifty years before,
and the extreme cold had never commenced until
about the 20th of December, twenty days later than
it began this time. While I was at Moscow, the
cold was at three degrees Ce. of the thermometer,
and was such as the French could with pleasure
bear; but on the march the thermometer sunk
eighteen degrees, and consequently nearly all the
horses perished. In one night I lost nearly thirty
thousand. The artillery, of which I had five hundred
pieces, was in a great measure obliged to be abandoned; neither ammunition nor provisions could be
carried. We could not, through the want of horses,
make a *reconnaissance*, or send out an advance
piquet of men on horseback to discover the way.
The soldiers lost their spirits and their senses, and
fell into confusion. The most trifling circumstance
alarmed them. Four or five men were sufficient

to terrify a whole battalion. Instead of keeping together, they wandered about in search of fire. Parties, when sent out on duty in advance, abandoned their posts, and went to seek the means of warming themselves in the houses. They separated in all directions, became helpless, and fell an easy prey to the enemy. Others lay down, fell asleep, a little blood came from their nostrils, and, sleeping, they died. In this manner thousands perished. The Poles saved some of their horses and artillery, but the French, and the soldiers of the other nations, were no longer the same men. In particular, the cavalry suffered. Out of forty thousand, I do not think that three thousand were saved.

' Had it not been for the burning of Moscow, I should have succeeded. I would have wintered there. There were in that city about forty thousand people who were practically slaves. For you must know that the Russian nobility keep their vassals in a sort of slavery. I would have proclaimed liberty to all the slaves in Russia, and abolished serfdom and nobility. This would have procured me the support of an immense and a powerful party. I would either have made peace at Moscow, or else I would have marched the next year to St. Petersburg. Alexander was so assured of it that he sent his diamonds, valuables, and ships to England. Had it not been for that fire, I should have succeeded in everything. Two days before I beat them in a great action at Moskwa; I attacked the Russian army of two hundred and fifty thousand

strong, intrenched up to their necks, with ninety
thousand, and totally defeated them.    Seventy
thousand Russians lay upon the field.    They had
the impudence to say that they had gained the
battle, although I marched into Moscow two days
after.    I was in the midst of a fine city, provisioned
for a year, for in Russia they always lay in provisions
for several months before the frost sets in.    Stores
of all kinds were in plenty.    The houses of the
inhabitants were well provided, and many had even
left their servants to attend upon us.    In most of
them there was a note left by the proprietor, begging
the French officers who took possession to be careful
of their furniture and other effects ; that they had
left every article necessary for our wants, and
hoped to return in a few days, when the Emperor
Alexander had accommodated matters, at which
time they would be happy to see us.

'Many ladies remained behind.    They knew that
I had been in Berlin and Vienna with my armies,
and that no injury had been done to the inhabitants;
and, moreover, they expected a speedy peace.    We
were in hopes of enjoying ourselves in winter quarters, with every prospect of success in the spring.
Two days after our arrival a fire was discovered,
which at first was not supposed to be alarming, but
to have been caused by the soldiers kindling their
fires too near to the houses, which were chiefly of
wood.    I was angry at this, and issued very strict
orders on the subject to the commandants of regi-
ments and others.    The next day it had increased,

but still not so as to give serious alarm.    However, afraid that it might gain upon us, I went out on horseback and gave every direction to extinguish it.

'The next morning a violent wind arose, and the fire spread with the greatest rapidity.    Some hundred miscreants, hired for that purpose, dispersed themselves in different parts of the town, and with matches,[1] which they concealed under their cloaks, set fire to as many houses to windward as they could, which was easily done, in consequence of the combustible materials of which they were built.    This, together with the violence of the wind, rendered every effort to extinguish the fire ineffectual.    I myself narrowly escaped with life.    In order to show an example, I ventured into the midst of the flames, and had my hair and eyebrows singed, and my clothes burnt off my back ; but it was in vain, as they had destroyed most of the pumps, of which there were above a thousand ; out of all these, I believe that we could only find one that was serviceable.    Besides, the wretches that had been hired by Rostopchin ran about in every quarter, disseminating fire with their matches ; in which they were but too much assisted by the wind.

'This terrible conflagration ruined everything. I was prepared for all but this.    It was unforeseen,

---

[1] The old-fashioned tinder probably.    Friction matches were invented by Walker of Stockton-upon-Tees in April 1827 ; and lucifer matches a few years later.

for who would have thought that a nation would have set its capital on fire ? The inhabitants themselves, however, did all they could to extinguish it, and several of them perished in their endeavours. They also brought before us numbers of the incendiaries with their matches, as amidst such a *popolazzo* we never could have discovered them ourselves. I caused about two hundred of these . wretches to be shot. Had it not been for this fatal fire, I possessed everything my army wanted— excellent winter quarters; stores of all kinds were in plenty ; and the next year would have decided the campaign. Alexander would have made peace, or I would have been in Petersburg.'

I asked if he thought that he could entirely subdue Russia. 'No,' replied Napoleon; 'but I would have caused Russia to make such a peace as suited the interests of France. I was five days too late ' in quitting Moscow. Several of the generals,' continued he, 'were burnt out of their beds. I myself remained in the Kremlin[1] until surrounded by flames. The fire advanced, seized the Chinese and India warehouses, ' and several stores of oil and spirits, which burst forth in flames and overwhelmed everything. I then re-

[1] General Gourgaud informed me that during the conflagration great numbers of crows (which are in myriads at Moscow) perched in flocks upon the towers of the Kremlin, from whence they frequently descended and hovered round the French soldiers, flapping their wings and screaming, as if menacing them with the destruction that followed. He added that the troops were dispirited by this, which they conceived to be a bad omen.—B. E. O'M.

tired to a country house of the Emperor Alexander,
distant about a league from Moscow, and you may
imagine the intensity of the fire when I tell you
that you could scarcely bear your hands upon the
walls or the windows on the side next to Moscow,
in consequence of their heated state. It was the
spectacle of a sea and billows of fire, a sky and
clouds of flame; mountains of red rolling flames,
like immense waves of the sea, alternately bursting
forth and elevating themselves to skies of fire, and
then sinking into the ocean of flame below.[1] Oh,
it was the most grand, the most sublime, and the
most terrific sight the world ever beheld! *Allons,
Docteur.*' This was Napoleon's general expression
when he wished me to retire.

*November* 9.—Had some conversation with
the Emperor on the subject of religion. I observed that in England there were different
opinions about his faith; that some had latterly
supposed him to be a Roman Catholic. '*Ebbene,*'
replied he, '*Credo tutto quel che crede la chiesa.*
I used,' continued he, 'to make the Bishop of
Nantes argue with the Pope frequently in my
presence. He wanted to re-establish the monks.
My bishop used to tell him that the Emperor had
no objection to persons being monks in their hearts,
but that he objected to allowing any society of them
to exist publicly. The Pope wanted me to confess,
which I always evaded by saying, "Holy father, I

---

[1] The reader is no doubt acquainted with Labaume's account of
the campaign of 1812.

am too much occupied at present. Perhaps when I get older." I took a pleasure in conversing with the Pope, who was a good old man, though obstinate.'

'There are so many different religions,' continued he, 'or modifications of them, that it is difficult to know which to choose. If one religion had existed from the beginning of the world, I should think that to be the true one.[1] As it is, I am of opinion that every person ought to continue in the religion in which he was brought up : in that of his fathers. What are you?'—'A Protestant,' I replied. 'Was your father so?' I said, 'Yes.' —'Then continue in that belief.'

'In France,' continued he, 'I received Catholics and Protestants alike at my *levée*. I paid their ministers alike. I gave the Protestants a fine church at Paris,[2] which had formerly belonged to the Jesuits. In order to prevent any religious disputes in places where there were both Catholic and Protestant churches, I prohibited them from tolling the bells to summon the people to worship in their respective churches, unless the ministers of the one and the other made a specific request for permission to do so, and stated that it was at the desire of the members of each religion. By

[1] 'All wise men are of the same religion, and that they never tell,' attributed to Talleyrand, was said as far back as Charles the Second's time. 'Men of sense are really but of one religion,' said Lord Shaftesbury. Upon which the lady to whom he said this remarked, 'Pray, my lord, what religion is that which men of sense agree in?'—'Madam,' said the Earl, 'men of sense never tell it.'— See Burnet's *History of My Own Time*, vol. i. p. 175.

[2] The Oratoire.

these means I prevented the squabbles which had previously existed, as the Catholic priests found that they could not have their own bells tolled, unless the Protestants had a similar privilege.'

'There is a link between animals and the Deity. Man,' added he, 'is merely a more perfect animal than the rest. He reasons better. But how do we know that animals have not a language of their own? My opinion is, that it is presumption in us to say no, because we do not understand them. A horse has memory, knowledge, and love. He knows his master from the servants, though the latter are more constantly with him. I had a horse myself, who knew me from any other person, and manifested by capering and proudly marching with his head erect, when I was on his back, his knowledge that he bore a person superior to the others by whom he was surrounded. Neither would he allow any other person to mount him, except one groom, who constantly took care of him, and when ridden by him, his motions were far different, and such as seemed to say that he was conscious he bore an inferior. When I lost my way, I was accustomed to throw the reins on his neck, and he always discovered it in places where I, with all my observation and boasted superior knowledge, could not. Who again can deny the sagacity of dogs? There is a link between all animals. Plants are so many animals who eat and drink, and there are gradations up to man, who is only the most perfect of them all.

The same spirit animates them all in a greater or a lesser degree.'

'That Governor,' added he, 'has closed up the path which led to the Company's gardens, where I used to walk sometimes, as it is the only spot sheltered from the *vento agro*, which I suppose he thought was too great an indulgence. But I do not give myself any uneasiness about it, for when a man's time is come he must go.' I took the liberty of asking if he was a predestinarian. '*Sicuro*,' replied Napoleon, 'as much so as the Turks are. I have been always so. When destiny wills, it must be obeyed.'

Asked him some questions about Blucher. 'Blucher,' said he, 'is a very brave soldier, *un bon sabreur*. He is like a bull who shuts his eyes, and, seeing no danger, rushes on. He committed a thousand faults, and had it not been for circumstances I could repeatedly have made him and the greatest part of his army prisoners. He is stubborn and indefatigable, afraid of nothing, and very much attached to his country; but as a general, he is without talent. I recollect that when I was in Prussia, he dined at my table after he had surrendered, and he was then considered to be a very ordinary man.'

Speaking about the English soldiers, he observed, 'The English soldier is brave, nobody more so, and the officers generally men of honour, but I do not think them yet capable of executing great manœuvres. I think that if I were at the head of them,

I could make them do anything. However, I do
not know them enough yet to speak decidedly. I
had a conversation with Bingham about it; and
although he is of a different opinion, I would alter
your system. Instead of the lash, I would lead
them by the stimulus of honour. I would instil a
degree of emulation into their minds. I would promote every deserving soldier, as I did in France.
After an action I assembled the officers and soldiers
and asked, Who have acquitted themselves best?
*Quels sont les braves?* and promoted such of them
as were capable of reading and writing.[1] Those who
were not, I ordered to study five hours a day until
they had learnt sufficiently, and then promoted them.
What might not be expected from the English army
if every soldier hoped to be made a general if he
behaved well? Bingham says, however, that the
greatest part of your soldiers are brutes, and must
be driven by the stick. But surely,' continued he,
' the English soldiers must be possessed of sentiments sufficient to put them at least upon a level
with the soldiers of other nations, where the degrading system of the lash is not used. Whatever
debases man cannot be serviceable. Bingham says
that none but the dregs of the populace voluntarily
enter as soldiers. This disgraceful punishment is
the cause of it. I would remove it, and make even
the situation of a private soldier be considered as
conferring honour upon the individual who bore it.

---

[1] This he constantly did, and in person, especially if he saw any
signs of the colonel of a regiment mentioning only officers for bravery.

I would act as I did in France. I would encourage
young men of education, the sons of merchants,
gentlemen, and others, to enter as private soldiers,
and promote them according to their merits. I
would substitute confinement, bread and water, the
contempt of his comrades, and similar punishments for
the lash. When a soldier has been debased and dishonoured by stripes, he cares but little for the glory
or the honour of his country. What honour can
a man possibly have who is flogged before his
comrades ? He loses all feeling, and would as soon
fight against as for his country, if he were better
paid by the opposite party.

'When the Austrians had possession of Italy, they
in vain attempted to make soldiers of the Italians.
They either deserted as fast as they raised them, or
else, when compelled to advance against an enemy,
they ran away on the first fire. It was impossible
to keep together a single regiment. When I got
Italy, and began to raise soldiers, the Austrians
laughed at me, and said that it was in vain, that
they had been trying for a long time, and that it
was not in the nature of the Italians to fight or to
make good soldiers. Notwithstanding this, I raised
many thousands of Italians who fought with a bravery
equal to the French, and did not desert me even in my
adversity. What was the cause ? I abolished flogging and the stick, which the Austrians had adopted.
I promoted those amongst the soldiers who had talents,
and made many of them generals. I substituted
honour and emulation for terror and the lash.'

I asked his opinion relative to the comparative merit of the Russians, Prussians, and Germans. Napoleon replied, ' Soldiers change, sometimes brave, sometimes *lâches*. I have seen the Russians at Eylau perform prodigies of valour : they were so many heroes. At Moscow, intrenched up to their necks, they allowed me to beat two hundred and fifty thousand men with ninety thousand.[1] At Jena, and at other battles in that campaign, the Prussians fled like sheep ; since that time they have fought bravely. My opinion is, that *now* the Prussian soldier is superior to the Austrian. The French cuirassiers were the. best cavalry in the world *pour enfoncer l'infanterie*. Individually, there is no horseman superior or perhaps equal to the Mameluke ; but they cannot act in a body. As partisans, the Cossacks excel, and the Poles as lancers.' This he said in reply to a question made by me regarding his opinion relative to the cavalry.

I asked who he thought was the best general amongst the Austrians. ' Prince Charles,' he replied, 'although he has committed a thousand faults. As to Schwartzenberg, he is not fit to command six thousand men !'

Napoleon then spoke about the siege of Toulon, and observed that he had made General O'Hara prisoner, ' I may say,' continued he, ' with my own hand. I had constructed a masked battery of eight twenty-four pounders, and four mortars, in order to

[1] The numbers on each side were probably about equal, the French having more regular troops.

open upon Fort Malbosquet (I think it was), which was in possession of the English.[1]   It was finished in the evening, and it was my intention to have opened fire upon them in the morning.   While I was giving directions at another part of the trenches, some of the Deputies from the Convention came down.   In those days they sometimes took upon them to direct the operations of the armies, and those imbeciles ordered the battery to commence, which was obeyed.   As soon as I saw this premature fire, . I immediately conceived that the English General would attack the battery and most probably carry it, as matters had not been yet arranged to support it.   In fact, O'Hara, seeing that the fire from that battery would dislodge his troops from Malbosquet, from which last I would have taken the fort which commanded the harbour, determined

---

[1] During the erection of one of the first batteries which Napoleon, on his arrival at Toulon, directed against the English, he asked whether there was a serjeant or corporal present who could write. A man advanced from the ranks and wrote by his dictation on the epaulement.

The note was scarcely ended when a cannon-ball, which had been fired in the direction of the battery, fell near the spot, and the paper was immediately covered by the loose earth thrown up by the ball.   'Well,' said the writer, 'I shall have no need of sand.'   This remark, together with the coolness with which it was made, fixed the attention of Napoleon and made the fortune of the serjeant.

This man was Junot, afterwards Duke of Abrantes, Colonel-General of the Hussars, Commandant in Portugal, and Governor-General in Illyria, where he evinced signs of mental alienation, which increased on his return to France, where he wounded himself in a horrible way. He died a victim of the intemperance which destroyed both his health and his reason.—*Las Cases*, vol i., part i., p. 154, English edition.

upon attacking it. Accordingly, early in the morning, he put himself at the head of his troops, sallied out, and actually carried the battery and the lines which I had formed' (*Napoleon here drew a plan upon a piece of paper of the situation of the batteries*) 'to the left, and those to the right were taken by the Neapolitans.

'While he was busy in spiking the guns, I advanced with three or four hundred grenadiers, unperceived, through a *boyau* covered with olive-trees, which communicated with the battery, and commenced a terrible fire upon his troops. The English, astonished, at first supposed that the Neapolitans, who had the lines on the right, had mistaken them for French, and said, "It is those *canaglie* of Neapolitans who are firing upon us" (for even at that time your troops despised the Neapolitans). O'Hara ran out of the battery and advanced towards us. In advancing he was wounded in the arm by the fire of a serjeant, and I, who stood at the mouth of the *boyau*, seized him by the coat and threw him back amongst my own men, thinking that he was a colonel, as he had two epaulettes on. While they were taking him to the rear, he cried out that he was the Commander-in-Chief of the English. He thought that they were going to massacre him, as there existed a horrible order at that time from the Convention to give no quarter to the English. I ran up and prevented the soldiers from ill-treating him. He spoke very bad French; and as I saw that he imagined they intended to butcher him, I

did everything in my power to console him, and
gave directions that his wound should be immediately dressed, and every attention paid to him.
He afterwards begged of me to give him a statement of how he had been taken, in order that he
might show it to his Government in his justification.'

'Those blockheads of Deputies,' continued he,
'wanted to attack and storm the town first; but I
explained to them that it was very strong, and that
we should lose many men; that the best way would
be to make ourselves masters of the forts which
commanded the harbour, and then the English
would either be taken, or be obliged to burn the
greatest part of the fleet, and escape. My advice
was taken; and the English, perceiving what would
be the result, set fire to the ships and abandoned
the town. If a south wind had come on, they
would have been all taken. It was Sidney Smith
who set them on fire, and they would have been all
burnt if the Spaniards had behaved well. It was
the finest *feu d'artifice* possible.'

'Those Neapolitans,' continued he, 'are the most
vile rabble in the world. Murat ruined me by
advancing against the Austrians with them. When
old Ferdinand heard of it, he laughed, and said in
his jargon that they would serve Murat as they had
done him before, when Championnet dispersed a
hundred thousand of them like so many sheep with
ten thousand Frenchmen. I had forbidden Murat
to act; for, after I returned from Elba, there was an
understanding between the Emperor of Austria and

me that if I gave him up Italy, he would not join the Coalition against me. This I had promised, and would have fulfilled it ; but that *imbécile*, in spite of the direction I had given him to remain quiet, advanced with his rabble into Italy, where he was blown away like a puff. The Emperor of Austria, seeing this, concluded directly that it was by my orders, and that I deceived him ; and being conscious that he had betrayed me himself before, supposed that I did not intend to keep faith with him, and determined to endeavour to crush me with all his forces.

'Twice Murat betrayed and ruined me. The first time, when he forsook me, he joined the Allies with sixty thousand men, and obliged me to leave thirty thousand in Italy, when I wanted them so much elsewhere. At that time his army was well officered by French. Had it not been for this rash step of Murat's, the Russians would have retreated, as their intentions were not to have advanced if Austria did not join the Coalition ; so that you would have been left to yourselves, and have gladly made a peace.' [1]

[1] After the defection of Murat, Madame (mother of the Emperor) refused to have anything more to do with either Murat or his wife ; to all their entreaties she invariably answered that she held traitors and treachery in abhorence. As soon as she was at Rome, after the disasters of 1814, Murat hastened to send her eight magnificent horses out of his stables at Naples ; but Madame would not accept them. She resisted in like manner every effort of her daughter Caroline, who constantly repeated that, after all, the fault was not hers ; that she had no share in it ; that she could not command her husband. But Madame answered, like Clytemnestra, ' If you could

He observed that he had always been willing
to conclude a peace with England. 'Let your
Ministers say what they like,' said he, ' I was always
ready to make a peace. At the time that Fox died
there was every prospect of effecting one. If Lord
Lauderdale had been sincere at first, it would also
have been concluded. Before the campaign in
Prussia, I caused it to be signified to him that he
had better persuade his countrymen to make peace,
as I would be master of Prussia in two months; for
this reason, that although Russia and Prussia united
might be able to oppose me, yet Prussia alone could
not. That the Russians were three months' march
distant ; and that, as I had intelligence that their
plan of campaign was to defend Berlin instead of
retiring, in order to obtain the support of the
Russians, I would destroy their army, and take
Berlin before the Russians came up, who alone I
would easily defeat afterwards. I therefore advised
him to take advantage of my offer of peace before
Prussia, who was your best friend on the Continent,
was destroyed. After this communication, I believe
that Lord Lauderdale was sincere, ánd that he
wrote to your Ministers recommending peace ; but
they would not agree to it, thinking that the King of
Prussia was at the head of a hundred thousand

not command him, you ought at least to have opposed him : but
what struggles have you made ? what blood has flown ? At the
expense of your own life you ought to have defended your brother,
your benefactor, your master, against the sanguinary attempts of
your husband.'—*Las Cases*, vol. ii., part iv., p. 354, English
edition.

men ; that I might be defeated, and that a defeat
would be my ruin. This was possible. A battle
sometimes decides everything ; and sometimes the
most trifling circumstance decides the fate of a
battle. The event, however, proved that I was
right ; after Jena, Prussia was mine. After Tilsit
and at Erfurth,' continued he, 'a letter containing
proposals of peace to England, and signed by the
Emperor Alexander and myself, was sent to your
Ministers, but they would not accept of them.'

He spoke of Sir Sidney Smith. 'Sidney Smith,'
said he, 'is a brave officer. He displayed considerable ability in the treaty for the evacuation
of Egypt by the French. He took advantage of
the discontent which he found prevailing amongst
the French troops, at being so long away from
France, and other circumstances. He also
manifested high honour in sending immediately to
Kléber the refusal of Lord Keith to ratify the
treaty, which saved the French army ; if he had
kept it a secret for seven or eight days longer,
Cairo would have been given up to the Turks, and
the French army necessarily obliged to surrender to
the English. He also showed great humanity and
courtesy in all his proceedings towards the French
who fell into his hands. He landed at Havre for
some *sottise* of a bet he had made, according to
some, to go to the theatre ; others said it was for
espionage ; however that may be, he was arrested
and confined in the Temple as a spy ; and at one
time it was intended to try and execute him.

Shortly after I returned from Italy, he wrote to me
from his prison, to request that I would intercede
for him ; but under the circumstances in which he
was taken, I could do nothing for him.  He is
active, intelligent, intriguing, and indefatigable ; but
I believe that he is *mezzo pazzo.*'

I asked if Sir Sidney had not displayed great
talent and bravery at Acre ?  Napoleon replied,
'Yes, the chief cause of the failure there was, that
he took all my battering train, which was on board
several small vessels.  Had it not been for that, I
should have taken Acre in spite of him.  He
behaved very bravely, and was well seconded by
Phillipeaux, a Frenchman of talent, who had studied
with me as an engineer.  There was a Major
Douglas also who behaved very gallantly.  The
acquisition of five or six hundred seamen as
cannoniers was a great advantage to the Turks,
whose spirits they revived, and whom they showed
how to defend the fortress.  But he committed a
great fault in making sorties, which cost the lives of
two or three hundred brave fellows, without the
possibility of success.  For it was impossible he
could succeed against the number of the French
who were before Acre.  I would lay a wager that
he lost half of his crew in them.  He dispersed
proclamations amongst my troops, which certainly
shook some of them, and I in consequence
published an order, stating that he was *mad*, and
forbidding all communication with him.  Some days
after he sent, by means of a flag of truce, a

lieutenant or a midshipman with a letter containing a challenge to me to meet him at some place he pointed out, in order to fight a duel. I laughed at this, and sent him back an intimation that when he brought Marlborough to fight me, I would meet him. Notwithstanding this, I like the character of the man.'

In answer to a remark of mine, that the invasion of Spain had been a measure very destructive to him, he replied, ' If the Government I established had remained, it would have been the best thing that ever happened for Spain. I would have regenerated the Spaniards ; I would have made them a great nation. Instead of a feeble, imbecile, and superstitious race of Bourbons, I would have given them a new dynasty, that would have no claim on the nation, except by the good it would have rendered unto it. In place of an hereditary race of asses, they would have had a monarch, with ability to revive the nation, sunk under the yoke of superstition and ignorance. Perhaps it is better for France that I did not succeed, as Spain would have been a formidable rival. I would have destroyed superstition and priestcraft, and abolished the inquisition and the monasteries of those lazy *bestie di frati.* I would at least have rendered the priests harmless. The guerillas, who fought so bravely against me, now lament their success. When I was last in Paris, I had letters from Mina and many other leaders of the guerillas, craving assistance to expel their *friar* from the throne.'

Napoleon afterwards made some observations relative to the Governor, whose suspicious and mysterious conduct he contrasted with the open and undisguised manner in which Sir George Cockburn conducted himself. 'Though the Admiral was severe and rough,' said he, 'yet he was incapable of a mean action. He had no atrocities in contemplation, and therefore made no mystery of his conduct. This Governor has a double correspondence with your Ministers, similar to that which all your ambassadors maintain; one written so as to deceive the world, should they ever be called upon to publish it, and the other, giving a true account, for themselves alone.' I observed that I believed all ambassadors and other official persons in all countries wrote two accounts ; one for the public, and the other containing matters which it might not be right to divulge.[1] 'True, *signor medico*,' replied Napoleon, taking me by the ear in a good-humoured manner, 'but there is not so Machiavellian a Ministry in the world as your own. *Cela tient à votre système.* That and the liberty of your press obliges your Ministers to render some account to the nation, and therefore they want to be able to deceive the public in many instances ; but as it is also necessary for them to know the truth *themselves*, they have a double correspondence ; one official and false, calculated to gull the nation, when published, or called for by

---

[1] O'Meara himself, be it remembered, all this time keeping up a private correspondence with persons in England unknown to Sir Hudson Lowe, and practically intended for the Ministers.

Parliament; the other, private and true, to be kept
locked up in their own possession, and not deposited
in the archives. In this way they manage to make
everything appear as they wish to John Bull. Now
this system of falsehood is not necessary in a country
where there is no obligation to publish, or to render
an account; if the Sovereign does not like to make
known any transaction officially, he keeps it to himself, and gives no explanation; therefore there is no
need of causing varnished accounts to be written, in
order to deceive the people. For these reasons
there are more falsifications in your official documents than in those of any other nation.'

*November* 10. — Wrote to Sir Hudson Lowe,
repeating my opinion that a further continuance of
confinement and want of exercise would be productive of some serious complaint to Napoleon, which
in all probability would prove fatal to him.

*November* 12.—Conversed with Napoleon, who
was in his bath, for a considerable time. On asking
his opinion of Talleyrand—' Talleyrand,' said he, '*le
plus vil des agioteurs, bas flatteur. C'est un homme
corrompu*, who has betrayed all parties and persons.
Wary and circumspect; always a traitor, but always
in conspiracy with fortune, Talleyrand treats his
enemies as if they were one day to become his
friends, and his friends as if they were to become
his enemies. He is a man of talent, but venal in
everything. Nothing could be done with him but
by means of bribery. The Kings of Wirtemberg
and Bavaria made so many complaints of his rapacity

and extortion that I took his *porte-feuille* from him : besides, I found that he had divulged to some *intrigants* a most important secret which I had confided to him alone.  He hates the Bourbons in his heart.  When I returned from Elba, Talleyrand wrote to me from Vienna, offering his services, and to betray the Bourbons, provided I would pardon and restore him to favour.  He rested his application upon a part of my proclamation, in which I said there were circumstances which it was impossible to resist, which he quoted.  But I considered that there were a few I was obliged to except, and refused, as it would have excited indignation if ·I had not punished somebody.'

I asked if it were true that Talleyrand had advised him to dethrone the King of Spain, and mentioned that the Duke of Rovigo (Savary) had told me that Talleyrand had said in his presence, 'Your Majesty will never be secure upon your throne, while a Bourbon is seated upon one.'  He replied, 'True, he advised me to do everything which would injure the Bourbons, whom he detests.'[1]

Napoleon showed me the marks of two wounds ;[2] one a very deep cicatrice above the left knee, which

[1] Napoleon invariably made this accusation against Talleyrand ; there is no reason for discrediting it.  It was after the failure in Spain that Talleyrand disclaimed any share in the matter, his disclaimer being first made publicly after a fresh tenure of power had given him the means of withdrawing all compromising documents.

[2] See footnote on the wounds of Napoleon towards the latter part of the second volume of this work ; also a footnote in Bourrienne's *Memoirs of Napoleon*, English edition of 1885, vol. ii. p. 468.

he said he had received in his first campaign of Italy, and was of so serious a nature that the surgeons were in doubt whether it might not be ultimately necessary to amputate. He observed that when he was wounded it was always kept a secret, in order not to discourage the soldiers. The other was on the toe, and had been received at Eckmühl. 'At the siege of Acre,' continued he, 'a shell thrown by Sidney Smith fell at my feet. Two soldiers, who were close by, seized and closely embraced me, one in front and the other on one side, and made a rampart of their bodies for me, against the effect of the shell, which exploded, and overwhelmed us with sand. We sank into the hole formed by its bursting; one of them was wounded. I made them both officers. One has since lost a leg at Moscow, and commanded at Vincennes when I left Paris.[1] When he was summoned by the Russians, he replied that as soon as they sent him back the leg he had lost at Moscow, he would surrender the fortress. Many times in my life,' continued he, 'have I been saved by soldiers and officers throwing themselves before me when I was in the most imminent danger. At Arcola, when I was advancing, Colonel Muiron, my aide-de-camp, threw himself before me, covered me with his body, and received the wound which was destined for me. He fell at my feet, and his blood spurted up in my face. He gave his life to preserve mine. Never yet, I believe, has there been such devotion shown by soldiers as mine have manifested for me.

[1] General Dumesnil, whose widow only died in 1884.

In all my misfortunes never has the soldier, even when expiring, been wanting to me—never has man been served more faithfully by his troops. With the last drop of blood gushing out of their veins, they exclaimed, *Vive l'Empereur!*'

I asked if he had gained the battle of Waterloo, whether he would have agreed to the treaty of Paris. Napoleon replied, 'I would certainly have ratified it. I would not have made such a peace myself. Sooner than agree to much better terms, I abdicated before ; but finding it already made, I would have kept it, because France had need of repose.'

*November* 13.—Sir Hudson Lowe sent orders to Count Las Cases to dismiss his present servant, and to replace him by a soldier whom he sent for that purpose. The Count replied that Sir Hudson Lowe had the power to take away his servant, but that he could not compel him (Las Cases) to receive another. That it would certainly be an inconvenience to lose his servant in the present state of health of his son ; but that if he were taken away, he would not accept one of Sir Hudson Lowe's choosing. Captain Poppleton wrote to Sir Hudson Lowe, stating the Count's disinclination ; and I informed him that the man he had sent to replace the Count's servant had formerly been employed at Longwood and turned away for drunkenness. Sir Hudson then desired me to tell Poppleton that the former servant might remain until he could find one that would answer, adding, that he would look out himself for a proper person, which he also desired me to tell the Count. Informed him that it was my intention to call in Mr. Baxter, to have the benefit of his advice in the case of young Las Cases, which presented some alarming symptoms.

Communicated to Count Las Cases the message I was charged with by Sir Hudson Lowe. The Count replied, 'If the Governor had told me that he did not wish my servant to remain with me, or that he would be glad if I sent him away, and that he would give me a fortnight to look out for another, I would immediately have dismissed him, and most probably have asked the Governor to send me another; but acting in the manner he has done, without saying a word to me, I will take no servant from his hands. He treats me as a corporal would. The Admiral, even if displeased, never would have taken my servant away out of revenge.'

Dined at Plantation House in company with the Marquis de Montchenu, who amused the company with the importance which he attached to *grande naissance*, relative to which he recounted some anecdotes.

*November* 16.—The *Adamant* transport arrived from the Cape, bringing news of the arrival of Sir George Cockburn in England, and that he had had an audience of the Prince Regent on the 2d of August.

An inspector of police named Rainsford[1] arrived from England and the Cape.

*November* 17.—The allowances for Longwood

[1] See vol. ii. p. 58.

diminished by order of Sir Hudson Lowe two
pounds of meat daily, in consequence of the departure of a servant, who had received but one
pound.   A bottle of wine also struck off.

The carters who bring up the provisions state
that the linen sent from Longwood is frequently inspected by Sir Thomas Reade on its arrival in town.
Countess Bertrand sent down in the trunk containing her soiled linen some novels which she had
borrowed from Miss Chesborough before the
arrival of Sir Hudson Lowe on the island.
They were placed on the top of the linen, and
the trunk was unlocked.   Sir Thomas Reade
said that it was a violation of the proclamation,
and that Miss Chesborough should be sent from
the island.

Mentioned to the Emperor that I had been informed he had saved the Grand Maréchal Duroc's
life during his first campaigns in Italy, when seized
and condemned to death as an emigrant; which
was asserted to have been the cause of the great
attachment subsequently displayed by Duroc to him
until the hour of his death.   Napoleon looked surprised and replied, 'No such thing—who told you
that tale?'   I said that I had heard the Marquis de
Montchenu repeat it at a public dinner.   'There is
not a word of truth in it,' replied Napoleon.   'I
took Duroc out of the artillery train when he was
a boy, and protected him until his death.   But I
suppose Montchenu said this because Duroc was of
an old family, which in that booby's eyes is the sole

source of merit.[1]   He despises everybody who has
not as many hundred years of nobility to boast of as
himself.[2]   It was such as Montchenu who were the
chief cause of the Revolution.   Before it such a man
as Bertrand, who is worth an army of Montchenus,
could not even be a *sous-lieutenant*, while *vieux
enfans* like him would be generals.   God help,' continued he, 'the nation that is governed by such !
In my time most of the generals of whose deeds
France is so proud sprang from that very class of
plebeians so much despised by him.   It surprises
me,' added he, 'that they have permitted the
Duchess of Reggio to be *première dame* to the
Duchess of Berri, as her husband was once a private
soldier, and did not spring from *grande naissance*.'
I asked his opinion of the Duke of Reggio (Oudinot).
'A brave man,' replied Napoleon, '*Ma di poca testa*.
He has been influenced latterly by his young wife,
who is of an old family, whose vanity and prejudices
she inherits.   However,' continued he, 'he offered
his services after my return from Elba, and took the

---

[1] When a marriage between Hortense Beauharnais (afterwards
Queen of Holland) and Duroc was contemplated, Napoleon said :
' They suit one another; they shall marry one another.   I like Duroc.
He is of good family.'   And Napoleon is said to have selected him
for missions to the Courts of Berlin and Russia on account of his good
education, agreeable manners, and power of expressing himself ' with
elegance and reserve.'—See *Bourrienne*, 1885 edition, vol. i. pp. 301,
469.

[2] On one occasion in Germany some elector or prince, when
showing Marshal Lannes over his picture-gallery, dilated at wearisome
length upon his ancestors and high descent, with the intention of an
obvious contrast.   ' But I,' retorted the Marshal haughtily, '*am* an
ancestor.'

oath of allegiance to me.'[1]     I asked him if he
thought that he was sincere.   ' It might have been
so, *signor medico*.   If I had succeeded, I daresay he
would have been.'

Napoleon very busily employed in dictating his
memoirs to Counts Bertrand and Montholon.

Sir Hudson Lowe objected to allowing the produce of the last plate which had been sold to be
placed at the disposal of the French, alleging that
it was too great a sum, viz. £295, and demanded
an explanation of the manner in which so *large* a
sum of money was to be expended.   It appeared
upon examination that instead of having £295 dis-
posable, there would be in reality only a few pounds,
as £85 were due to Marchand, £45 to Cipriani, and
£16 to Gentilini, for money advanced by them to
purchase extra articles of food, previous to the sale
of the last plate ; also £70 to Mr. Balcombe's concern, £10 to Le Page, and £20 to Archambaud,
for fowls, etc.

*November* 22.—Orders sent up by Sir Hudson
Lowe for a fresh reduction in the allowance of meat
and wine.

Saw Baron Sturmer in the town, with whom I
had some conversation.   He was very desirous of
seeing Napoleon, and informed me that Sir Hudson
Lowe, in granting the Commissioners permission to
enter as far as the inner gate of Longwood, had

---

[1] This is not correct.   Oudinot did not take the oath to Napoleon,
and is believed not to have offered his services to him, retiring to his
country seat during the Cent Jours.   His non-employment is proof
that Napoleon was wrong, or misunderstood in this passage.

required them to pledge their honour that they would not speak to Napoleon without having first obtained his permission.

*November* 23.—Sir Pulteney Malcolm arrived from the Cape. Napoleon very anxious to obtain some newspapers. Tried to procure some, but was informed that the Governor had got all that were to be had.

*November* 25.—On my return from town to Longwood met Sir Hudson Lowe, who was riding up and down the road. When I came near to His Excellency, he observed, with an air of triumph, 'You will meet your friend Las Cases in custody.' A few minutes afterwards met the Count, under charge of the Governor's aide-de-camp, Prichard, on his way to Hut's Gate. His arrest had been effected in the following manner :—About three o'clock Sir Hudson Lowe, accompanied by Sir Thomas Reade, Major Gorrequer, and three dragoons, entered Longwood. Shortly afterwards Captain Blakeney and the Inspector of Police followed them. Sir Hudson and Major Gorrequer rode off a little to the left, while the others proceeded to Captain Poppleton's room, having first ordered a corporal and party from the guard to follow them up to the house. Sir Thomas ordered Captain Poppleton to send for Count Las Cases, who was with Napoleon. After they had waited a short time Las Cases came out, and was arrested while going into his room by Reade and the Inspector of Police, who took possession of his clothes and effects. His papers were sealed up by his son, who afterwards proceeded to Hut's Gate under custody, where he remained with his father in charge of an officer of the 66th Regiment, with orders not to be allowed to see anybody except the Governor and his staff. [It appeared that the Count had given a letter, written upon silk, to Scott his servant, with which he was to proceed to England.[1]   Scott told this to his father, who had him brought to a Mr. Barker, and from thence to the Governor, by whom, after undergoing an examination, he was committed to prison.]

Saw Napoleon in the evening, who appeared to have been wholly ignorant of Las Cases's intentions. 'I am convinced,' said he, 'however, that there is nothing of consequence in the letter, as Las Cases is an honest man, and too much attached to me to undertake anything of consequence without first having acquainted me with his project. You may depend upon it that it is some letter of complaints to *Miladi* about the conduct of this Governor, and the vexations which he inflicts upon us, or to his banker, as he has four or five thousand pounds in some banker's hands in London, which I was to have

---

[1] See *Forsyth*, vol. i. p. 476, for the letter sent by Las Cases. Sturmer, in his report to the Austrian Government, remarks on the facility given to the former servant, already removed for a similar offence, to communicate with Las Cases : 'It is hard to conceive, after the causes of offence he had previously given, and which led to his removal from Longwood, how he has been permitted to return there, and to see his former master without escort or witness.   This carelessness contrasts strikingly with the harshness of the rules fixed in the island, and with the extreme strictness often extended to the most minute details.'—*Sturmer*, Vienna edition, 1886, p. 47.

had for my necessities, and he did not like his letter
to go through the Governor's hands, as none of us
will trust him.    If Las Cases had made his project
known to me, I would have stopped him ; not that
I disapprove of his endeavouring to make our situation known—on the contrary; but I disapprove of the
bungling manner in which he attempted it.    For a
man of talent, like Las Cases, to make an ambassador of a slave, who could not read or write,
to go upon a six months' embassy to England, where
he never has been, knows nobody, and who, unless
the Governor was a *scioccone*, would not be permitted
to leave the island, is to me incomprehensible.    I
can only account for it by supposing that the weight
of afflictions which presses upon us, together with
the melancholy situation of his son, condemned to
die of an incurable malady, have impaired his judgment.    All this I wish to be known.    I am sorry
for it, because people will accuse me of having been
privy to the plan, and will have a poor opinion of
my understanding ; supposing me to have consented
to so shallow a plot.    I would have recommended
him to request some man of honour to make our
situation known in England, and to take a letter to
the Prince Regent ; first asking him to pledge his
honour to observe secrecy if he did not choose to
undertake the mission.    If he betrayed us, so much
the worse for himself.    Las Cases has with him my
campaigns in Italy, and all the official correspondence between the Admiral, Governor, and
Longwood ; and I am told that he has made a

journal, containing an account of what passes here, with many anecdotes of myself. I have desired Bertrand to go to Plantation House and ask for them. It is the least interesting part of my life, as it only relates the commencement of it; but I should not like this Governor to have it. ' I am sure,' continued he, ' that there is nothing of consequence in Las Cases's letter, or he would have made me acquainted with it; although I daresay Lowe will write a hundred falsehoods to England about it.

'When in Paris, after my return from Elba, I found in M. Blacas's private papers, which he left behind when he ran away from the Tuileries, a letter which had been written in Elba by one of my sister Pauline's chambermaids, and appeared to have been composed in a moment of anger.[1] Pauline is very handsome and graceful. There was a description of her habits, of her dress, her wardrobe, and of everything that she liked; of how fond I was of contributing to her happiness; and that I had superintended the furnishing of her *boudoir* myself; what an extraordinary man I was; that one night I had burnt my finger dreadfully, and had merely poured a bottle of ink over it, without appearing to regard the pain, and many little *bêtises*, true enough perhaps. This letter M. Blacas had got interpolated with horrid stories; in fact, insinuating that I slept with my sister; and in the margin, in the handwriting of the interpolator, was written "*to be printed*." '

---

[1] Pauline Bonaparte was at Elba when Napoleon left the island.

*November* 26.—Napoleon in his bath. Asked
if I had heard anything more respecting Las
Cases; professed his sorrow to lose him.[1] 'Las
Cases,' said he, 'is the only one of the French
who can speak English well, or explain it to my
satisfaction. I cannot now read an English newspaper. Madame Bertrand understands English
perfectly; but you know one cannot trouble a lady.
Las Cases was necessary to me. Ask the Admiral
to interest himself for that poor man, who, I am
convinced, has not said as much as there was in
Montholon's letter. He will die under all these
afflictions, for he has no bodily strength, and his
unfortunate son will finish his existence a little
sooner.'

He asked if Madame Bertrand had not been
unwell, and said he believed she suspected that
her mother was either dead or most alarmingly
ill. 'Those Creoles,' said he, 'are very susceptible.
Josephine was subject to nervous attacks when
in trouble. She was really an amiable woman—
elegant, charming, and affable. *Era la dama la
più graziosa di Francia.* She was the goddess
of the toilet; all the fashions originated with her;
everything she put on appeared elegant; and she
was so kind, so humane—she was the best woman
in France.' [2]

[1] Napoleon's regret is the more easy to conceive as there was no
one at Longwood capable of replacing Las Cases, and that he could
successfully employ in the work he had commenced.—*Sturmer*, p. 52.

[2] Napoleon paid heavily for the perfection of Josephine's toilettes.
Bourrienne, who often had to arrange her financial difficulties, says

He then spoke about the distress prevailing
in England, and said that it was caused by the
abuses of the Ministry. 'You have done wonders,'
said he; 'you have effected impossibilities, I may
say; but I think that England, encumbered with
a national debt, which will take forty years of
peace and commerce to pay off,[1] may be compared
to a man who has drunk large quantities of brandy
to give him courage and strength; but afterwards,
weakened by the stimulus which had imparted
energy for the moment, his powers are exhausted
by the unnatural means used to excite them.'

Some conversation then took place relative to
the battle of Austerlitz. Napoleon said that,
prior to the battle, the King of Prussia had

that the extent to which her bills were overcharged, owing to the
fear of not being paid for a long period, and of deductions being
made from the amount, was inconceivable. 'It appeared to me also
that there must be some exaggeration in the number of articles supplied. I observed in the milliner's bill thirty-eight new hats, of great
price, in one month. There was likewise a charge of eighteen hundred
francs for heron plumes, and eight hundred francs for perfumes. I
asked Josephine whether she wore out two hats in one day? . . . This
inconceivable mania for spending money was almost the sole cause
of her unhappiness.'—Bourrienne's *Memoirs of Napoleon Bonaparte*,
1885 edition, vol. i. p. 354.

[1] 'In January 1816, when stock was taken after the great continental wars, it was found that the total amount of our indebtedness
was over nine hundred millions sterling. Within a few years this
was largely reduced, and subsequently a comparatively small sum was
paid off every year until it now stands at seven hundred and thirty-six
millions. In 1813 alone forty millions were added to the National
Debt, and upwards of six hundred millions were raised during the
French war. In 1816 the debt amounted to £45 a head of the
population—its proportion to the present population is £20 a head.'
—Whitaker's *Almanack*, 1888.

signed the Coalition against him. 'Haugwitz,' said he, 'came to inform me of it, and advised me to think of peace. I replied, "The issue of the battle which is imminent will decide everything. I expect that I shall gain it, and if so, I shall be able to dictate such a peace as answers my purposes. *Now* I will hear nothing." The event answered my expectation : I gained a victory so decisive as to enable me to dictate what terms I pleased.' I asked him if Haugwitz had been gained by him? He replied, 'No; but he was of opinion that Prussia should never play the first fiddle in the affairs of the Continent; that she was only a second-rate power, and ought to act as such. Even if I had lost the battle, I expected that Prussia would not cordially join the Allies, as it would naturally be her interest to preserve an equilibrium in Europe, which would not result from her joining those who, on my being defeated, would be much the strongest. Besides, jealousies and suspicions would arise, and the Allies would not have trusted to the King of Prussia, who had betrayed them before.

'I gave Hanover to the Prussians,' continued he, 'on purpose to embroil them with you, produce a war, and shut you out from the Continent. The King of Prussia was blockhead enough to believe that he could keep Hanover and still remain at peace with you. Like a madman, he made war upon me afterwards, induced by the Queen and Prince Louis, with some other young

men, who persuaded him that Prussia was strong
enough even without Russia. A few weeks convinced him of the contrary.' I asked him what
he would have done if the King of Prussia had
joined the Allies with his army previous to the
battle of Austerlitz? 'Ah, Mr. Doctor, that would
have entirely altered the face of things!'

He eulogised the King of Saxony, who, he
said, was a truly good man ; the King of Bavaria,
a plain good man ; the King of Wurtemberg, a
man of considerable talent, but unprincipled and
wicked. 'Alexander and the latter,' said he, 'are
the only sovereigns in Europe possessed of talents.
Lord ——, *un mauvais sujet, un agioteur.* While
negotiating in Paris, he sent couriers away every
day to London, for the purposes of stock-jobbing,
which was solely what he interested himself about.
Had there been an honest man, instead of an
intriguing stock-jobber, it is very likely the negotiation would have succeeded. I was much grieved
afterwards to have had any business with such a
contemptible character.' This was pronounced with
an air of disdain.

*November* 27.—Napoleon very much concerned
about the treatment which Las Cases had suffered,
and the detention of his own papers. He observed
that if there had been any plot in Las Cases's
letter, the Governor could have perceived it in
ten minutes' perusal.[1] That in a few moments

---

[1] The reader will remark that Las Cases was arrested on 25th
November. On the 27th November Lowe states that he would send

he could also see that the campaigns of Italy, etc., contained nothing treasonable ; and that it was contrary to all law to detain papers belonging to him (Napoleon). 'Perhaps,' said he, 'he will come up here some day and say that he has received intimation that a plot to effect my escape is in agitation. What guarantee have I that when I have nearly finished my history, he will not seize the whole of it ? It is true that I can keep my manuscripts in my own room, and with a couple of brace of pistols I can despatch the first who enters. I must burn the whole of what I have written. It served as an amusement to me in this dismal abode, and might perhaps have been interesting to the world, but with this *sbirro Siciliano* there is no guarantee nor security. While surrounding the house with his staff, he reminded me of the savages of the South Sea Islands, dancing round the prisoners whom they were going to devour. Tell him,' continued he, 'what I say about his conduct.'

Went to Hut's Gate to see Sir Hudson Lowe, who had sent a dragoon for me. On my arrival, His Excellency told me that the campaigns of Italy and the official documents would be sent to Longwood the following day, and desired me to tell General Bonaparte that all his papers had

back the documents belonging to Napoleon on the 28th November, but they do not seem to have been all returned till much later ; see 10th December. What right he had to retain these papers for an hour does not appear ; he must have known how galling it was to Napoleon.

been kept sacred,[1] and that all his personal ones should be returned. As to Las Cases's journal, he said that he would have some conversation with Count Bertrand concerning it.

I informed His Excellency that Napoleon had disclaimed all knowledge of the project which Count Las Cases had formed, and added my own conviction, that until the moment that the latter had been arrested, he was wholly ignorant of his intentions. Sir Hudson replied that he acquitted him of any knowledge of the matter, which he desired me to tell him, and congratulated himself much on his own discernment in the opinion he had formed of Count Las Cases's servant.

Saw young Las Cases afterwards, who was very unwell. During the time that I was examining him professionally, Sir Thomas Reade remained in the room. On my going out, Sir Thomas said that 'old Las Cases had been so impertinent to the Governor, that the latter had ordered that he should not be permitted to see any person, unless in the presence of some of the Governor's staff.'

On my return, explained to Napoleon the Governor's message, and informed him that I had seen part of his papers sealed up. When I said

---

[1] The papers had not been kept sacred. Lowe says that all he did was 'to satisfy myself they were really the papers specified.'— *Forsyth*, vol. i. p. 383. Lowe informed Earl Bathurst that he had run over the whole of the papers with Las Cases's acquiescence (see *Forsyth*, vol. i. p. 383), but Forsyth goes on to tell us that Las Cases '*frequently protested.*'—*Forsyth*, vol. i. p. 387.

that the Governor had acquitted him of any
participation in the business,—' If,' said he, ' I had
known of it, and had not put a stop to it, I should
have been worse than a *pazzo da catena*.    I
suppose he thinks there was some plot for my
escape.   I can safely say that I left Elba with
eight hundred men, and arrived at Paris, through
France, without any other plot than that of knowing
the sentiments of the French nation.'

He then sent for St. Denis, who had copied Las
Cases's journal, and asked him the nature of it.
St. Denis replied that it was a journal of everything remarkable that had taken place since the
embarkation on board the *Bellerophon*, and contained divers anecdotes of different persons, of Sir
George Cockburn, etc.   ' How is he treated ? ' says
Napoleon, ' *Comme ça, sire.*'   ' Has he said that I
called him a *requin ?* '—' Yes, sire.'—' Sir George
Bingham ? ' —' Very well spoken of, also Colonel
Wilks.' — ' Is there anything to compromise any
person ? ' (naming three or four).   ' No, sire.'—'Anything about Admiral Malcolm ? ' — ' Yes, sire.'—
' Does it say that I observed, Behold the countenance of a real Englishman ? '—' Yes, sire, he is very
well treated.'—' Anything about the Governor ? '—
' A great deal, sire,' replied St. Denis, who could
not help smiling.   ' Does it say that I said, *C'est
un homme ignoble*, and that his face was the most
*ignoble* I had ever seen ? '   St. Denis replied in the
affirmative, but added, that his expressions were
very frequently *moderated*.   Napoleon asked if the

anecdote of the coffee-cup was in it; St. Denis
replied, he did not recollect it. ' Does it say that I
called him, *sbire Sicilien ?*'—'*Oui, sire.*'—'*C'est son
nom,*' said the Emperor.

Napoleon conversed about his brother Joseph,
whom he described as being a most excellent
character. 'His virtues and talents are those of a
private character; and for such nature intended
him : he is too good to be a great man. He has no
ambition. He is very like me in person, but hand-
somer. He is extremely well informed.' On all
occasions I have observed that Napoleon spoke of
his brother Joseph in terms of warm affection.[1]

*November* 29. — Having been unwell for some
days with a liver complaint, a disease extremely
prevalent and frequently fatal in the island, and finding the symptoms considerably aggravated by the
frequent journeys I was obliged to make to town
and Plantation House, I felt it necessary to apply to
Dr. M'Lean of the 53d Regiment to bleed me very
profusely. Before the abstraction of blood was well
over, Sir Hudson Lowe came into my apartment.

[1] 'One of Bonaparte's greatest misfortunes was that he neither
believed in friendship nor felt the necessity of loving. How often
have I heard him say : "Friendship is but a name; I love nobody;
I do not even love my brothers. Perhaps Joseph a little, from habit,
and because he is my elder. And Duroc, I love him too, but why?
Because his character pleases me. He is stern and resolute, and I
really believe the fellow never shed a tear. For my part, I know
very well that I have no true friends. . . . Leave sensibility to
women; it is their business. But men should be firm in heart
and in purpose, or they should have nothing to do with war or
government."'—Bourrienne's *Memoirs of Napoleon Bonaparte,* 1885
edition, vol. i. p. 285.

I informed him that Napoleon had said, 'What guarantee can I have that he will not come up some day when I have nearly finished my history, and under some pretext seize it?' which he had desired might be communicated to him. Sir Hudson replied, 'The guarantee of his good conduct!'

Shortly afterwards I saw Napoleon in his dressing-room. He was much pleased at having received the campaigns of Italy, and added that he would reclaim the other papers. 'This Governor,' said he, 'if he had any delicacy, would not have continued to read a work in which his conduct was depicted in its true light. He must have been little satisfied with the comparisons made between Cockburn and him. I am glad, however, that he has read it, because he will see the real opinion that we have of him.' While he was speaking, my vision became indistinct, everything appeared to swim before my eyes, and I fell upon the floor in a fainting fit.

When I recovered my senses and opened my eyes, the first object which presented itself to my view I shall never forget: it was the countenance of Napoleon, bending over my face, and regarding me with an expression of great concern and anxiety. With one hand he was opening my shirt-collar, and with the other holding a bottle *de vinaigre des quatre voleurs*[1] to my nostrils. He had taken off my cravat, and dashed the contents of a bottle of

---

[1] Littré traces it back only to 1720, the time of the Plague at Toulouse.

*eau de Cologne* over my face. 'When I saw you
fall,' said he, 'I at first thought that your foot had
slipped ; but seeing you remain without motion, I
apprehended that it was a fit of apoplexy ; observing, however, that your face was the colour of death,
your lips white and without motion, and no apparent
respiration or empurpled countenance, I concluded
directly that it was a fit, or that your soul had
departed.'

Marchand now came into the room, whom he
ordered to give me some orange-flower water, which
was a favourite remedy of his. When he saw me
fall, in his haste he broke the bell riband. He told
me that he had lifted me up, placed me in a chair,
torn off my cravat, dashed some *eau de Cologne* and
water over my face, etc., and asked if he had done
right. I informed him that he had done everything
proper, and as a surgeon would have done under
similar circumstances ; except that instead of allowing me to remain in a recumbent posture, he had
placed me in a chair. When I was leaving the
room, I heard him tell Marchand in a undertone to
follow me, for fear I should have another fit.

*December* 1. — Napoleon, after some inquiries
touching my health, and the effects of the mercury
upon me, observed that he wished Las Cases to go
away, as three or four months' stay in St. Helena
would be of little utility either to Las Cases or himself. 'The next,' said he, 'to be removed under some
pretext, will be Montholon, as they see that he is a
most useful and consoling friend to me, and that he

always endeavours to anticipate my wants. I am
less unfortunate than they. I see nobody ; they
are subject to daily insults and vexations. They
cannot speak, they cannot write, they cannot stir
out without submitting to degrading restrictions.
I am sorry that two months ago they did not
all go. I have sufficient strength to resist all
this tyranny alone. After they have been taken
away, you will be sent off, *et alors le crime sera
consommé.*[1]

'Lowe is at once *geôlier*, governor, accuser, judge,
and sometimes executioner ; for example, when he
seized that East Indian, who was recommended
by that *brave homme*, Colonel Skelton, to General
Montholon, as a good servant. He came up here
and seized the man with his own hands under my
windows. He did justice to himself certainly ; *le
metier d'un sbire lui convient beaucoup mieux que
celui de représentant d'une grande nation.* A soldier is
better off than they are, as, if he is accused, he must
be tried according to known forms before he can be
punished. In the worst dungeon in England a
prisoner is not denied printed papers and books.
Except obliging me to see him, he has done everything to annoy me.

'Instead of allowing us to be subject to the
caprice of an individual,' added he, 'there ought to be
a committee composed of the Admiral, Sir George
Bingham, and two members of the Council, to debate

[1] It is at least curious that Napoleon should have foretold
O'Meara's removal.

and decide upon the measures necessary to be adopted towards us.'

*December* 3.—Napoleon sent for me at one o'clock P.M.   Found him in bed suffering from headache and general uneasiness, which had been preceded by shiverings.   Had a little fever during the night.   I recommended some remedies, and pointed out in strong terms the necessity there was of his following my advice, and especially in taking exercise, and my firm conviction that in the contrary case he would soon be seized with an alarming fit of illness.   '*Tanto meglio*,' replied Napoleon ; *più presto si finirà.*'

*December* 4.—Wrote an account of the state of Napoleon's health, and of the advice which I had given him, to Sir Hudson Lowe.   Napoleon somewhat better.

He gave his opinions about Moreau and others.[1] 'Moreau,' said he, 'was an excellent general of division, but not fit to command a large army. With a hundred thousand men Moreau would divide his army in different positions, covering roads, and would not do more than if he had only thirty thousand.   He did not know how to profit either by the number of his troops, or by their positions.   Very calm and cool in the field, he was more collected and better able to command in the heat of an action than to make dispositions prior to it.   He was often seen smoking his pipe in battle.

---

[1] 'What a number of great generals arose suddenly during the Revolution : Pichegru, Kléber, Masséna, Marceau, Desaix, Hoche, etc.'—*Las Cases*, vol. ii., part iii., p. 229, English edition.

Moreau was not naturally a man of bad heart ; *Un bon vivant, mais il n'avait pas beaucoup de caractère.* He was led away by his wife and another intriguing Creole. His having joined Pichegru and Georges in the conspiracy, and subsequently having closed his life fighting against his country, will ever disgrace his memory. As a general, Moreau was infinitely inferior to Desaix, or to Kléber, or even to Soult. Of all the generals I ever had under me, Desaix and Kléber possessed the greatest talents ;[1]

---

[1] 'Desaix was surnamed by the Arabs the *just Sultan;* at the funeral of Marceau the Austrians observed an armistice, on account of the respect they entertained for him ; and young Duphot was the model of perfect virtue.

'But the same commendations cannot be bestowed on those who were further advanced in life, for they belonged in some measure to the era that had just passed away. Masséna, Augereau, Brune, and many others, were merely intrepid depredators. Masséna was, moreover, distinguished for the most sordid avarice. It was asserted that I played him a trick which might have proved a hanging matter ; that being one day indignant at his depredations, I drew on his banker for two or three millions. Great embarrassment ensued ; for my name was not without its due weight. The banker wrote to intimate that he could not pay the sum without the authority of Masséna. On the other hand, he was urged to pay it without hesitation, as Masséna, if he were wronged, could appeal to the courts of law for justice. Masséna, however, resorted to no legal steps, and consoled himself as well as he could for the payment of the money. Oudinot, Murat, and Ney were commonplace kind of generals, having no recommendation save personal courage.

'Moncey was an honest man ; Macdonald was distinguished for firm loyalty ; I was deceived with respect to the character of Bernadotte ; Soult also had his faults as well as his merits. The whole of his campaign of the south of France was admirably conducted.'—*Las Cases*, vol. ii., part iii., p. 230, English edition.

'Kléber,' said he, 'was endowed with the highest talent; but he was merely the man of the moment; he pursued glory as the only especially Desaix, as Kléber only loved glory, inasmuch as it was the means of procuring him riches and pleasures, whereas Desaix loved glory for itself, and despised everything else. Desaix was wholly wrapt up in war and glory. To him riches and pleasure were valueless, nor did he give them a moment's thought. He was a little black-looking man, about an inch shorter than I am, always badly dressed, sometimes even ragged, and despising comfort or convenience. When in Egypt, I made

road to enjoyment ; but he had no national sentiment, and he could, without any sacrifice, have devoted himself to foreign service.' Kléber had commenced his youthful career among the Prussians, to whom he continued much attached. Desaix possessed, in a very superior degree, the important equilibrium above described. Moreau scarcely deserved to be placed in the first rank of generals ; in him Nature had left her work unfinished ; he possessed more instinct than genius. In Lannes courage at first predominated over judgment; but the latter was every day gaining ground, and approaching the equilibrium. He had become a very able commander at the period of his death. 'I found him a dwarf,' said the Emperor, 'but I lost him a giant.' In another general, whom he named, judgment was, on the contrary, superior to courage ; it could not be denied that he was a brave man ; but he, like many others, did not forget the chance of the cannon ball.

Speaking of military ardour and courage the Emperor said, ' I know the depth, or what I call the *draught of water*, of all my generals ; some,' added he, joining action to his words, ' will sink to the waist, some to the chin, others over the head; but the number of the latter is very small, I assure you. Suchet,' he said, ' was one whose courage and judgment had been surprisingly improved. Masséna was a very superior man, and by a strange peculiarity of temperament, he possessed the desired equilibrium only in the heat of battle ; it was created in the midst of danger. The generals,' finally observed the Emperor, ' who seemed destined to future distinction were Gerard, Clausel, Foy, Lamarque, etc. These were my new marshals.'—*Las Cases*, vol. i., part ii., p. 9, English edition ; see also vol. ii. p. 45 of this work.

him a present of a complete field-equipage several
times, but he always lost it. Wrapt up in a cloak,
Desaix threw himself under a gun, and slept as
contentedly as if he were in a palace. For him
luxury had no charms. Upright and honest in all
his proceedings, he was called by the Arabs, *the just
Sultan*. He was intended by nature for a great
general. Kléber and Desaix were a loss irreparable
to France. Had Kléber lived, your army in Egypt
would have perished. Had that imbecile Menou
attacked you on your landing with twenty thousand
men, as he might have done, instead of the division
Lanusse, your army would have been only a meal
for them. You were seventeen or eighteen thousand
strong, without cavalry.

'Lannes, when I first took him by the hand, was
an *ignorantaccio*. His education had been much
neglected. However, he improved greatly; and to
judge from the astonishing progress he made, he
would have been a general of the first class. He
had great experience in war, and had been in fifty-
four pitched battles, and in three hundred combats
of different kinds. He was a man of uncommon
bravery; cool in the midst of fire; and possessed of
a clear, penetrating eye, ready to take advantage of
any opportunity which might present itself. Violent
and hasty in his expressions, sometimes even in my
presence, he was ardently attached to me. In the
midst of his anger he would not suffer any person
to make any rejoinder to his remarks. On that
account, when he was in a choleric mood, it was

dangerous to speak to him, as he used to come to me in his rage, and say that such and such persons were not to be trusted.   As a general he was greatly superior to Moreau or to Soult.

'Masséna,' said he, 'was a man of superior talent.   He generally, however, made bad dispositions previous to a battle; and it was not until the dead fell around him that he began to act with that judgment which he ought to have displayed before. In the midst of the dying and the dead, of balls sweeping away those who encircled him, then Masséna was himself—gave his orders and made his dispositions with the greatest *sang froid* and judgment.   This is *la vera nobilità di sangue.*   It was truly said of Masséna that he never began to act with judgment until the battle was going against him.[1]   He was, however, *un voleur.*   He went halves along with the contractors and commissaries of the army.   I signified to him often, that if he would discontinue his peculations I would make him a present of eight hundred thousand or a million of francs; but he had acquired such a habit that he could not keep his hands from money.[2]   On this account he was hated by the soldiers, who mutinied against him three or four times.   However,

---

[1] It was, however, through the ability of his dispositions that the Allies were defeated at Zurich in 1799, and Souvaroff was defeated by inferior forces, and a few years afterwards the Duke of Wellington forced to retire to the lines of Torres Vedras.   The siege of Genoa attests his gallantry for all time.

[2] See also letters from Napoleon to Joseph at Naples in *Du Casse* on this point.

considering the circumstances of the times, he was precious ; and had not his bright parts been soiled with the vice of avarice, he would have been a great man.

'Pichegru,' continued Napoleon, 'was *répétiteur* at Brienne, and instructed me in mathematics, when I was about ten years old. He possessed considerable knowledge in that science. As a general, Pichegru was a man of no ordinary talent, far superior to Moreau, although he had never done anything extraordinarily great, as the success of the campaigns in Holland was in a great measure owing to the battle of Fleurus.[1] Pichegru, after he had allied himself with the Bourbons, sacrificed the lives of upwards of twenty thousand of his soldiers, by throwing them purposely into the enemy's hands, whom he had informed beforehand of his intentions. He had a dispute once with Kléber, at a time when, instead of marching his army upon Mayence, as he ought to have done, he marched the greatest part of them to another point, where Kléber observed that it would only be necessary to send the *ambulances* with a few men to make a show. At that time it was thought to be stupidity, but afterwards it was discovered to be treachery. One of Pichegru's projects was for Louis to come and join the army under his command, and to cause himself to be proclaimed King. To ensure success he signified to Louis that it was necessary for him to bring a large sum of money ; as he said that

[1] Gained by General, afterwards Marshal, Jourdan, for whom Joseph asked the title of Duke of Fleurus.

*Vive le Roi* lay at the bottom of the *gosier*, and that it would require a great quantity of wine to bring it out of the mouth. If Louis *had* come,' continued the Emperor, 'he would have been shot.'

Sir Hudson Lowe came up to Longwood and observed to me that General Bonaparte had adopted a very bad mode of procedure, by, in a manner, declaring war against him (Sir Hudson), when he was the *only* person who had it in his power to render him a service, or to make his situation comfortable. Count Las Cases had, he said, much altered his opinion concerning him since the intercourse they had had together, and no longer looked upon him in the light of an arbitrary tyrant, who did everything to annoy them ; which change of opinion the Count had signified to him, and confessed that they had represented everything to General Bonaparte '*par un voile de sang*.'[1] That I should do well to remove any false impressions under which General Bonaparte might labour. His Excellency then made some remarks upon ' General Bonaparte's constantly confining himself to his room,' and asked what I supposed would induce him to go out ? I replied, an enlargement of his boundaries, taking off some of the restrictions, and giving him a house at the other side of the island. I observed also that the allowance of provisions was totally insufficient, as the French laid out seven or eight pounds a day in articles which were indispensable, and which I enumerated. Sir Hudson Lowe answered, 'That with respect to this last, he had

---

[1] Sir Hudson Lowe's own words.

exceeded by one half what was allowed by the Ministers, who were answerable to Parliament that the expenses of Longwood did not exceed £8000 per annum, and that perhaps he (Sir Hudson) might be obliged hereafter to pay the surplus out of his own salary. That his instructions were much more rigid than those of his predecessor. But unfortunately General Bonaparte had thought that he had come out furnished with instructions of a much more lenient nature than those of the Admiral, when the fact was directly the reverse. That all his actions had been misconstrued and misrepresented, and malicious constructions put upon them. That the British Government did not wish to render General Bonaparte's existence miserable, or to torment him. That it was not so much himself (Bonaparte) they were afraid of; but that turbulent and disaffected people in Europe would make use of his name and influence, to excite rebellion and disturbances in France and elsewhere, in order to aggrandise themselves, and otherwise answer their own purposes; also, that Las Cases was very well treated, and wanted for nothing.' This he desired I would communicate to General Bonaparte.

I communicated some of those remarks of the Governor's to Napoleon, who replied, 'I do not believe that he acts according to his instructions. A Government two thousand leagues off, and ignorant of the localities of the island, can never give orders in detail; they can only give general and discretionary ones. They have only directed

him to adopt every measure he may think necessary
to prevent my escape.    Instead of that, I am
treated in a manner dishonourable to humanity.
To kill and bury a man is intelligible, but this
slow torture, this killing in detail, is much less
humane than if they ordered me to be shot at once.
I have often heard,' continued he, 'of the tyranny
and oppressions practised in your colonies; but I
never thought that there could exist such violations
of law and of justice as are practised here.    From
what I have seen of you English, I think there is
not a nation on earth more enslaved, as I told
Colonel Wilks, the former Governor of this island.'
Here I observed that I begged of him not to form
his opinion of the English nation by a little colony,
placed under peculiar circumstances, and subject
to military law; that to judge correctly of England,
one must be *there*, and *there* he would see how
little a person with a brown or a black coat cared
about the Ministers.    'So said the old colonel,'
replied Napoleon, 'but I only speak of you as I
have seen you, and I find you to be the greatest
slaves upon earth.    All trembling with fear at the
sight of that Governor.[1]    There is Sir George
Bingham, who is a well-disposed man, yet he is
so much afraid that he will not come and see me,
through fear that he might give umbrage to the
Governor; the rest of the officers run away at

---

[1] Napoleon might have added the foreign Commissioners to his
list.    In fact no one seems to have known how to escape the
suspicions of Lowe.

the sight of us.' I replied that it was not fear, but delicacy, which prevented Sir George Bingham from coming, and that as to the other officers, they must obey the orders which they had received. Napoleon replied, 'If they were French officers, they would not be afraid of expressing their opinion as to the barbarity of the treatment pursued here; and a French general, second in command, would, if he saw his country dishonoured in the manner yours is, write a complaint of it himself to his Government. As to myself,' continued he, 'I would never make a complaint if I did not know that, were an inquiry demanded by the nation, your Ministers would say, "He has never complained, and *therefore* he is conscious that he is well treated, and that there are no grounds for it." Otherwise, I should conceive it degrading to me to utter a word; though I am so disgusted with the conduct of this *sbirro*, that I should, with the greatest pleasure, receive the intimation that orders had arrived to shoot me—I should esteem it a blessing.'

I observed that Sir Hudson Lowe had professed himself very desirous to accommodate and arrange matters in an amicable manner. Napoleon replied, 'If he wishes to accommodate, let him put things upon the same footing as they were during the time of Admiral Cockburn. Let no person be permitted to enter here for the purpose of seeing me without a letter from Bertrand. If he does not like to give Bertrand liberty to pass people in, let him make out a list himself of such persons in the island as he will allow to visit, and send it to Bertrand, and let the latter have the power to grant them permission to enter, and to write to them. When strangers arrive, in like manner let him make out a list of such as he will permit to see us, and during their stay let them be allowed to visit with Bertrand's pass. Perhaps I should see very few of them, as it is difficult to distinguish between those who come up to see me as they would a wild boar, and others who are actuated by motives of respect; but still, I should like to have the privilege. It is for him to accommodate if he likes; he has the power—I have none; I am not Governor—I have no places to give away. Let him take off his restrictions that I shall not quit the high-road, or speak to a lady if I meet one. I would wager my life,' continued he, 'that if I sent for Sir George Bingham, or the Admiral, to ride out with me, before I had gone out three times with either the one or the other this Governor would make some insinuations to them which would render me liable to be affronted by their refusing to accompany me any longer. He says that Las Cases is well treated, and wants for nothing, because he does not starve him. He pays no attention to the moral wants which distinguish the man from the brute; he only looks to the physical and grosser ones. Just as if Las Cases were a horse, or an ass, and a bundle of hay was sufficient to entitle him to say, he is happy.'

*December* 5.—Had a long conversation with the Emperor in his bath. Asked his opinion of the Czar Alexander. ' *C'est un homme extrêmement faux. Un Grec du bas empire,*' replied Napoleon. ' He is the only one of the three,[1] who has any talent. He is plausible, a great dissimulator, very ambitious, and a man who studies to make himself popular. It is his foible to believe himself skilled in the art of war, and he likes nothing so well as to be complimented upon it, although everything that originated with himself relative to military operations was ill-judged and absurd.

' At Tilsit, Alexander and the King of Prussia used frequently to occupy themselves in contriving dresses for dragoons; debating upon what button the crosses of the orders ought to be hung, and such other fooleries. They fancied themselves on an equality with the best generals in Europe, because they knew how many rows of buttons there were upon a dragoon's jacket. I could scarcely keep from laughing sometimes when I heard them discussing these *coglionerie* with as much gravity and earnestness as if they were planning an impending action between two hundred thousand men. However, I encouraged them in their arguments, as I saw it was their weak point. We rode out every day together. The King of Prussia was *une bête, et nous a tellement ennuyés*, that Alexander and myself frequently galloped away in order to get rid of him.'

[1] Alexander, Francis, and the King of Prussia.

Napoleon afterwards recounted to me some part of his early life: said that after having been at school at Brienne, he was sent to Paris at the age of fifteen or sixteen, 'where at the general examination,' continued he, 'being found to have given the best answers in mathematics,[1] I was appointed to the artillery. After the Revolution about one-third of the artillery officers emigrated, and I became *chef de bataillon* at the siege of Toulon; having been proposed by the artillery officers themselves as the person who, amongst them, possessed most scientific knowledge. During the siege I commanded the artillery and directed the operations against the town. After the siege I was made commandant of the artillery of the army of Italy, and my plans led to the capture of many important fortresses in Switzerland and Italy.

'On my return to Paris I was made General, and the command of the army[2] in La Vendée

---

[1] Only one individual formed a mistaken idea of him; that was M. Bauer, the dull, heavy German master.

Young Napoleon never made much progress in the German language, which offended M. Bauer, who ranked German above all things, and he in consequence formed a most contemptible opinion of his pupil's abilities. One day Napoleon not being in his place, M. Bauer inquired where he was, and was told that he was attending his examination in the class for artillery. 'What! does he anything?' said M. Bauer ironically. 'Why, sir, he is the best mathematician in the school,' was the reply. 'Ah, I have always heard it remarked, and I have always believed, that none but a fool could learn mathematics.' 'It would be curious,' said the Emperor, 'to know whether M. Bauer lived 'long enough to see me rise in the world, and to enjoy the confirmation of his own judgment.'—*Las Cases*, vol. i., part i., p. 124, English edition.

[2] Really the command of a brigade.

offered to me, which I refused, and replied that such a command was only fit for a general of *gendarmerie*.[1]  On the 13th of Vendemiaire I commanded the army of the Convention in Paris against the Sections, whom I defeated after an action of a few minutes.  Subsequently I got the command of the Army of Italy, where I established my reputation.  Nothing,' continued he, 'has been more simple than my elevation.  It was not the result of intrigue or crime.  It was owing to the peculiar circumstances of the times, and because I fought successfully against the enemies of my country.  What is most extraordinary, and I believe unparalleled in history, is that I rose from being a private person to the astonishing height of power I possessed without having committed a single crime to obtain it.[2]  If I were on my deathbed, I could make the same declaration.'

I asked if it were true that he was indebted to Barras for employment at Toulon, and if he had ever offered his services to the English.  'Both reports are untrue,' replied Napoleon.  'I had no connection with Barras until after the affair of Toulon.

[1] There are several errors in this paragraph, probably from Napoleon being misunderstood.  His mathematical proficiency is doubtful, and there is much question as to his real part in the capture of Toulon.  It was only the command of an infantry brigade in La Vendée, that was not offered, but to which he was nominated, and for not joining which he was struck off the employed list.  But this account of his early connection with the plans for the operations of the army of Italy, a matter too often overlooked, is quite correct.

[2] The bitterest enemy of Napoleon must allow that this boast was justified.  Not a drop of blood was shed for the sake of his elevation to the consulship.  And, if we except the death of the Duc d'Enghien, what monarch in disturbed times had shed less blood?

It was Gasparin, Deputy for Orange, and a man of talent, to whom I was chiefly indebted for protection at Toulon, and support against a set of *ignorantacci* sent down by the Convention. I never in my life offered my services to England, nor ever intended it. Nor did I ever intend to go to Constantinople : all those accounts *sont des romans.*[1] I passed a short time with Paoli in Corsica, in the year 17—, who was very partial to me, and to whom I was then much attached. Paoli espoused the cause of the English faction, and I that of the French, and consequently most of my family were driven away from Corsica. Paoli often patted me on the head, saying, "You are one of Plutarch's men." He divined that I should be something extraordinary.' Of General Dugommier he spoke in terms of great affection as a personal friend, describing him as a brave and intrepid officer, who had judgment enough to carry into execution the plan proposed by him, in opposition to those directed by the Committee of Public Safety.

He spoke about the expedition to Copenhagen, ' which,' said he, ' showed great energy on the part of your Ministers ; but setting aside the violation of the law of nations which you committed (for, in fact, it was nothing but a robbery), I think that it was injurious to your interests, as it made the Danish nation irreconcilable enemies to you, and, in fact, shut you out of the North for three years. When I

---

[1] He did certainly once apply to be sent to Constantinople. See Colonel Iung's *Bonaparte et sa temps*, vol. iii, p. 64.

heard of it, I said, I am glad of it, as it will embroil England irrecoverably with the Northern Powers. The Danes being able to join me with sixteen sail of the line was of but little consequence. I had plenty of ships, and only wanted seamen, whom you did not take, and whom I obtained afterwards; while by the expedition your Ministers established their characters as faithless, and as persons with whom no engagements, no laws, were binding.'

' During the war with you,' said he, 'all the intelligence I received from England came through the smugglers. They are people who have courage and ability to do anything for money. They had at first a part of Dunkirk allotted to them, to which they were restricted; but as they latterly went out of their limits, committed riots, and insulted everybody, I ordered Gravelines to be prepared for their reception, where they had a little camp for their accommodation, beyond which they were not permitted to go. At one time there were upwards of five hundred of them in Dunkirk. I had every information I wanted through them. They brought over newspapers and despatches from the spies that we had in London. They took over spies from France, landed and kept them in their houses for some days, then dispersed them over the country, and brought them back when wanted. The police had in their pay a number of French emigrants, who gave constant information of the actions of the Vendean party, Georges, and others, at the time they were preparing to assassinate me. All their movements were made

known.   Besides, the police had in their pay many
English spies, some of high quality, amongst whom
there were many ladies.   There was one lady in
particular of very high rank who furnished considerable information, and was sometimes paid
£3000 in one month.   They came over,' continued
he, 'in boats not broader than this bath.   It was
really astonishing to see them passing your seventy-
four gun ships in defiance.'   I observed that they
were double spies, and that they brought intelligence from France to the British Government.
'That is very likely,' replied Napoleon.   'They
brought you newspapers ; but I believe that, as
spies, they did not convey much intelligence to you.
They are *genti terribili*, and did great mischief to
your Government.   They took from France annually
forty or fifty millions of silks and brandy.   They
assisted the French prisoners to escape from
England.   The relations of Frenchmen, prisoners
in your country, were accustomed to go to Dunkirk, and to make a bargain with them to bring
over a certain prisoner.   All that they wanted was
the name, age, and a private token, by means of
which the prisoner might repose confidence in them.
Generally, in a short time afterwards, they effected
it ; as, for men like them, they had a great deal of
honour in their dealings.   They offered several
times to bring over Louis and the rest of the Bourbons for a sum of money ; but they wanted to
stipulate that if they met with any accident, or
interruption to their design, they might be allowed

to massacre them. This I would not consent to.
Besides, I despised the Bourbons too much, and had
no fear of them ; indeed, at that time, they were no
more thought of in France than the Stuarts were
in England. They also offered to bring over
Dumouriez, Sarrazin, and others, whom they thought
I hated, but I held them in too much contempt to
take any trouble about them.'

This conversation was brought about by my
telling him that Lefebvre-Desnouettes had arrived
at New York, and was with his brother Joseph.
When I asked if Lefebvre had not broken his parole
in England, Napoleon replied that he had, and
then observed, 'A great deal has been said about
French officers having been employed after having
broken their parole in England. Now the fact is,
that the English themselves were the first to break
their parole at a time when twelve of them ran
away. I proposed afterwards to your Ministers
that both Governments should reciprocally send back
every prisoner of whatsoever rank he might be, who
had broken his parole and escaped. This they
refused to do, and I became indifferent about it. I
did not receive at Court those who escaped ; or encourage them, nor discourage them, after this refusal.
Your Ministers made a great fuss about officers who
broke their parole having been employed in my
armies, although they refused to agree to the only
measure which could put a stop to it, viz. that both
sides should send them back immediately ; and afterwards had the impudence to attempt to throw all

the odium upon me.   But you English can never do any wrong.'

I asked if he thought that the expedition to Walcheren might, if it had been well conducted, have taken Antwerp ?   Napoleon replied, ' I am of opinion that if you had landed a few thousand men at first at Williamstadt, and marched directly for Antwerp, between consternation, want of preparation, and the uncertainty of the number of assailants, you might have taken it by a *coup de main*.  But after the fleet had got up it was impossible ; as the crews of the ships, united to the National Guard, workmen, and others, amounted to upwards of fifteen thousand men.   The ships would have been sunk, or taken into the docks, and the crews employed upon the batteries.   Besides, Antwerp, though old, is strongly fortified.[1]  It is true that Lord Chatham did everything possible to ensure the failure of the object of the expedition ; but after the delay of a few days, it would have been impossible for any man to have effected it. You had too many men for a *coup de main*, and too few for a regular siege.   The inhabitants were against you, as they saw that your object was to get possession of the town, to burn and destroy everything, and then go on board your ships and get away.   It was a very unlucky expedition for you.   Your Ministers were very badly informed about the country.   You had afterwards the *bêtise*

---

[1] It was successfully defended (as Hamburg was by Davoût) by Carnot in 1814.

to remain in that pestilential place until you lost some thousands of men. *C'était le comble de la bêtise et de l'inhumanité.* I was very glad of it, as I knew that disease would carry you off by thousands, and oblige you to evacuate it without any exertion being made on my part. I sent none but deserters and *mauvais sujets* to garrison it, and gave orders that they should sleep in two frigates I had sent there for that purpose. I also had water conveyed to them at a great expense, but still it was most unhealthy. The General who commanded Flushing,' added he, 'did not defend it as long as he ought to have done. He had made a large fortune by the smugglers (as there was another depot of them there), and had been guilty of some malpractices, for which he was afraid of being brought to a court-martial, and I believe was glad to get away.'

I asked him if it were true that a Corsican, named Masseri, had been sent with some proposals to him once by our Government? Napoleon replied, 'Masseri? Yes, I recollect perfectly well that he was brought to me when I was First Consul. He was introduced with great mystery and secrecy into my room, when I was in a bath, as I am now. I think he began to speak about some political matters, and to make some insinuations about peace, but I stopped him, as it had been published in the English papers that he was coming upon some mission to me, which I did not like. Besides, Masseri, though *un bravissimo uomo*, was a great *bavard*. I believe that he was sent by King

George himself. He was a Republican, and maintained that the death of Charles the First was just and necessary.'

Lady Lowe came up to Longwood, and for the first time paid a visit to Countesses Bertrand and Montholon.

*December* 6.—Napoleon observed to me that the visit of Lady Lowe yesterday appeared to him to be an artifice of her husband, to throw dust in people's eyes, and to make them believe that, notwithstanding the arrest of Las Cases, the Governor was very well esteemed at Longwood, and had only done his duty ; and that there was no foundation for the reports which had been spread of the ill-treatment said to be inflicted upon the inhabitants of Longwood. I informed him that Lady Lowe had been always desirous to call upon Countesses Bertrand and Montholon, and had embraced the first opportunity which presented itself after her accouchement. Napoleon replied, ' I am far from thinking that she participates in the designs of her husband, but she has chosen the time badly. At the moment when Sir Hudson treats Las Cases so barbarously and illegally he sends her up. It is either an artifice of her husband's to blind the world, or else he mocks our misfortunes.' I observed that more probably it was a preliminary step of the Governor's towards an accommodation. ' No,' replied Napoleon, ' that cannot be. If he really wished to be accommodating, the first step would be to take away some of his useless and oppressive restrictions. Yesterday, after his wife had been here, Madame Bertrand and family went out to walk. On their return, they were stopped and seized by the sentinels, who refused to let them in because it was six o'clock. Now, in God's name, if he had a mind to accommodate, would he continue to prevent us from walking at the only time of the day when, at this season, it is agreeable? Tell him,' continued Napoleon, 'candidly the observations I have made, if he asks you what I thought of the visit.'

*December* 7.—Wrote to Sir Hudson Lowe that a statement of what Napoleon had informed me on the 4th inst. would be the best mode of effecting an accommodation.

Had a long conversation with Napoleon upon the anatomy of the human body. He desired to see some anatomical plates, which I explained to him. I observed that plates only served to remind a person of what he had already learned from actual dissection, for which they could never be entirely substituted. In this Napoleon perfectly agreed with me, and gave me some account of the encouragement which he had given to the schools of anatomy and surgery, and of the facilities which he had afforded to medical students to learn their profession at a trifling expense.

Heard him express some opinions afterwards relative to a few of the characters who had figured in the Revolution. 'Robespierre,' said he, 'though a bloodthirsty monster, was not so bad as Collot

d'Herbois, Billaud de Varennes, Hébert, Fouquier
Tinville, and many others. Latterly Robespierre
wished to be more moderate, and actually some
time before his death said that he was tired of
executions and suggested moderation. When
Hébert accused the Queen *de contrarier la nature*,
Robespierre proposed that he should be denounced,
as having made such an improbable accusation purposely to excite a sympathy amongst the people, that
they might rise and rescue her.

‘From the beginning of the Revolution Louis had
constantly the life of Charles the First before his
eyes.[1] The example of Charles, who had come to
extremities with the Parliament and lost his head,
prevented Louis on many occasions from making
the defence which he ought to have done against
the revolutionists. When brought to trial, he
ought merely to have said that by the laws he could
do no wrong, and that his person was sacred. The
Queen ought to have done the same. It would
have had no effect in saving their lives ; but they
would have died with more dignity. Robespierre
was of opinion that the King ought· to have been
despatched privately. “What is the use,” said

---

[1] Bertrand de Molleville states that ‘the King's usual book was
the *History of Charles I.;*’ and Madame Campan says the Queen
told her that the King had observed to her that ‘all which was going
forward in France,’ during the early days of the Revolution, was an
imitation of the Revolution in England in the time of Charles I., and
that he was incessantly reading the history of that unfortunate
monarch in order that he might act better than Charles had done at
a similar crisis.—*The Private Life of Marie Antoinette*, by Madame
Campan, 1884 edition, vol. ii. p. 228.

Robespierre, "of this mockery of forms, when you go to the trial prepared to condemn him to death, whether he deserves it or not." The Queen,' added Napoleon, 'went to the scaffold with some sensations of welcome; and truly it must have been a relief to her to depart from a life in which she was treated with such execrable barbarity. Had I,' continued he, 'been four or five years older, I have no doubt that I should have been guillotined along with numbers of others.'

*December* 10.—Water very scarce at Longwood. Sir Hudson Lowe gave directions that the horses of the establishment should be ridden to water to Hut's Gate, instead of getting it from the tubs that were placed for the use of Napoleon's household. The water in them is extremely muddy, green, and nauseous. In Deadwood it is much more easy to get a bottle of wine than one of water. Parties of the 53d are employed daily in rolling butts of water to their camp. It reminded me of my former residence in Egypt, where we were obliged to buy bad water at an exorbitant rate.

Charles, a mulatto servant, discharged from Longwood. Orders given by Sir Hudson Lowe that he should be sent to his house. Underwent a long interrogation from His Excellency as to what he had seen and heard during the time he had been at Longwood. Application made to the Governor by the orderly officer to allow a cart for the purpose of bringing water to the establishment, that in the tubs being so very scanty and bad.

Napoleon rather depressed and annoyed, that instead of the whole of the campaigns of Italy having been returned by Sir Hudson Lowe, only three or four chapters had been sent. Desired me to tell Sir Hudson Lowe that he supposed he was getting them copied, and that, according as they were finished, he would send them back.

*December* 11.—Went to Plantation House and acquainted Sir Hudson Lowe with the message I was charged to deliver to him. His Excellency waxed very wroth, and said, 'That if General Bonaparte persisted in his belief that the papers had been kept for the purpose of copying, after the assurance to the contrary, which he had yesterday had from young Las Cases, he (Sir Hudson) considered *him unworthy of being treated like a man of honour, and undeserving the consideration due from one gentleman to another.'* This he not only repeated twice, but obliged me to insert it in my pocket-book; desiring me not on any account to omit communicating those expressions to General Bonaparte.

After having cooled a little, however, His Excellency rescinded his directions, gave me some explanations which he desired me to make known to Napoleon, and ordered me to rub out of my pocket-book the obnoxious expressions. He then walked about with me in the library and said, 'That in reference and reply to what I had written to him, General Bonaparte could not be permitted to run about the country. That if the intentions of Ministers were only to prevent his escape from the island, a Company's Governor would have answered as well as any other person; but that there were other objects in view, and material ones, which he had been sent out to fulfil. That there were several reasons for not allowing him to communicate with any one on the island. That any man might secure his person by planting sentries about him, but that much more was to be done.' When I was about to leave the room, he called me back and said, 'Tell General Bonaparte that it is very fortunate for him that he has so good a man for Governor over him; that others with the instructions I have would have put him in chains for his conduct.' He concluded by desiring me to endeavour to get Sir Thomas Strange introduced to Napoleon.

Cipriani in town, purchasing provisions.

*December* 12.—Explained to Napoleon in the least offensive manner I could the message I had been ordered by Sir Hudson Lowe to deliver, with an assurance from the Governor that his papers had been kept sacred; which I observed had been confirmed by a letter from Emanuel de Las Cases, accompanying those that had been returned, testifying that the papers had been respected. That Sir Hudson Lowe had told me, that during the examination of the papers, which took place always in presence of Las Cases, whenever the

latter pointed out one as belonging to him
(Napoleon), it was immediately put aside without
being looked at ; and that when the examination
was finished, the papers were sealed up with Las
Cases's seal, and not opened again, unless in his
presence.    That Sir Hudson had said, that so
far from being instigated by malice or revenge
he had written to the Ministry to ameliorate his
condition, etc.    Napoleon replied that he did
not believe it ; that no assertion from a man who
had told so many falsehoods could be credited ;
and that the letter from young Las Cases was
not satisfactory, as it merely contained an assurance from Sir Hudson Lowe that they would be
respected.

I then informed him that Sir Thomas Strange,
who had been Chief Judge in the East Indies,
was desirous of paying his respects to him, and
that his intended visit did not arise from curiosity,
but was a mark of that attention which every
person ought to show towards so great a man, and
one who had filled so high a station in the world.
Napoleon replied, ' I will see no person who does
not first go to Bertrand.    Persons sent direct by
the Governor I will not see, as it would have the
appearance of obeying a command from him.'

Count Bertrand now came in, and mentioned
that the Governor was at Longwood, and wanted
to see me.    Napoleon then said, ' If he asks you
any questions about my thoughts, tell him that I
intend writing a protest to the Prince Regent

against his barbarous conduct. That his keeping Las Cases in custody, when there is nothing against him, is illegal. That he ought either to be sent back here, or sent off the island, or tried. If he wishes to accommodate differences, as he informed you, let him alter his conduct, and put matters upon the footing they were during the time of Admiral Cockburn. As to the visit of the judge, whom he wishes me to see, tell him *que les gens qui sont dans un tombeau ne reçoivent pas de visites*, as he has literally immured me in a tomb. Besides, according to his restrictions, if the judge does not speak French, I cannot employ one of my officers to interpret, for he has prohibited strangers who may visit me from speaking or communicating with any person of my suite, and, moreover, I have lost Las Cases.'

Count Bertrand desired me to say that if he saw Sir Thomas Strange, he should be obliged to show him those parts of the Governor's restrictions, signed by himself, in which he had prohibited those who had a pass to see the Emperor, from holding any communication with others of his household unless specially permitted.

Informed Sir Hudson Lowe of what I had been desired, which he said he would communicate to Lord Bathurst. He then observed, ' That Count Las Cases had not followed General Bonaparte out of affection, but merely to have an opportunity of obtaining materials from him to publish his life ; that General Bonaparte did not know what

Las Cases had written, or the expressions which had dropped from him; that he had already collected some very curious materials for his history; and that Ministers feared that some turbulent, intriguing persons in France, or on the Continent, would endeavour to excite rebellion and new wars in Europe, by making use of his (Napoleon's) name to ensure their purposes.'

He added again that he could not tell me the nature of his orders; that he had an important object to fulfil, independently of the detention of General Bonaparte; and, after some more conversation upon similiar subjects, said, that he would give permission to-morrow to Sir Thomas Strange and family to communicate with Bertrand, or with any others of the suite.

Saw Sir Thomas Reade, to whom I mentioned Napoleon's answer relative to the interview which the Governor was desirous to obtain for Sir Thomas Strange. Sir Thomas replied, 'If I were Governor, I'll be d——d if I would not make him feel that he was a prisoner.' I observed, 'Why, you cannot do much more to him than you have already done, unless you put him in irons.'—'Oh,' answered Reade, 'if he did not comply with what I wanted, I'll be d——d if I wouldn't take his books from him, which I'll advise the Governor to do. He is a d——d outlaw and a prisoner, and the Governor has a right to treat him with as much severity as he likes, and nobody has any business to interfere with him in the execution of his duty.'

*December* 13.—A sealed letter from Napoleon to Las Cases given by Count Bertrand to Captain Poppleton, for the purpose of being forwarded through the Governor to the Count. At 6 P.M. a dragoon brought two letters from Sir Hudson Lowe to Count Bertrand, one returning Napoleon's letter to Count Las Cases, because it was sealed, adding, that he would not forward any sealed letter; and that even if it were open, it would depend upon the nature of the contents, whether it would be forwarded or not; as he (the Governor) did not wish that any communication should take place between Longwood and Count Las Cases. In the other the Governor intimated that probably he should not take any steps with respect to Las Cases until he heard from the British Government.

Saw Napoleon, who conversed upon the probability of a revolution in France. 'Ere twenty years have elapsed, when I am dead and buried,' said he, 'you will witness another revolution in France. It is impossible that twenty-nine millions of Frenchmen can live contented under the yoke of sovereigns imposed upon them by foreigners, and against whom they have fought and bled for nearly thirty years. Can you blame the French for not being willing to submit to the yoke of such asses as Montchenu? You are very fond in England of making a comparison between the restoration of Charles the Second and that of Louis; but there is not the smallest resemblance. Charles was recalled by the mass of the English nation to the throne which his

successor afterwards lost for a *mass;* but as to the
Bourbons, there is not a village in France which has
not lost thirty or forty of the flower of its youth in
endeavouring to prevent their return.   The sentiments of the nation are:  "*Ce n'est pas nous qui
avons ramené ces misérables; non, ceux qui ont ravagé
notre pays, qui ont brûlé nos maisons, qui ont violé
nos femmes et nos filles, les ont mis sur le trône par
la force.*"'

I asked him some questions about the share that
Moreau had in Georges's conspiracy.  'Moreau,' said
he, 'confessed to his advocate that he had seen and
conversed with Georges and Pichegru, and that on
his trial he intended to avow it.   His counsel, however, dissuaded him from doing so, and observed
that if he confessed having seen Georges, nothing
could save him from being condemned to death.
Moreau, in an interview with the other two conspirators, insisted that the first step to be taken was
to kill me;[1] that when I was disposed of, he should
have great power and influence with the army; but
that as long as I lived he could do nothing.   When
he was arrested, the paper of accusation against him
was given to him, in which his crime was stated to
be, the having conspired against the life of the First

---

[1] Moreau had practically suggested the murder of Napoleon by
using in his communication with the conspirators the phrase, 'Il
faudrait que les consuls . . . disparussent,' watered down by Lanfrey
(vol. iii. p. 185) to 'Il faudrait qu'ils (les Consuls) disparaissent,' when
he, the virtuous patriot, would have been ready to act.   Moreau had
met Georges and Pichegru by night.   See *Thiers*, vol. v. p. 144, or a
note on page 166 of *Bourrienne*, 1885 edition, vol. ii.

Consul and the security of the Republic, in complicity with Pichegru and Georges. On reading the names of those two he dropt the paper and fainted.

‘In the battle before Dresden,’ said Napoleon, ‘I ordered an attack to be made upon the Allies by both flanks of my army. While the manœuvres for this purpose were executing, the centre remained motionless. At the distance of about from this to the outer gate,[1] I observed a group of persons collected together on horseback. Concluding that they were endeavouring to observe my manœuvres, I resolved to disturb them, and called to a captain of artillery, who commanded a field battery of eighteen or twenty pieces—“Throw a dozen balls at once into that group; perhaps there are some staff officers in it.” It was done instantly. One of the balls struck Moreau, carried off both his legs, and went through his horse.[2] Many more, I believe, who were near him were killed and wounded. A moment before Alexander had been speaking to him. Moreau’s legs were amputated not far from the spot. One of his feet, with the boot upon it, which the surgeon had thrown upon the ground, was brought by a peasant to the King of Saxony, with information that some officer of great distinction had been struck by a cannon-shot. The King, conceiv-

[1] About five hundred yards.

[2] This was a mistake of Napoleon’s. Cathcart (*War in Russia and Germany*, pp. 229, 231), who was an eyewitness, says the shot came from a field battery about a quarter of a mile distant, and not from Napoleon’s own position at all. Thus *Thiers*, vol. xvi. p. 315, is wrong.

ing that the name of the person might perhaps be discovered by the boot, sent it to me. It was examined at my headquarters, but all that could be ascertained was, that the boot was neither of English nor of French manufacture. The next day we were informed that it was the leg of Moreau.

'It is not a little extraordinary,' continued Napoleon, 'that in an action a short time afterwards I ordered the same artillery officer, with the same guns, and under nearly similar circumstances, to throw eighteen or twenty balls at once into a concourse of officers collected together, by which General St. Priest, another Frenchman, a traitor and a man of talent, who had a command in the Russian army, was killed, along with many others. Nothing,' continued the Emperor, 'is more destructive than a discharge of a dozen or more guns at once amongst a group of persons. From one or two they may escape ; but from a number discharged at a time, it is almost impossible. After Essling, when I had caused my army to cross over to the isle of Lobau, there was for weeks, by common and tacit consent on both sides between the soldiers, not by any agreement between the generals, a cessation of firing, which indeed had produced no benefit, and only killed a few unfortunate sentinels. I rode out every day in different directions. No person was molested on either side. One day, however, riding along with Oudinot, I stopped for a moment upon the edge of the island, which was about eighty

toises[1] distant from the opposite bank, where the
enemy was. They perceived us, and knowing me
by the little hat and gray coat, they pointed a three-
pounder at us. The ball passed between Oudinot
and me, and was very close to both of us. We put
spurs to our horses, and speedily got out of sight.
Under the actual circumstances the attack was little
better than murder ; but if they had fired a dozen
guns at once, they must have killed us.'[2]

Count Bertrand brought back Napoleon's letter
to Captain Poppleton, broke the seal before him, and
desired that it might be sent in that state to Sir
Hudson Lowe.

Some oranges sent to Longwood by the Admiral.

*December* 14.—Napoleon very unwell. Found
him in bed at 11 P.M. 'Doctor,' said he, 'I had a
nervous attack last night, which kept me continually
uneasy and restless, with a severe headache and
involuntary agitations. I was insensible for a few
moments. I verily thought and hoped that a more
violent attack would have carried me off before morning. It seemed as if a fit of apoplexy was coming on.
I felt a heaviness and giddiness of my head (as if it
were overloaded with blood), with a desire to put myself in an upright posture. I felt a heat in my head,
and called to those about me to pour some cold water
over it, which they did not comprehend for some
time. Afterwards the water felt hot, and I thought

---

[1] Equal to about 160 yards or 480 feet.

[2] See note in the second volume on the escapes and wounds of
the Emperor.

it smelt of sulphur, though in reality it was cold.'
At this time he was in a free perspiration, which I
recommended him to encourage, and his headache
was much diminished. After I had recommended
everything I thought necessary or advisable, he
replied, ' *Si viverebbe troppo lungamente.*' He afterwards spoke about funeral rites, and added, that
when he died, he would wish that his body might be
burned. ' It is the best mode,' said he, ' as then the
corpse does not occasion any inconvenience ; and as
to the resurrection, that must be accomplished by a
miracle, and it is easy for the Being who has it in
His power to perform such a miracle as bringing the
remains of the bodies together, also to shape again
the ashes of the dead.'

*December* 15.— Had a long conversation with
Sir Hudson Lowe relative to the affairs of Longwood and to Napoleon's health. His Excellency
said that he supposed it was Count Bertrand who
had informed Count Las Cases that he (Sir
Hudson) would send him away from the island if
he persisted in writing any more injurious reflections upon the way that General Bonaparte was
treated. That he would hold him (Bertrand)
answerable for the consequences. He also observed that as to the restrictions which had been
so much complained of, there was in reality but
little difference ; that with respect to the prohibition
to speak, which General Bonaparte complained
of, it was not an *order* to him not to speak, *but
merely a request ! ! !* He also added that Las

Cases had attempted to send a secret accusation against him, which was like stabbing a man in the back, and that they must be conscious they were telling lies, or they would not be afraid to send them to England through him, as he had offered to forward them.[1] In his conversation with Bertrand he had merely observed that, according to his instructions, he *ought* to have sent Las Cases off the island, in consequence of the letters he had written. His instructions, he said, were of such a nature that it was impossible to draw a line between some which directed that General Bonaparte should be treated with great indulgence, and others, prescribing regulations and restrictions impossible to be reconciled with the first. That he had in consequence written for further explanations, and had recommended the relaxation of the existing restrictions.

*December* 16.—Saw Napoleon, to whom I repeated what the Governor had desired. Napoleon replied, ' He sent back, and refused to forward, a letter of complaints sent to him by Montholon ; he told Bertrand that he would receive no letters

---

[1] Lowe seems to have taken any 'injurious reflections on either myself' or the Government (*Forsyth*, vol. i. p. 465) as a crime to occasion the return of the letter containing them. Earl Bathurst, in his reply to Lord Holland on 18th March 1817 (*Forsyth*, vol. ii. p. 335), implies that Lowe was forced to forward all letters. But this does not seem to have been ever understood at Longwood, and this is one of the most important points. Lowe certainly took on himself to refuse even to receive letters if they contained anything he disapproved of, the title of Emperor for example.

in which I was not styled as his Government wished; and he sent up by his *chef d'état major* a paper, threatening with transportation from the island all who should make reflections upon him or his Government; besides giving Bertrand clearly to understand that if Las Cases continued his complaints he would send him from St. Helena.'

*December* 18.—Went with Mr. Baxter to visit Count Las Cases and his son. The Count informed me that the Governor had given him permission to return to Longwood under certain conditions, but that he had not decided what he would do. Young Las Cases said that his father feared he would be looked upon slightingly at Longwood if he returned, in consequence of the disgraceful manner in which he had been arrested and dragged away by the Governor's police.

Informed the Emperor on my return that the Governor had offered to allow Las Cases to return to Longwood. After some discussion on the subject, he observed that he would give no advice to Las Cases about it. If he came back, he would receive him with pleasure; if he went away, he would hear of it with pleasure; but that in the latter case, he should wish to see him once more before he left the island. He added, that since the arrest of Las Cases, he had ordered all his generals to go away; that he should be more independent without them, as then he should not labour under the fear of their suffering ill-treatment by the Governor, in order thereby to revenge himself upon him. ' I,' continued he, ' am not afraid that they will send *me* off the island.'

Saw Sir Hudson Lowe, who said, that with the exception of certain necessary restrictions he had orders from Government to treat General Bonaparte with all possible indulgence, which he thought he had done! That if some restrictions had been imposed, it was his own fault and that of Las Cases. That he had been very mild!! This he desired me to communicate. Shortly afterwards he said that if Count Bertrand had shown his (Sir Hudson's) restrictions to Sir Thomas Strange, he, the Governor, would have been authorised to send him off the island. Nearly in the same breath he asked if I thought that the interference of Sir George Bingham as an intermediator would be of any service? I replied that probably it might, but as Sir George Bingham did not speak French with sufficient fluency to enter into long discussions or reasonings, I was of opinion that Admiral Sir Pulteney Malcolm would be a much better intermediator.

Told Napoleon what Sir Hudson Lowe had directed. ' Doctor,' replied he, ' when this man has the audacity to tell *you, who know everything that has been done*, that he treats me with indulgence, I need not suggest to you what he writes to his Government.'

He informed me that last night he had suffered another attack similar to that of the 13th, but

more violent. 'Ali,'[1] said he, 'frightened, threw
some *eau de Cologne* in my face, mistaking it for
water. This getting into my eyes gave me
intolerable pain, and certainly brought me to
myself.'

Told him what Sir Hudson Lowe had said
relative to the intermediation of Sir George
Bingham. He replied, 'Perhaps it might be of
some service; but all he has to do is, conduct
himself no longer as a jailer, but behave like a
gentleman. If any person were to undertake the
office of intermediator, the most fit would be the
Admiral, both because he is independent of Sir
Hudson Lowe, and because he is a man with
whom I can reason and argue. When your
Ministry is insincere, wants to shuffle, or has
nothing good to carry out, a *polisson* like Drake,
or Hudson Lowe, is sent as Ambassador or
Governor; when it is the contrary, and it wishes
to conciliate or treat, such a man as Lord Cornwallis is employed. A Cornwallis here would
be of more avail than all the restrictions that
could be imagined.' He then observed that he
thought it would be better for Las Cases to come
back to Longwood than either to remain in the
island separated from them, or be sent to the
Cape.

*December* 21.—A letter received from Major
Gorrequer, stating that the Governor would permit
Archambaud to see his brother (who, with Santini

---

[1] St. Denis was commonly called Ali, after a previous valet.

and Rousseau, had arrived in the *Orontes* frigate from the Cape[1])—on the following day.

*December* 23.—Sir Hudson Lowe at Longwood ; informed him what Napoleon had said about Las Cases. He told me that Las Cases wanted to make *terms*, previous to returning to Longwood, and desired me to 'go to Hut's Gate and tell him what General Bonaparte had said; but not to hold any other communication with him.' I mentioned to His Excellency the fit of syncope with which Napoleon had been attacked : 'It would be lucky,'[2] replied Sir Hudson Lowe, 'if he went off some night in a fit of the kind.'

I remarked that I thought it very probable he would be attacked with a fit of apoplexy, which would end his career, and that continuing to lead his present mode of life, if the restrictions were not modified, it was impossible he could remain in health. His Excellency observed that he would have some conversation with Count Bertrand on the subjects complained of.

On his return Sir Hudson appeared in a very bad humour, and said that Count Bertrand had for a short time spoken very reasonably, but that afterwards he had broken out foolishly about *nôtre situation*, just as if it were of any consequence to England, or to Europe, what became of Count Bertrand ; or as if it were not *Bonaparte* alone who

---

[1] This request had been at first refused by Sir Hudson Lowe.

[2] The French *translation* of O'Meara reads differently here— ' *Fâcheux*,' but three different English editions all have ' lucky.'

was looked after,—that he did not know what business he had to couple *his* situation with Bonaparte's.

Mrs. Balcombe and her eldest daughter came to see Countess Bertrand. They were desirous of paying a visit to Napoleon and to Countess Montholon, but as their pass specified Count Bertrand's house, and did not mention either of the others, it was not permitted by the orderly officer.

Saw Napoleon afterwards. 'What a fool I was to give myself up to you,' said he; 'I had a mistaken notion of your national character; I had formed a romantic idea of the English. There entered into it also a portion of pride. I disdained to give myself up to any of those sovereigns whose countries I had conquered, and whose capitals I had entered in triumph; and I determined to confide in you, whom I had never vanquished. Doctor, I am well punished for the good opinion I had of you, and for the confidence which I reposed in you, instead of giving myself up to my father-in-law, or to the Emperor Alexander, either of whom would have treated me with the greatest respect.'

I observed that it was possible that Alexander might have sent him to Siberia. 'Not at all,' replied Napoleon, 'setting aside other motives, Alexander would, through policy, and from the desire which he has to make himself popular, have treated me like a King, and I should have had palaces at command. Besides, the Czar is a generous man, and would have taken a pleasure in treating me well; and my father-in-law, though not gifted with ability, is still a conscientious man, and incapable of committing such acts of cruelty as are practised here.'

Saw Las Cases and his son with Mr. Baxter. Wrote a letter afterwards to Sir Hudson Lowe respecting the state of health of the younger Las Cases, and recommended his removal to Europe for the recovery of his health. Mr. Baxter also wrote a report of a similar tendency, and one about the Count himself, in which he said, that in consequence of his being afflicted with dyspepsia, it was probable that a change to a colder climate would be beneficial, and that that of Europe would be preferable.

*December* 25.—Napoleon in very good spirits. Asked many questions in English, which he pronounced as he would have done French ; yet the words were correct, and applied in their proper sense.

*December* 26.—Sir Hudson Lowe sent for me. Found him in town. He observed that I had put too much political feeling into my letter respecting young Las Cases ; that my opinion must have related to what would have happened had he remained at Longwood ; and that it appeared to enter too much into the feelings of *those* people. I replied that I could not separate my opinion from the cause of his complaints, and that he himself had said, if the state of young Las Cases absolutely required his removal to Europe, he would not oppose it. Sir Hudson answered that he had certainly said that if it *absolutely* required such a measure, he would not oppose it ; but that I had entered into a discussion not called for in the letter.

He then spoke about the restrictions, and showed me a letter which he said he intended to send to Bertrand, and upon which he desired to know my opinion. After reading it, I observed to His Excellency that I thought it calculated to produce some severe remarks from Napoleon; as, in fact, it left matters in nearly the same state as they had been before, after having nominally removed some of the restrictions. On a little reflection, His Excellency appeared to be of the same opinion, and said that he would reconsider the matter. In the meantime he authorised me to tell General Bonaparte that several of the restrictions should be removed, especially those relative to speaking; that the limits should be enlarged, and that liberty should be granted to people to visit him much as in former times under the Admiral.

Informed Napoleon of this, who replied that he desired no more than to have matters put as nearly as possible as they were under the Admiral. That he thought it right and just if the Governor suspected either an inhabitant of the island, or a passenger, or any of them, that he should not allow them to enter Longwood; but that what he (Napoleon) meant was, that the majority of respectable passengers or inhabitants should be allowed to visit him, and not one or two who had been picked out and sent up to Longwood by the Governor, or by his staff, as a keeper of galley-slaves would send a curious traveller to his galleys to see some extraordinary criminal. ' If,' continued he, ' I met a man

whose conversation pleased me (like the Admiral,
for example), I should wish to see him again, and
perhaps ask him to dinner or breakfast, as was done
before this Governor's arrival; therefore I wish
that a list should be sent in the first place by the
Governor to Bertrand, containing the names of the
persons that he will allow to visit us; and that afterwards Bertrand shall have the privilege of asking
any person again whose name is upon that list. I
will never see any one coming up with a pass in
which the day is fixed, which is a way of saying,
Come out this day and exhibit yourself. I want also
that our situation may be clearly defined, so that my
household shall not be liable to the insults which
they have all suffered, and continue to suffer, either
from being kept in the dark respecting the restrictions which he imposes, or from misconception of
sentinels, or the orders given being of a discretional
nature, which may make a sentinel responsible and
constitute him an arbitrary judge. The trifling
vexations and humiliations which he makes us
undergo are worse to us than the greater. I am
willing,' continued he, 'to listen to accommodation,
and not to insist upon too much. But he has no
heart or feeling. His policy is that of the petty
states of Italy; to write and promise fairly, apparently give liberty, but afterwards by insinuations
change everything. His is the policy of insinuations.'

I then asked if the Governor consented, and the
Admiral were satisfied, would he hold a conference
with that officer as an intermediator, in order to

bring about an arrangement? Napoleon replied,
'Willingly. With the greatest pleasure I would treat
personally with the Admiral, and I think that we
could settle it in half an hour. I have so much confidence in him, that if the English Government would
allow it, and the Admiral would pledge his word of
honour that no one but himself should know the
contents (unless there was some plot or intrigue
against his Government), I would write a letter,
putting him in possession of everything I know
relative to my property, in order that I might be
able to make use of it. To-morrow,' continued he,
'I shall let you know whether I am of the same
opinion as to the intermediation. If I continue the
same, you shall go to the Governor and propose it
to him.'

A letter sent by Count Bertrand to Sir Hudson
Lowe, requesting that Count Las Cases might be
permitted to visit Longwood previous to his
departure, to take leave of the Emperor.

*December* 27.—Gave Napoleon some newspapers.
On looking over them he observed an article about
Pozzo di Borgo. 'Pozzo di Borgo,' said he, 'was
deputy to the Legislative Body during the Revolution. He is a man of talent, an intriguer, and knows
France well. As long as he remains there as
Ambassador, you may be sure that Alexander does
not consider Louis to be firmly seated upon the
throne. When you see a Russian nominated as
Ambassador, you may then conclude that Alexander
thinks the Bourbons likely to continue in France.'

Went to Plantation House to inform Sir Hudson Lowe of Napoleon's willingness to accept the Admiral's intermediation. He said that he would accept the proposal, but that he had previously to decide upon a very delicate point, which might break off any purposed arrangement. That General Bonaparte had asked to see Count Las Cases before his departure, which would do away with the great object he had had in view for a month back, viz. that of cutting off all communication between Longwood and Las Cases. That General Bonaparte might make important and dangerous communications to Las Cases; to obviate which he would propose that a staff officer should be present at the demanded interview, which it was likely might anger General Bonaparte.

He then wrote the following words on a piece of paper, which he desired me to copy, and to show the copy: 'The Governor is not conscious of ever having wilfully given to General Bonaparte any just cause of offence or disagreement. He has seen with pain misunderstandings arise on points where his duty would not allow him to pursue any other course, and which might have been frequently removed by a single word of explanation.

'Any channel by which he may think such misunderstandings may be removed, the Governor is perfectly ready and willing to avail himself of.'

*December* 28.—Napoleon indisposed. Had passed a very uneasy night, and had suffered considerably from headache. Saw him at 3 P.M., when he was still in bed, and afflicted with severe headache. He had not seen any one. Informed him what Sir Hudson Lowe said respecting the proposed intermediation. I did not like to communicate what His Excellency had said about the interview which he had desired to have with Las Cases, as I thought it would both aggravate his illness and tend to impede the desired accommodation. While I was in his bedroom, Marchand came in and informed him that the bath which he had ordered could not be got ready on account of the total want of water at Longwood. However, he appeared satisfied, and expressed his fear that if Sir Pulteney came up this day, his indisposition might prevent his seeing and conversing with him. He desired me, therefore, to tell Count Bertrand, in case the Admiral came, to take him to his house, show him the necessary papers, and talk the matter over ; adding, that if he found himself well enough, he would send for him, but if not, that he would appoint a future day.

Sir Pulteney and Lady Malcolm came to Longwood and paid a visit to Counts and Countesses Bertrand and Montholon. No communication had been yet made by the Governor to Sir Pulteney, who, when informed of the proposal, expressed his ardent wish that something might be done to put things upon a better footing between Napoleon and the Governor ; adding, that he thought if the matter were left to him, he could arrange it satisfactorily in a very little time. He observed, however, that until the Governor authorised him, he would have no conversation on the subject either with Napoleon or with any of his suite.

Sir Thomas Reade all day in consultation at Plantation House.

*December* 29.—A letter from Sir Hudson Lowe for Count Bertrand arrived at eight o'clock in the morning. Saw Napoleon at 2 P.M. Informed me, that as the Governor had fourteen or fifteen days ago expressed a wish to know what the French complained of, he had directed Bertrand to send him a copy of his restrictions, with some observations thereupon.

' The Governor,' said he, ' is a man totally unfit to fill the situation he holds. He has a good deal of cunning, but no talent or steadiness. He ought to be sent to Goa. Bertrand wrote that he hoped he would not refuse his consent to a matter of so little consequence as that of permitting Las Cases to come up here. If he refuses, Bertrand will go down to see him with an officer, which I could not consent to do.'

A letter superscribed ' in haste,' from Sir Hudson was given to Captain Poppleton, containing one for Count Bertrand, signifying that ' in consequence of the manner[1] in which Count Las Cases had been removed from Longwood, the Governor could not permit him to take leave of General Bonaparte,'

[1] The Emperor then took some turns in the garden ; the wind had become cold; he went into the house again and bade me follow him alone into the drawing-room and the billiard-room, whilst he paced up and down the whole extent of the two rooms. He was talking to me again about the manner in which he had passed his

etc.   Shortly afterwards Count Bertrand and
Baron Gourgaud went to town, accompanied by

day, and asked me how I had spent mine ; then, the conversation
having turned on his marriage, he was speaking of the *fêtes* which
had taken place on that occasion, and which had ended in the terrible
accident that happened at M. de Schwartzenberg's ball.   I was listen-
ing, and inwardly proposing to make an interesting article in my
journal on the subject, when the Emperor suddenly interrupted his
conversation, to observe through the window a great number of
English officers, who were advancing towards us from the gate of
our enclosure ; it was the Governor, surrounded by several of his
staff.   The Grand Marshal, who at this moment came into the room,
observed that the Governor had already been there in the morning,
and that he had been at his house, and remained there some time ;
he added, that a movement of the troops was spoken of.   These
circumstances appeared singular, and—mark the effect of a guilty
conscience—the idea of my letter clandestinely sent, immediately
occurred to my mind, and a secret foreboding instantly warned me
that all these strange proceedings concerned me.   Such, in fact, was
the case, for a few minutes after, a message was brought to me,
informing me that the English Colonel, the creature of Sir Hudson
Lowe, was waiting for me in my own apartment.   I made a sign
that I was with the Emperor, who, a few minutes afterwards, said to
me, 'Go, Las Cases, and see what that animal wants of you.'   And
as I was going, he added, '*and come back soon.*'   These were for me
the last words of Napoleon.   Alas, I have never seen him since !
but his accent, the tone of his voice, still sound in my ears.

   ' The Colonel who wished to see me was a man entirely devoted to
the Governor's wishes,—his factotum,—and with whom I had frequently to communicate as interpreter.   I had no sooner entered the
room than, with an expression of benevolence and kindness both in his
voice and countenance, he inquired after my health with a tender
interest.   This was the kiss of Judas ; for having made a sign to
him with my hand to sit down on the sofa, and having also taken a
seat on it myself, he seized this opportunity to place himself between
me and the door, and altering at once his tone and expression he
informed me that he arrested me in the name of the Governor, Sir
Hudson Lowe, on the deposition of my servant, who had charged
me with having carried on a secret correspondence.'—*Las Cases*,
vol. iv., part vii., p. 283, English edition.

Captain Poppleton, to take leave of Count Las Cases.

It is difficult to reconcile the conduct pursued towards them there, with the other measures practised by Sir Hudson Lowe, and with the importance which he professed to attach to '*cutting off* all communication with Longwood.' At breakfast they were left to themselves, with the exception of Captain Poppleton, who understands French with difficulty, and not at all when spoken in the quick manner in which Frenchmen usually converse with each other. For some hours they remained together in the large room of the castle, which is about fifty feet by twenty, walking up one side, while Colonel Wynyard and Major Gorrequer, who were to watch them, remained on the opposite side of the room ; so that Las Cases might just as well have been permitted to come to Longwood, and thereby a refusal, which was considered as an insult, would have been spared to Napoleon.

About 3 P.M. Las Cases and his son embarked on board the *Griffon* sloop of war, Captain Wright, for the Cape of Good Hope. He was accompanied to the seashore by Sir Hudson Lowe, Sir Thomas Reade, etc. His journal and papers, except a few of no consequence, were detained by the Governor. Previous to his departure he made over £4000 (which he had in a banker's hands in London) for Napoleon's use.

I saw Sir Hudson Lowe on horseback in the street, who called out to me when passing, 'Your negotiation has failed.'

About £500 worth of plate brought down by
Cipriani in the morning to be sold. When Sir
Hudson Lowe saw it he sent for Cipriani,
from whom he demanded, in what manner they
could spend so much money? Cipriani (an arch,
intelligent Corsican) replied, 'To buy food.' His
Excellency affected surprise, and said, 'What, have
you not enough?'—'We have purchased,' said
Cipriani, 'so many fowls, so much butter, bread,
meat, and divers other articles of food daily for some
months; and I have to thank your *chef d'état major*,
Colonel Reade, for his goodness in not only procuring me many things that I wanted, but for his kindness in seeing that the people did not impose upon
me when I was paying for them.' Sir Hudson was
a little disconcerted at this reply at first, but afterwards, resuming an appearance of astonishment,
asked, 'Why do you buy so much butter, or so many
fowls?'—'Because,' replied Cipriani, 'the allowance
granted by *vostra eccellenza* does not give us enough
to eat. You have taken off nearly half of what the
Admiral allowed us.' Cipriani then gave him an
account in detail of their wants, explained the
difference between the French and English mode of
living, and accounted satisfactorily for everything.
Sir Hudson said that the scheme of allowances had
been hastily made out; that he would look into it,
and endeavour to increase the quantity of those
articles of provisions of which they stood most in
need; and that on the next arrival from England he
expected a change for the better.

*December* 31.—Sir Hudson Lowe sent for me at six in the morning. Soon after my arrival he called me into a private room, and in a very solemn manner said that he had sent for me about a very extraordinary circumstance; that last evening the Baron Sturmer had written a note to Major Gorrequer, stating that General Bonaparte had had a fainting fit, *accompanied by fever!* some time back, detailing the fact of the *eau de Cologne* having been thrown in his face, and some other circumstances, and begging to know if it were true, as such stories *were good to send to his Court.* His Excellency said that he was very much surprised how Baron Sturmer could know that General Bonaparte had experienced a fit, or any of the circumstances attending it; and asked me to whom I had told it? I replied, ' I mentioned it to none but yourself, your staff, possibly the Admiral, and Baxter, whom I consulted professionally upon the matter; that, moreover, many of the circumstances detailed in the baron's letter were falsehoods; also that everybody at Longwood knew that Napoleon had had a fainting fit on the night he had mentioned, as well as the circumstances which accompanied it.' His Excellency then gave me some advice about the necessity of secrecy, and desired me to write him a statement of the business, in order that, as it had unfortunately got abroad, he might be able to contradict any incorrect account of it; he supposed the Admiral had repeated it to Montchenu or Sturmer.

Saw the Admiral in town, who told me that I had not mentioned the circumstance to him, nor had he done so either to Montchenu or Sturmer; but that half the town knew it, which I was soon convinced of by the number of questions put to me by divers persons before leaving it.

# CHAPTER III

## 1817

*January* 1.—Saw Napoleon in the drawing-room. Wished him a Happy New Year. He said he hoped that the succeeding one would find him better situated ; and added, laughing, 'Perhaps I shall be dead, which will be still better. Worse than this cannot be.' He was in very good spirits, spoke about hunting the stag and the wild boar.[1] Showed

[1] 'During our ride the Emperor mentioned several serious accidents by which, at one time or other, his life had been endangered.

'At St. Cloud he once wished to drive his calash six-in-hand. The horses were startled by the aide-de-camp, Caffarelli, inadvertently crossing the road in front of them. Before the Emperor had time to recover the reins, the horses set off at full speed, and the calash, which rolled along with extreme velocity, struck against a railing. The Emperor was thrown out to the distance of eight or ten feet, and lay stretched on the ground with his face downwards. He was, he said, dead for a few seconds. He felt the moment at which life became extinct, which he called the *negative moment.* The first individual of the suite who alighted immediately revived him by a touch. He observed that the mere contact suddenly restored him to life, as in the nightmare the sufferer is relieved as soon as he can utter a cry.

'On another occasion the Emperor said he had nearly been drowned when in garrison at Auxonne in 1786 ; while he was one day amusing himself with swimming, a sudden numbness came over him,

me the scar of a wound in the inside of the ring-
finger, which he told me he had received from a
wild boar while hunting, accompanied by the Duke
of Dalmatia (Soult).  Count Montholon came in, to
whom Napoleon whispered something; after which
he went out and returned with a snuff-box, which
he gave to the Emperor, who presented it to me
with his own hands, saying, 'Here, Doctor, is a
present I make to you for the attention which you
manifested towards me during my illness.'  It is
needless to say that a gift from the hands of such a
man was received with sensations of pride, and that
I endeavoured to express the sentiments which
filled my mind.

    Napoleon also made some elegant presents to

he lost his self-possession, and being alone, he was carried along by
the current in a senseless state.  He felt life escape him, and even
heard his comrades on the shore call out that he was drowned, and
hasten in quest of boats to drag for his body.  In this case too a
sudden shock restored him to life.  His breast struck against a sand-
bank, and by a miracle, his head being above the water, he recovered
himself sufficiently to swim ashore.  The water dislodged itself from
his stomach; he regained the spot where he had left his clothes, and
having dressed himself, he got home, while his friends were still in
search of his body.

  'Another time while hunting the wild boar at Marly, all his suite
were put to flight; it was like the rout of an army.  The Emperor,
with Soult and Berthier maintained their ground against three
enormous boars.  "We killed all three, but I received a hurt from
my adversary, and nearly lost this finger," said the Emperor, pointing
to the third finger of his left hand, which, indeed, bore the mark of a
severe wound.  "But the most laughable circumstance of all was
to see the multitude of men, surrounded by their dogs, screening
themselves behind the three heroes, and calling out lustily: *Save
the Emperor! save the Emperor!* while not one advanced to my
assistance."'—*Las Cases*, vol. ii., part iii., p. 324, English edition.

the Countesses Bertrand and Montholon, consisting of some of the beautiful porcelain, I believe unique, presented to him by the city of Paris, with some handsome *crêpes;* to Count Bertrand, a fine set of chessmen ; to Count Montholon, a handsome ornament, etc. All the children also were gratified with some elegant gift from him. The weather was so bad and so foggy that the signal from Deadwood could not be discerned.

*January* 3.—Napoleon had been ill during the night, but felt better. In pretty good spirits. After some conversation, I asked his opinion about Georges. 'Georges,' said he, 'was *una bestia ignorante.* He had courage, and that was all. After the peace with the Chouans I endeavoured to gain him over, as then he would have been useful to me, and I was anxious to calm all parties. I sent for and spoke to him for a long time. His father was a miller, and he was an ignorant fellow himself. I asked him, "Why do you want to restore those Bourbons ? If even you were to succeed in placing them upon the throne, you would still be only a miller's son in their eyes. They would hold you in contempt, because you are not of noble birth." But I found that he had no heart ; in fact, that he was *not a Frenchman.* A few days after he went over to London.' '

*January* 4.—The *Spey* man of war arrived, and brought the news of the destruction of the Algerine ships, and the treaty which the Dey had been obliged to make.

*January* 5.—Had a long conversation with Sir Hudson Lowe at Longwood concerning the restrictions. His Excellency said that he had no objection to allow General Bonaparte to ride to the left of Hut's Gate, in the direction of Miss Mason's ; but that he did not like to grant the same permission to his attendants. I observed that it would be difficult to make such a distinction, as Napoleon never rode out without being accompanied by two or three of them. Sir Hudson Lowe replied that he had no objection to their being permitted to ride in that direction when in company with General Bonaparte ; but without him, he would not grant it. He then desired me to tell General Bonaparte that *he* might ride in that direction whenever he pleased, that there would be no impediment to his movements. I observed that he had better make Count Bertrand acquainted with it ; and also that some notice ought to be given to the sentinel at Hut's Gate, otherwise he would stop Napoleon if he attempted to avail himself of the permission. Sir Hudson Lowe replied that the sentinel had no orders to stop him. I said that Generals Montholon and Gourgaud had been stopped several times when going to the alarm-house, although within the limits. The Governor replied that this must be a mistake, as the sentinels had no orders to stop them. I observed that I had been twice stopped myself by the sentinels in that spot. ' How can that be,' said Sir Hudson, ' as the sentinels *have orders* only *to stop French people ?*' I answered that the sentinel had said that he had

orders to stop *all suspicious people;* and that
conceiving me to be one, he had stopped me, for
which I could not blame him. His Excellency
laughed at this, then observed that he would *not*
enlarge the limits, that they were fixed; but that he
would give *General Bonaparte leave to extend his
rides in different directions,* and ordered me to tell
him, 'That he might ride within the old limits
unaccompanied, and that no impediment would be
placed in his way.'

Saw Napoleon shortly after, to whom I conveyed
His Excellency's message. He asked me if the
piquets had been placed upon the hills as formerly,
when he used to ride in that direction. I replied that I had not observed them. He took
out his glass and looked towards the spot for a
moment.

Informed Napoleon of the Algerine affair, and
gave him a paper which contained the official detail.
After reading it he professed great pleasure that
the barbarians had been chastised, but observed
that the victory we had gained did not alter his
opinion as to the best mode of acting with them.
'You might,' said he, 'have settled it equally well by
a blockade. It no doubt reflects great credit upon
the English sailors for their bravery and skill;
yet still I think that it was hazarding too much.
To be sure you effected a great deal and
got away, because your seamen are so good;
but that is an additional reason why you should
not run the risk of sacrificing them against such

*canaille.*[1]   There are no other seamen (except the
Americans) who would have done what yours effected,
or perhaps have attempted it.   Notwithstanding this,
and that you have succeeded, it was madness and an
abuse of the navy to attack batteries elevated above
your ships, which you could not injure ; to tackle red-
hot balls and shells, and run the hazard of losing a
fleet and so many brave seamen against such *canaille.*'

He spoke in very high terms of Lord Nelson,
and indeed attempted to palliate that only stigma on
his memory, the execution of Caracciolo ; which he
attributed entirely to his having been deceived by
that wicked woman, Queen Caroline, through Lady
Hamilton, and to the influence which the latter had
over him.

While conversing with the Emperor, General
Gourgaud sent in his name and entered.   He
communicated some information rather at variance
with the message which the Governor had directed
me to deliver.   It appeared that while taking a ride
*within* the limits, he was stopped about five o'clock
P.M. by the sentinel at Hut's Gate, and detained
until released by the serjeant commanding the
guard.   He added that almost every time he went
out the same thing occurred, the sentinels wishing
to screen themselves from any responsibility.

*January* 6.—Communicated this to Sir Hudson

---

[1] 'The loss of the Allied Fleets at the battle of Algiers was—Dutch,
thirteen killed, fifty-two wounded ; English, one hundred and twenty-six
killed, six hundred and ninety wounded.   The loss of the enemy was
supposed to be nearly four thousand killed and wounded.   See
James's *Naval History*, 1878 edition, vol. vi. p. 289.

Lowe, and brought him a letter from Captain Poppleton on the subject. His Excellency denied that the sentinels had ever received any new orders, and stated that it was the fault of the sentinel.

Cipriani informed me that Pozzo di Borgo was the son of a shepherd in Corsica, who used to bring eggs, milk, and butter to the Bonaparte family. Being a smart boy, he was noticed by Madame Mère, who paid for his schooling. Afterwards, through the interest of the family, he was chosen Deputy to the Legislative Body, as their sons were too young to be elected. He returned to Corsica as *procuratore generale*, where he united himself with Peraldi, an implacable enemy of the Bonapartes, and consequently became one himself.

By the same authority I was informed that Masseria, on his arrival in Paris from Corsica, in order to obtain an interview with Napoleon, had applied to him (Cipriani) for advice how to accomplish this object, stating that he intended to apply to the Arch Chancellor. Cipriani advised him by no means to do so, as possibly he might be arrested and tried (being an *émigré*), in which case he must be condemned to death ; but to apply to Madame Mère, to whom he was known. Masseria followed his advice, and succeeded in obtaining an interview, although he failed in the attempt to open a negotiation. In a subsequent endeavour to obtain another he received a hint to quit France.

On making inquiry at Hut's Gate, the serjeant commanding the guard showed a scrap of paper

containing the orders to the sentinels, which were,
'That none of the French, not even Bonaparte
himself, were to be permitted to pass that post,
unless accompanied by a British officer.' The
serjeant also said, what indeed was notorious, that
Sir Hudson Lowe frequently gave verbal orders
himself, not only to the non-commissioned officers of
the guard, but sometimes to the sentinels themselves. That those orders might be written down
afterwards, or they might not.

*January* 7.—Napoleon did not retire to rest until
three in the morning, having been employed dictating
and writing until that hour. He got up again at five,
and went into a warm bath. Ate nothing until seven
in the evening, and went to bed before eight.

*January* 8.—Asked Napoleon if it were true
that Desaix had, a little before his death, sent
a message of the following purport to him: 'Tell
the First Consul that I regret dying before I have
done sufficient to make my name known to posterity.' He replied, 'It was true,' and accompanied
it with some warm eulogiums on Desaix.[1] He
breakfasted this morning in the English manner,
upon a little toast and tea. Weather so foggy
that signals could not be passed.

*January* 10.—Sir Pulteney Malcolm, accompanied by Captains Meynel and Wauchope, R.N.,
came to Longwood, and had an interview with
Napoleon. He recounted to the Admiral a sketch
of his life.

---

[1] Desaix really fell without a word.

Went to town and asked Sir Thomas Reade that permission might be granted to the French to purchase two cows, that a little good milk might be provided for the establishment.

The fog so thick, and the weather so bad, that the signal of *all's well* could not be seen. Orderlies sent to acquaint the Governor and Admiral.

*January* 12.—Saw Napoleon in his dressing-room. Gave him a newspaper of the 3d of October 1816. Had some conversation with him relative to Chateaubriand, Sir Robert Wilson, etc. I observed that some persons were surprised that he had never written, or caused to be written, an answer to Sir Robert Wilson's work, and to others containing similar assertions. He replied that it was unnecessary; that they would fall to the ground of themselves; that Sir Robert had already contradicted it by the answer which he had given in his interrogation, when tried in Paris for having assisted Lavalette in his escape; and that he was convinced Wilson was now sorry for having published what he then had been led to believe was true. That, moreover, the English, who travelled in France, would return undeceived as to his character, and would undeceive their countrymen.

I asked if he had not been very thin when he was in Egypt. He answered that he was at that time extremely thin, although possessed of a strong and robust constitution. That he had supported what would have killed most other men.   After his thirty-sixth year he began to grow fat.

He told me that he had frequently laboured in State affairs for fifteen hours without a moment's cessation, or even having taken any nourishment. On one occasion he had continued at his labours for three days and nights without lying down to sleep.[1]

[1] The Emperor was almost always in his closet; it might be said that he spent the whole day and part of the night in it. He usually went to bed at ten or eleven o'clock, and got up again at about twelve to work for a few hours more. Sometimes he sent for M. Meneval, but most frequently he did not; and aware of his zeal, he would sometimes say to him, 'You must not kill yourself.'

When the Emperor went into his cabinet in the morning, he found bundles of papers already arranged and prepared for him by Meneval, who had been there before him. If the Emperor sometimes allowed twenty-four hours, or two days, to elapse without going into it, his secretary would remind him of it, and tell him that he would suffer himself to be overwhelmed with the mass of papers that were accumulating, and that the closet would soon be full of them. To this the Emperor usually answered good-humouredly, 'Do not alarm yourself, it will soon be cleared;' and so indeed it was, for in a few hours the Emperor had despatched all the answers, and was even with the current business. It is true that he got through a great deal by not answering many things and throwing away all that he considered useless, even when coming from his Ministers. To this they were accustomed; and when they received no answer, they knew what it meant. He himself read all letters that were addressed to him; to some he answered by writing a few words in the margin, and to others he dictated an answer. Those that were of great importance were always put by and read a second time, and were never answered until some time had elapsed. When leaving his closet he generally recapitulated those affairs that were of greatest consequence, and fixed the hour at which they must be ready for him, which was always punctually attended to. If at that hour the Emperor did not come, M. Meneval followed him about from place to place through the palace several times to remind him of it. On some of these occasions the Emperor would go and settle the affair,

When Napoleon was rising up from table this
day, and in the act of taking his hat off the side-
at other times he would say, ' *To-morrow; night is a good adviser.*'
This was his usual phrase ; and he often said that he had indeed
worked much more at night than during the day ; not that thoughts
of business prevented him from sleeping, but because he slept at
intervals, according as he wanted rest, and a little sufficed for him.

It often happened to the Emperor, in the course of his campaigns,
to be roused suddenly upon some emergency of business ; he would
then immediately get up, and it would have been impossible to guess
from the appearance of his eyes that he had just been sleeping.   He
then gave his decision, or dictated his answer, with as much clearness, and with his mind as free and unembarrassed, as at any other
moment.   This he called the *after-midnight presence of mind;* and
he possessed it in a most extraordinary degree.   It has sometimes
happened that he has been perhaps called up as often as ten times
in the same night, and each time he was always found to have fallen
asleep again, not having as yet taken his quantum of rest.

Boasting one day to one of his Ministers (General Clarke) of the
faculty which he possessed of sleeping almost at pleasure, and how
little rest he required, Clarke answered in a jocular tone, ' Yes, Sire,
and that is a source of torment to us, for it is often at our expense ; we
feel our share of it sometimes.'—*Las Cases*, vol. iii., part vi., p. 238.

Meneval says of the night-work of the Emperor, ' I would find
him in his white dressing-gown, with a Madras handkerchief on his
head, walking up and down his cabinet, with his hands crossed
behind his back, or else dipping in his snuff-box, less from liking
than from preoccupation, for he only smelt the snuff, and his hand-
kerchiefs of white cambric were not soiled by it.   His ideas developed
under his dictation with an abundance and a clearness that showed
his attention was closely fixed upon the object of his work.   When
the work was ended, and sometimes in the middle of it, he had ices
or sherbet brought.   He asked me which I preferred, and his care
went so far as to advise me which he thought best for my health.
After this he returned to bed, if it were only for an hour, and fell
asleep again as if he had not been interrupted. . . . When the
Emperor rose in the night, he forbade my being awakened before
seven o'clock in the morning.   Then I found my desk covered with reports and papers annotated by him.'—*Meneval*, tome i. pp. 134, 135.

On one occasion in 1812 (*Las Cases*, English edition of 1824, part
vi., p. 21), after many hours of protracted labour, Count Daru fell

board, a large rat sprang out of it, and ran between his legs, to the surprise of those present.

*January* 13.—Made inquiries from the purveyor if credit were given to the establishment on any articles allowed them by Government during the week, which had not been consumed, and whether they might be permitted to appropriate the value of such articles as had not been used to increase the allowance of others, of which they had not a sufficient quantity; or whether the savings so made were to be credited to Government? The reply was, 'Any saving made by the establishment upon the English confectionery allowed to them may be carried to increase the quantity of vegetables allowed; but all and every other saving is to be credited to Government, and not to the French.' That some weeks back no saving of any description was permitted to be appropriated to increase the allowances in which there might be a deficiency; but after several representations had been made by me during Napoleon's illness of the deficiency of vegetables, Sir Hudson Lowe had directed that the value of the confectionery *not* used by them [1]

asleep in middle of writing a despatch in the Emperor's cabinet. On awaking between two and three in the morning he saw Napoleon at the adjoining desk rapidly completing the despatch. The Emperor good-humouredly reproached him for having supped too heartily, whereupon Daru explained that he had been kept up for the greater part of three nights in succession by the pressure of official business. Napoleon read him a lecture upon not overtasking his resources.

[1] The French rarely used any of the confectionery sent from England, as Piéron, the *chef d'office*, was very superior in his art.— B. E. O'M.

might be carried over to increase the allowance of
provisions ; that a very severe reprimand had been
given to the purveyors, in a letter from Major
Gorrequer, for having credited the value of the fruit
allowed (when none was to be procured on the
island), to increase the quantity of vegetables,
accompanied by a strict order never to repeat it.'

*January* 14.—Made inquiries from Brigade-
Major Harrison, who was stationed at Hut's
Gate, if any alteration had been made in the
orders, so as to allow Napoleon to pass the piquet
at that gate, and to go round by Miss Mason's
and Woody Range, *unaccompanièd* by a British
officer ? Major Harrison replied that no change
of orders to that effect had been given, and that
if he attempted to pass he would be stopped by
the sentinels. He added that General Gourgaud
had asked him the same question yesterday, to
whom he had returned a similar answer. Cipriani
in town purchasing sheep.

*January* 15.—Saw Napoleon in his bath. He
was rather low-spirited and thoughtful. Made
some observations about the Governor's not having
kept his word relative to the proposed intermediation through the medium of the Admiral.

*January* 17.—Madame Bertrand delivered of
a fine boy at half-past four o'clock. Her accouchement was followed by some dangerous symptoms.

Sir Hudson Lowe came up to Longwood
and asked me 'if I had had any conversation
with Napoleon touching the Admiral since he

had seen me?' I replied that he 'appeared much surprised that the Governor had not acted upon the proposed intermediation by means of the Admiral.' Sir Hudson Lowe observed, 'That he had considered the negotiation to be broken off, by General Bonaparte's having sent to him a number of strictures upon the restrictions of October last, written in a violent manner; and that the frequent use of the word "*Emperor*," in the strictures written by Count Bertrand, was sufficient for him to break off the affair.' I replied that the strictures had merely been sent by Napoleon for his own consideration. His Excellency then began to inveigh against Count Las Cases, whom he accused of 'having been the cause of much mischief between Bonaparte and himself; said he had asserted in his journal that Bonaparte had declared that he abhorred the sight of the British uniform; and that I had better take an opportunity to tell him this, and add, that I heard him (the Governor) say that he did not believe that he had ever said so.'

Sir Hudson then asked me if 'I had informed General Bonaparte that he was at liberty to ride round by Miss Mason's and Woody Range unaccompanied?' I replied that I had, but that Major Harrison had asserted the contrary to General Gourgaud and myself. His Excellency said that since that time permission had been granted, of which he desired me to inform General Bonaparte, as well as of his reasons for not having gone on any further with the proposed mediation. Also, 'That he daily expected good news from England for the French, and hoped he should be permitted by the English Government to render their situation more comfortable.'

In the evening, however, His Excellency changed his mind, and ordered me 'not to communicate anything to General Bonaparte on the subject of the ride to the left of Hut's Gate, but to mention everything else he had directed me.'

*January* 18.—Napoleon sent for me. Complained of severe headache, and made many inquiries concerning Madame Bertrand, about whose state of health he appeared very anxious.

Acquainted him with the causes which the Governor had assigned yesterday, as his reasons for not having proceeded further in the proposed intermediation, and the other matters that I was directed to tell him. Napoleon replied, 'I never intended to break off the negotiation. The observations were sent to him because he asked for them himself, and desired to know what we complained of. It was never intended as a refusal, nor to be sent to England, as it was only a copy of what I once intended to send. I wished,' continued he, 'to have had the Admiral present at any agreement which might be made, in order to be able to call upon him hereafter as a man of honour and an Englishman to bear witness to whatever was agreed upon, that the Governor might not be able to change the orders and directions, subsequently deny what had been settled, and then say that he had changed nothing. But this Governor never intended to call in the Admiral. It was all a trick. *E un uomo senza fede.'*

I said that the Governor had informed me that he had written to England, and daily expected orders to ameliorate his condition. 'He has never written for any such thing,' replied Napoleon ; 'he sees that he has gone too far, and now he awaits the arrival of some ship from England, in order that he may throw the weight and odium of those restrictions upon the Ministers, and say that he has written and got them taken off. The Ministers have merely given him directions to take every precaution to prevent me from escaping; all the rest is discretional. He treats us as if we were so many peasants, or poor simple creatures, who could be duped by his shallow artifices.'

The *Adamant* arrived from the Cape. A present of some fruit sent by Lady Malcolm to Napoleon. Went to town and procured some newspapers, which I gave to Napoleon on my return. Assisted in explaining some of the passages to him. Repeated an anecdote which I had heard about his son, at which he laughed much, appeared entertained, and brightened up.[1] Made

---

[1] 'I give you Madame Bertrand's description of young Napoleon as very beautiful, in order to introduce his father's laconic English account of him. The boy, he says, resembles him only in the upper part of his form: "He has one grand, big head."'—Warden's *Letters from St. Helena*, p. 43.

me repeat it again; asked about the Empress
Marie Louise, and desired me to endeavour to *see*
all the newspapers that arrived, in order that if
I could not procure the loan of them, I should
be able to inform him of anything they might
contain relative to his wife and child. 'For,'
added he, 'one reason that the Governor does
not send up a regular series of papers, is to prevent
me from seeing any article which he thinks would
give me pleasure, especially such as contain some
little information about my son or my wife.'

*January* 19.—Sir Hudson Lowe sent for me.
Communicated to him Napoleon's reply to the
message he had charged me to deliver on the
17th, moderating the tone of it. Sir Hudson said,
'That he had never asked for the observations on
the restrictions. That he believed he had asked
what they complained of, and that he was glad
to know they had not intended to break off the
accommodation by sending them.'

A little afterwards, however, His Excellency
began to wax warm, and said, 'That the person
who had ordered observations to be written couched
in such language, and containing lies, could not
be actuated by any conciliatory views, and he
should take no positive steps in the matter. That
he conceived a person's proposing another for a
mediator could have no other object in view than
to *make some concession or apology;* if such were
General Bonaparte's views, he (Sir Hudson) should
think it advisable to employ one, and not other-

wise.' He then asked me 'if such were General Bonaparte's intentions?' I told His Excellency that I could assure him Napoleon had no such intention, and never had.

Sir Hudson, after some hazardous assertions relative to Napoleon's motives, got up, walked into another room, from whence he returned with a volume of the *Quarterly Review*, containing an article on Miot's work upon Egypt, which he put into my hands, and with a triumphant laugh pointed out the following passage, which he desired me to read aloud :—

'He (Bonaparte) understands enough of mankind to dazzle the weak, to dupe the vain, to overawe the timid, and to make the wicked his instruments. But of all beyond this, Bonaparte is grossly and brutally ignorant. Of the strength of patriotism, the enthusiasm of virtue, the fortitude of duty, he knows nothing, and can comprehend nothing.'

During the time I was reading this he indulged in bursts of laughter. He afterwards made me observe a definition of the word *caractère* in a posthumous work of Voltaire's (I think), of which he said General Bonaparte must have been ignorant, or he would not be so fond of using the word.

Subsequently Sir Hudson Lowe said that 'General Bonaparte ought to send the Admiral to him.' I observed that Sir Pulteney Malcolm would not undertake any office of the kind unless first authorised by him (Sir Hudson) to undertake it. That as he had now the complaints of the

French in his possession, he might let the Admiral know how far he would agree to their demands; and by making that officer acquainted with his intentions, the latter would know how to act and what answer to make. Sir Hudson recurred again to the language in which the observations on his restrictions were couched, and gave me a message, similar to that of the 17th, with the addition, 'That at the time he had foreseen that the request to see Las Cases, which he could not grant, would probably break off the proposed accommodation.'

He then told me that I might borrow any books I liked in his library, excepting such as flattered Bonaparte too much. Shortly after he gave me Pillet's *Libel upon England,* Miot's *Expedition to Egypt, Amours secrètes de Napoléon,* etc. I asked him if I might lend Pillet to Napoleon. He said, 'Yes; and tell him that Pillet knows just as much about England as Las Cases.' His Excellency then took from a shelf a book called *Les Imposteurs insignes, ou Histoires de plusieurs Hommes de néant de toutes Nations, qui ont usurpé la Qualité d'Empereur, de Roi, et de Prince,* put it into my hand, and with a peculiar grin said, 'You had better take General Bonaparte this also. Perhaps he may find some characters in it resembling himself.'

*January* 20.—Cipriani in town, purchasing meat, butter, and other necessaries. Sir Thomas Reade very active in assisting him to procure them.

*January* 21.—Saw Napoleon in the evening.

Gave him Pillet's *Libel,* mentioning at the same time some of the falsehoods contained in it. He appeared surprised and shocked, and observed that malice frequently defeated itself. When I mentioned that Pillet had asserted that the French naval officers were more skilful and manœuvred better than the English, he smiled contemptuously and observed, 'Truly, they have proved it by the result of their actions.'

I then told him that I had got a book entitled *Amours secrètes de Napoléon Bonaparte,* but that it was a foolish work. He laughed, and desired me to bring it to him. 'It will at least make me laugh,' said he. He observed a print in the book which represented him plunging a sword into a balloon, because the manager of it would not let him ascend, and remarked, 'It is believed by some that I did what is represented here, and I have heard that it was asserted by persons who knew me well, but it is not true.' [1]

Some one then came into the room, to whom he cried, '*Eh bien, voilà mes amours secrètes.*' He then ran through the book, read out some parts, and laughed heartily, but observed that it was monstrously silly ; that they had not even described him as a wicked man. After having perused a portion of it which I had not read, he shut the book and returned it, observing that there was not a single word of truth in the anecdotes ; that

[1] The circumstance represented really occurred, but the actor was one of the *comité,* a young man of great bravery.

even the names of the greatest number of the
females mentioned were unknown to him.

Napoleon sat up until late at night reading
Pillet, and I was informed that he was heard
repeatedly to burst out into loud fits of laughter.

*January* 22.—Napoleon employed a considerable
portion of the day in dictating his memoirs to
Counts Bertrand and Montholon in the billiard-
room, which he has converted into a *cabinet de
travail.* Occasionally he amuses himself with
collecting the balls together and endeavouring to
roll them all into the opposite corner-pocket.

Sir Hudson Lowe sent me up some coffee for
Napoleon's own use, which he strongly recommended
as of very good quality.

*January* 23.—Napoleon in good spirits. Spoke
about Pillet's book. Observed that he had no recollection whatever of such a person. ' Probably,' said
he, ' Pillet is some one who has been harshly treated
by you in the prison-ships, and has written in a bad
humour and full of malice against the English, which
is evidently displayed in his work. There is,' continued he, ' only one statement in the book which I
believe to be correct, viz. that relative to the treatment of the prisoners in the *pontons.* It was barbarous on the part of your Government to immure
a number of poor wretches of soldiers, who had not
been accustomed to the sea, on board ship so many
hours every night without fresh air. There was
something horrid,' continued he, ' in the treatment
of the prisoners in England. The very idea of

being put on board a ship, and kept there for several
years, has something dreadful in it.   Even your
seamen hate the idea of being always on board ships,
and run to seek the delights of the shore whenever
they can.   There was nothing which so much irritated
the nations of the Continent against you.   For your
Ministers not only crowded Frenchmen in them, but
also prisoners of all other nations at war with you.
I received so many complaints about the barbarous
treatment to which they were subjected in the
*pontons*—a treatment so contrary to that practised in
France towards the English—that at last I gave
orders that all the English prisoners should be put
on board *pontons*, which were to be prepared for
that purpose, and to be treated precisely as you
treated mine in England.   Had I remained in
France it would have been carried into execution,
and would have had a good effect, for I would have
given every liberty and facility to the English so
confined to vent their complaints, and your Ministry
would, in spite of themselves, have been obliged to
remove the French from the *pontons*, in order that
a similar measure might be adopted towards the
English in France.'

I observed that the treatment of the French
prisoners in England had not been nearly so bad as
was stated by many, especially by Pillet.   Napoleon
replied, 'I have no doubt that the statement is
exaggerated; but still they were treated in a most
oppressive manner.   The mere putting soldiers on
board ships is of itself cruel.   Now, in France, all

the English were treated well. It is impossible that
any Government could have given more lenient
directions for the treatment of prisoners of war than
those issued by me; but I could not help some
abuses being practised. I always punished the
authors of them when they came to my knowledge.
There was Viriòn; as soon as I found out his
robberies, I gave orders to have him tried, and I
would have had him hanged, if, dreading the result,
he had not shot himself. Let the thousands of
English prisoners who were in France be asked to
state candidly the manner in which they were treated.
There are some of them now in this island. When
they attempted to escape and were retaken, then,
indeed, they were closely confined, but never were
treated in such a barbarous manner as you treated
mine in your *pontons.*

'Your Ministers made a great noise about my
having employed French prisoners who had broken
their parole and escaped.[1] But the prisoners of
your nation were the first to set the example of
escaping, and your Ministers employed them afterwards. In retaliation I of course did the same. I
published the names of several Englishmen who
broke their parole previous to the French having
done so, and who were afterwards employed by you;
nay, I did more,—I made an offer to your Ministers
to send back all the French prisoners who had
violated their parole from the beginning of the war,
provided they would in like manner send back all

[1] General Lefebvre-Desnouettes amongst others.

the English who had done the like. They, however,
refused to consent to this. Your Ministers made a
great outcry about the English travellers that I
detained in France; although they themselves had
set the example, by seizing upon all the French
vessels and persons on board of them, upon whom
they could lay their hands, either in their harbours,
or at sea, before the Declaration of War, and before
I had detained the English in France. I said then,
If you detain my travellers at sea, where you can do
what you like, I will detain yours on land, where I
am equally powerful. But after this I offered to
release all the English I had seized in France before
the Declaration of War, provided you would in like
manner release the French and their property which
you had seized on board the ships. Your Ministers
refused.'

I asked the Emperor if he had ever read Miot's
*History of the Expedition to Egypt.* 'What, the
Commissary?' replied he. 'I believe Las Cases
gave me a copy; moreover, it was published in
my time.' He then desired me to bring the one
which I had, that he might compare them. He
observed, 'Miot was a *polisson*, whom, together
with his brother, I raised from the dirt. He says
that I threatened him for writing the book, which is
a falsehood. I said to his brother once that he
might as well not have published untruths. What
does he say about the poisoning affair and the
shooting at Jaffa?' I replied that as to the poisoning
Miot declared he could say no more than that such

had been the current report; but that he positively
asserted that he (Napoleon) had caused between
three and four thousand Turks to be shot some
days after the capture of Jaffa. Napoleon answered,
'It is not true that there were so many. I ordered
about a thousand or twelve hundred to be shot,
which was done. The reason was, that amongst
the garrison of Jaffa a number of Turkish troops
were discovered, whom I had taken a short time
before at El-Arish and sent to Bagdad upon their
parole not to serve again, or to be found in arms
against me for a year. I had caused them to be
escorted twelve leagues on their way to Bagdad by
a division of my army. But those Turks, instead
of proceeding to Bagdad, threw themselves into
Jaffa, defended it to the last, and cost me a number
of brave men to take it, whose lives would have
been spared if the others had not reinforced the
garrison of Jaffa. Moreover, before I attacked the
town, I sent them a flag of truce. Immediately
afterwards we saw the head of the bearer elevated
on a pole over the wall. Now if I had spared them
again, and sent them away upon their parole, they
would directly have gone to St. Jean d'Acre, where
they would have played over again the same scene
that they had done at Jaffa. In justice to the lives
of my soldiers, as every general ought to consider
himself as their father, I could not allow this. To
leave as a guard a portion of my army, already small
and reduced in number, in consequence of the breach
of faith of those wretches, was impossible. Indeed,

to have acted otherwise than as I did would probably have caused the destruction of my whole
army. I therefore, availing myself of the rights of
war, which authorise the putting to death prisoners
taken under such circumstances, independently of
the right given to me by having taken the city by
assault, and that of retaliation on the Turks, ordered
that the prisoners taken at El-Arish, who, in defiance
of their capitulation, had been found bearing arms
against me, should be selected and shot. The rest,
amounting to a considerable number, were spared.
I would,' continued he, 'do the same thing again
to-morrow, and so would Wellington, or any general
commanding an army under similar circumstances.

' Previously to leaving Jaffa,' continued Napoleon,
'and after the greatest number of the sick and
wounded had been embarked, it was reported to me
that there were some men in the hospital so dangerously ill as not to be able to be moved. I immediately ordered the chiefs of the medical staff to
consult together upon what was best to be done, and to
give me their opinion on the subject. Accordingly
they met, and found that there were seven or eight
men so dangerously ill, that they conceived it impossible for them to recover ; and also that they could not
exist twenty-four or thirty-six hours longer ; that,
moreover, being afflicted with the plague, they would
spread that complaint amongst all those who
approached them. Some of them, who were sensible,
perceiving that they were about to be abandoned,
earnestly entreated to be put to death. Larrey was

of opinion that recovery was impossible, and that
those poor fellows could not exist many hours ; but
as they might live until the Turks entered, and experience the dreadful torments which they were
accustomed to inflict upon their prisoners, he thought
it would be an act of charity to comply with their
desires, and accelerate their end by a few hours.
Desgenettes did not approve of this, and replied
that his profession was to cure the sick and not to
destroy them. Larrey came to me immediately
afterwards, informed me of the circumstances, and of
what Desgenettes had said ; adding, that perhaps
Desgenettes was right. " But," continued Larry,
"those men cannot live for more than a few hours,
twenty-four or thirty-six at most ; and if you will
leave a rearguard of cavalry, to stay and protect
them from advanced parties, it will be sufficient."
Accordingly I ordered four or five hundred cavalry
to remain behind, and not to quit the place until all
were dead. They did remain, and informed me
that all had expired before they had left the town ;
but I have heard since that Sidney Smith found
one or two alive when he entered it. This is the
truth of the business. Wilson himself, I daresay,
knows now that he was mistaken. Sidney Smith
never asserted it.

' I have no doubt that this story of the poisoning
originated in something said by Desgenettes, who
was a *bavard*, which was afterwards misunderstood
or incorrectly repeated. Desgenettes,' continued he,
' was a good man, and notwithstanding that he had

given rise to this story, I was not offended, and had him near my person in different campaigns afterwards.    Not that I think it would have been a crime had opium been given to them.    To leave a few *misérables*, who could not recover, in order that they might be massacred by the Turks with the most dreadful tortures, as was their custom, would, I think, have been cruelty.    A general ought to act to his soldiers as he would wish should be done to himself.    You have been amongst the Turks and know what they are ; I ask you now to place yourself in the situation of one of those sick men, and imagine that you were asked which you would prefer, to be left to suffer the tortures of those miscreants, or to have opium administered to you ?'    I replied, 'Most undoubtedly I should prefer the latter.'—'Certainly, so would any man,' answered Napoleon ; 'if my *own son* (and I believe I love my son as well as any father does his child) were in a similar situation with those men, I would advise it to be done ; and if so situated myself, I would insist upon it, if I had sense enough and strength enough to demand it.    If I had thought such a measure as that of giving opium necessary, I would have called a council of war, have stated the necessity of it, and have published it in the order of the day.    It should have been no secret.    Do you think that if I had been capable of secretly poisoning my soldiers, or of such barbarities as driving my carriage over the dead, and the still bleeding bodies of the wounded, my troops would have fought for me with an enthusiasm and affection without a parallel? Even some of the wounded, who had sufficient strength left to pull a trigger, would have despatched me.

'I have been accused in like manner,' continued the Emperor, 'of having committed such unnecessary crimes as causing Pichegru, Wright, and others to be assassinated. Instead of desiring the death of Wright, I was anxious to bring to light by his testimony that Pitt had caused assassins to be landed in France, purposely to murder me. Wright killed himself, probably that he might not compromise his Government. What motive could I have in assassinating Pichegru? A man who was evidently guilty—against whom every proof was ready. His condemnation was certain. Perhaps I should have pardoned him. If, indeed, Moreau had been put to death, then people might have said that I had caused his assassination, and with great apparent justice, for he was the only man I had much reason to fear; and until then he was judged innocent. He was "*blue*," like me; Pichegru was "*white*," known to be in the pay of England, and his death certain.' Here Napoleon described the way in which he had been found, and observed that the very uncommon mode of his death was a proof that he had not been murdered.

'There never has been,' continued he, 'a man who has attained the height of power to which I have risen without having been sullied by crimes except myself. An English lord, a relation of the

Duke of Bedford, who dined with me at Elba,[1] told me that it was generally believed in England that the Duc d'Enghien had not been tried, but assassinated in prison in the night; and was surprised when I told him that he had had a regular trial, and that the sentence had been published before execution.'

I now asked if it were true that Talleyrand had detained a letter written by the Duc d'Enghien to him until two days after the Duke's execution? Napoleon's reply was, 'It is true; the Duke had written a letter, offering his services, and asking a command in the army from me, which Talleyrand did not make known until two days after his execution.' I observed that Talleyrand, by his culpable concealment of the letter, was virtually guilty of the death of the Duke. 'I,' replied Napoleon, 'caused the Duc d'Enghien to be arrested in consequence of the Bourbons having landed assassins in France to murder me. I was resolved to let them see that the blood of one of their princes should pay for their attempts, and he was accordingly tried for having borne arms against the Republic, found guilty, and shot, according to the existing laws against such a crime.'

*January* 26.—Napoleon went out of the house (being the first time since the 20th of November last) to pay a visit to Countess Bertrand, whom he complimented much upon her beautiful child. 'Sire,' said the Countess, 'I have the honour to present to Your Majesty *le premier Français* who, since your

[1] Query, Lord Ebrington.

arrival, has entered Longwood without Lord Bathurst's permission.'

*January* 27.—Informed the Emperor that I had a book containing an account of a society named 'Philadelphi,' which had been formed against him, and expressed my surprise that he had never fallen by the hands of conspirators. He replied, 'No person knew five minutes before I put it into execution that I intended to go out, or where I should go. For this reason the conspirators were baffled, as they were ignorant where to lay the scene of their enterprise. Shortly after I was made Consul there was a conspiracy formed against me by about fifty persons, the greater number of whom had once been very much attached to me, and consisted of officers of the army, men of science, painters, and sculptors. They were all stern Republicans ; their minds were heated ; each fancied himself a Brutus, and me a tyrant and another Cæsar. Amongst them was Arena, a countryman of mine, a Republican, and a man who had been much attached to me before ; but thinking me a tyrant, he determined to get rid of me, imagining that by doing so he should render a service to France. There was also one Ceracchi, another Corsican, and a famous sculptor, who, when I was at Milan, had made a statue of me. He too had been greatly attached to me, but being a fanatical Republican, determined to kill me, for which purpose he came to Paris, and begged to have the honour of making another statue for me, alleging that the first was not sufficiently well executed for so

great a man. Though I then knew nothing of the
conspiracy which had been formed, I refused to give
my consent, as I did not like the trouble of sitting
for two or three hours in the same posture for some
days, especially as I had sat before to him.[1] This
saved my life, his intention being to poniard me
whilst I was sitting. In the meantime, they had
arranged their plans. Amongst them there was a
captain who had been a great admirer of mine.
This man agreed with the rest that it was necessary
to overturn the tyrant, but he would not consent that
I should be killed, although he strenuously joined in
everything else. All the others, however, differed
with him in opinion, and insisted that it was absolutely necessary to despatch me, as the only means
of preventing France from being enslaved. This
captain, finding that they were determined to shed
my blood, notwithstanding all his arguments and
entreaties, gave information of their names and
plans. They were to assassinate me on the first
night that I went to the theatre, in the passage, as I
was returning. Everything was arranged with the

---

[1] Napoleon was never a good or patient sitter. 'Canova,' says
Bourrienne, 'came to St. Cloud to model the figure of the First
Consul, of whom he was about to make a colossal statue. . . . But
Bonaparte was so tired, disgusted, and fretted by the process that he
very seldom put himself in the required attitude, and then only for a
short time. . . . Whenever Canova was announced he would shrug
his shoulders and say, "More modelling! Good heavens, how vexatious!" Canova expressed great displeasure at not being able to study
his model as he wished to do, and the little anxiety of Bonaparte on
the subject damped the ardour of his imagination.'—*Memoirs of
Napoleon Bonaparte*, 1885 edition, vol. i. pp. 506, 507.

police—I went the same evening to the theatre, and actually passed through the conspirators ; some of whom I knew by sight, and who were armed with poniards under their cloaks in order to despatch me when I was going out. Shortly after my arrival the police seized them all. They were searched and the poniards found upon them. In France a person cannot be found guilty of a conspiracy to murder unless the instruments of death are found upon him. They were afterwards tried, and some were executed.'

I asked several questions about the infernal-machine incident. Napoleon replied, ' It was about Christmas time, and great festivities were going on. I was much pressed to go to the Opera. I had been greatly occupied all day, and in the evening found myself tired. I threw myself on a sofa in my wife's salon and fell asleep. Josephine came down some time after, awoke me, and insisted that I should go to the theatre. She was an excellent woman, and wished me to do everything to ingratiate myself with the people. You know that when women take a thing into their heads, they will go through with it, and you must gratify them. Well, I got up, much against my inclination, and went in my carriage, accompanied by Lannes and Bessières. I was so drowsy that I fell asleep again in the coach. I was asleep when the explosion took place, and I recollect, when I awoke, experiencing a sensation as if the vehicle had been raised up, and was passing through a great body of water. The

contrivers of this were a man named Saint Régant,
Limoelan, a *religious* man, who has since gone
to America and turned priest, and some others.
They procured a cart and a barrel resembling that
with which water is supplied through the streets of
Paris, with this exception, that the barrel was put
crossways.    This they filled with gunpowder, and
placed it at the turning of the street through which
I was to pass.    What saved me was, that my wife's
carriage was the same in appearance as mine, and
there was a guard of fifteen men to each.    Limoelan
did not know which I was in, and indeed was not
certain that I should be in either of them.    In order
to ascertain this, he stepped forward to look into the
carriage, and assure himself of my presence.    One
of my guards, a great tall strong fellow, impatient
and angry at seeing a man stopping up the way and
staring into the carriage, rode up, and gave him a
kick with his great boot, crying, "Get out of the way,
*pékin*," which knocked him down.    Before he could
get up the carriage had passed a little on.    Limoelan
being confused I suppose by his fall, and not perceiving that the carriage had passed, ran to the cart
and exploded his machine between the two carriages.
It killed the horse of one of my guards and wounded
the rider, knocked down several houses, and killed
and wounded about forty or fifty *badauds*, who were
waiting to see me pass.    The police collected all the
remnants of the cart and the machine, and invited
all the workmen in Paris to come and look at them.
The pieces were recognised by several.    One said,

I made this, another that, and all agreed that they had sold them to two men, who by their accent were *Bas Brêtons ;* but nothing more could then be ascertained.[1]

'Shortly after the hackney coachmen and others of that description gave a great dinner in the Champs Elysées to Cæsar, my coachman, thinking that he had saved my life by his skill and activity at the moment of the explosion, which was not the case, for he was drunk at the time. It was the guardsman who saved it by knocking the fellow down. Possibly my coachman may have assisted by driving furiously round the corner, as he was drunk and not afraid of anything. He was so far gone that he thought the report of the explosion was that of a salute fired in honour of my visit to the theatre !

'At this dinner they all took their bottle freely, and drank to Cæsar's health. One of them, when he was drunk, said, "Cæsar, I know the men who tried to blow the First Consul up the other day. In such a street and such a house (naming them) I saw on that day a cart like a water-cart coming out of a passage, which attracted my attention, as I had never seen one there before. I observed the men and the horse, and should know them again." The

[1] Count Rapp, who attended Madame Bonaparte to the Opera on this memorable occasion, says : 'When I entered the theatre Napoleon was seated in his box, calm and composed, and looking at the audience through his opera-glass. Fouché was beside him. "Josephine ? " said he, as soon as he observed me. She entered at that moment, and he did not finish his question. "The rascals," said he very coolly, "wanted to blow me up. Bring me a book of the oratorio."'—*Memoirs of General Count Rapp*, p. 19.

Minister of Police was sent for ; he was interrogated, and brought them to the house which he had mentioned, where they found the measure with which the conspirators had put the powder into the barrel, with some of the powder still adhering to it. A little also was found scattered about. The master of the house, on being questioned, said that there had been people there for some time, whom he took to be smugglers ; that on the day in question they had gone out with the cart, which he supposed to contain a loading of smuggled goods. He added that they were *Bas Brêtons*, and that one of them had the appearance of being master over the other two. Having now a description of their persons, every search was made for them, and Saint Régant and Carbon were taken, tried, and executed. It was a singular circumstance that an Inspector of Police had noticed the cart standing at the corner of the street for a long time, and had ordered the person who was with it to drive it away ; but he made some excuse, and said that there was plenty of room, and the other seeing what he thought to be a water-cart, with a miserable horse, not worth twenty francs, did not suspect any mischief.

'At Schoenbrunn,' continued the Emperor, ' I also had a narrow escape. Shortly after the capture of Vienna, I reviewed my troops at Schoenbrunn. A young man about eighteen years of age presented himself to me. He came so close at one time as to touch me, and said that he wanted to speak to me. Berthier, who did not like to see me disturbed then, pushed him to one side, saying, " If you want to say anything to the Emperor, you cannot do it now." He then called Rapp, who was a German, and said, "Here is a young man who wishes to speak to the Emperor ; see what he wants and do not let him annoy the Emperor ;" after which he called the young man, and told him that Rapp spoke German, and would answer him. Rapp went up to him, and asked him what he wanted ? He replied that he had a memorial to give to the Emperor. Rapp told him that I was busy, and that he could not speak to me then. He had his hand in his breast all this time, as if he had some paper in it to give to me. Finding that notwithstanding his refusal he insisted upon seeing me, and was pushing on, Rapp, who is a vigorous man, gave him a blow with his fist and knocked him down.

'He approached again afterwards when the troops were passing. Rapp, who watched him, ordered some of the guards to seize and keep him in custody until after the review, and then bring him to his quarters, that he might learn what he complained of. The guards, observing that he always kept his right hand in his breast, made him draw it out and examined him. Under his coat they found a knife as long as my arm. When asked what he intended to do with it, he replied instantly, " To kill the Emperor."

'Some short time afterwards he was brought before me. I asked him what he wanted ? He replied, "To kill you." I asked him what I had done to him to make him desire to take away my life? He answered that I had done a great deal of mischief to his country; that I had desolated and ruined it by the war which I had waged against it. I inquired of him why he did not kill the Emperor of Austria instead of me, as *he* was the cause of the war and not I? He replied, "Oh, he is a blockhead, and if he were killed another like him would be put upon the throne; but if you were dead, it would not be easy to find such another." He said that he had been called upon by God to kill me, and quoted Judith and Holofernes. He was the son of a Protestant clergyman at Erfurth named Staps. He had not made his father privy to his design, and had left his house without money. I believe that he had sold his watch to purchase the knife with which he intended to kill me. He said that he trusted in God to find him the means to effect it. I called Corvisart, ordered him to feel his pulse, and see if he were mad. He did so, and everything was calm. I desired him to be taken away and locked up in a room with a *gendarme*, to have no sort of food for twenty-four hours, but as much cold water as he liked. I wished to give him time to cool and reflect, and then to examine him when he was fasting and when he might not be supposed to be under the influence of anything that would heat his imagination. After the twenty-four hours had expired, I sent for him and asked, "If I were to pardon you, would you make another attempt upon my life?" He hesitated for a long time, and at last, but with great difficulty, said that he would not, as it would not appear to be the intention of God that he should kill me, otherwise He would have allowed him to have done it at first. I ordered him to be taken away. It was my intention at first to pardon him ; but it was represented to me that his hesitation after twenty-four hours' fasting was a certain sign that his intentions were bad, and that he still intended to assassinate me ; that he was a fanatic, and that it would set a very bad example. Nothing,' continued he, ' is more dangerous than one of those religious enthusiasts.

' Another time,' proceeded the Emperor, ' a letter was sent to me by the King of Saxony, containing information that a certain person [1] was to leave Stuttgard on a particular day for Paris, where he would probably arrive on a day that was pointed out, and whose intentions were to murder me. A minute description of his person was also given. The police took its measures ; and on the day pointed out he arrived. They had him watched. He was seen to enter my chapel, to which I had gone for the celebration of some festival. He was arrested and examined. He confessed his intentions, and said that when the people knelt down, on the elevation of the Host, he intended to advance and fire at me (in fact he had advanced near to me at the moment) ; but upon a little reflection thought that would not be sure enough, and he determined

---

[1] La Sahla, see *Bourrienne*, vol. ii. p. 522.

to stab me with a knife which he had brought for that purpose. I did not like to have him executed, and ordered that he should be kept in prison.

'When I was no longer at the head of affairs, this man, who had been detained in prison for seven months after I left Paris, and ill-treated, I believe, got his liberty. Soon after he said that his designs were no longer to kill me, but that he would murder the King of Prussia for having ill-treated the Saxons and Saxony. On my return from Elba I was to be present at the opening of the Legislative Body, which was to be done with great state and ceremony. When I went to open the chamber this same man, who had got in, fell down by some accident, and a parcel, containing some chemical preparation, exploded in his pocket, and wounded him severely. It never has been clearly ascertained what his intentions were at this time. It caused great alarm amongst the Legislative Body, and he was again arrested. I have since heard that he threw himself into the Seine.'

I then asked Napoleon if he had really intended to invade England, and if so, what were his plans? He replied, 'I would have headed the Expedition myself. I had given orders for two fleets to proceed to the West Indies. Instead of remaining there, they were merely to show themselves amongst the islands, and return directly to Europe, raise the blockade of Ferrol, and release the ships there, proceed to Brest, where there were about forty sail of the line, unite and sail to the Channel, where they would not have met with anything strong enough to engage them, and clear it of all English men-of-war. By false intelligence, adroitly managed, I calculated that you would have sent squadrons to the East and West Indies and Mediterranean in search of my fleets. Before they could return I would have had the command of the Channel for two months, as I should have had about seventy sail of the line, besides frigates. I would have hurried over my flotilla with two hundred thousand men, landed as near Chatham as possible, and proceeded direct to London, where I calculated on arriving in four days from the time of my landing. I should have proclaimed a Republic (I was First Consul then), the abolition of the Nobility and House of Lords, the distribution of the property of such of the latter as opposed me amongst my partisans, liberty, equality, and the sovereignty of the people. I would have allowed the House of Commons to remain; but would have introduced a great reform. I would have issued a proclamation, declaring that we came as friends to the English, to free the nation from a corrupt and flagitious aristocracy, and to restore the Government of the democracy, all which would have been confirmed by the conduct of my army, as I would not have allowed the slightest outrage to be committed by my troops. Marauding or ill-treating the inhabitants, or the most trifling infringement of my orders, I would have punished with instant death.

'I think,' continued he, 'that with my promises,
together with what I would actually have effected,
I should have had the support of a great many.
In a large city like London, where there are so
many *canaille* and so many disaffected, I should
have been joined by a formidable body ; I would
at the same time have excited an insurrection in
Ireland.' I observed that his army would have
been destroyed piecemeal, that he would have had
a million of men-in-arms against him in a short
time ; and, moreover, that the English would have
burnt London rather than have suffered it to fall
into his hands. 'No, no,' said Napoleon, 'I do not
believe it. You are too rich and too fond of money.
A nation will not so readily burn its capital. How
often have the Parisians sworn to bury themselves
under the ruins of their capital rather than suffer
it to fall into the hands of the enemies of France,
and yet twice it has been taken. There is no
knowing what would have happened, Mr. Doctor.
Neither Pitt, nor you, nor I, could have foretold
what would have been the result. The hope of
a change for the better, and of a division of property,
would have operated wonderfully amongst the
*canaille*, especially that of London. The lower
orders of all rich nations are nearly alike. I would
have made such promises as would have had a
great effect. What resistance could an undisciplined
army make against mine in a country like England,
abounding in plains ? I weighed all you have said ;
but I calculated on the effect that would be produced

by the possession of a great and rich capital, the
bank and all your riches, the ships in the river, and
at Chatham.    I expected that I should have had
the command of the Channel for two months, by
which I should have had supplies of troops; and
when your fleet came back, they would have found
their capital in the hands of an enemy, and their
country overwhelmed by my armies.    I would have
abolished flogging, and promised your seamen everything, which would have made a great impression
upon their minds.'

I ventured to ask if he had aimed at universal
dominion.    ' No,' replied Napoleon ; ' my intention
was to make France greater than any other nation ;
but universal dominion I did not aim at.    For
example, it was not my intention to have passed the
Alps.    I purposed, when I had a second son, which
I had reason to hope for, to have made him King
of Italy, with Rome for his capital, uniting all Italy,
Naples, and Sicily into one kingdom, and putting
Murat out of Naples.'    I asked if he would have
given another kingdom to Murat.    ' Oh,' replied
he, ' that would have been easily settled.'

*January* 30.—Saw Napoleon in the billiard-room.
He directed me to bear the following message to
the Governor : ' Tell him that in consequence of his
conduct in having accepted the proposed intermediation of the Admiral, declaring that he would
charge the Admiral with it, and afterwards doing
nothing, I conceive him to be a man without
honour and without faith.    That he has broken his

word with me, broken a compact which is held sacred by robbers and Bedouin Arabs, but not by the agents of the British Ministers. Independently,' continued he, 'of his conduct with respect to the Admiral, he has broken his word about the limits. He charged you to inform me that we were permitted to ride anywhere through the old bounds, and specifically named the path by Miss Mason's. Now Gourgaud went a few days ago and asked the question from the Major at Hut's Gate, who told him that he could not pass, and that no change had been made in the orders by the Governor.'

I now informed Napoleon, 'That since the time he alluded to, Sir Hudson Lowe had given directions to allow the Emperor and any of his suite to pass by the road leading to Miss Mason's, but that they could not pass unless accompanied by him.' Napoleon replied, 'Then it is an unjust order, and beyond his power to give. For by the paper which those generals have signed, by order of his Government, they bind themselves to undergo such restrictions as it may be thought necessary to impose upon *me*, and not any more. Now this is a restriction not imposed upon me, and consequently cannot be inflicted upon them, and is illegal.'

Went to town to deliver this message. On my arrival found that Sir Hudson Lowe had left it. Conceiving that Napoleon might alter his mind, and finding that the *Julia* had arrived, bringing news from England, I did not proceed to Plantation House. Got some newspapers and returned to

word' with us ... ... ... ... which is ...
sacred by ... ... Bedouin Arabs, but ...
the agents of the British Ministers. Independently
continued ... of his conduct with respect to the
Admiral, he has broken his word about the limits
He charged you to inform me that we were ...
suited to ... anywhere through the old bounds
and specifically named the path by Miss Mason's.
Now Gourgaud went a few days ago and asked 'the
question from the Major at Hut's Gate, who told
him that he could not pass, and that no change had
been made in the orders by the Governor.'

I now informed Napoleon, 'That since the time
he alluded to, Sir Hudson Lowe had given directions to allow the Emperor and any of his suite to
pass by the road leading to Miss Mason's, but that
they could not pass when accompanied by him.'
Napoleon said 'But it is an unjust order, and
beyond ... ... ... For by the paper which
... ... back again by order of his Government, ... bind ... to undergo such
restrictions as it may be thought necessary to
impose upon him, ... can any more.' Now this is
restriction ... upon me, and consequently
cannot be laid ... from, and is illegal.'

Went to ... to deliver this message. On my
arrival found that Sir Hudson Lowe had left it.
Conceiving that Napoleon might alter his mind, and
finding that the ... had arrived, bringing news
from England. I did not proceed to Plantation
House. Got some newspapers and returned to

VIEW OF LONGWOOD, FROM BALCOMBE'S COTTAGE

LONDON: RICHARD BENTLEY & SON. 1887.

Longwood. Found Napoleon in a warm bath. His legs were swollen. On my recommending exercise, he said that he had some idea of asking the Admiral to ride out with him, but was afraid that it might get him into a scrape with the Governor.

In one of the papers there was a report that the sovereignty of Spanish South America had been offered to his brother Joseph. 'Joseph,' said he, 'although he has *beaucoup de talent, et d'esprit*, is too good a man, and too fond of amusements and literature, to be a king. However, it would be of great advantage to England, as you would have all the commerce of Spanish America. Joseph would not, and indeed could not, trade with either France or Spain, for evident reasons; and South America cannot do without importing immense quantities of European goods. By having me in your hands, you could always make advantageous terms with Joseph, who loves me sincerely, and would do anything for me.'

*January* 31.—Went to Plantation House, and made known to Sir Hudson Lowe the message I was charged with in as moderate language as circumstances would admit. After a long discussion the Governor determined upon giving the following reply : ' The Governor is employed in writing an answer to the observations of Count Bertrand, and to the paper containing the remarks on his answer to the proposition for the intervention of the Admiral ; and also in arranging how far his instructions will permit him to accede to General Bonaparte's wishes. When these are finished, he will send them to Count Bertrand, and then, if any other arrangement is deemed necessary, the Governor will have no objection to authorise the Admiral, or any other person General Bonaparte may think proper, to act as mediator, although the intermediation of any person will have no influence whatsoever in inducing the Governor to grant more or less than he would do of his own free will and judgment. This, with the alterations already made in the restrictions, and the general tenor of the observations and remarks received from Longwood, since the Governor expressed his readiness to employ a mediator, and the expectation of an arrival from England, has been the cause of the delay in authorising the Admiral to undertake the office.'

Sir Hudson desired me to show this to Napoleon, and at the same time gave me a copy of his own answer to the original proposition, and one of the remarks that had been made upon it by Napoleon, which, together with the tenor of the observations, he desired me to explain, 'were of a nature to induce a belief that a refusal had been intended by General Bonaparte.'

I said that Napoleon had also remarked that it was impossible that all the restrictions could have been imposed in obedience to specific instructions from the Ministers, as he had of his own power taken some of them off, which, had they been ordered by Ministers, he could not have done without having first obtained their sanction, for which there had not been yet sufficient time. His Excellency appeared to be taken unawares, as he immediately replied, 'They were not ordered by Ministers; there were no minute details given, either to me, or to Sir George Cockburn. In fact, it is left entirely to my judgment, and I may take what measures I think proper, and, indeed, do as I like. I have been ordered to take particular care that he does not escape, and to prevent correspondence of any kind with him, except through me. The rest is left to myself.'

Admiral and Lady Malcolm, with Captain Meynel, had an interview at Longwood.

*February* 1.—Informed Napoleon of what I had been directed by Sir Hudson Lowe. Showed him His Excellency's answer to the proposition for intermediation, with his remarks opposite to it. 'I maintained, and will maintain,' replied the Emperor, 'that his last restrictions are worse than any in force at Botany Bay, because even there it is not attempted to prohibit people from speaking. It is useless for him to endeavour to persuade us that we have not been ill-treated by him. There is not a freeborn man whose hair would not stand on end with horror, on reading such an atrocious proceeding as that prohibition against speaking. His assertion, that it was intended as civility, is a mockery, and adds irony and insult to injury. I know well that if he really intended to grant anything, it is in his power to do so without a mediator. It was a mark of imbecility in him to have accepted the proposition, but having once accepted it, he ought not to have broken his word. Sometimes I believe that he is an executioner who has come to assassinate me ; but most probably he is a man of incapacity and without heart who does not comprehend his office.'

Saw Sir Hudson Lowe on the hill above Hut's Gate, to whom I communicated Napoleon's reply. His Excellency repeated that the prohibition to speak, which had been so much complained of, was not an order but rather a request, and an instance of civility on his (Sir Hudson's) part, in order to prevent the necessity, which would otherwise exist, of the interference of a British officer. 'Did you tell him that ? ' said Sir Hudson Lowe. I answered that I had. 'Well, what reply did he make ?' I gave his reply, which did not appear to please the Governor. I subsequently informed him that water was so scarce at Longwood as to make it sometimes impossible to procure a sufficiency for a bath for Napoleon's use, and that it was generally a matter of great difficulty to obtain the necessary quantity. Sir Hudson Lowe replied, ' That he did not know what business General Bonaparte had to *stew himself in hot water* for so many hours, and so often, at a time when the 53d Regiment could scarcely procure enough water to cook their food.'

Napoleon went down to pay a visit to Count and Countess Bertrand, where he remained nearly two hours.

`February 2.   Napoleon in a bath.   Conversed
upon various topics.

*February 4.*—The scarcity of water at Longwood has daily increased, and the greatest part of
what has been brought up is sour, turbid, and of a
very disagreeable taste, in consequence of having
been conveyed in old wine and rum casks, which necessarily communicate an unpleasant taste to the water.

*February 6.*—Lady Lowe paid a visit to Countess
Bertrand.

Sir Hudson Lowe had a long conversation with
me relative to Napoleon ; the purport of which was,
that if he put the limits on their old footing,
Napoleon should not make a practice of visiting the
houses that were situated in them, and at the same
time that he (Napoleon) should not know that any
restriction existed to prevent him.   His Excellency
said that there was a great difference between limits
for exercise and limits for correspondence and communication ; that if he gave larger limits, they must
be subject to the restriction of not entering a house
unless accompanied by a British officer.   I observed
that there were only four houses within the limits of
Woody Range.   Sir Hudson said that perhaps it
might be settled by his giving General Bonaparte a
list of such houses as he would permit him to enter.
I informed him that Napoleon had said that if he
were disposed to intrigue with the Commissioners, or
with others, he might easily do so by instructing
them to meet him within the limits of the alarm-
house, which was always in his power to effect ; but

that he (Napoleon) would never do anything which
had the appearance of an intrigue. Sir Hudson
replied that 'General Bonaparte had never been
without intriguing, and never would.' He then
desired me to say that he daily expected a ship with
fresh orders, and permission to grant an extension
of limits. That he should have no objection to
allow General Bonaparte to enter into certain houses
which he (Sir H.) would point out, nor indeed to
send a list of them to Count Bertrand.

*February 7.*—Communicated Sir Hudson's Lowe's
ideas to Napoleon. 'If he were to give me the
whole of the island, on condition that I would pledge
my word not to attempt an escape,' replied he, ' I
would not accept it, because it would be equivalent
to the acknowledging myself a prisoner, although
at the same time I would not make the attempt. I
am here by force and not by right. If I had been
taken at Waterloo, perhaps I might have had no
hesitation in accepting it, although even in that case
it would be contrary to the law of nations, as now
there is no war. If they were to offer me permission to reside in England on similar conditions, I
would refuse it. I do not understand what he
means by correspondence. What is he afraid of ?
Perhaps the Commissioners. The Admiral never
was afraid of his conduct being made public. I
hope,' continued Napoleon, 'that you told him I
said that he had not the right to impose any
restrictions unless they were signed by the Ministers.' I replied that I had, and that the Governor

had said that he had it in his power to impose whatever restrictions he thought necessary. ' By the
Bill,' replied Napoleon, ' he has not the right. By
the law of force he can do what he likes, in the same
manner as the English Parliament have passed a
Bill to legalise illegality, and to authorise a proscrip-
tion contrary to the laws of nations, to good faith,
and to their own honour. But even in that it is not
allowed to delegate the authority.'

After some further observations Napoleon desired me to communicate to the Governor, ' That if
he sent a list to Count Bertrand, or told him that
within the limits there were two or more houses
which he either suspected or was unwilling that I
should visit, I shall not enter either them, or those
of the Commissioners. If he arranges it in this
manner, it will be understood ; but if he sent a list of
all the houses in the island except one, and specified
that I might enter all but that one, I would not
accept it. Whereas, on the contrary, if he made
another list of every house in the island except one,
and said that he did not wish me to go into any of
those mentioned in that list, and made no observation about the remaining one, I would sooner accept
it than the first, although I could go only into one
house, whereas, by the other, I could enter all on the
island excepting one. Availing myself of the first
would appear like visiting by his permission,
whereas the other would seem to be voluntary, as in
consequence of nothing having been mentioned, it
would be left at my option to go in or not. It

would be like a free will. Tell him this,' continued
he; 'although I am sure that it is merely some
shuffling trick on his part, and will come to nothing.

'I think,' added Napoleon, 'that it is owing to
some small remains of the influence *of my star* that
the English have treated me so ill; at least that
this man whom they have sent out as Governor has
conducted himself in such a manner. At all events
posterity will avenge me.'

*February* 8.—Went to Plantation House and
communicated to Sir Hudson Lowe the purport of
the above-mentioned conversation. His Excellency
replied that, by the proposed arrangement, the principal difficulties were removed, and that he would
speak to Count Bertrand about it. Cipriani in
town endeavouring to procure some good meat.

The meat sent has been of so bad a quality for
some days that the orderly officer has thought it
incumbent upon him to return it, accompanied with
official complaints.

*February* 9.—Scott, the servant, to whom Count
Las Cases had given the letter, released from prison
under the following conditions, viz. his father to
be security for him, and to forfeit £100 if his son
ever went beyond the enclosure of the father's little
property.

*February* 10.—Told Napoleon that I had communicated his desires to Sir Hudson Lowe, who
had promised to talk the matter over with Count
Bertrand. Napoleon replied, 'You may depend
upon it that it will end in nothing. It is merely

to deceive *you*.   He will act as he has done in that
affair with the Admiral.

'Gourgaud,' added Napoleon, 'is stopped at Hut's
Gate every day.  The sentinel cries "*Halt;*" then the
serjeant comes out, and after a sort of consultation
together says "*Pass.*"'

Had some conversation about Alexandria.   'Your
Ministers,' said he, 'acted most unwisely in not having
retained possession of Alexandria.   For if you had
kept it *then*, it would now be an old robbery like
Malta, and would have remained with you quietly.
Five thousand men would be sufficient to garrison
it, and it would pay itself by the great trade you
would have in Egypt.   You could prohibit the
introduction of all manufactures except English, and
consequently you would have all the commerce of
Egypt, as there is no other seaport town in the
country.   In my opinion, it would be to you an
acquisition far preferable to Gibraltar or Malta.
Egypt once in possession of the French, farewell
India to the English.[1]   This was one of the great
projects I aimed at.   I know not why you set
so great a value upon Gibraltar; you cannot
prevent a fleet from passing from it into the Mediterranean.   When I was sovereign of France, I
would much rather have seen Gibraltar in your
hands than in those of the Spaniards ; because your

---

[1] A pertinent passage at the present moment, seventy years afterwards.  Modern artillery will carry across the Straits of Gibraltar ;
and if Tangier had been properly retained by England the entrance
to the Mediterranean might be sealed in time of war.

having possession of it always incensed the Spaniards against you.' I observed that it had been reported he had intended to besiege it, and for that purpose had marched a great army into Spain; although others said that his object was merely to get his troops a footing in that country. He laughed, and said, '*C'est vrai.* Turkey,' added he, 'must soon fall, and it will be impossible to divide it without allotting some portion to France, which will be Egypt. But if you had kept Alexandria, you would have prevented the French from obtaining it, and from ultimately gaining possession of India, which will certainly follow their possession of Egypt.'

*February* 12.—Found Sir Hudson Lowe at Plantation House closeted with Sir Thomas Reade. Had a conversation with him afterwards in the library relative to the proposition which had been made to him on the 8th. His Excellency, however, would not understand that only visiting such houses into which entrance had not been prohibited by him, and abstaining from entering all which were marked as objectionable in a list made by himself, was in the end precisely the same as the mode which he had suggested of only visiting certain houses that were specifically named in a list. He said, with considerable ill-humour, that General Bonaparte had some *design* in it, and that he would not grant his consent. I observed that it was rather unfortunate that he had desired me to make any proposition on the subject, as it might afford a foundation for another charge of shuffling. His Excellency replied by desiring me to tell General Bonaparte, as he had done on former occasions, that he might consider himself very fortunate in having so good a man to deal with, etc.

Mrs. and Misses Balcombe arrived at Longwood. I dined with Napoleon in company with them. He was extremely lively and chatty, and displayed a fund of *causerie* rarely to be met with. He instructed Miss Eliza Balcombe how to play at billiards.[1]

Application made on the 10th to Sir Hudson Lowe to allow Cipriani to go down into the valley (guarded by a soldier) to purchase sheep and vegetables from the farmers, as the meat sent by the Government was not eatable. Refused by Sir Hudson Lowe. The daily allowance of meat, vegetables, wines, etc. being carted up in the sun to Longwood, many of the articles are rendered unfit for use on the road.

*February* 14.—Breakfasted with Napoleon, with whom I had a conversation about Russia. ' If the Emperor Paul had lived,' said he, 'there would have been a peace with England in a short time, as you would not have been long able to contend with the united Northern Powers. I wrote to Paul to continue building ships, and to endeavour to unite the North against you ; not to hazard any battles, as

---

[1] ' Billiards was a game much played by Napoleon and his suite. I had the honour of being instructed in its mysteries by him ; but when tired of my lesson my amusement consisted in aiming the balls at his fingers, and I was never more pleased than when I succeeded in making him cry out.'—Mrs. Abell's *Recollections*, p. 176, 1873 edition.

the English would gain them, but allow you to exhaust yourselves, and by all means to get a large Russian fleet into the Mediterranean.'

Some conversation then took place relative to the manner in which the British Ministers had treated him, which he asserted to be much worse than that which had been practised towards Queen Mary.

'Mary,' said he, 'was better treated. She was permitted to write to whom she pleased, and she was confined in England, which of itself was everything ; it appears that she was persecuted more on account of her religion by the Puritans than from any other cause.' I observed that Mary was accused of having been an accomplice in the murder of her husband. He replied, 'Of that there is not the smallest doubt. She even married his murderer afterwards. Alexander employs the murderers of his father. One of them O—— is now his aide-de-camp. I must, however, do him the justice to say, that at Tilsit he observed to me that I paid a great deal of attention to B——, and begged to know my reasons for it ? I answered, because he is your General. "*Cependant*," said the Czar, "*c'est un vilain coquin. C'est lui qui a assassiné mon père*, and policy alone obliges me to employ him, although I wish him dead, and in a short time will send him about his business." Alexander and the King of Prussia,' continued he, 'dined with me every day, and in order to pay a compliment to the former, I had intended, on the day that this conversation took

place, to have asked B—— to dinner, as being the
Commander-in-Chief of his army. This displeased
the Czar, who, although he asked B—— to his own
table, did not wish me to do so, because it would
have raised him too high in the eyes of the Russians.

'Paul,' continued he, 'was murdered by B——,
O——, P——, and others. There was a Cossack,
in whom Paul had confidence, stationed at his door.
The conspirators came up and demanded entrance.
P—— told him who he was, and that he wanted to
see the Emperor upon immediate business. The
faithful Cossack refused. The conspirators fell upon
him, and after a desperate resistance, overpowered
and cut him to pieces. Paul, who was in bed,
hearing the noise, got out and endeavoured to
escape to the Empress's apartments. Unluckily
for himself he, in his suspicions, a day or two before,
had ordered the door of communication to be closed
up. He then went and concealed himself in a press.
Meanwhile the conspirators broke open the door,
and running to the bed perceived that there was
nobody in it. "We are lost," they cried, "he has
escaped." P——, who had more presence of mind
than the rest, went to the bed, and putting his hands
under the bedclothes said, 'The nest is warm; the
bird cannot be far off.' They then began to search,
and finally dragged Paul out of his hiding-place.
They presented him a paper containing his abdication, which they wanted him to sign. He refused
at first, but said that he would abdicate if they
would release him. They then seized and knocked

him down and tried to suffocate him.   Paul made a
desperate resistance, and fearful that assistance might
arrive, B—— despatched him by stamping his heel
into his eyes, and thus beating his brains out, while
the others held him down.   Paul, in his struggles
for life, once got B——'s heel into his mouth, and
bit a piece out of the skin of it.'

I asked him if he thought that Paul had been
mad?  'Latterly,' said Napoleon, 'I believe that he
was.   At first  he was strongly prejudiced against
the Revolution and every person concerned in it;
but afterwards I had rendered him reasonable, and
had changed his opinions altogether.   If Paul had
lived, you would have lost India before now.   An
agreement was made between Paul and myself to
invade it.   I furnished the plan.   I was to have
sent thirty thousand good troops.   He was to have
sent a similar number of the best Russian soldiers,
and forty thousand Cossacks.   I was to subscribe
ten millions for the purchase of camels and other
requisites for crossing the desert.   The King of
Prussia was to have been applied to by both of
us to grant a passage for my troops through his
dominions, which would have been immediately
granted.   I had at the same time made a demand
to the Shah of Persia for a passage through his
country, which would also have been granted, as the
Persians were desirous of profiting by it themselves.
My troops were to have gone to Warsaw, to be
joined by the Russians and Cossacks, and to have
marched from thence to the Caspian Sea, where

they would have either embarked, or have proceeded by land, according to circumstances.   I was
beforehand with you, in sending an ambassador to
Persia to make interest there.   Since that time your
Ministers have been *imbéciles* enough to allow the
Russians to get four provinces, which increase their
territories beyond the mountains.   The first year of
war that you will have with the Russians, they will
take India from you.'

I asked then if it were true that Alexander had
intended to have seized upon Turkey ?   Napoleon
answered, 'All his thoughts are directed to the
conquest of Turkey.   We have had many discussions about it ; at first I was pleased with his
proposals, because I thought it would enlighten the
world to drive those brutes, the Turks, out of
Europe.   But when I reflected upon the consequences, and saw what a tremendous access of
power it would give to Russia, on account of the
numbers of Greeks in the Turkish dominions who
would naturally join the Russians, I refused to
consent to it, especially as Alexander wanted to
get Constantinople, which I would not allow, as
it would have destroyed the balance of power in
Europe.   I reflected that France would gain
Egypt, Syria, and the islands, which would have
been nothing in comparison with what Russia
would have obtained.   I considered that the
barbarians of the North were already too powerful,
and probably in the course of time would over-
whelm all Europe, as I now think they will.

Austria already trembles; Russia and Prussia
united, Austria falls, and England cannot prevent
it. France under the present family is nothing,
and the Austrians are so *lâche* that they will be
easily overpowered. Russia is the more formidable,
because she can never disarm. In Russia, once
a soldier, always a soldier. They are barbarians,
who, one may say, have no country, and to whom
every country is better than the one which gave
them birth. Moreover the Russians are poor, and
it is necessary for them to conquer. When I am
dead, my memory will be esteemed and I shall be
revered in consequence of having foreseen and endeavoured to put a stop to that which will yet take
place. It will be revered when the barbarians of the
North will possess Europe, which would not have
happened, had it not been for you, *signori Inglesi.'*

Napoleon expressed great anxiety relative to
Count Montholon, as the Governor had made
some insinuations that his removal was in contemplation. 'I should feel,' continued he, 'the
loss of Montholon most sensibly; as, independently
of his attachment to me, he is most useful, and
endeavours to anticipate all my wants. I know
that it would grieve him much to leave me, though
in truth it would render him a great service if he
were removed from this desolate place, and restored
to the bosom of his friends, as he is not proscribed,
and has nothing to fear in France. Moreover,
being of a noble family, he might readily find
favour with the Bourbons if he chose.'

Accompanied Countess Montholon to Plantation House, to pay a visit to Lady Lowe. Saw Sir Hudson, who said that 'he would not place any confidence in the assurances of General Bonaparte, and was determined that he should not enter any house unaccompanied by a British officer.' Some discussion then took place relative to the *passes* which His Excellency had formerly given to persons who were desirous to visit Longwood. Sir Hudson Lowe wished to persuade me that he had never given a pass for one day only,[1] and that Major Gorrequer could testify to the truth of that. I remarked that several persons to whom he had granted passes had shown them to Count Bertrand at Hut's Gate, and pointed out to him that on the pass itself the day had been specified, and on that account they had begged Bertrand to exert himself to induce Napoleon to see them, as their passes were null after that day. Sir Hudson angrily replied that 'they were *liars.*'

Before my departure, Sir Hudson Lowe told me that I might take some of the numbers of the *Ambigu* and show them to General Bonaparte.

On my return informed Napoleon that I had received some numbers of a periodical work called *l'Ambigu*, which, I added, were extremely abusive of him. He laughed, and said, 'Only children mind abuse;' and then desired me to bring them to him. When he saw them, he said, 'Ah! Pelletier.

---

[1] This was a matter of public notoriety both at St. Helena and amongst the passengers to and from England.

He has been libelling me these twenty years.   But
I am very glad to get them all the same.'

Countess Montholon · and Mrs. ˙and Miss
Balcombe passed an hour in conversation with
Napoleon after dinner yesterday.

*February* 17.—Napoleon observed that he found
Pelletier's *Ambigu* very. interesting, although it
contained many falsehoods and *bêtises*.   'I have
been reading,' continued he, 'the account of the
battle of Waterloo contained in it, which is nearly
correct.   I have been considering who could have
been the author.   It must have been some person
about me.   Had it not been for Grouchy,' added
he, 'I should have gained the day!'[1]

I asked if he thought that Marshal Grouchy
had betrayed him intentionally.   'No, no,' replied
Napoleon, 'but there was a want of energy on
his part.[2]   There was also treason amongst the
staff.   I believe that some of the staff officers
whom I had sent to Grouchy betrayed me,[3] and
went over to the enemy.   Of this, however, I am
not certain, as I have never seen Grouchy since.'[4]

---

[1] See also p. 161, and vol. ii. p. 25.

[2] An unfair charge, as the Marquis of Grouchy was preparing to
march upon Brussels after his victory over the Prussians at Wavres.

[3] Like General Bourmont, who incurred the lasting stigma of
going over to the enemy immediately before an action, and whose
promotion in subsequent years is equally discreditable to the French
Government.

[4] Dorsey Gardner, a recent and most painstaking American
authority on the Campaign of 1815, sums up the position thus
(pp. 170, 171):—(*a*) Napoleon's delays allowed the Prussians fifteen
hours for their undisturbed retreat from Ligny—time enough to

I asked if he had thought Marshal Soult to have been loyal to his interest? Napoleon answered, 'Certainly. But Soult did not betray Louis, as has been supposed, nor was he privy to my return and landing in France. For some days Soult thought that I was *mad*, and that I must certainly be lost. Notwithstanding this, appearances were so much against Soult, and without intending it his acts turned out to be so favourable to my projects that, were I trying him, and ignorant of what I know, I should condemn

ensure their junction with the English; (*b*) Napoleon sent off Grouchy, against his earnest protest, to march in a false direction; (*c*) Napoleon and Grouchy were both equally remiss in patrolling the country between them, and so were in ignorance of the Prussian cross march until too late; (*d*) Grouchy could not, after he knew of the cross march, have prevented half, or perhaps three-quarters of Blucher's army from joining Wellington. Mathematically stated, any censure should be apportioned in the ratio of five parts to Napoleon and one to Grouchy.

'The notion,' says Colonel Chesney, a very high English authority, 'that Grouchy is responsible for the Waterloo defeat must be dismissed, by those who choose to weigh the evidence, from the domain of authentic history to the limbo of national figments; in plain truth, never has a single reputation been so grossly sacrificed to save national vanity. So far from earning for him blame, the marshal's conduct, weighing all the circumstances of the campaign, should have crowned his old age with honour. That the result has been so different is due simply to the demand by the French for a popular scapegoat, and to the readiness with which Napoleon supplied it in his lieutenant.'

See also Hamley's *Operations of War*, pp. 196, 197. Siborne's *Campaign of Waterloo*. Grouchy's *Fragments Historiques*.

Charras, the best French authority, also supports this view; while Marshal Grouchy's exploits in the ever memorable campaign of 1814, and his able handling of his troops when retiring in 1815 after Waterloo, are no slight testimony in his favour.

him for having betrayed Louis. But he really
was not privy to it, although Ney, in his defence,
stated that I told him so. As to the proclamation
which Ney said that I had sent to him, it is not
true. I sent him nothing but orders. I would
have stopped the proclamation had it been in
my power, as it was unworthy of me. When
Ney promised the King to bring me back in an
iron cage, he really meant what he said, and
continued to say until two days before he actually
joined me. He ought to have acted like Oudinot,
who asked his troops if they might be depended
upon, to which they unanimously replied, "We
will not fight against the Emperor, nor for the
Bourbons." He could not prevent the troops
from joining me, nor indeed the peasants, but he
went too far.

'Mouton Duvernet,' said he, 'suffered unjustly;
at least considering all circumstances, he did not
deserve it more than another. He hung upon
the flanks of my little army for two days, and his
intentions were for the King. But every one
joined me. The enthusiasm was astonishing. I
might have entered Paris with four hundred
thousand men if I had liked. What is still more
surprising, and I believe unparalleled in history
is, that it was effected without any intrigues.
There was no plot, no understanding with any of
the generals in France. Not one of them knew
my intentions. In my proclamations consisted
the whole of my conspiracy. With them I effected

everything. With them I led the nation. Not
even Masséna knew of my intention. When he
was informed of my having landed with a few
hundred men he disbelieved it, and pronounced
it impossible, thinking that if I had entertained
such a project I should have made him acquainted
with it. The Bourbons want to make it appear
that a conspiracy existed in the army, which is
the reason they have shot Mouton-Duvernet, Ney,
and others, because my having effected what I
did, not by the aid of a conspiracy, or by force,
as not a musket was fired, but by the general
wish of the nation, reflects such disgrace upon them.

'There never was yet,' continued Napoleon,
'a king who was more the sovereign of the *people*
than I was. If I were not possessed of the
smallest talent, it would be more easy for me to
reign in France than for Louis and the Bourbons,
endowed with the greatest abilities. The mass
of the French nation hate the old nobles and the
priests. I have not sprung from the *ancienne
noblesse*, nor have I ever too much encouraged
the priests. The French nation have predominant
in them *la vanità, la leggerezza, l'independenza, ed
il capriccio*, with an unconquerable passion for
glory. They will as soon do without bread as
without glory; and a proclamation will draw them
on. Unlike England, where the inhabitants of a
whole county may be inflamed by and will follow
the opinion of two or three noble families, they
must be themselves courted.

'At Waterloo not a single soldier betrayed me. Whatever treason there was, existed among the generals, and not among the soldiers or the regimental officers; these last were acquainted with each other's sentiments, and turned out those they suspected.

'Your nation,' continued Napoleon, 'is chiefly guided by interest in all its actions. I have found since I have fallen into your hands, that you have no more liberty than other countries. I have paid dearly for the romantic and chivalrous opinion which I had formed of you.'

Here I repeated nearly what I had said upon former occasions. Napoleon shook his head, and replied, 'I recollect that Paoli, who was a great friend to your nation,—in fact, who was almost an Englishman,—said, on hearing the English extolled as the most generous, the most liberal, and the most unprejudiced nation on earth, "Softly, you go too far; they are not so generous nor so unprejudiced as you imagine; they are very self-interested; they are a nation of merchants, and generally have gain in view. Whenever they do anything, they always calculate what profit they shall derive from it. They are the most calculating people in existence." This Paoli said, not without at the same time giving you credit for the good national qualities which you really possess. *Now* I believe that Paoli was right.'

Napoleon then made some remarks upon Longwood, and expressed his surprise that some person had not made a contract to bring a supply of water to it and to the camp ; stipulating that he should be permitted to establish a garden in the valley, by means of which a sufficiency of vegetables might be produced at a cheap rate, not only for Longwood and the camp, but also for the ships. 'Here,' continued he, 'if water were brought by a conduit, Noverraz, with the help of two or three Chinese, would produce a sufficiency of the vegetables which we so much want. How much better would it be to dispose of the public money in conducting water to those poor soldiers in camp than in digging ditches and throwing up fortifications round this house, just as if an army were coming to attack it! A man who has no regard for his soldiers ought never to have a command. One of the greatest necessities of the soldier is water.'

*February* 18.—Saw Sir Hudson Lowe at Plantation House. Found him busied in examining some newspapers for Longwood, several of which he put aside, as not being, in his opinion, proper to be sent to Napoleon, observing to me at the same time, 'That however strange it might appear, General Bonaparte ought to be obliged to him for not sending him newspapers indiscriminately, as the perusal of articles written in his own favour might excite hopes which, when not ultimately realised, could not fail to afflict him ; that, moreover, the British Government thought it improper to let him know everything that appeared in the newspapers.'

*February* 19.—Sir Thomas Reade very busy in

circulating reports in the town that 'General Bonaparte was sulky and would see nobody; that the Governor was too good, and that the villain ought to be put in chains.'

*February* 21.—The *David* transport brought the news of the arrival of the *Adolphus* at the Cape, laden chiefly with iron rails, to surround Napoleon's house, for which the Governor had sent to England.

Sir Hudson Lowe came up to Longwood and inspected the works throwing up about the stables, and the sentinels that he had placed. Held a long conversation with me afterwards about the restrictions and limits without coming to any determination.

His Excellency then told me, in order, as he said, to show the good opinion that he entertained of me, that 'he had no scruple in informing me that the Commissioners were to be looked upon with great suspicion; that they were, in fact, spies upon everybody and upon everything, and only wanted to get something out of me, in order to send it to their Courts; that I had better be very cautious, as in all probability they would report to their employers everything that I said, as they had already done to him; in proof of which he repeated to me the tenor of the conversation which I had held with Baron Sturmer at Plantation House on the 21st of October 1816, adding his satisfaction at having found that I had been cautious in my remarks. He also said that he had written to Lord Bathurst in very favourable terms about me, and had recom-

mended that my salary should be augmented to
£500 per annum.'

After this His Excellency acquainted me that he
had received a letter from young Las Cases for me,
which he would send.

*February* 24.—Mr. Vernon came up to Longwood to *ondoyer* Count Bertrand's child.   Napoleon
played at billiards in the evening.

*February* 28.—Napoleon had very little rest
during the night.   Got up at five o'clock and walked
about in the billiard-room for some time.   Found
him lying on his sofa.   Looked low, and out of
spirits.   Greeted me with a faint voice.   Gave him
a Portsmouth paper of the 18th of November last.
On reading some remarks made about the injury
that was likely to accrue to the French interest by
the marriage of the Emperor of Austria and the
Princess of Bavaria, together with an observation
that he, Napoleon, had prevented it even when in
the plenitude of his power, Napoleon said, ' *C'est
vrai*, I was apprehensive of the consequences of the
alliance between the two houses.   But what signifies
it now ?   Under the Bourbons, France will never be
a first-rate power.

' Nature,' he remarked later on when a change of
topic occurred, ' in forming some men, intended that
they should always remain in a subaltern situation.
Such was Berthier.   There was not in the world so
good a *chef d'état major;* but change his occupation,
he was not fit to command five hundred men.   A
good scribbler, like this Governor, an excellent

*commis.* You may see how unfit for command he is,
when he allows himself to be led by the nose by
such a contemptible *imbécile* as that Colonel Reade.
Have you ever read *Gil Blas ?'* I replied that I
had. 'That eternal smile on Reade's lips,' rejoined
Napoleon, 'is not natural, and reminds me of
Ambrose de Lamela. Like Lamela's going to
church while he was plotting to rob his master, it
masks his real intentions. I have been informed,'
continued he, 'that the Balcombes were interrogated
and cross-examined both by the Governor and by
his privy councillor, Reade, touching what they had
heard and seen at Longwood, and that the father
replied that his daughters had come here to have
the honour of visiting us, and not as spies.'

*March* 1.—Napoleon conversed with me for
some time relative to the iron railing said to have
been brought out in the *Adolphus.* I told him that
it was customary in England to put rails round the
country-houses of gentlemen, at which he looked
rather incredulous.

*March* 2.—Saw Napoleon in his dressing-room,
lying on his sofa. He was rather low-spirited, and
looked pale.

During the course of conversation he observed
that he saw a change in the system of the Bourbons
favourable to them, as, instead of employing the
ultrafaction, and other violent characters, they
had appointed men who had been formerly employed
by him, and who had the confidence of the nation.
Amongst others he mentioned Molé.

Asked Napoleon whether the statement contained in the *Observer* relative to Clarke's conduct towards Carnot, in having withheld his pension, and the manner in which he himself was reported to have acted, were true. Napoleon replied, ' It is perfectly true. But I was surprised to see the papers occupied so much about Clarke, who is not of sufficient importance for people to trouble themselves about him.' I asked his opinion of Clarke. He replied, ' He is not a man of talent, but he is laborious and useful in the *bureau*. He is, moreover, incorruptible, and careful of the public money, which he never has appropriated to his own use. He is an excellent *redacteur*. He is not a soldier, however, nor do I believe that he ever saw a shot fired in his life. He is infatuated with his nobility. He pretends that he is descended from the ancient kings of Scotland, or Ireland, and constantly boasts of his nobility. He was an admirable clerk. I sent him to Florence as Ambassador, where he employed himself in nothing but turning over the old musty records of the place, in search of proofs of the nobility of my family, which you may know came from Florence.[1] He plagued me with letters upon this subject, and caused me to write to him not to trouble his head or mine with his nonsense about nobility ; that I was the *first* of my family.

[1] Comte d'Hérisson says that the Bonapartes originated in Sarzane, a town in the Genoese territory, where he found records of a Bonaparte de Cianfardo, a notary, in 1250 ; and deeds proving that Francesco di Giovanno, or François de Bonaparte, left Sarzane for Corsica ' about the year 1512.'—*The Black Cabinet*, pp. 111, 112.

Notwithstanding this, he still continued his inquiries. When I returned from Elba, he offered his services to me, but I sent him word that I would not employ any traitors, and dismissed him to his estates.' I asked if he thought that Clarke would have served him faithfully. 'Yes,' replied the Emperor, 'so long as I was the strongest, like a great many others.' I inquired if it were true that he had written the letter which had been attributed to him, announcing to Clarke the death of his nephew? He replied that he had, and that his name was Elliot.

I remarked that his ancestors were noble. He replied they were senators of Florence.

*March* 3.—Saw Napoleon in very high spirits while dressing. Free from any complaint. Laughed and quizzed me about some young ladies, and asked me to give him all the gossip of the town. Appeared to be in better spirits than he had been for a long time.

He then asked some medical questions, went into the billiard-room, ordered some bottled porter, took a glass of it, saying in English, *Your health*, and made me take another. Asked many questions about porter, and was much surprised at its low price in England. While walking about the room, 'What sort of a man did you take me to be before you became my surgeon?' said he, 'What did you think of my character, and what I was capable of? Give me your real opinion frankly.' I replied, 'I thought you to be a man whose stupendous talents

were only to be equalled by your measureless
ambition; and although I did not give credit to a
tenth part of the libels which I had read against
you, still I believed that you would not hesitate to
commit a crime, when you found it to be necessary,
or thought it might be useful to you.'—'This is just
the answer that I expected,' replied Napoleon, 'and
is perhaps the opinion of Lord Holland, and even
of numbers of the French.    I have risen to too
great a pitch of human glory and elevation not to
have excited the envy and jealousy of mankind.
They will say, "It is true that he has raised himself
to the highest pinnacle of glory, but to attain it he
has committed many crimes."    The fact is, I have
always gone with the opinion of great masses, and
with events.    I have always made little of the
opinion of individuals—a great deal of that of the
public; of what use then would crime have been to
me?    I am too much a fatalist, and have always
despised mankind too much to have had recourse
to crime to frustrate their attempts.

'In spite of all the libels,' continued he, 'I have
no fear whatever about my fame.    Posterity will do
me justice.    The truth will be known, and the good
that I have done will be compared with the faults
that I have committed.    I am not afraid of the
result.    Had I succeeded, I should have died with
the reputation of having been the greatest man that
ever existed.    As it is, although I have failed, I
shall be considered as an extraordinary man: my
elevation was unparalleled, *because* unaccompanied

by crime.   I have fought fifty pitched battles,
almost all of which I have gained.   I have framed
and carried into effect a code of laws that will carry
my name down to the most distant generations.
From nothing I raised myself to be the most
powerful monarch in the world.   Europe was at
my feet.   My ambition was great, I admit, but it
was of a dispassionate nature, and caused by events
and the opinion of great bodies.   I have always
been of opinion that sovereignty lay in the people.
In fact, the Imperial Government was a kind of
republic.   Called to the head of it by the voice of
the nation, my maxim was, *la carrière ouverte aux
talens*, without distinction of birth or fortune, and
this system of equality is the reason why your
oligarchy hate me so much.

   ' Those,' continued he, ·' who consented to the
union of Poland with Russia, will be the execration
of posterity, while my name will be pronounced with
respect when the fine Southern countries of Europe
are a prey to the barbarians of the North.   Perhaps
my greatest fault was, not having deprived the King
of Prussia of his throne, which I might easily have
done.   After Friedland, I ought to have taken
Silesia and —— from Prussia, and given them to
Saxony, as the King and the Prussians were too
much humiliated not to revenge themselves the first
opportunity.   Had I done this, given them a free
constitution, and delivered the peasants from feudal
slavery, they would have been contented.'

   Napoleon afterwards walked down to Count

Bertrand's. For two or three days he has taken much more exercise than formerly.

*March* 4.—Saw Napoleon in the billiard-room. He was in extremely good spirits. Returned me the *Ambigu* for 1816, and desired me to endeavour to obtain the numbers for 1815.

In answer to a question of mine he said, ' P—— would write for anybody that would pay him. He made offers to me to change his style, and write for me in such a manner that the British Government would not be aware that he was employed by me. One time in particular he sent to the police a MS. copy of a book written against me, with an offer that it should not be printed provided he were paid a certain sum of money. This was made known to me. I ordered the police to answer, that if he paid the expenses of printing, the work should be published in Paris for him. He was not the only one who made offers of the kind to me when I was in power. Some of the editors of the English newspapers made similar advances, and declared that they could render me most essential services, but I *then* did not attach sufficient importance to their offers, and refused them. Not so the Bourbons. In 1814 the editor of one of them was paid about £3000 of English money, besides having a great number of copies taken. I told you before that I found his receipt amongst Blacas's papers on my return from Elba.[1] I do not know

---

[1] When Louis XVIII. was in exile at Hartwell, a continuous record of his movements was transmitted to the Tuileries. The King is

if he is in their pay now. In that year also a great number of pamphlets were printed in London against the Bourbons, and copies of each sent over to them, with a threat of publication if they were not paid. The Bourbons were greatly frightened, and greedily bought them up. There was one pamphlet in particular, a terrible libel against the late Queen of France, which it cost them a large sum of money to suppress.[1]

'When I was on the throne,' continued he, 'there were thirty clerks employed in translating the English newspapers, and in making extracts from English works of merit. Matters which appeared of importance were extracted from the newspapers and daily submitted to me. But I never had it done in my presence, or endeavoured to accompany the translator in his progress, as has been asserted. I did not even know the English article "*the*" at that time. Indeed, to me it was not of sufficient importance to learn the language purposely to read the papers, especially as I had letters and intelligence constantly from the spies in England. The papers, however, served to corroborate their information relative to the movements of troops, assembling and sailing of men of war, and other measures of Government.'[2]

said to have divided the amount paid by the Imperial Police for the reports with the informer. There are many versions of the story and different informers named, but all do credit to the shrewdness of the King.

[1] See Campan's *Memoirs of Marie Antoinette*, vol. ii. p. 211.

[2] There are frequent references to the English newspapers in the correspondence of Napoleon.

The Governor at Longwood. Explained his intention of putting the iron railing round the house, the doors of which he said he should cause to be locked at seven or eight o'clock at night, and the keys sent to Plantation House, where they should remain until daybreak the next morning.

*March* 5. — The *Tortoise* storeship, Captain Cook, arrived direct from England, which she had left on the 18th of December 1816.

On my return to Longwood I found Napoleon in very different spirits from yesterday. He was reclining on his sofa, in a pensive attitude, his head resting upon one of his hands, and apparently melancholy. His morning gown was on, a Madras handkerchief round his head, and his beard un-shaved. In rather a desponding manner he asked me, 'What news?' and if any ship had arrived from England? I replied that one had arrived direct from that country. After having related what I heard and conceived to be most interesting, I mentioned that a book had been published respecting him by Warden, which had excited great interest. At the name of Warden he raised his head and said, 'What, Warden of the *Northumberland?*' I replied in the affirmative. 'What is the nature of the work? Is it for or against me? Is it well written?' I replied that it was a description of what had passed on board of the *Northumberland* and at St. Helena; that it was in his favour, and well written, and contained many curious statements, and also refutations of some accusations that had been made against him, an explanation about the affair of the Duc d'Enghien, etc. ' Have you seen it ? ' I replied, ' No.' —' Then how do you know that it is in my favour, or that it is well written ? ' I replied that I had seen some extracts from it in the newspapers, which I gave to him. He sat down to read the papers, asked the explanation of a few passages, and said they were true; inquired what Warden had said of the affair of the Duc d'Enghein ? I replied that he asserted that Talleyrand had detained a letter from the Duke for a considerable time after his execution, and that he had attributed his death to Talleyrand. ' Of this there is no doubt,' replied Napoleon.

Napoleon then asked how the work had been received in England ? I replied, ' I had heard that it had succeeded very well.' He asked, ' Whether the Ministers were pleased with it ? ' I answered, ' That they had not as yet shown any displeasure, as Warden had been recently appointed to a ship.'—' I suppose,' said Napoleon, ' that he has arranged it so as to please the Ministers ? ' I replied that from what I had been able to learn, he had endeavoured to state the truth.

I then assisted him in reading over some extracts which were in the *Observer*, the correctness of which he admitted. He perused very attentively and made me explain to him three times an article which stated that the Empress Marie Louise had fallen from her horse into the Po, and with difficulty had been saved from a watery grave, and appeared considerably affected by the perusal.

Some odd numbers of the *Times* and a few letters sent up by the Governor. General Gourgaud received a letter from his sister, which informed him that Sir George Cockburn had called twice to see his mother in Paris. This mark of attention on the part of the Admiral quite enchanted General Gourgaud. Count and Countess Bertrand in raptures, as the same letter stated that Madame Dillon, the Countess's mother, was doing well. Though myself for many years a wanderer, I never observed so forcibly before the satisfaction and consolation afforded by a letter from distant relations or friends to those who are separated from their home. By the joy in the countenances of some at Longwood, it was easy to distinguish those who had received intelligence, as the melancholy and dissatisfaction portrayed in the others denoted the contrary. There was no necessity for asking any questions. A line of writing from Europe is, at Longwood, a treasure above all price.[1]

---

[1] '*May* 29, 1816.—A letter was delivered to me from the Grand Marshal. It had just arrived from Europe, and was addressed to the Emperor. I handed it to him. He read it over once and sighed ; and then having read it a second time, he tore it, and threw fragments beneath the table. This letter was delivered open ! . . . The Emperor then resumed his perusal of the journals, and suddenly stopping, he said, after a few moments' silence : " That letter was from poor Madame : she is well, and wishes to come to reside with me at St. Helena ! . . ."

'After this he continued his reading. This, which was the first

*March* 6.—Some French newspapers sent up
to Napoleon by the Admiral, through the Governor.
Napoleon very anxious to hear some further
intelligence of Marie Louise. The circumstance
he observed yesterday appeared to have excited
some apprehensions for her safety in his mind,
which was not much relieved when he perceived
that only odd numbers of the newspapers had
been sent up by the Governor. On coming
afterwards to an article · in the French papers,
which stated that the project for supplying Paris
with water by an · English company had been
abandoned, he called out to me, 'Have I not
told you so, and that the people would not suffer
it?' Informed him that the Governor had sent
up Mr. Warden's book to me, with instructions
to deliver it to him. He looked at the facsimile
of his own handwriting and laughed heartily.

At night Napoleon sent for me. Said that he
was convinced the Governor had kept back some
letters and newspapers. That he had no doubt
that Sir Hudson Lowe had himself received a
complete series of papers, but that he had kept
back some according to his usual habit, because
there might have been an article which would
prove agreeable to him. 'At first,' said he, 'I
thought that there might have been some bad
news of my wife, but a moment's reflection taught

letter that the Emperor had received from any individual of his family,
was in the handwriting of Cardinal Fesch. The Emperor was
evidently much hurt by its having been delivered to him open.'—*Las
Cases*, vol. ii., part iii., p. 354, English edition.

me, that if so, this man would not have failed
to send it directly, in order to afflict me.  Perhaps
there may be some news of my son ; when you
go to town to-morrow, endeavour to see a complete
series of papers, and look attentively at them.
You can find out ten articles in your papers, while
I am searching for one.  Try and get some more
of the Portsmouth papers, as the news is more
condensed in them, and I do not lose myself as
in looking over a number of the *Times.*'

*March* 8.—Mrs. and Misses Balcombe at Longwood.  Napoleon sent for and conversed with
them for a few minutes.  Sir Hudson Lowe, when
informed of this, said, ' That they had no business
to have spoken to General Bonaparte, as their
pass had only specified Count Bertrand's family.'[1]

*March* 10.—Napoleon in good spirits.  Had
some conversation relative to Warden's book.  I
asked him about that part which treats of the

[1] 'One day our pass from Sir Hudson Lowe only specified a visit
to General Bertrand, but my anxiety to see Napoleon caused me to
break through the rule laid down, and the consequences of my
imprudence were nearly proving very serious, as my father *all but*
lost the appointment he then held under Government.  I had caught
sight of the Emperor in his favourite billiard-room, and not being
able to resist having a game with him I bounded off, leaving my
father in dismay at the consequences likely to ensue.  Instead of my
anticipated game I was requested to read a book by Dr. Warden,
surgeon of the *Northumberland*, that had just come out.  It was in
English, and I had the task of wading through several chapters, and
making it as intelligible as my ungrammatical French permitted.
Napoleon was much pleased with Dr. Warden's book, and said it
was a very true one.  I finished reading it to him whilst we remained
with Madame Bertrand.'—Mrs. Abell's *Recollections of the Emperor
Napoleon*, 1873 edition, pp. 176, 177.

Governor's physiognomy; and Warden's reply, that he liked Lady Lowe's better. He laughed, and replied, 'As well as I recollect, it is true.[1] But I said much worse than what Warden has stated there, which I believe is to be found in Las Cases's journal, where the Governor must have seen my remarks.'

I then asked his opinion of Warden's book. He replied, 'The foundation of it is true, but he has misunderstood all that was said to him; Warden does not understand French. He was wrong to make me speak in the manner he has done. For, instead of having stated that it had been conveyed through an interpreter, he puts down almost everything as if I had been speaking to him, and as if he could have understood me; consequently he has often put into my mouth expressions unworthy of me, and not in my style. He has said that Massena had stormed the village of Esling thirteen times, which, if the work is translated into French, will make every French officer acquainted with the battle laugh, as Massena was not at that particular spot during the whole of the action. What he says about the prisoners

[1] '"Have you," Napoleon exclaimed, "any knowledge of physiognomy?"—"Not from study. . . ."—"Can you judge whether a man possesses talents from observing his features?"—"All I can say, General, is this, that I know when a face is pleasing or displeasing to me."—"Ah!" he replied in an instant, "there it is—you have found it out! Have you observed Sir Hudson Lowe's face?"—"Yes, I have." —"And what does it promise?"—"If I am to speak the truth, I like Lady Lowe's much better!" He now laughed.'—Warden's *Letters from St. Helena*, 1816 edition, pp. 176, 177.

that had been made at Jaffa is also incorrect, as
they were marched on twelve leagues in the
direction of Bagdad, and not to Nazareth.   They
were Maugrabins from near Algiers, and not natives
of the country that he mentions : he is incorrect in
stating that I proposed to give the sick opium ; I
did not propose it.   The proposal was first made
by one of the medical officers.   He is wrong in
the explanation which he has given of the reason
why I wished Wright to live.   My principal reason
was, to be able to prove, as I told you before, by
Wright's evidence, that —— had caused assassins,
hired by the Comte d'——, to be landed in France,
to murder me.   This I thought I should have
effected by Wright's own evidence at a trial in
presence of the Ambassadors of the Powers in
friendship with me.   Now there was something
glorious in Wright's death.   He preferred taking away his own life to compromising his
Government.

'The Duc d'Enghien was to have come to
Paris to assist the assassins.   The Duc de Berri
also was to have landed in Picardy to have excited
insurrection.   I received information of this, and
Savary was despatched to the spot to arrest him.
If he had been taken, he would have been instantly
shot.   He was on board an English vessel which
came in close to the coast, but a certain signal which
had been previously agreed upon not having been
made from Béville, he became afraid and stood off.
The place where they were to have landed was

called the *falaise de Béville*, near Dieppe, at the foot
of a steep precipice, up which people are obliged to
climb by the help of ropes.   It was chosen by them
on this account, as they were not likely to be
interrupted by the custom-house officers.   The
Comte d'——— and the Duc de B——— were
always endeavouring to procure my assassination.
Louis, I believe, was not privy to it.   They thought,
I suppose, that they were at liberty to make as
many attempts to assassinate me as they chose, with
impunity.   As head of the French Government, by
the laws of politics, and by the laws of nature, I
should have been justified in retaliating by assassination in turn, which it would have been most easy
for me to have effected.

'Shortly after Marengo,' continued Napoleon,
'Louis wrote a letter to me, which was delivered by
the Abbé Montesquieu,[1] in which he said that I
delayed for a long time to restore him to his throne ;
that the happiness of France could never be complete without him ; neither could the glory of the
country be complete without me ; that one was as
necessary to it as the other ; and concluded by
desiring me to choose whatever I thought proper,
which would be granted under him, provided I
restored to him his throne.   I sent him back a very
handsome answer, in which I stated that I was
extremely sorry for the misfortunes of himself and
his family ; that I was ready to do everything in my
power to relieve them, and would interest myself

[1] *Vide Bourrienne*, vol. ii. pp. 47, 48.

about providing a suitable income for them, but that
he might abandon the thought of ever returning to
France as a sovereign, as that could not be effected
without his having passed over the bodies of five
hundred thousand Frenchmen.

'Warden has been incorrectly informed that
Maret was privy to my return to France. He
knew nothing about it, and such a statement may
injure his relations in France. He has acted also
unguardedly in asserting matters upon the authority
of Count and Countess Bertrand, as it may make
them many enemies. He ought to have said, " I
have been told at Longwood." As to his saying
that the information came from me, I care not, as I
*fear nobody*, but he ought to have been cautious
about the others.

'Gourgaud was very angry yesterday about what
was said of him. I told him that he ought to take
example by me, and observe with what patience
I bore the libels on me with which the press·
was overwhelmed; that they had made me out a
poisoner, an assassin, a violator; a monster who
was guilty of incest, and of every horrid crime.
That he ought to reflect upon this, and be silent.

'I see,' continued he, 'by some answers in the
*Times*, that the *Morning Chronicle* appears to
defend me. What harm could it possibly do to let
me see that paper — to let me read something
favourable of myself? It is very seldom that I now
see anything of the kind, but it is a cruelty to
withhold so slender a consolation.'

He then made some observations respecting
Talleyrand. '*C'est un coquin, un homme corrompu,
mais homme d'esprit.* A man who seeks every
opportunity to betray. After the marriage of
Prince Eugene, I was obliged to turn him out of
office, on account of complaints made against him
by the Kings of Bavaria and Wurtemberg. Nothing
was to be done, no treaty to be made, without first
having bribed him. There were some commercial
treaties on foot at the time, to conclude which he
demanded enormous sums. The Bourbons have
done wisely to get rid of him, as he would have
betrayed them on the first opportunity, if he saw
that there was any probability of success, as he had
offered to do after my return from Elba.

'I see,' said Napoleon, 'no feasible measure to
remedy the distresses of your manufacturers, except
endeavouring by all means in your power to promote
the separation of the Spanish South American
colonies from the mother country.[1] By means of this
you would have an opportunity of opening a most
extensive and lucrative commerce with the South
Americans, which would be productive of great
advantages to you. If you do not adopt some steps
of the kind, the Americans will be beforehand with
you. If you act as I have said, they could trade
with no other nation than you. Both Spain and
France must be shut to them.

'If the war with England had lasted two or

---

[1] 'To call the new world into existence to redress the balance of
the old.'—*Canning.*

three years longer,' added he, 'France would not·
have had any further occasion for colonies. In
consequence of the great encouragement I gave, and
the premiums I paid, to those who devoted their
chemical labours to the making of sugar,[1] especially
from the beetroot, it was sold so low as fifteen sous
a pound ; and when the process should have been a
little more matured, sugar would have been made in
France as cheaply as it could have been imported
from the West Indies.'

I remarked that the French could with difficulty
have done without coffee. 'They could very well
have contented themselves with several kinds of
herbs, as tea,' replied the Emperor. 'It would
have been possible to have grown coffee in the
southern part of France, and an inferior kind of
coffee of grain might have been substituted.'

A few moments afterwards Napoleon observed
that it was true, as had been stated in the papers,
that the Belgians were sorry that the English had
gained the battle of Waterloo.[2] 'They considered
themselves Frenchmen,' said he, 'and in truth they
were such. The greater part of the nation loved
me, and wished that I might succeed. The stories
that your Ministers have taken such pains to
circulate respecting the nations that I had united to
France having hated me and detested my tyranny

[1] A concentrated substitute for sugar has lately been produced
from tar !

[2] The Belgian troops certainly took to flight during the battle.—
*Siborne*, pp. 248, 249.

are falsehoods. The Italians, Piedmontese, Belgians, and others, are an example of what I say. You will learn hereafter the opinions of those English who have visited the Continent. You will find that what I tell you is correct, and that *millions* in Europe now *weep* for me. The Piedmontese preferred being as a province of France, to being an independent kingdom under the King of Sardinia.'

Count Bertrand's cook went to camp and got so drunk as to be totally incapable of cooking the dinner for the family. Napoleon, when informed of this at dinner, sent some dishes from the table to Countess Bertrand, with his compliments.

*March* 11.—The *Griffon* sloop of war arrived from the Cape with a mail, in which were some letters for the French. Count Bertrand received the pleasing intelligence that his brother was no longer in exile, but had been permitted to return to his home, and to remain there under *surveillance.*

Informed by one of the partners that last week an official letter had been sent to the house of Balcombe and Co., to demand an explanation why *fourteen shillings* more than the sum that had been allowed by Government had been expended for fish for the establishment of Longwood in the preceding fortnight. Also to know why two shillings and sixpence more than the allowance had been expended for twine. Moreover, that forty pounds of barley had been sent up to Longwood by order of the surgeon, for the use of Countess

Bertrand, a repetition of which in future was prohibited, unless the order was first approved at
Plantation House.

Last Sunday Mr. Balcombe and myself had a
conversation with Sir Hudson Lowe, in the library
at Plantation House, relative to the affairs of
Longwood. Mr. Balcombe presented two sets of
bills drawn by Count Bertrand for his approval.
His Excellency professed himself to be greatly
surprised at the large sums of money laid out by the
French, and said that twelve thousand a year ought
to cover all expenses. He was informed by Mr.
Balcombe and myself that it was chiefly expended
in the purchase of provisions and various necessaries of life, as the allowance granted by Government was not sufficient. Amongst many other
articles I mentioned that only seventy-two pounds
of beef were allowed. Sir Hudson said that he
would increase the quantity to one hundred, and
would confer with Count Bertrand on the subject.
He was apparently in a very bad humour, and
railed at what he termed the *impudence* of Las
Cases, in having presumed to send from the Cape to
Longwood some wine, Florence oil, and other
articles of a similar nature, for the use of the
French, which he said was an insult to the British
Government, and concluded by refusing to approve
of more than one set of bills.[1]

---

[1] Sir Hudson Lowe would not allow any bill of exchange drawn
by any of the inhabitants of Longwood to be cashed, unless it had
been previously approved of and indorsed by himself.

*March* 12.—Saw the Emperor at 11 A.M. in a very good humour.

I asked Napoleon if it were true, as had been stated, that he was once in danger of being taken by the Cossacks? 'At the battle of Brienne,' replied he, 'I recollect that about twenty or twenty-five Uhlans, not Cossacks, got round one of the wings of my army, and endeavoured to fall upon a part of the artillery. It was at the close of the day, and beginning to be dark. The Uhlans stumbled somehow or other upon me and my *état-major*. When they saw us, they were quite lost, and did not know how to act. They did not, however, know who I was, neither was I myself for some time aware of who they were. I thought they were some of my own troops. Caulaincourt, however, perceived who they were, and called out to me that we were amongst enemies. Just at this moment the Uhlans being frightened, and not knowing what to do, tried to escape in all directions. My staff began to fire upon them. One of them galloped up so close to me (without knowing me) as to strike my knee violently with his hand. He had a spear in his hand at the charge, but it was with the reverse end that he struck me. At first I thought that it was one of my own staff who was riding roughly by me, but looking round, I perceived that he was an enemy. I put my hand down to draw out one of my pistols to fire at him, but he was gone. Whether he was killed or escaped I know not. That day I drew my sword, which was a circumstance that rarely had occurred, as I gained battles with my eye and not with my arms. Those Uhlans were afterwards, I believe, cut to pieces.' I asked if he considered himself to have been in any great peril on that day? 'No,' said he, 'it was an accident. My cavalry was in another part of the field at the time. It was possible certainly that I might have been killed, but they were more intent upon running away themselves than upon killing any of us.'[1]

I asked if during the retreat from Moscow he had ever been in danger of being taken by the Cossacks? 'Never,' replied Napoleon, 'I had always with me a guard sufficient to repel any attack, or even to prevent any apprehension as to the result in case one was made.'

*March* 13.—Napoleon in his bath. In very good spirits. After some conversation on the subject of what had been lately published respecting him, 'I suppose,' said he, 'that when

[1] It has been said that on the same night, when the French had in their turn stormed the village of Brienne, Blucher and his staff fell in with a party of their cavalry, and were only prevented from being taken by two Cossacks who had seen them, and who stopped Blucher at the foot of a flight of stairs when on the point of going out, who otherwise would have been killed or made prisoner. That they had drawn their swords, and were prepared to fall upon the French, but after having made a *reconnaissance*, they were found to be so numerous as not to admit of a probability of success. This, if true, forms a singular coincidence with what I have related above ; but as I had it from Sir Hudson Lowe, I cannot be responsible for the correctness of the statement.—B. E. O'M.

you go to England, you will publish *your* book. You certainly have a better right to publish about me than Warden, and you can say that you have had long conversations with me. You would gain a great deal of money, and everybody would believe you. Truly, no French physician has ever been so much about me as you have been. I saw them only for a few minutes. The world is anxious to know every little circumstance about a man who has happened to make any figure in it, such as all the trifles about how he eats, drinks, sleeps, his general habits, and manners.[1] People are more anxious to learn those *sottises* than to know what good or bad qualities he may possess.'

Napoleon walked out about five, and paid a visit to Countess Montholon. He remained a few minutes looking at Captain Poppleton, who was busily employed in digging some potatoes out of a little garden that we had endeavoured to cultivate in front of the house.

*March* 14.—Told Napoleon that a letter had appeared in the French papers, which was attributed to the Marquis de Montchenu, stating that upon his arrival he (Napoleon) had given him an invitation to dine, to which he had replied that he had been sent to St. Helena to guard, and not to dine with him. '*Ces messieurs sont toujours les mêmes,*' replied the Emperor; 'it is

---

[1] See Bourrienne's *Memoirs*, English edition of 1885, vol. i. chap. xxviii., and vol. iii. p. 479.

very likely that he has been *bête* enough to write it. Those old French noblesse are capable of any *bêtise*. Montchenu is worthy of being one of the *grande naissance* of France!'

Mentioned to him that in one of the papers it had been stated that Sir George Cockburn had gone to Paris impressed with a poor opinion of his (Napoleon's) abilities, and had said that on the score of talent he was an ordinary character, and by no means to be feared. Napoleon replied, ' Probably and with reason he does not suppose me to be a god, or to be endowed with supernatural talents ; but I will venture to say that he gives me credit for possessing *some*. If he has really expressed the opinion attributed to him, it pays a poor compliment to the discernment of the greatest part of the world.'

He then desired me to get him the paper which contained the report of Sir George Cockburn's opinion, adding that he was now so much accustomed to read libels, that he cared but little what was said, or what calumnies were published about him.

I asked him about the shooting of Palm, and said I had been informed that he had given a satisfactory explanation of every sanguinary act that he had been accused of having committed excepting that. Napoleon replied, ' I never have been asked any explanation about it. All that I recollect is, that Palm was arrested by order of Davoût, I believe, tried, condemned, and shot, for having, while the country was in possession of the French, and under military occupation, not only excited rebellion amongst the inhabitants, and urged them to rise and massacre the soldiers, but also attempted to instigate the soldiers themselves to refuse obedience to their orders, and to mutiny against their generals. I believe that he met with a fair trial. I should like,' continued he, 'to read the principal libels which have been published against me in England, if I could have them in French. There is Pelletier,' added he, laughing, 'who *proves* that I was *myself* the contriver of the infernal machine.'

Major Hodson paid a visit to Countess Bertrand. Informed her that both himself and his wife would be most happy to call frequently upon her; but that it had been hinted to him that it would not be liked at Plantation House.

*March* 15.—Sir Hudson Lowe gave directions to Captain Poppleton that General Bonaparte, or any of his suite might go unaccompanied along the road to Woody Range, and to Miss Mason's; but that they were not permitted to quit the path, and that they might re-enter Longwood at the bottom of the wood. That the two sentinels at the end of the wood were still to remain. He then asked what were the orders of those sentinels? Captain Poppleton replied, 'To let no person in or out of Longwood.' Sir Hudson desired that those orders should *still be continued in force,* adding, that he did not think that the path by

which the French were to be permitted to
enter was *near* enough to the sentinels to allow
them to interfere with them.   He desired also
that the sentinels should be posted a little before
sunset.

END OF VOL. I

*Printed by* R. & R. CLARK, *Edinburgh.*